Archibald Chesterfield and the Whispers
of the Aztec Scroll by R.A. Moak

Published by R.A. Moak
Alpharetta, Georgia

Archibald Chesterfield and the Whispers of the Aztec Scroll
First Edition
ISBN 979-8-9994732-0-2 (Paperback)
ISBN 979-8-9994732-2-6 (Ebook)
Cover and concept art by Robert Jarocki
Published by R.A. Moak
Alpharetta, Georgia
For more information, visit: subscribepage.io/GMEeiK
Printed in the United States of America

Acknowledgments

Writing a book is never a solitary journey, no matter how many hours are spent alone at the desk. I owe my deepest gratitude to those who supported and encouraged me along the way.

To my wife, **Melissa Moak**—your love, patience, and unwavering belief in me gave me the strength to see this through. This book could not exist without your constant encouragement and partnership.

To my family—thank you for standing by me, for your patience, and for reminding me why stories matter.

To Amy, whose sharp eye and thoughtful edits elevated this story to a higher standard—your contribution means more than I can say.

To Robert, whose artistry helped bring Archibald Chesterfield's world to life—you gave shape and color to a vision that once lived only in my imagination.

And finally, to every friend and reader who cheered me on, thank you. This book exists because of your encouragement and belief that the story was worth telling.

—R.A. Moak

Archibald Chesterfield and the Whispers of the Aztec Scroll

by R.A. Moak

Journal Entry

Florence, Italy — April 17, 1952

I've just arrived in Florence. The city hums with beauty and history, but I'm not here to admire cathedrals or sip wine by the Arno. I'm following the trail of a tomcat named Marius — elusive, sharp, and far too quiet for someone due at a meeting this afternoon. Two o'clock came and went. No sign of him.

What little I've uncovered suggests Marius has a knack for appearing just before things go missing — sculptures, manuscripts, a painting or two. Nothing definitive, but enough to raise suspicion. His name surfaces in the margins of unrelated reports — half-erased, peripheral, but always nearby.

I worry I'm stepping into something larger than I understand. But I need to know more.

— J.C.

Prologue

The wind howled through the peaks as Archibald Chesterfield struck a match with shaking paws. The end of his pipe flared to life, casting a faint orange glow across his tired face. The fire crackled low in the hearth behind him, barely pushing back the chill that crept through the old cabin's stones. On the table sat James's journal, worn and frayed at the edges. Beside it lay the scroll whole now. Two halves, reunited. The secrets no longer hidden. And tucked behind them, glinting faintly in the firelight, the emerald sphere. It didn't hum. It didn't glow.

It just sat there ancient, perfect, impossibly still. Archie stared at it for a long time. He thought of Nora. Of her laugh. Her steady paws. The moment she slipped the key into his coat pocket without saying a word. He tightened his grip on the pipe. And then there was Roxanne. There had been a moment just one when he'd thought it was finished. But she was still out there. Somewhere. Watching. Waiting. He shifted in the wooden chair, the bones in his back aching from the climb. Outside, snow battered the windows.

The others would arrive soon once the roads cleared. Mabel, Eddie, Teddy, Dolores. Even Vince. All of them coming because he'd asked. Because there was still one truth left to face. Not long ago, he'd been a professor chasing footnotes. Now he was something else. He exhaled, smoke curling like a ghost in the firelight, and rested a paw on the closed scroll. Tomorrow, if the storm broke, he'd hike down the mountain and meet Vince before the others arrived. Just a few more hours of quiet of solitude before the final chapter began.

1

The students were quiet alert, even. Archibald Chesterfield set down his chalk and turned to face the rows of eyes staring back at him from the lecture benches. Dust filtered through the tall arched windows of the hall, catching the late light and hanging like a curtain in the air. Behind him, a blackboard bore the faded scrawl of today's final word: Legacy. "Civilizations," he said, adjusting his waistcoat, "are remembered not by what they conquered, but by what they left behind. Stones, scrolls, scars. Their greatest truths aren't written in laws or ledgers— they're found in fragments." Pens moved briskly across lined paper. He let the silence stretch a beat longer before tapping the chalk tray with a knuckle.

"Your essays on the Olmec codices are due Friday. I expect proper citations, full footnotes, and no heroic last-minute excuses. If your flat floods, write by candlelight. History waits for no one." The bell outside chimed softly through the windows. The students stood, some grumbling under their breath, others still scribbling as they filed out. Archie remained still at the front of the hall, watching them go, one paw resting absently on the edge of the desk.

3

He exhaled slowly. They were listening. That was rare. He gathered his notes into a neat bundle and tucked them into his satchel. A folded flyer peeked out between pages—a university bulletin for an upcoming seminar: Illicit Trade in Antiquities—A Modern Crisis. He traced the edge of it with a claw, then smiled faintly. It brought back memories.

During his final years at Oxford, he'd spent time abroad—months wandering archives in Florence, studying museum theft reports in Madrid, walking the damp marble floors of Lisbon's vaults with ink-stained paws and questions that kept him awake at night. He'd picked up fluent Spanish, conversational Italian, and a taste for espresso strong enough to strip paint.

Those were good years. Restless, but good. His path hadn't always been so clear. After the accident—the car crash that took both of their parents, James and Olivia Chesterfield— he and Teddy had been left to piece things together. Olivia, once a police officer, had been the strong one, steady and unshakable. James, a brilliant historian with a meticulous eye for detail, had filled their home with books, old documents, and gentle wisdom. They had been the foundation. And suddenly, they were gone.

Archie had poured himself into James's notebooks, hoping to find meaning or at least structure. Teddy had taken a quieter path, sorting through dusty records and hiding behind clean lines and labeled boxes. They'd both ended up in the business of memory, in their own ways. Now, Archie taught. Teddy curated. And tonight, they'd sit across a dinner table together for the first time in months, glasses raised, plates full.

Archie tightened his coat against the wind and stepped out into the fading day. The drive across London was uneventful. His coupe hummed through the narrow lanes, tires spitting rainwater as the mist thickened. On the seat beside him, wrapped carefully in cloth, sat two things: a velvet box, and a bottle of Clawridge Reserve 15-year-old Scotch.

The letter opener had belonged to Olivia—sterling silver, engraved with delicate vinework along the handle. It had sat on her desk for years, slicing open invitations, holiday cards, handwritten letters. Archie had cleaned it the night before and packed it carefully in its original box. A gift. A keepsake. Something personal for Teddy and Dolores, late but meaningful and the Clawridge Reserve well, that was for the table. For the toasts. For the silence that came after the talking, when the fire dimmed and no one felt the need to fill the air.

He turned onto his street, slowed the car, and frowned. Police lights. Three cruisers idled near the curb, their engines murmuring. Red and blue flashes lit up the wet bricks of his building. Yellow tape fluttered like a torn banner across the front steps. Two constables stood at the entrance, ears twitching, eyes alert. Archie pulled in a few doors down and cut the engine. He stepped out into the damp and looked up. His window—fourth floor—was dark, just as he'd left it. He adjusted his scarf, pulled his jacket tight, and walked forward.

One of the officers raised a paw. "Evening, sir. Building's closed. You'll need to step back." "I live here," Archie said evenly. "Flat twenty-three. Just stopping in to collect something before dinner with family." The officer glanced toward the entryway, where a tall tom emerged from the shadows.

Broad shouldered, black and white fur, long coat, and a scar over one brow. His eyes were sharp but not unkind. "Name?" the tom asked. "Archibald Chesterfield." The tom produced a badge. "Detective Edward. You can call me Ed." Archie offered his university identification and driver's license. "I left the college a little after five. Drove straight here. My brother's expecting me—I'm running a bit behind."

Ed nodded, flipping open a small notebook. "You planning to stay the night?"

"No. Just came to collect a gift I'd forgotten. Then I'll be on my way." "Sorry," Ed said. "Whole floor's closed." Archie hesitated. "Might I ask what's happened?" "Murder," the detective said plainly. There was no drama in the word—just weight. Archie's breath stilled. "Who?" "David Smit. Flat twenty-five." His grip tightened on the bottle beneath his coat. David had been quiet. Soft-spoken. He read The Times and always passed it to Archie when he was finished, folded neatly. They'd shared idle conversation. Weather, books, the occasional commentary on the state of traffic in the city. Nothing deep. But kind. "He wasn't the sort to cause trouble," Archie said after a beat. "No," Ed agreed. "And yet." The detective scribbled something in his notebook, then snapped it shut. "You'll need to make arrangements elsewhere. And if you think of anything unusual—anything at all—you report it." Archie nodded slowly. "Of course." "Have a good evening, Mr. Chesterfield." Archie stepped back, the cold mist clinging to his fur, the lights from the cruisers painting streaks across the wet ground. He walked to his car and opened the door, pausing before sliding into the driver's seat. The letter opener would have to wait. And the Clawridge Reserve, it seemed, would be poured under different circumstances.

6

Archie didn't go to Teddy and Dolores's right away. He should have—he knew that. The bottle of Clawridge Reserve still sat carefully wrapped on the passenger seat, and the silver letter opener—meant to be a symbol of warmth and memory—rested in his flat guarded by Scotland Yards finest, untouched. The dinner would go on without him, delayed perhaps, but not derailed.

Still, something kept his paws on the wheel. Something unfinished.

Before he made his way back to the building, he stopped at a corner pub two blocks away. The bar was nearly empty. The barkeep, a wiry grey cat with a checkered scarf and a limp, barely looked up as Archie entered. "Telephone?" Archie asked. The barkeep jerked his chin toward the back. The payphone hung on the wall near the lavatory. Archie dropped in a coin and dialed from memory. The line rang twice before Teddy picked up. "Hello?"

"It's me," Archie said. His voice was low but steady. "Listen, I won't make dinner.

Something's happened at my building. Police have cordoned it off. There's been a murder." "Bloody hell. Are you alright?" "I'm fine. I wasn't there. I was on my way to yours when I stopped to grab the letter opener." "Should I come get you?" "No. Not necessary. I'll sort myself out. But I'll be very late." "Archie, what are you planning to do?" "Nothing reckless. I promise. Just—don't wait up." A pause. Then Teddy exhaled. "Be careful."

"I always am." He wasn't. But it was the only answer Teddy ever let go unchallenged.

Archie returned the receiver to its cradle and stepped back into the night.

By the time he reached the building again, it was nearly two in the morning.

The rain had stopped, leaving a thin sheen on the street. The last of the cruisers had gone. Only one constable remained in a parked car down the block, sipping from a thermos, his hat tilted low. The yellow tape still fluttered faintly on the stair railings, but the urgency had passed. The building looked quiet again—sleeping, almost.

Archie circled around to the alley, stepping over a loose brick and ducking beneath a fire escape he hadn't used in years.

During the blackout three summers ago, he'd climbed this very ladder when the elevators failed and the stairwell was flooded. He remembered the feel of the rust beneath his claws, the way the fourth-floor window creaked when opened from the outside.

Now, he slipped off his shoes and flexed his paws. The brick was cold, the iron rungs damp, but he moved with practiced precision. Climbing wasn't his strength—but Archibald's curiosity was and curiosity made him brave.

He reached the fourth floor ledge and edged toward his own window. A string-based latch something he'd rigged in his early days here, more a novelty than a necessity—was still in place. With a flick of a claw, the catch popped free.

The window creaked as it opened, slow and hesitant. He slipped inside. The flat smelled of rain and old paper. Everything was as he'd left it—books stacked by the armchair, a coat draped over the sofa, a brass lamp half-lit on the desk. He stood still a moment, listening. Nothing. No footsteps. No voices. Just the steady tick of the wall clock and the faint rattle of the windowpane in its frame. He padded to the fireplace mantle, retrieved the box he'd set aside for the letter opener, and slipped it into his coat pocket. Then he moved to the door and pressed an ear to the wood. Silence.

Archie turned the knob slowly, opened the door a crack, and stepped into the hallway.

Down the corridor, the yellow tape still hung limp in front of David Smit's door. Flat twenty-five.

Archie moved toward it, careful not to let his claws click against the floor. He paused at the threshold, knelt beside the lock, and reached into the inner pocket of his coat. A slender steel pick. A tension wrench. Not standard issue for a university professor—but Archie believed in being prepared. The lock gave after a few careful turns. The door creaked open. The scent of blood hit him first. It was faint now, but unmistakable—metallic, sour, threaded through the air like something spilled and forgotten.

The flat was dim. The main lamp in the sitting room had been switched off. Police had already swept the scene— Archie could tell by the light scuff marks on the floor, the shifted stack of books by the armrest, the slightly open desk drawer, but the room hadn't been ransacked.

Whoever had done this had known what they were after. Archie stepped carefully across the rug, avoiding the darkest stains, and moved toward the desk.

David's workspace was methodical letters arranged by size, envelopes neatly tied in twine. A small brass reading lamp, still warm, sat next to an ink blotter. Nothing that screamed danger. Nothing that explained a murder. He opened the lower drawer.

Papers. Receipts. A ledger of some sort, handwritten in sharp, careful script. He flipped through quickly—names, meeting locations, payment schedules. A few entries were blacked out with ink. He frowned.

Then he noticed something odd: the drawer had more depth than its contents required.

He tapped gently along the inside. A hollow thud. False bottom. Archie used the pick again, wedging the tip beneath the edge. It shifted with a pop, revealing a slim cavity lined with felt. Inside: a folder, thin and tightly packed.

He opened it.

Documents. Lists. Names he recognized—some tied to known criminal syndicates in East London. Others he didn't, but the details were clear. Financial exchanges. Schedules. One page outlined an arms shipment—military-grade weapons—scheduled for Friday evening. The location was circled. This wasn't petty crime. This was infrastructure. David Smit had stumbled into something massive.
Or worse—he'd been part of it. And changed his mind.
Archie sat back on his heels, folder pressed to his chest.

"What were you planning to do with this, David?" he whispered. "Were you going to turn it in? Or run?" He didn't have time to answer the question. Not now. Footsteps echoed down the stairwell. Archie shut the folder, slid it into his coat, and crept back into the hallway. He locked the door behind him, quick but careful, and returned to the fire escape without being seen. By the time the constable down the block looked up from his thermos, Archie was halfway down the alley, boots in hand, blending with the fog.

It was nearly three by the time Archie arrived at Teddy's house.

The streets were quiet. The wind had calmed. Fog clung to the corners of the old stone terrace homes, muffling the sound of his footsteps as he walked up the narrow path, silver letter opener tucked under his arm with the still wrapped bottle of Clawridge Reserve.

He knocked twice sharp but light.

A moment later, the door opened. Teddy stood in his robe, spectacles pushed up into his mane, his fur slightly rumpled. He took one look at Archie and frowned. "You look like hell," he said. "I feel like it," Archie replied.

Teddy stepped aside to let him in. The hallway smelled faintly of roast and rosemary— Dolores's doing, no doubt. The kitchen light was still on, though the rest of the house had gone to sleep. Archie shrugged off his coat and boots, setting the bottle on the counter with a soft thunk. His fur was damp, his sleeves dusted with ash and old wallpaper.

"Dolores asleep?" he asked. Teddy nodded. "Since midnight. She tried to wait up. I told her not to bother." Archie reached into his satchel and pulled out the velvet box.

"I didn't forget," he said, handing it over. Teddy took the box, opened it, and stared down at the silver letter opener. His expression shifted—first surprise, then something quieter, harder to name.

"Wasn't sure you still had this," he murmured. "I kept it safe. Figured it should be yours now." Teddy closed the box carefully and set it on the table.

They stood in silence for a moment, then Archie poured two glasses of Scotch. He handed one to his brother and leaned against the counter, swirling the amber liquid before taking a long sip. Teddy followed suit. Then: "So. What happened?"

Archie's voice stayed low. "The victim was David Smit. Lived two doors down. I knew him— quiet fellow. We shared papers. Pleasant, if distant." "And?"

Archie glanced toward the stairwell, then lowered his voice further. "After the officers cleared out, I went back." Teddy's brow furrowed. "You didn't." "I had to know."

Teddy exhaled sharply. "You broke into a sealed crime scene?" "I didn't touch anything I didn't have to," Archie said. "But yes."

Teddy dragged a paw over his face. "You're going to get yourself arrested one of these days." "Only if I'm sloppy."

"And—were you sloppy tonight?"

12

Archie didn't answer right away. He reached into the inner lining of his coat and pulled out the folder—now wrapped in waxed cloth and tied with a bit of twine.

He set it on the kitchen table between them. Teddy stared. "What is it?"

"Records," Archie said. "Meetings. Names. A planned arms shipment—military-grade, East London. If even half of it is legitimate, it's enough to make headlines and destroy half the city's underworld." Teddy didn't reach for the folder. "You're not taking this to the police?" "I am," Archie said. "But not as myself. If they tie me to the break-in, the best I can hope for is obstruction. At worst, they think I planted evidence." *"So what's the plan?"*

"I have a courier I trust. Anonymity guaranteed. It'll be at Scotland Yard by sunrise, with a note addressed to Detective Edward." Teddy took another sip of Scotch, slower this time. "You're still dancing along the edge, Archie." "I know." "You could help people. Do this properly. Open a practice. Work with the Yard."

"Perhaps," Archie said. "But not tonight." A long silence passed between them.

Then Teddy stood, gently gathered the folder, and nodded once. "I'll fetch the wrapping paper from the study. If you're going to play hero, at least do it in clean lines." Archie smiled faintly. Some things never changed.

By dawn, the city stirred. Milk carts clattered along narrow lanes. Gas lamps flickered and dimmed in the haze. A weak sun pressed against the rooftops, but the fog hadn't yet lifted.

Archie stood at the edge of a quiet post alley near Scotland Yard, coat collar turned up, paws tucked deep in his pockets. Beside him, a small brown parcel sat neatly on a bench— twine wrapped, wax-sealed, and marked in bold, careful print:

TO: DETECTIVE EDWARD – CONFIDENTIAL

He'd included no return address. No paw prints. Nothing that tied him directly to the documents tucked inside. Just the truth, or as close as one could come to it in the dark.

His courier—a sharp-eyed she-cat named Mae who owed him a favor from a scroll acquisition in Seville—would arrive at six sharp. She was quiet, precise, and didn't ask questions. He trusted her.

As the first constable rounded the block on patrol, Archie turned from the bench and disappeared into the morning fog.

He said nothing. He left no note. But the city was no longer as quiet as it had been.

Something had shifted. That evening, Archie returned to his flat.

The fourth floor had reopened. The tape was gone. The air inside still held a strange stillness, as though the walls themselves were uncertain what had changed. His coat remained draped over the sofa.

He poured himself a modest glass of the Tabbymore Single Malt Reserve and sat by the window, watching the sky dim into gray.

The knock came just after sunset. He opened the door to find Detective Ed standing there, arms folded, hat in one paw, eyes sharp but unreadable. "Mr. Chesterfield," Ed said with a small nod. "We received a package this morning. No name. Just instructions to bring it to my desk."

Archie raised an eyebrow, not unkindly. "A surprise, then?"

"You might say that," Ed said. "It contained enough intelligence to stop a major arms deal before it ever left the warehouse. Names, locations, hard evidence. Someone put in a great deal of effort to make sure it got into the right hands."

"I'm glad to hear it," Archie said, stepping back. "Would you like to come in?"

Ed shook his head. "Not tonight. Just thought I'd say thank you, in my own way."

Archie nodded once. "Of course." Ed hesitated, then added, "You're a history man, right?"

"I am."

"Well, I've got a case on my desk with roots going back a few centuries. Art theft. Strange symbols. Ancient references. Nothing official yet, but... I could use someone who knows the difference between a fake and a relic."

Archie smiled, slow and dry. "You know where to find me."

Ed tipped his head, turned, and descended the stairs without another word.

Archie closed the door and leaned against it, letting his eyes fall shut. The city was waking in ways it hadn't for years. And Archibald Chesterfield professor, historian, and something quietly more was ready.

2

Five Years Later ◆

The sun rose early over London, casting a golden glow through the tall windows of Archibald Chesterfield's flat. He squinted and groaned as the light hit his face. Mornings were not his strong suit never had been. And yet, somehow, he had chosen a profession that required him to be upright, dressed, and coherent by seven o'clock sharp. He glanced at the bedside clock: 5:30 a.m. With a sigh, he rolled out of bed and reached for the robe hanging on the door. A long day of teaching awaited him at Cambridge, one of the most prestigious universities in the country. Prestige, however, did little to ease the sting of an early alarm. Archie shuffled into the kitchen and started the coffee pot—the most critical step of his morning routine. While it brewed, he slipped out to check the community mailbox and retrieve his morning paper, always the highlight of his routine. As he made his way back up the stairs, the aroma of freshly brewed coffee wafted through the air and brought a small, satisfied smile to his whiskered face.

Back inside, he laid the paper on the breakfast table and moved to the kitchen. Eggs, cream, and a few slices of toast were assembled quickly, and soon the comforting sounds of breakfast sizzling filled the flat. He poured himself a hot cup of coffee and stirred it slowly, already feeling more like himself.

By the time breakfast hit the plate, he realized he'd need to eat fast. He was running late and would have to save the paper for a break later in the day. Eggs on toast disappeared in record time, and within minutes, Archie was dressed, briefcase in hand, and headed out the door.

By day, Archibald Chesterfield was a respected history professor. But on weekends and holidays, he wore a different hat a private investigator. Over the years, he'd assisted the police in several peculiar cases, especially the ones that didn't quite make sense. He had an eye for details others overlooked. It wasn't a profession most would associate with an academic, but Archie thrived in that duality.

He picked up the pace as he neared the train station. "Should've just grabbed a takeaway," he muttered. The day was already shaping up to be a long one he had dinner plans at his brother Theodore's house. Dolores, Theodore's wife, was an exceptional cook. Archie grinned at the thought. I hope she's making roast chicken tonight...

The train ride passed uneventfully, and Archie arrived at the university just after 7:20 A.M. From down the hall, he could already hear the chatter and occasional hissing coming from his classroom. He sighed. He entered the room, cleared his throat, and addressed the noisy students. "Settle down, please. And apologies for my delay this morning."

The rest of the morning went smoothly enough. When the bell rang to signal the lunch break, Archie felt a wave of relief. He dismissed the students with a reminder, "Papers on the Queen of England are due Friday. No exceptions."

With a hop in his step, he made his way down the corridor, grabbed a quick tuna sandwich, and retreated to the teachers' quarters for a bit of peace. He unwrapped his lunch and opened the paper, finally ready to enjoy a moment of stillness. But one headline stopped him cold:

THE HOLLOW COIN STRIKES AGAIN!!!

Archie's ears perked up. He'd read about the Hollow Coin before an elusive organization rumored to be behind high-profile art thefts, forgeries, and the black-market trade in rare documents. Most dismissed the group as myth, including the police, but Archie knew better. There was often truth behind whispered legends.

He read on. According to the article, the authorities were skeptical of the group's existence. No concrete evidence had ever tied any crime directly to the Hollow Coin. Still, something about the timing and details made Archie's instincts stir. This was no ordinary heist.

He scanned the article for the byline: Nora Slate.
He didn't know the name, but maybe he could track her down and get more information. If she was confident enough to mention the Hollow Coin in print something the police wouldn't even acknowledge she either had a source or had stumbled across something big.

Archie glanced at his pocket watch. Back to class now, he thought, but later tonight, I'll do some digging. He had Thursday off plenty of time to visit the British Museum, see what he could uncover, and maybe even meet Miss Slate.

With a small chuckle, he pulled a pen from his jacket and circled her name. "Well, Miss Slate," he muttered. "You may not know it yet, but you've got an appointment with Archibald Chesterfield."

The final bell rang, dismissing the last class of the day. Archie returned to his office or what passed for one. It was more of a glorified broom closet with a desk. He closed the door and sat down, reaching for the phone. Most faculty offices had direct lines, a rare modern convenience he appreciated.

He dialed the number to Eddie Mason's office. After a few rings, a familiar gravelly voice answered. "This is Eddie." Archie cleared his throat. "Ed, how've you been? It's your pal, Archie." "I don't have anything for you," Eddie interrupted. "If this is about the museum, my higher-ups are breathing down my neck. I can't even touch the case."

Archie raised an eyebrow. "Do you at least know what was stolen? The article didn't mention it." Eddie sighed. "What did I just say, Archie? I can't talk about the painting"

He paused, then cursed under his breath. "Forget it. Just stay out of it. And don't even think about showing up at the museum." Archie smiled. So it was a painting... "Wouldn't dream of it," he said cheerfully. "Thanks, Eddie." He hung up, leaned back in his chair, and let the pieces fall into place. He had a lead. Eddie wouldn't talk but maybe the museum staff would. And he had a name: Nora Slate. For now, though, he had a dinner to get to.

Archie left the college with the newspaper tucked under his arm. The Hollowed Coin he hadn't had a case this intriguing in quite some time. Curiosity swelled inside him as he made his way to the train station. He couldn't wait to tell Teddy. He boarded the train and took a seat by the window, flipping open the paper again, scanning for more details about the theft that had occurred just a few nights ago.

When the train pulled into his stop, Archie hopped off and flagged down a taxi to take him to his brother's house. During the ride, he opened his briefcase and pulled out a worn brown journal. Flipping it open, he checked to see if he had any pressing engagements. To his relief, the week and weekend were wide open. Perfect. He could spend Thursday through Sunday digging into the mystery starting with Nora Slate.

The taxi pulled up to his brother's house. Archie tucked the newspaper under his arm and stepped out, giving the front door a quick knock. It swung open a moment later to reveal a tall, bright-orange feline. Her calm, welcoming eyes lit up, and a warm smile spread across her face. She wore a white apron dusted with flour, and her tufted ears twitched with delight enough to make any male cat blush.

"Don't just stand there, get in here!" Dolores beamed, pulling Archie into a big hug and planting a kiss on his cheek. The house smelled incredible rich spices, roasted vegetables, and what Archie immediately recognized as roast chicken. His stomach growled. That tuna sandwich earlier had barely made a dent. "Dinner'll be ready soon," Dolores said with a wink. "Teddy's working in the study." "Thanks, Dolores," Archie replied, making his way upstairs. "Teddy!" Archie called halfway up the staircase. "In here!" came the muffled reply.

As Archie climbed, he glanced at the walls lined with family photos snapshots of him and Teddy over the years, and a few of Mom and Dad. He smiled softly. Those were happy times, he thought. Rounding the corner, he found Teddy buried in a pile of documents, sleeves rolled up to his elbows, tie and jacket discarded on the couch. He wore a crisp white dress shirt, and his tan, furry forearms rested on the edge of the desk. It looked like he'd been at it for hours.

Archie took a seat across from him, setting his briefcase and the folded paper on the chair beside him. Teddy looked up and grinned. "You're always a sight for sore eyes." He stood, walked around the desk, and pulled his brother into a strong hug. "Glad you made it tonight. I'm starving Dolores is making a feast down there." Archie chuckled. "I could smell it from the street. Can't wait."

"Make yourself comfortable," Teddy said, gesturing to the armchairs. "Oh—and close the door. We've got a little time before dinner." Archie shut the door behind him as Teddy opened a cabinet built into the desk. From inside, he pulled out a bottle of Silver Tabby Vintage 1979 whiskey. Archie's eyes lit up. "No way! Where did you find that?" he gasped. "I've been searching for a bottle for months." Teddy laughed, retrieving two glasses. "I was picking up some wine for tonight, and there it was just sitting on the back shelf. Couldn't leave without it."

He cut the foil seal with a claw and uncorked the bottle with practiced ease. "Also grabbed these," he added, opening a small leather case. Inside were six finely rolled cigars from Fumar, their favorite club. "Catnip-infused. Figured you'd want one." Archie picked one up and brought it to his nose. It was perfectly blended. He smiled but set it back. Teddy gave him a look. "After dinner," he said with a smirk, handing Archie a glass of scotch.

Archie took it and inhaled deeply, then sipped. He closed his eyes, letting the taste settle on his tongue. "Absolutely exquisite," he murmured, taking another drink. Then he leaned forward, eyes glinting. "I have news, brother. A case."

Teddy's ears perked up immediately. He always lit up when Archie had something brewing. He took a seat beside him, scotch in hand. "Well, go on," he said, grinning. "Don't leave me hanging." Archie grabbed the newspaper sitting beside his briefcase.

"Have you read this yet?" he asked Teddy. Teddy adjusted his glasses. "No, not yet. What am I looking for?" Then he spotted the headline. "The Hollowed Coin," he read aloud. His eyes narrowed. "I hear about them from time to time through the grapevine at work. But Archie, there's no guarantee they're even real. This might not have anything to do with them."

Archie leaned forward. "Normally, I'd agree with you. But I haven't even spoken to the article's author, Nora Slate, and already I've been told rather forcefully to stay away from the case. My contact in the department wants me nowhere near it." Teddy peered over the rim of his glasses. "We talking about Detective Edward?" Archie smirked and took a sip of his drink. "The very one," he said with a chuckle.

Teddy let out a low laugh. "Then there's got to be something to it. Ed's been more willing to talk in the past— especially when it benefited him. If he's clamming up now, that's a red flag." He looked at Archie, concern creeping into his voice. "I can't poke around at work, though. If the wrong cats catch wind that I'm digging into this, I could lose my job." He sighed, then added, "That being said, I'll keep my ears open. There's always gossip floating around the office. I might overhear something useful."

Archie stood and placed a paw on his brother's shoulder. "That's good enough for me. I'll start chasing down leads, beginning with the reporter. There's a reason she wrote about that group in connection with the robbery I just have to find it." He gestured toward the door, his ears twitching as Dolores called up from downstairs. Teddy rubbed his belly and grinned. "We'll table this discussion until after dinner." Archie laughed as they made their way down the stairs. "You've put on a few pounds, haven't you?" "Shut up," Teddy barked, swatting at him playfully.

Dolores, having overheard, called from the kitchen, "Oh, you haven't, huh? Then what happened to the slice or three of pie I made for dessert?" Teddy blushed, and Archie cackled. Teddy had always had a healthy appetite. Maybe too healthy. But none of that mattered as they reached the dinning room. The table was a thing of beauty---- roast chicken, mashed potatoes, asparagus, and golden butter-glazed carrots. Everyone was going to leave full tonight.

Archie sat down, letting the rich aromas wash over him. Dolores poured him a glass of red wine, then did the same for Teddy and herself. She'd changed into jeans and a soft blouse and took her seat beside her husband.

The meal felt like a pause in time. They laughed, talked about life, shared future plans. Archie briefly mentioned that a new case might be forming but didn't go into details—he didn't want to worry Dolores.

Dinner ended with most of the cherry pie still intact though a suspicious few slices were missing.

Later, Archie and Teddy retired to the living room, where a warm fire was crackling. Teddy opened the cigar case from earlier and offered one to Archie, then took one for himself.

He breathed in the scent with satisfaction. "Been waiting all week for this. Dolores usually doesn't let me have these unless I've earned them." "And?" Archie asked, raising a brow.

"I did the chores. Even raked the yard." Teddy snipped off the end of his cigar and passed the cutter to Archie. Archie did the same, then leaned toward the fire as Teddy lit a match and took a long, slow drag. He unbuttoned his collar and let his fluff breathe.

Archie sank into his chair, took a deep pull from his cigar, and exhaled a perfect smoke ring.

Teddy, now pouring their second glass of that glorious Silver Tabby Vintage, handed one to Archie, who placed it gently on the side table.

"Hey Ted," Archie said, "do you know anyone over at The Daily Paw? I know you're not familiar with the reporter, but maybe someone else who could lead me to her?"

Teddy took a sip, scratching his head. "Not at the paper, no.

But I do know the newsstand owner—Morty Clawthorne. Older cat. Bit of a skeptic. Doesn't believe half of what he sells, but he hears a lot."

Archie nodded, taking another puff. "I've bought a paper or two from him, but don't really know the guy. Still… it's a start. He might know someone on the inside."

Another hour slipped by in the comfort of cigars, good scotch, and quiet company. When Archie had finished both, he stood. It was getting late, and he still had a class to teach in the morning. Tomorrow was Wednesday. He'd swing by Morty's stand on the way in.

He gave Dolores and Teddy a warm hug, then stepped out into the night and climbed into a cab.

As the city lights drifted past the window, Archie reflected on the evening. Teddy might be able to help more down the road, but for now, Morty was his best lead.

When he got home, Archie slipped out of his coat and boots and headed straight for the shower. It had been a long day a little too much pie and a little too much whiskey but a good day nonetheless.

The hot water melted the weariness from his muscles, and before long, he was in bed, fast asleep, already looking forward to tomorrow.

Archie woke up with a surge of purpose for today was supposed to be a day of results. He and Morty were going to have a chat about the latest story in The Daily Paw.

He looked out his window and took in the view of London in all her usual, moody charm. He downed the last of his coffee, grabbed his briefcase, and headed out.

He took the train, like always. On his way to Cambridge, he stopped by a small pastry shop and picked up a couple of jelly-filled cheese danishes. He was a bit excited—he hadn't had anything sweet in a while. Well... not since Dolores' cherry pie. That made him chuckle.

He licked his lips and took a bite, letting the warm filling melt in his mouth. His ears perked slightly, and his whiskers twitched with satisfaction. If this didn't get Morty talking, nothing would. A few blocks later, he spotted him.

Morty was a tall, skinny, gray-and-white cat. He wore his usual black visor cap, his short gray ears poking through. A blue button-down shirt with the sleeves rolled up like he was ready to sell out his whole stand. Archie could already hear him: "Come get your papers! Best news in London! Affordable prices!"

Morty's back was turned, so he hadn't seen Archie yet. Archie leaned against the back of the stand, finishing the last bite of his danish and licking the jelly off his orange paws.

He cleared his throat. "Hey! What you selling?" Morty spun around, surprised. It took him a second. "Well, look at that. If it isn't Archibald Chesterfield," Morty said with a smirk. He stepped forward to shake Archie's paw. Archie took it and laughed. "How are ya?"

Morty gave a half shrug, took off his cap, scratched his head. "Trying to make a living, you know how it goes." Then he leaned in a bit. "You know there's a conspiracy in the police department. Can't trust a single one of 'em." Archie smiled. That was the Morty he remembered always suspicious, always ranting. Sometimes a bit much, but today, that kind of talk might be useful. "You don't say," Archie said. "And what makes you think that?"

Morty opened his mouth, ready to go on a tear, then paused. He narrowed his eyes, like he was trying to figure out if Archie was poking fun.

Archie held up the second danish."Relax. I come bearing gifts," he said. He leaned in, slipped a folded £100 note into Morty's tip jar, and grabbed a fresh paper and the latest Super Tom comic. Morty took the pastry, barely noticing the overpayment. He bit into it, licked the filling off his whiskers, then glanced into the crowd. "So," he said. "What is it you want to know, Archie?"

Archie opened the paper, casually flipping through it. "You still got contacts at The Daily Paw?" Morty paused mid-bite to help a customer. Archie kept his eyes on the paper but wasn't reading a word. "Management? No," Morty finally said. "That bridge burned when I accused the head editor of covering up a story. But I still talk to a couple of the writers now and then." Archie kept his tone light. "Would you happen to know Nora Slate?"

Morty smirked. "Now why would you want to talk to Miss Slate?" Archie cleared his throat, not wanting to give too much away. "I'm working a case with the police. She's a potential witness."

Morty squinted. "That so? Funny, haven't heard anything about that in the news."

Archie folded the paper and pulled his glasses from his jacket, cleaning them on a cloth. "That's because it's not an official case," he said. "I'm running point, and that's all I can say." He put the glasses back on and looked up. "Can you set up a meeting?" Morty lit a cigarette and took a slow drag."No chance. We're not exactly friendly. We only talk if I've got a story lead. She hasn't called in months. I do have a number for her, though—it rarely gets picked up. Might be dead."

It wasn't much, but Archie figured a maybe was better than nothing. Morty pulled out a crumpled notepad, scribbled something down, folded the paper, and handed it over.
Archie tucked the number into the newspaper and slipped his glasses back into his jacket. "Good to see you again, Morty," he said. "I've got a class to teach."

Morty tipped his cap. "Always a pleasure, Mr. Chesterfield. Don't be a stranger."

Archie nodded and headed toward the university. It wasn't much of a lead, but it was something.
He'd make the call later using a pay phone his home line and office line weren't an option; too many ears at the university, and at home, the neighbors had a habit of listening in on shared lines.

As he walked the hall toward his classroom, his mind was elsewhere. He was glad he had the next few days off. He needed time to figure out what really happened at the museum… and what that stolen painting was all about.

3

Eddie Mason shifted in his chair, tail flicking with irritation as he stared at the case file on his desk. He was supposed to be reviewing a missing person report, but his focus kept slipping. His thoughts were fixed on the museum robbery from earlier in the week.

He'd barely stepped onto the scene, just enough time to glance at the records on the stolen painting, when the call came in direct from the chief. The message was curt: back off. The department would be handling the investigation personally.

Eddie's ears twitched. Something about it didn't sit right.

He closed his eyes and let out a quiet sigh, claws tapping once against the file folder. The whole thing echoed a case he could never quite shake one that had haunted him ever since.

His gaze drifted to a photo on his desk edges worn, frame a bit chipped. A different time. A different Eddie. This museum case... it was too familiar.
It took him back to the case that changed the course of his life. It happened ten years before he ever crossed paths with the ever-clever Mr. Chesterfield.

It was a bitter night in London, cold enough to sting through fur. Eddie was out on patrol with his partner, Jimmy. Jimmy was driving that night. Eddie glanced over.

"Quiet night, huh?" Jimmy turned a corner, the cruiser humming softly down the damp street. "Yeah," he said, "but it's cold as the dickens out here."

Eddie grunted. "We've probably got time for a quick coffee. There's a cafe a couple blocks up could use something to warm the whiskers." Jimmy smirked. He was a bit younger than Eddie a cool cat, quite literally. Maine Coon, with those good genes: tall, broad-shouldered, and built like he'd walked off a movie poster.

A few minutes later, they pulled up to the cafe. Jimmy threw the car into park, then looked over. "I got this one," he said.

Eddie didn't argue. Free coffee was a rare blessing in their line of work.

Jimmy stepped out, his thick orange fur puffed up against the cold. He practically looked like a lion—his mane spilling out from his collar, nearly bursting through his uniform.

While Jimmy went inside, Eddie decided it was as good a time as any for a smoke. He pulled out a battered pack of cigarettes, slid one between his lips, cracked the window, and struck a match. The first few drags hit hard, smoke curling into the frigid night air.

Jimmy returned a few minutes later with two steaming cups. Here," he said, handing one over. Eddie flicked ash out the window, then stubbed the cigarette out and took the cup. Out of habit, he went to pop the lid off.

"Don't worry," Jimmy grinned, "extra cream. I remember." Eddie chuckled. "You're a lifesaver." He took a sip, letting the heat spread through him. Jimmy sighed contentedly. "This hits the spot. Good call."

They sat in comfortable silence for a moment, warming up and letting the night breathe. "It's a slow one," Eddie said. "No rush finishing our rounds."

Jimmy had been his partner for four years. It hadn't always been smooth, but over time, they'd become a well-oiled team. Reliable. Trustworthy. "Hey Eddie," Jimmy said. "You got plans this weekend? I'm grilling steaks. Picked up a few cigars that've been begging to be smoked."

Before Eddie could answer, the radio crackled to life— loud, abrupt, and sharp enough to make him jump. His coffee spilled across his lap. "Son of a !" he hissed, letting out a loud meow followed by a curse. He snatched up the radio, voice low and growling. "This is Whisker 2751, dispatch, go ahead."

A moment of static. Then: "We've got a homicide. Holborn and Farringdon. Caller reports came from a third-floor apartment." Eddie tensed. "Any detectives en route?" "Negative. They're held up. Forensics ETA twenty-five minutes." "Understood," Eddie said. "We'll secure the scene."

Jimmy flicked the lights on, and they tore off through the fog-slicked streets. Fifteen minutes later, they arrived— first on scene. The building was a crumbling old block, brickwork worn and windows dim. They exited the cruiser, both drawing their service revolvers. "On me," Eddie said.

Jimmy fell in behind, covering Eddie as they approached the entrance. The hallway inside was poorly lit, a single flickering bulb overhead. Eddie pulled out his flashlight, sweeping it ahead as they moved in tandem.

The place felt dead. No noise, no movement. Like the tenants had vanished.

They reached the third floor, scanning for signs of forced entry. Halfway down the corridor, Jimmy pointed silently at a door slightly ajar. Eddie whispered, "Hold." Then louder: "This is Scotland Yard. Identify yourself!" He barely finished the sentence when Jimmy broke formation and rushed toward the door. "Damn it," Eddie muttered, following close behind. Jimmy could be too eager at times— but he had good instincts. Jimmy pressed his back to the wall beside the door, gun drawn.

"This is the police!" he shouted, then pushed the door open and swept the room with his light. What he saw froze him in place.

Two detectives Johnson and Manny tied back-to-back in chairs. Throats slit. Blood pooled at their feet. Then Jimmy saw it—the bomb. The red numbers read: 5 seconds. All he had time to do was shout: "EDDIE STAY BACK!"
Eddie sprinted forward, but BOOM. And then Darkness.

Eddie's ears rang. His vision swam in a haze of smoke and fire. The taste of ash filled his mouth. He tried to move— pain flared in his side—and then the thought struck him like a lightning bolt. Jimmy.

"Jimmy!" he shouted, though the name barely left his throat...

His voice was hoarse, broken. He knew in his gut it was too late. But he had to try.

Eddie pushed himself upright, propping his back against the scorched wall. His head pounded concussion, maybe worse but there was no time to think about that now. He glanced forward, eyes stinging. The hallway was gone. The blast had blown half the apartment to rubble. There was no clear path to where Jimmy had been.

The sound of the street—sirens, shouting—bled in around the ringing in his ears.

He scanned the floor. His service weapon was a few feet away, flung across the hall. He crawled toward it, grabbed it, holstered it. Then he staggered toward the stairwell, barely staying upright. Halfway down, his foot caught the edge of a broken step. He fell. Hard.

He crashed down the last few stairs, landing in a heap at the bottom. The air rushed from his lungs. Pain lit up his side. A rib—maybe two—felt wrong. He groaned, reached for the railing, and dragged himself upright.

He shoved the door open. Cold night air hit him like a slap. He stumbled outside, coughing violently. Blood splattered against the back of his paw. The world spun—sirens screamed in the distance—and then everything went black.

When Eddie opened his eyes, he felt like he'd been asleep for years.

The room was white. Sterile. Machines beeped softly beside him. Tubes ran from his arm. His chest ached with every breath. Then it all rushed back in.

Jimmy. The bomb. The setup. He tried to sit up, but pain clamped down on his body like a vice.

A voice cut through the fog. Low. Familiar. "Easy, son. Just rest."

Eddie blinked. The blurry shape leaning over him slowly came into focus.

Captain Grimwhisker. "Captain..." Eddie rasped, trying to sit again. The older tom gently placed a paw on his shoulder. "Take it easy, Mason. Don't strain yourself."

Cedric Grimwhisker was a commanding figure—grey and black fur, broad shoulders, steady eyes. He carried himself with quiet authority, but Eddie had always known him as fair. Firm when needed, but compassionate when it mattered.

Now, for the first time Eddie could remember, the captain looked shaken. His ears drooped slightly. His eyes held something Eddie had never seen in them before. Sadness.

Real, heavy sadness. "Eddie..." Grimwhisker said quietly. "I'm so sorry. Jimmy was killed in action."

The words didn't land at first. They just hovered there, like smoke after a fire.

Eddie didn't answer. He couldn't. His throat closed, his vision blurred again—but this time, not from smoke. He turned his head and broke.

Tears spilled from his eyes in silent waves. His ears drooped, shoulders trembling as a broken meow escaped him.

The captain sat beside the bed and placed a paw gently on Eddie's forearm.

"Let it out, son," he said. "He was a good cop. He did his duty to the end."

Eddie sobbed. Quiet, helpless sobs that wracked his whole body. Minutes passed before he could speak. He wiped his face with a shaking paw, voice cracking as he asked, "What happened? We were set up. Someone knew we were coming. Someone killed those detectives... it was a trap." Grimwhisker gave a slow, heavy nod. "Evidence is still being collected. Most of it... was destroyed in the blast. The three bodies we recovered were... in pieces."

Eddie winced. Tears welled up again. "Oh, Jimmy..." After another moment, the captain straightened.

"I need you to tell me everything. Every detail you can remember. Unfortunately, we're working with almost nothing." Eddie nodded and took a shaky breath. He forced himself to recall everything—every stop they made, every call, every sound—right up until the moment Jimmy shouted his name.

Grimwhisker took notes quietly, never interrupting. When Eddie finished, the captain capped his pen and stood. "You're on leave," he said. "Until the doctors say otherwise.

Get rest. Leave this with me— I'm taking it straight to the Commissioner. We'll get to the bottom of it."

Eddie nodded weakly. There wasn't much else he could do, and that alone made him feel helpless. He watched the captain leave.

Then he whispered into the empty room: "I swear, Jimmy... if it's the last thing I ever do, I'll get justice for you."

Later that day, Eddie sat up slowly, despite the protests from his body. Pain stabbed through his ribs, but he didn't care. Jimmy was gone. And his parents deserved to know.

He reached for the call button and paged the nurse. A young white-furred nurse with kind eyes entered the room. "What can I do for you, Mr. Mason?" "I need to sit up," he said, pushing against the mattress. "Please don't strain yourself—" He raised a paw. "I'll be fine. I just... I need the phone."

She hesitated, then nodded. "Of course." She brought the phone over and set it gently on the table.

Eddie looked at her. "Can I have a little privacy?" "Of course," she said softly. She closed the door behind her as she left.

Eddie stared at the phone for a long moment, then picked up the receiver. He took a breath, steadied his paw, and dialed. The line rang twice.

Then a She-cats voice answered. "Hello?" Eddie swallowed hard. "Hi, Liz... it's Eddie." "Eddie?" she laughed softly. "Hey! How are you?" His heart dropped. She didn't know. She hadn't been told. "Not great," he said, his voice already breaking. There was a pause. Then her voice turned quiet. "Eddie? What's wrong?" Time slowed. Everything around him faded as he told her. He hung up with shaking paws and lay back against the pillows, eyes burning. And then he cried. Until sleep finally took him.

A week had passed. Eddie was recovered enough to return to duty, though he'd been cleared only for desk work until the doctors signed off on field assignments. He hated it. He wanted to get back into the case—to find out who had set him and Jimmy up.

When he arrived at Scotland Yard headquarters, he passed through security and was met with familiar faces. A few officers came up to ask how he was doing.

Eddie smiled, nodded, and gave the same practiced lie each time. "I'm fine. Thanks for checking in." He wasn't fine.

He barely made it to his desk before his lieutenant, Fanghorn, approached him. Eddie was already dreading the task ahead writing his full report on the incident. The wounds were still fresh, and putting it all into words again felt like tearing them open.

"Lieutenant," Eddie said, standing. Fanghorn waved him off. "Relax, Mason."

He paused for a moment, then added, "You can write up your report later. The Captain wants to see you in his office once you're settled." Eddie nodded, and Fanghorn moved on down the hall.

He pulled a fresh sheet of paper into the typewriter and stared at it. He didn't know how he was supposed to put that day into words. But it had to be done.

Still... it could wait. Grimwhisker had called him in. Maybe he had a lead. Maybe someone had cracked something about the attack. Or maybe... Eddie didn't know.

He walked down the corridor and climbed the stairs to the fifth floor. When he reached the Captain's door, he knocked lightly.

From inside, Grimwhisker's muffled voice called, "Come in." Eddie stepped into the office.

The Captain was behind his desk, sorting through a few papers. Eddie took a moment to glance around— Commendation plaques, framed photos with the Chief, and a few with highranking government officials. There had been talk that Cedric Grimwhisker might be the next commissioner.

Eddie smiled to himself. He'd be the right cat for the job.

Grimwhisker looked up, nodded once, and gestured toward the door. "Close it behind you, would you?

Eddie did. As he turned back, he noticed the Captain walking over to the radio in the corner. He turned it up—loud. Too loud. The volume filled the room with static and chatter, and Eddie winced as the noise hit his still-sensitive ears.

Grimwhisker didn't speak. He simply motioned to the chair.

Eddie sat, the whole thing striking him as strange. The radio, the silence, the way the Captain was moving—it didn't feel like a routine check-in. Then Grimwhisker slid a piece of paper across the desk.

Eddie glanced at it, eyes narrowing. His stomach twisted as he read the message:

We are being watched. Meet me at this address outside of town at midnight.

Memorize this. I will destroy the message. Eddie looked up, eyes searching the Captain's face for confirmation.

Grimwhisker didn't blink.

Without a word, Eddie studied the address, committed it to memory, then nodded once.

Grimwhisker took the paper, walked over to the fireplace, and tossed it in. Eddie watched the message blacken and curl into ash.

Then the Captain returned to the radio and turned the volume down. His whole demeanor changed—suddenly casual, even a little cheerful.

"Sorry about that, Eddie," he said. "Just wanted to catch the end of the broadcast. Hope the volume wasn't too much."

Eddie gave a faint laugh, still rubbing one of his ears. "No worries, sir. Still a bit sensitive."

Grimwhisker tapped a pen against his desk. "This won't take long. I just wanted to check in— see how you're doing. I'm sure you'll be back in the field in no time."

Eddie nodded slowly, trying to match the Captain's tone. "Thank you. It's good to be back. I'll have my report on your desk by the end of the day." The Captain nodded once. "Appreciate it."

Eddie stood and left the office, the door clicking softly shut behind him.

He walked back to his desk in a fog. Something was going on. Something bigger than just the bombing. Bigger than the detectives who'd died. Bigger than Jimmy.

And whatever it was, it wasn't safe to talk about it here. Even the walls of Scotland Yard couldn't be trusted.

Eddie spent the rest of the day trying to recap the report. It was too soon—far too soon— but the information regarding the setup and attack was critical. Every detail might be evidence.

Once the report was done, he decided to make a hard copy. After the strange meeting with Grimwhisker, he didn't trust a single document to remain untouched. Something told him it was smart to have a version no one else could alter.

He left work early—his CO had no issue with it, considering it was his first day back. He had a few hours before the midnight meeting, and he desperately needed a nap.

The drive home was quiet. Almost too quiet. His mind kept drifting back to the day of the explosion. He asked himself the same question over and over: What did I miss? At first, nothing came.

Then, like a switch flipped, a memory zoomed into focus: he was passing the evidence room. Jimmy had been arguing with someone—Lieutenant Fanghorn.

At the time, he hadn't thought much of it. Jimmy had a talent for pissing people off, and his relationship with Fanghorn had always been rocky. But now? Now it felt... off.

He tried to remember—had he seen Fanghorn anywhere else that day?

A loud car horn snapped him back to the present. His ears rang. The light had turned green, and the cars behind him were blaring.

He muttered an apology no one could hear and drove the rest of the way home in silence.

He parked in his usual spot and took the stairs instead of the elevator. He needed to be alone with his thoughts.

As he reached the third-floor landing, another memory struck him—this one even sharper. He had seen Detective Johnson talking to Fanghorn outside the courthouse. Jimmy had been inside, testifying on a separate case that was about to wrap. Johnson looked frustrated. Fanghorn had stormed off.

Two arguments in one day. Two different officers. Both with Fanghorn.

Coincidence? Maybe. But that's all Eddie had to go on. He reached the fourth floor and turned down the hallway. That's when he noticed it—his apartment door was ajar. Not wide open. Not kicked in. Just... cracked.

His instincts kicked in. Without thinking, he leaned against the wall, weapon drawn. He tilted his head and focused his ears. Even with lingering damage from the blast, he could make out two muffled voices coming from inside. He strained harder.

The first voice was deep. Gruff. The kind of voice that came from a cat twice his size.

"Fanghorn asked us to clean this up. The two detectives and those two street cops were supposed to die in that explosion. I don't see anything here about the weapons deal—but we've got a living witness. Fanghorn wants Eddie and Grimwhisker to meet with an accident." Eddie's stomach turned. Grimwhisker? What did the Captain have to do with this?

He considered his options. Even if he caught them by surprise, there was no guarantee he'd walk out alive. And if things went sideways, the neighbors could be caught in the crossfire. Worse—he wasn't anywhere close to 100 percent. He started to back away, slowly—

That's when the door across from his apartment opened.

43

It was Hazel, his landlady. Mid-50s, dark brown fur, with eyes that could cut you in half if rent was late.

She blinked in surprise. "Hey Eddie, good to see you—"

"Run!" he barked. Hazel froze.

The two cats inside his apartment burst through the door— guns drawn. Eddie didn't hesitate.

He fired first, hitting the smaller cat in the chest. The intruder crumpled without a sound. Eddie turned on the larger one— but it was too late. The black-furred brute was already on him. The gun went flying from Eddie's paw.

The impact sent Eddie to the floor. Pain lanced through his jaw and ribs.

He looked up—just in time to see the bigger cat reaching for a concealed pistol in his coat.

No time to think. Eddie launched himself forward, claws out.

The black cat smirked, raising the gun—he hadn't expected Eddie to charge, but he was ready for it.

At the last second, Eddie dove low. The shot rang out— missed by inches. Eddie's claws hit home—right into the tom's lower stomach. The big cat howled.

Eddie's ribs screamed, but he didn't stop. He reached for the small pistol in his ankle holster— a .32—just as the black cat turned to fire again. Three shots. Two in the chest. One in the head. The brute dropped like a sack of bricks.

Eddie pushed himself up, clutching his side. Hazel was crouched against the wall, trembling. He went to her, lifted her gently. "Are you alright?" She nodded slowly. "Who were they?"

Eddie shook his head. "I don't know. But I'm going to find out."

She opened her mouth to speak again, but he stopped her.

"Don't call the police. We can't be sure who'd answer that call. I'll handle this."

Hazel nodded. She had no reason not to trust Eddie. He was a good tenant—and a cop and she'd seen the look in his eyes. These cats hadn't come to rob him. They'd come to kill.

Eddie dragged the bodies into his apartment. Normally, it would be a breach of protocol— tampering with a crime scene—but this wasn't a normal night. His apartment was completely trashed. Files overturned. Drawers open. The place was torn apart. They were looking for something. Jimmy had stumbled into something. And at the center of it all... Fanghorn.

Eddie checked the clock. He had four hours until the meeting with Grimwhisker. He'd play it carefully.
Because after tonight, he couldn't be sure who to trust. Not even the Captain.

Eddie stormed out of his building and slid into his car, his heart still racing. He couldn't believe what had just happened—twice in one week, someone had tried to kill him.

As he pulled away from the curb, his mind flashed back to what he'd overheard: something about a major arms deal, and Fanghorn was smack in the middle of it. No wonder he didn't mind me leaving early... Eddie thought. He knew they'd be waiting for me. Probably gave them my damn address. And then there was Grimwhisker. Somehow, he was connected too—but it felt like he might be a target himself.

Eddie exited the parking lot, deciding he needed to lay low until the meeting. There was a bar about five miles from the address Grimwhisker had given him—a crowded place, full of other cats. Less chance anyone would try something in public.

The drive felt like a lifetime. After the shootout, every car behind him made his fur stand on end. He kept checking his rearview mirror, his nerves fraying by the mile.

An hour later, Eddie arrived at the bar. It was packed. Good. The busier, the better.

He checked his watch—two hours until the meeting. Inside, the bar was loud and full of younger cats already deep into their drinks. Eddie found a table in the far corner where he had a clear view of the entrance. A waitress came by and he ordered a Ferocious Fowl 101, neat. After the day he'd had, he figured he'd need more than one.

The music blurred into background noise as he kept his paw under his coat, pawtips resting on the grip of his gun.

Time crawled. Eventually, Eddie looked down at his watch. It was time.

He left the bar, got back in his car, and drove to the address Grimwhisker had provided. It turned out to be a worn-down old hotel on the edge of town. A few rough-looking cats loitered outside. The kind of place where the receptionist never asked questions. Eddie parked and waited, eyes scanning the lot. A few minutes passed. Then he saw him.

Grimwhisker emerged from the shadows, wearing jeans and a hooded sweatshirt. His face was partially covered, but Eddie recognized him instantly. You didn't work under Cedric Grimwhisker without knowing that towering frame and no-nonsense walk.

Eddie exhaled slowly, then stepped out. As he moved closer, he pulled his gun and stayed low along the wall. He wasn't taking chances—not tonight.

He watched Grimwhisker head up the stairs. The Captain's own sidearm was tucked in the back of his waistband.

Eddie waited for his moment—then stepped out and raised his weapon. "Hold it right there, Captain." Grimwhisker froze, confused. He turned slowly, hands visible. Eddie stepped closer. "Turn around, but keep your paws where I can see them." Grimwhisker complied, opening his mouth to speak. "Shut it," Eddie snapped. "We'll talk. On my terms." He disarmed Grimwhisker and motioned toward the room. "Open the door."

Inside, Eddie kept the gun trained on him and locked the door. He pulled a chair near the bed while Grimwhisker sat on the edge of the mattress. For a moment, silence hung in the air, thick and tense.

"I'm sorry it has to go down like this, Captain," Eddie said finally, "but after today? I don't know who I can trust." Grimwhisker studied him, then nodded. "Seems to me we're both in a bit of a situation."

"A bit of a situation?" Eddie let out a dry laugh. "This is the second time someone's tried to kill me in a week. I'm past 'situations.' I want answers. Now."

Grimwhisker let him cool off before responding. "I get it, son. This place was the safest I could think of. While you were in the hospital, I started digging. Quietly. An internal investigation. But I kept coming up dry... until one afternoon I caught Fanghorn snooping through my office." Eddie narrowed his eyes.

"Said he was waiting to talk to me about your return to active duty," Grimwhisker continued. "Didn't sit right with me. So that night, I stayed late and went down to his office. Caught him on the phone with someone, looking irritated, flipping through a black book—it looked like a journal."

"And?"

"Once he left, I tried to find it. Drawer was empty. But I noticed something odd about the cabinet—it opened up into a hidden compartment." Grimwhisker pointed to the bathroom vent. "It's all in there. You should see it." Eddie stayed cautious. "You get it. I'm not turning my back."

Grimwhisker nodded and removed the vent cover, pulling out a thick file stuffed with documents. He handed it to Eddie, who stepped back and sat on the edge of the bed, still keeping his gun within reach.

As Eddie flipped through the papers, his expression darkened.

"Gun running... bribery... extortion... This is a damn criminal operation," he muttered. "I accused you, and I was wrong. I'm sorry, sir. I didn't know who to trust."

Grimwhisker's face softened. "It's alright. I'd have done the same. But yeah... Fanghorn's been using the force to cover this up for a while. I think Jimmy stumbled onto it. So

48

did those detectives. Fanghorn couldn't risk it spreading—he started tying up loose ends. That meant Jimmy… and you."

Eddie's ears perked at the sound of tires screeching outside. He moved to the window and peeked through the blinds.

"We've got company," he said, tossing Grimwhisker's gun back to him. "Looks like we're gonna have to shoot our way out."

Grimwhisker caught it with a grin and checked the chamber. "Wouldn't be the first time."

Eddie tucked the file back into the vent. "We can't let it fall into the wrong paws. First, we survive." Grimwhisker peeked out the window. "I count five." Eddie pulled back. "Let's assume seven." "You ready?" Grimwhisker asked. Eddie flashed a grin. "Who do you think taught me?"

They moved out together—Eddie in front, Grimwhisker covering the rear. The moment they hit the stairwell, a shot rang out, splintering the railing. Eddie returned fire, dropping the first assailant. Grimwhisker spotted two more coming from the back—he fired, catching one in the leg, the other in the shoulder.

Eddie reached the stairs and met a wave of Fanghorn's men. He took down three in quick succession. The fourth raised his weapon as Eddie ran dry—but Grimwhisker nailed him with a clean headshot, spinning around to finish off the wounded cat behind him.

By the time they hit the bottom floor, another one was down. Then Eddie saw him—Fanghorn, bolting toward a car. Eddie chased him. "Stop!" he shouted.

Fanghorn spun around, sneering. "You just wouldn't die, huh? You ruined everything."

"You're a disgrace," Eddie growled. "Jimmy didn't deserve this. None of them did. You sold us all out—for money. For guns. For nothing."

Fanghorn laughed. "Jimmy was a fool who stuck his nose where it didn't belong."

Eddie didn't hesitate. Fanghorn reached for his gun, but Eddie's shot hit center mass before Fanghorn even cleared his holster. Grimwhisker caught up, breathing hard."I got the rest," he said, looking down at Fanghorn's body. "Seems he got what was coming." He looked at Eddie, his voice steady. "And you got justice for Jimmy."

Eddie snapped back to the present, dragging himself out of what felt like a long fall into a painful memory. His eyes settled on the old photo—Jimmy's face, frozen in time. For a fleeting second, it reminded him of Archie Chesterfield.

Archie wasn't a cop, but sometimes Eddie wondered if he'd missed his calling. The orange tabby had a knack for seeing things others didn't, for sniffing out the truth buried under layers of noise. And, like Jimmy, trouble had a habit of finding him. This case was no exception.

Eddie had already taken it up with Grimwhisker—now Commissioner Grimwhisker—but the response had been clear: the matter was under wraps, and Eddie was advised to stay clear until official clearance was given. The stonewalling only made him more certain he was on the right trail.

"Well," he muttered, leaning back in his chair, "guess it's time for a little off-the-books work."

He rose, grabbed his jacket from the coat rack, and slid open his desk drawer. His badge and sidearm sat where he left them, waiting like old friends. Time to head back to the scene of the crime.

4

Archie stood at the window, watching the early light stretch across the rooftops of London. The city always looked its best in the morning—dressed in gold and still half-asleep, like a queen just rising from slumber. He took the last sip of his coffee, savoring the quiet. Then he grabbed his jacket, fixed his hat, and set out.

It was time to pay The Daily Paw a visit. Maybe, just maybe, she would be there.

Today, Archie was operating in an official capacity—as a private investigator, not just a curious academic.

The towering glass-and-brick headquarters of The Daily Paw loomed ahead. He hadn't set foot inside in years, not since university. He'd written a term paper once on the paper's role during the Great Fish Market Strike, and even toured the building. Strange how familiar and alien a place could feel at once.

Inside, the lobby was sleek but worn at the edges—polished tile floors scuffed by years of hurried feet, the scent of ink and old paper hanging faintly in the air. Behind the reception desk, a young cat flipped through a stack of documents. He looked up as Archie approached— mostly white with scattered orange spots and a large patch over one eye.

"Hello, sir. How can I help you?"

Archie smiled with just the right touch of charm. "Yes, I'm here to see Nora Slate."

The receptionist raised a brow. "Do you have an appointment?"

Archie leaned in slightly, lowering his voice. "Of course I do. She said she'd be at the office today."

He straightened and added a note of mock offense. "Honestly... do you know who I am? I'm a key witness in her next story. We've got an interview scheduled and—" he flicked open his pocket watch, "—I'm already late. Now, what floor is her office on?"

The receptionist blinked, caught off guard by Archie's confidence. He fumbled through a Rolodex, pulled a card, and dialed the number listed. It rang. And rang. And rang.

After several moments, he hung up and gave a small shrug. "I'm sorry, sir. She didn't answer her line. I can't let you up without management's approval. But I can call them if you'd like"

Archie cut him off with a wave. "No need. Miss Slate will hear from me—mark my words."

He spun on his heel and marched out of the building, biting back a grin.

"I really should've been an actor," he muttered to himself, amused by his own performance.

Outside, traffic picked up—carriages and cabs weaving through the morning rush. Across the street, Archie spotted a dusty old payphone beside what used to be a tobacconist's shop, now boarded up and forgotten. He darted across and stepped inside, the booth barely muffling the city's growing noise. Outside, traffic picked up—carriages the city's growing noise.

He pulled the slip of paper Morty had given him from his coat and inserted a coin. The rotary dial clicked as he turned the numbers. It rang twice. Then again. He sighed, about to hang up. Click.

A soft voice came through, barely louder than the hum of the city behind him. "...Hello? Morty, is that you?"

The voice was young. Fragile. She spoke like someone afraid the sound might give her away.

Archie hesitated, surprised. This wasn't the confident, take-no-nonsense reporter who wrote last week's explosive article. Still, he kept his tone even. "No. I'm a friend of Morty's. He gave me this number."

There was silence on the other end—long enough that Archie considered she might already be gone.

Then, more uncertain than before: "What... what can I do for you, Archie?"

He could hear the fear under her words. Whatever she'd written, whatever she'd uncovered— it had clearly come at a cost. He chose his next words carefully.

"I'm Archibald Chesterfield. I work with the police in an unofficial capacity. Nora... are you safe?"

A pause. Then a whisper so faint he had to press the receiver tighter to his ear.

"I feel like I'm being watched. Followed, even. I haven't been to the office in—I don't know how long."

Archie took a breath, calming his voice. "Listen, I have an idea. Would you be open to meeting at my brother's estate? He works with Parliament. It's just outside the city—quiet, secure. I'll arrange a car to pick you up tonight."

More silence. He waited.

Finally, she said, "Okay. I'll wait for your call. Write this down—I change hotels every couple of days. Too scared to go back to my apartment."

Archie reached into his coat and pulled out his notepad. "Go ahead." She gave him the address. He jotted it down.

"Don't answer the door for anyone," he added. "Wait for my call. The driver's name is Francis. He'll be there at eight sharp." "Okay," she whispered. "Thank you."

Archie hung up and immediately dropped another coin into the machine. He dialed a second number. One ring. Then a cheerful voice answered. "This is Frank!" "Francis, it's Archie."

There was a warm chuckle. "Archie! Haven't heard from you in a year. You still keeping the family in line?"

"Sorry, not a social call," Archie interrupted. "I've got a client who needs transport. Pickup at 8 p.m. tonight." Francis's tone shifted without missing a beat. "Understood.

Address?" Archie read it out. "She suspect she's being followed?" "Yes," Archie replied. "Or at least watched."

"Drop-off location?"

Archie gave him the destination. Then added, "I'd like you to keep an eye on the hotel until pickup. A lot can happen in the next few hours. And if something feels off—get her out of the city. Make contact with me later."

Francis's voice was calm. "Got it. I'll be in place early. Talk tonight."

Archie hung up, slipping the notepad back into his coat. He still had one more stop to make today. The scene of the crime.

Thirty minutes later, Archie arrived at the museum. The midday crowd had grown, with tourists and locals flowing in and out like water through a leaky pipe. As he stepped through the tall glass doors, a familiar calm settled over him.

The air inside smelled faintly of polished wood and aged paper—like time itself had left a trace. Soft pawsteps echoed on marble floors, and hushed conversations drifted across the atrium. No matter how many times he came here, the place always pulled a quiet awe from him. It was a temple of history, and Archie was a devout worshipper.

He approached the front desk and set a crisp twenty-pound note down. "One ticket, please."

The young attendant, a tabby with faint stripes and alert green eyes, handed him a ticket. Archie leaned forward slightly. "I'd also like to speak with the museum manager."

Her ears twitched, eyes narrowing in concern. "Did I do something wrong, sir?"

Archie softened his tone, giving her a gentle smile. "Not at all. This is something else— nothing you'd have clearance to approve."

Her ears relaxed, the tension leaving her shoulders. "One moment," she said, disappearing into the back.

Archie tapped his claws against the desk absentmindedly, then checked his watch. 4:00 p.m. If he was here much longer, he'd need to call Miss Slate from the museum's phone to confirm the pickup arrangements with Francis.

A tall cat appeared from a side corridor. Jet-black fur, sleek and well-kept, gave him a ghostlike presence under the gallery lights. His voice was calm and measured. "How may I assist you, sir?"

Archie handed over his card. "Archibald Chesterfield. I'm working with the police. I need to examine the crime scene."

The manager scanned the card, his face unreadable. "I'll need to verify that with the authorities."

Archie's polite demeanor cooled. "Feel free, but I wouldn't take long. Detective Eddie Mason gave me direct instructions to examine the site."

The manager's eyes narrowed slightly at the name, a flicker of recognition showing in the twitch of his whiskers. He had met Eddie during the initial investigation—hard to forget someone like him. After a brief pause, he gave a small nod and gestured toward a roped-off exhibit. "This way."

Archie ducked under the police tape and moved into the cordoned space. The empty wall where the stolen painting had hung loomed like a blank page.

"Do you have a picture of the piece?" he asked, turning back to the manager. "A brochure or catalog entry?"

The manager walked to a nearby drawer beneath one of the displays, pulled it open, and returned with a glossy museum brochure. Archie took it, nodded his thanks, and added, "If you wouldn't mind, I'll need some privacy." The manager gave a short nod and quietly stepped away.

Now alone, Archie moved through the room with care. Yellow police markers still dotted the floor—evidence tags long since cataloged. He crouched to inspect one, then another, making his way methodically toward the bare wall.

No damage. No scuff marks. No tool scratches. No chipped paint. Nothing.

Normally, in a rushed art theft, you'd expect signs of struggle—ripped frame edges, a crooked nail, even dust streaks where the painting used to rest. But here? It was as if the thief had tiptoed in, gently lifted the piece, and vanished into thin air.

Archie's brow furrowed. "Too clean," he whispered to himself. "This wasn't a smash-and grab.

Either someone from the inside took their time… or a bloody ghost stole it."

He turned to scan the rest of the room. The other artifacts— priceless statues, ancient relics— hadn't been touched. Only one painting was missing. Why this one?

He opened the brochure and studied the image of the stolen piece. A regal feline stood tall, draped in vibrant Aztec garb, adorned with gold and jade. Acamapichtli, the name read in bold print.

Archie frowned. Aztec history wasn't his strongest subject, but something felt off. He'd assumed this ruler belonged to the 1500s, around the time of the Spanish conquest. But Acamapichtli had ruled centuries earlier—late 1300s into the early 1400s—founding Tenochtitlan and laying the groundwork for what would become the Aztec Empire. So why had this particular painting been taken?

There was a story buried here. A thread that someone didn't want unraveled.

Archie tucked the brochure into his coat pocket. His instincts told him this case went deeper than stolen art. Much deeper.

The museum manager returned to the front desk and told the young feline attendant he'd be in his office if she needed anything. Once inside, he let out a long sigh and slumped into his chair, the weight of unease settling over him. He removed his jacket, loosened the top two buttons of his shirt, and pulled off his tie. With a quick swipe of his claw, he rolled up his sleeve and turned his wrist upward, revealing a dark red symbol burned into his fur — a hollowed coin. It was still clearly visible despite his dark coat. Fortunately, he wore gloves most of the time to keep it concealed.

Now he had a problem. Some nosy orange tabby was poking his ears where they didn't belong.

The manager shut the office door, picked up the phone, and dialed a number. It rang twice before a deep growl came through the receiver — the kind of voice that made your fur stand on end. He sounded like a lion. "We have a problem," the manager said, his voice shaky. "Someone's poking around the crime scene." "Is it the cops?" the voice rumbled back. "No," he replied quickly. "A private investigator... goes by Archibald Chesterfield."

There was a short silence before the voice returned, cool and low. "We'll take care of it." "Understood," the manager said, then hung up. He leaned back in his chair and exhaled, visibly rattled. He hated dealing with that cat — always so intense. But they couldn't afford more witnesses. They still hadn't pinned down the reporter. She'd been slippery.

There was a knock at the door. He quickly straightened, throwing his jacket back on and slipping into his curator gloves before opening it. "Yes?" he asked.

The young employee stood in the doorway. "Sorry to bother you, sir... but Detective Eddie is here to see you."

The manager blinked, then nodded. "I'll be right out," he said through clenched teeth.

He cursed under his breath. First the snooper, now the detective. What was his luck today?

Outside, he greeted Eddie with a forced smile. "Ah, Detective. How may I help you?" He couldn't help but look into those steely, intimidating eyes.

"I'm just here to take another look at the crime scene," Eddie said coolly.

The manager gestured with a paw. "Of course, Detective. I believe your partner is already in there."

Eddie blinked. "Oh, is he now?" he said, the sarcasm barely hidden. The manager handed him Archie's business card.

Eddie's face darkened, the blood visibly rushing to his ears. "Thanks," he said stiffly, and stormed off toward the roped-off exhibit.

Archie stood in the center of the gallery, deep in thought. Why this painting? Why take nothing else?

The stolen piece wasn't priceless. Valuable, sure — but not enough to justify a lone theft. He needed to find the painting. Only by studying it further could he hope to understand why it had been taken. Just then, a booming voice shook the room. "CHESTERFIELD!" Archie spun around, eyes wide. Bloody hell. It was Eddie.

He didn't even have time to brace — Eddie was on him in seconds. "Now, Eddie—" Archie started.

"Don't 'Eddie' me!" the detective barked, grabbing Archie by the scruff and twisting his ear. Archie winced in pain.

"What the hell are you doing here? I told you — stay out of this case!" Archie, still grimacing, couldn't help himself. "Sorry, Eddie... must be my hearing. I don't recall you saying that."

Eddie's eyes flashed — for a second, he saw Jimmy's face in Archie's. That same infuriating smirk. He let go, and Archie rubbed his ear, muttering.

"Explain," Eddie snapped. "Before I drag you out of here — and you know I will."

Archie straightened his coat. "I get it, Eddie, but something's off about this. Just look." He pointed at the empty wall. "No damage. No scratches. Nothing else in the room touched. And the dates on the plaque — they're wrong."

Eddie turned to the wall, jaw clenched. He didn't want to admit Archie had a point, but the spotless surface was damning. It was almost as if the painting had never been there. No scrape marks, no dust outlines. Just... gone.

"Bloody ghost must've taken it," Archie muttered under his breath.

Eddie exhaled. "You're right. But we can't discuss this officially. You need to leave — now. I'll call you in a few days." He escorted Archie out of the room.

Archie glanced at his watch and cursed. Five 'til eight. He turned to the museum manager. "Do you have a phone I could use? I need to make a quick call." The manager frowned. "It's not for personal use."

Eddie stepped in. "Apologies. It'll be quick — my responsibility." With a huff, the manager relented. "Fine. This way." Archie followed him into the office and picked up the phone. "Thanks. Just a minute — can you shut the door?" The manager did, and Archie quickly dialed Nora.

"Hello?" came the soft voice on the other end, tense with worry.

"Sorry I'm late. The car is downstairs — black sedan. Francis is a black and grey Maine Coon. You can't miss him. Good luck, Nora. I'll see you soon."

He hung up and stepped out. The manager was speaking quietly with Eddie. "All done," Archie said. "Thanks again."

Eddie walked him to the entrance, lit a cigarette, and took a slow drag. "Try staying out of trouble, especially police matters."

Archie grinned. "Be honest — would you have noticed there were no marks or that the painting's historical context was off?" Eddie grumbled. "The historical part? Not a chance." Archie tipped his hat. "Take care, Eddie." Eddie nodded. "I'll call in a few days. Stay sharp."

Archie walked down the sidewalk, satisfied. He had leads, he'd be meeting Nora soon — things were looking up. He muttered to himself, "Damn, forgot to call Teddy... oh well. Francis will fill him in." Then — tires screeched.

Before he could turn, a dark paw clamped over his mouth. He felt a sharp prick in his neck. His vision swam. Then, darkness.

Archie woke with a brutal, pounding ache behind his eyes. His skull throbbed in time with his heartbeat, every pulse like a drumbeat against bone. He tried to move but felt the tug of restraints. His paws were bound—rough rope, not plastic cuffs—and a blindfold dug uncomfortably into the fur behind his ears.

Where was he?

The last thing he remembered was walking away from the museum, trying to hail a cab to his brother's flat. Then— tires, a dark paw, the sting of a needle. "Focus," he whispered to himself. "Use your senses."

He forced himself to breathe, slow and deep, despite the pain. The air was thick with the scent of damp concrete, rust, and mildew. It was stifling—hot and musty, like a space sealed too long. The floor beneath him was cold, hard. Concrete, probably. Far from clean. But outside---- there. Faintly, he heard the muffled hum of cars. Honking. Voices. Street noise. He wasn't far from the city center.

That narrowed things. A basement? Maybe a derelict warehouse. Old factory, possibly. Somewhere forgotten by most—but still close enough to the beating heart of London.

Archie twisted his wrists experimentally. The rope bit into his fur. Tied tight, but not anchored to anything. Not yet.

He rolled to his side and rubbed the blindfold against the floor, grinding it against the concrete until it loosened. After a few rough scrapes, it slid up over one eye, and then the other. Blinking against the murky light, Archie pulled himself into a seated position against the wall. Across the room, he spotted a short set of stairs leading upward to a bolted door.

Wherever he was—it wasn't just underground. It was hidden. The door creaked. Archie stilled.

Two figures came down the stairs—both feline, both large. The first was a sleek black cat, tall and wiry, with a tattered eyepatch over his right eye. The second was stockier— burnt orange fur, dressed in slacks and a tight black T-shirt.

The black cat stepped into the light, revealing a mark scorched into the underside of his forearm. It was angry and red, still healing. A circular burn—no, more than a burn. A brand. The edges were blistered, raw. At the center of the ring was a hollowed-out core, like a coin missing its middle. Archie's breath caught. The Hollowed Coin.

He'd read about it once—tucked away in the back of a banned anthropology text. A mark used by a secret society thought to be defunct. Even the professor who'd written about it had called it myth. A fanciful idea. But here it was. Burned into flesh. They were real. "Pick him up," the black cat growled.

The orange one moved fast, hauling Archie upright and driving a fist into his gut. Archie doubled over, coughing violently. Blood rose in his throat.

The black cat followed with a right hook, then a left. Archie's world spun, ears ringing. His head lolled, and he spit blood to the floor. "What do you want?" he managed. The black cat leaned in, voice smooth and cold.

"Seems you've been sniffing where you don't belong, Mr. Chesterfield. We can't have that." He threw another punch— across the jaw. Archie laughed, blood on his lips.

"You're going to have to hit harder than that," he slurred, faking strength he didn't have. The black cat drew back, lining up a real knockout. Archie moved.

He slammed his boot heel down on the orange cat's foot. Hard. The thug yelped and recoiled— just enough. Archie ducked, and the black cat's punch missed him and caught the orange one clean in the snout. The orange cat toppled.

Archie surged forward, trying to ram the black cat, but he wasn't quick enough. A fist crashed into his ribs, sending him sprawling. He wheezed, clutching his chest. The black cat stepped in, towering. Three gunshots rang out. The black cat collapsed like a sack of bricks.

Archie blinked in disbelief. Slowly, painfully, he turned toward the stairs.

Eddie stood there—gun still raised, eyes sharp and scanning the room. Once he was sure no one else was coming, he rushed to Archie's side and started untying him. "You alright?" Eddie asked.

Archie winced. "Oh, I've been better. But I've also been worse." Eddie gave him a look. "You look like hell." "I feel like it too."

Eddie helped him up. The orange cat was out cold on the floor, blood leaking from his nose. "What happened to him?" Eddie asked.

Archie smirked. "Let's just say your friend's aim isn't great." "C'mon," Eddie said. "Let's get you to a hospital."

Archie pulled his arm free. "Wait. Not yet. We've got a chance here, Eddie. Let's look around before backup shows up."

"I already called it in," Eddie replied. "We've got fifteen minutes, tops."

Archie limped through the room, scanning for anything unusual. At first glance, it was just a dusty, disused basement. But something wasn't right. He passed a far wall. Stopped. Then turned back. "Eddie. Here." Eddie stepped away from the stairs, eyeing the wall. "Looks... off."

"False wall, maybe?" Archie ran his paw along the stonework, feeling for irregularities. "Help me."

They pushed together. One of the bricks gave under Archie's touch. He pressed it in. A section of wall slid back, groaning on hidden hinges.

Beyond it: a narrow tunnel, descending stone steps, and flickering lights ahead. They shared a glance, then stepped through.

The chamber was larger than it should've been. Shelves and pedestals lined the space, cluttered with crates, boxes, and items carefully covered in cloth. Archie pulled one aside and stared. Artifacts. Old. Rare. Some priceless. There—center stage—the missing painting from the museum.

Archie's eyes lit up. "Well, Detective. Looks like we're not going home empty-pawed." Eddie stared, stunned. "How the hell does this exist here? Has it always been under the city?"

Archie approached the painting and began inspecting the frame. Something didn't feel right. He ran a claw along the edge and—crack—a piece snapped loose. Eddie flinched. "Don't tell me you broke it."

But Archie didn't respond. His paw slipped inside the hollow space behind the frame and pulled something free. A book. A journal. Worn, leather-bound, and thick with dust. "What's in it?" Eddie stepped in behind him.

Archie shook off the grime, coughing as dust clouded the air. No title. No markings.

Then he saw it—small, near the bottom corner of the front cover. Two letters faded but unmistakable. J.C. Archie gasped. He flipped open the cover.

The first entry was dated, handwritten in a style he knew intimately. There was no doubt. "This was my father's." Eddie stared at him. "You sure?"

Archie's expression changed—no wit, no grin. Just something deep and solemn. Eddie had seen that look before.

It was the same one he wore the night they found Jimmy's body.

Eddie sighed. "Alright. I don't know what this is yet, but I'm with you. Let's get your statement in, then I'll get you home."

Archie nodded, sliding the journal into his coat as they turned back toward the stairs.

By the time they reached the surface, sirens were wailing down the block. Police vans. Uniforms. Medics.

The next twenty minutes blurred by. Paramedics patched Archie up while Eddie gave a short debrief. Archie, still in shock, kept a paw on his coat pocket like a soldier guarding something sacred.

When the medic finally cleared him to leave, Eddie asked, "You good to walk?" The doctor nodded. "More or less. He just needs rest." Eddie opened the cruiser door. Archie climbed in, sore and silent, his mind racing. Whatever this was... it had just become personal.

5

The drive to Teddy's house was dead quiet. Archie sat slumped in the passenger seat, wincing with every bump in the road. His ribs screamed. His head throbbed. But it wasn't just the pain — his mind was racing.

After a few long minutes, he finally broke the silence.

"How did you know where to find me?" he asked, voice hoarse. "I thought I was done for."

Eddie let out a low chuckle. "Truth be told, I got lucky. I was outside grabbing a smoke when I saw you get taken. Van pulled off fast, but I tailed it—kept back far enough to not get spotted. Then I followed the noise."

Archie managed a crooked grin. "So much for my brilliant plan to get kidnapped," he muttered, then winced. "Next time I'll think of something less painful." Eddie smirked. "Maybe stick to lectures."

They turned onto Teddy's Street. Archie caught sight of Francis's car in the driveway and felt a wave of relief. He hadn't realized how much he'd been holding his breath. After everything, he was just glad to be home — or close to it.

Eddie eased the cruiser to a stop. "Don't move. Let me help you out."

Archie gave a shallow nod. His body felt like it had been thrown down a flight of stairs. He kept one paw pressed against his jacket, holding the journal tight to his chest.

As Eddie helped him out of the car, the front door flew open.

Teddy came barreling down the walkway, panic plain on his face. Dolores followed just behind him.

Teddy reached Archie first, throwing his arms around him. "I thought I lost you!" he cried.

Archie groaned but returned the hug, even as pain flared down his side. "I'm alright," he said. "Really. I'm alright."

Eddie stood back, arms crossed. "Hate to break up the reunion," he said, "but he's banged up bad. He needs to lie down." Teddy nodded and slipped under Archie's other arm. "Dolores! Hot bath. First aid kit!" "I'm on it," she called, already halfway back inside.

Francis held the door open as they helped Archie through. Nora stood behind him, quiet but watching.

She was a sleek gray tabby with striking emerald eyes, her fur neatly kept beneath a tailored trench coat that hinted at style without excess.

A leather satchel hung from one shoulder—worn, but organized—while her gaze carried the sharpness of someone used to observing details others missed. Young, poised, and undeniably beautiful, she had the look of a cat who didn't just chase stories—she lived them.

Archie gave Francis a nod. "Thanks for getting her here." "Of course," Francis said.

Nora didn't speak but followed Dolores into the house.

Inside, Archie eased into the armchair, teeth gritted against the pain. His coat sagged open slightly, revealing the edge of the old leather-bound journal.

"I've got your payment in the safe," he said to Francis, voice low. Francis shook his head. "This one's on the house, Archie. Just glad you made it back." Archie exhaled hard, too drained to argue.

He looked at Francis, then Eddie. "Give me a minute with Teddy?"

The two of them nodded and stepped into the kitchen without a word.

Archie leaned back, closed his eyes, and waited. He knew Teddy was about to let loose. He could feel it in the air — that tightly coiled tension that only a brother could carry.

Teddy stepped in front of him, mouth half open, already mid lecture.

Archie held up a paw and reached into his coat. "Before you say it…" He pulled the journal out and handed it over.

Teddy's face went still. He adjusted his glasses and stared at the worn cover. His paw hovered over the faded initials. "J.C.…" he murmured. "Open it," Archie said. "First page." Teddy did.

His eyes moved across the handwritten lines, slow and deliberate. His jaw tightened. His breathing hitched. When he finally looked up, his eyes were glassy. "This… this is Dad's…"

Teddy handed the journal back to Archie, then sank into the chair across from him, tears still streaming down his face.

For a long moment, neither of them spoke. Then Archie broke the silence.

"I have to solve this, Teddy. I have to know how Dad was mixed up in all of this…"

He paused, the weight of the journal pressing against his lap.

"The accident—Teddy, what if it wasn't an accident? After what happened tonight, I can't ignore the possibility that there was foul play involved. And the Hollowed Coin… it's at the center of it."

Teddy wiped his face with the back of his paw. He hated that Archie might be right. As much as he wanted to tell him to drop it, there was no going back now.

"First thing's first," Teddy said quietly. "We've got to get you back to one hundred percent."

Eddie stepped back into the room, followed by Dolores carrying the first aid kit. Francis lingered by the door. "I'll take off," Francis said. "But if you need anything, Archie—anything—you just call." Archie gave him a grateful nod. "Thanks again."

Dolores spent the next several minutes tending to Archie's wounds with careful precision. Afterward, she helped him into the bath, where the hot water eased the tension in his battered body. Archie let himself exhale, letting the steam work through the stiffness in his bones.

When the bath was done, Dolores had already turned down the guest bed for him. Archie changed, crawled under the covers, and sank into the mattress. All he wanted was sleep. It had been the longest day of his life. But sleep didn't come easily.

He stared up at the ceiling, the shadows dancing across the plaster. Thoughts swirled—his father's journal, the Hollowed Coin, the danger that was creeping too close to the people he loved. He let out a slow breath and finally closed his eyes. Sleep found him at last.

The morning light crept in through the curtains, slow and quiet.

Archie stirred, groggy and aching. He couldn't remember the last time he'd slept this late— or felt this drained. He reached for his pocket watch. Nearly 11 A.M.

Archie groaned and sat up, easing out of bed. He grabbed his robe and shuffled toward the stairs. Every step sent a jolt of soreness through his ribs. They say the day after a hard workout—or getting severely beaten—hurts worse than the injury itself. Archie winced and coughed. "Bloody hell," he muttered.

Teddy's voice called from downstairs, alarmed. "Wait there! Let me help you."

Archie sighed, leaning against the wall. A moment later, Teddy was bounding up the steps and slipping under his brother's arm.

"Come on, slow down," Teddy said, guiding him to the kitchen table.

Dolores appeared with a warm smile and a fresh cup of coffee. "Hungry?"

Archie's stomach growled loud enough to answer for him. "Absolutely famished, my dear," he said, eyes half-closed in gratitude.

Dolores chuckled, gave his shoulder a gentle pat, and returned to the kitchen.

Archie sat back, savoring the quiet. The coffee was perfect— strong, earthy, just a touch of sugar. He let himself settle into the moment, grateful to be upright, grateful to be alive. Then came a long, exaggerated yawn. Archie looked up to see Eddie stretching, still bleary-eyed.

"Well," Eddie said, grinning, "look who finally woke up." Teddy shot him a glare. Eddie ignored it completely. Archie raised an eyebrow and sipped again.

"Says the one who also just rolled out of bed," he quipped, chuckling despite the pain.

Teddy chuckled too, despite himself. In the kitchen, Dolores and Nora shared a laugh over something out of view. Archie watched them for a moment—this strange little mix of family, friends, and fugitives—and felt a rare sense of peace. They were safe. For now. And they were in it together.

About an hour later, Dolores and Nora brought out a spread that could feed a dozen:

pancakes, sausage, French toast, eggs, jam, buttered toast— if you could think of it, it was on the table.

Dolores leaned close to Archie and whispered, "Archie... you're drooling."

He flushed, grabbed a napkin, and wiped his mouth, half-laughing, half-embarrassed.

After a short blessing, they all began to eat. Archie looked across the table at Nora. She still seemed tense, but less so than the night before. Being around Teddy and Dolores— kind, grounded, warm—had softened her guard.

Archie forked a piece of pancake into his mouth, followed it with a sip of coffee, and spoke gently. "How are you holding up, Nora?" She blinked, surprised by the question. "I'm... okay. I think. I'm still not sure what I've walked into."

Archie nodded. "When we spoke on the phone, I was focused on getting you somewhere safe.

I didn't expect everything to turn out the way it has. For that, I'm sorry." Nora stopped him with a shake of her head.

"If it weren't for you, I might not even be here right now. I just hope I can help—with whatever information I've got."

Archie smiled, finishing his bite. "You have my word—I'll do everything I can to protect you."

Teddy spoke up. "And you're welcome to stay with us as long as you need, Nora. No pressure. No danger." Nora looked between them, then to Dolores. "Thank you... all of you. This means more than I can say."

As the meal wound down, Archie pushed back from the table and gave Teddy a glance. It was time. Teddy knew that look.

Archie had a particular way of analyzing things—laying out information, seeing how it fit together, spotting patterns no one else could. It was as if his mind could take scattered fragments and make sense of them in a way that felt effortless.

That, Teddy thought, was what made his brother dangerous.

Archie calmly moved the plates and coffee cups to the side. Dolores stepped in behind him, collecting the dishes and carrying them into the kitchen. She'd seen Archie in this mode before, but it still caught her off guard—this switch he flipped when the puzzle pieces finally started lining up.

Not everyone got to see Archibald Chesterfield in his element.

Archie placed the old journal down on the table like it was a relic. His fingers moved across the worn leather with care. He opened it slowly, as if it might fall apart in his hands.

From the main floor storage closet, Teddy rolled in a dry erase board, parking it near the table. Then he stepped beside Dolores and watched in silence.

"This," Archie said, tapping a faded sketch in the journal, "is the earliest record I've found of the Hollowed Coin." They all leaned in to look.

Journal Entry — 25 Years Ago — Inked in faded black cursive

March 4th — Met with a contact outside Holloway Market. Claims the coin isn't just a myth. Symbol carved in bone, passed through generations like a curse. He spoke of 'The Marked'— those branded with the coin's shape. When I asked why they were chosen, he only said: "Because they knew too much."

Eddie narrowed his eyes. "So this mark—the one you saw at the warehouse—it's the same?"

Archie nodded. "Every detail. The circle, the break through the center, even the way it was burned in. It wasn't random. Someone meant for me to see it."

He turned another page, revealing frantic scribbles— maps, names, cities all connected by desperate lines.

"My father followed this symbol across continents. He thought it was just historical... until it started to feel like something else. Something real."

Nora scanned the notes. "And you think the people who grabbed you are tied to this group?" "They didn't just grab me," Archie said. "They wanted to send a message. They're part of something that's been hiding in plain sight for generations."

Journal Entry – 18 Years Ago – Smudged, ink running slightly

Something wrong with the Marseille coin— looks newer, too clean. A replica, perhaps? But why place it in the hands of another 'Marked'? I fear I'm no longer chasing history—I'm trespassing on someone's territory. They don't want this known. The deeper I dig, the more the shadows close in.

Teddy scratched behind his ear. "So… the real coin is still out there?"

"That's the question, isn't it?" Archie stepped to the whiteboard and uncapped a marker. He drew the symbol—clean and exact: a perfect circle, broken through the middle with a jagged hollow gap.

"They've tried to bury their trail. But they missed something."

He flipped to the back of the journal and pulled out a sketch. He pinned it to the board. A coin, surrounded by carved stone pillars and ancient glyphs. "This came from Peru," he said. "A site deep in the Andes.

My father believed it was connected to the Aztec Scroll." Nora leaned in. "Wait—the Aztec Scroll?"

"He thought the coin and the Scroll were part of the same system," Archie said. "The coin not just as a mark… but a key."

Eddie looked over the sketch again. "And your parents? This all connects back to them?" Archie paused, his paw resting on the journal. "They were killed. James and Olivia Chesterfield. The report said car accident—brake failure. But the timing's too clean. My father's notes stop… and then they're gone."

Dolores spoke up quietly. "I knew how they died. Teddy told me. But I wasn't there. I didn't know them. And I never saw this side of it."

Archie looked up. "They didn't just die. They were erased."

For a moment, no one said a word. Then Nora stepped closer to the board, eyes scanning the layers of symbols and scribbled theories.

"You figured all this out from a handful of notes and half a symbol?" Archie nodded once.

Eddie exhaled, shaking his head. "Remind me never to underestimate a quiet professor again."

Teddy gave a soft laugh. "This is why I always lose arguments with him."

Dolores smiled faintly. "This is who he is when the dust starts to settle. He sees things no one else does."

Journal Entry — Final Entry — Writing shaky, stained

The coin is not just a warning or a mark—it's a key. A physical one. Crafted with precision, likely in limited number. I found references to it in stonework along the Veracruz corridor— pre-Columbian etchings that match the Hollowed Coin symbol, but with grooves, like a lock. What does it open? The Scroll, or perhaps only part of it. I no longer believe the Scroll is a single piece. If I'm right, it was split—deliberately. Half is hidden somewhere in the mountains, the other... still unknown. But the coin key must come first. The site near Cempoala holds promise. I'll start there.

Archie closed the journal with a soft thud. Then, calmly, he looked up.

"My father believed the Hollowed Coin was a key. A real one. Carvings he found in Mexico— grooved, mechanical— lined up with the coin's pattern. He thought it might unlock part of the Scroll. But the Scroll was split. Half of it's missing. He traced that lead to a site near Cempoala."

Nora stared at the map he unfurled, showing a faded red X near the Gulf Coast.

"Cempoala," Archie said. "An ancient Totonac city, later absorbed by the Aztec Empire. If the key still exists, it's buried there." Eddie straightened. "Then we head to Mexico." Archie turned toward Teddy and Dolores. "You two are staying here."

Teddy raised a brow. "Not going to argue. If I disappear, it'll raise alarms in Parliament. But I can look into this from the other side—dig through old funding records, quiet reports.

If this thing ever crossed into government hands, I'll find it." Archie nodded. "That's exactly what I need from you." He turned to Dolores. "Watch his back. And yours."

She smiled. "We'll keep the home front steady. Just don't get yourselves killed chasing myths."

Archie tucked the map under his arm and looked at the team. "Nora. Eddie. Pack light. We leave in the morning."

He let the silence settle for a moment—then added, with a quiet certainty that none of them would forget:

"They've already taken too much from us. It's time we take something back."

6

The day passed in a hush of contemplation. No one said it aloud, but the weight of what was coming pressed on them all.

Archie stood by the window, his eyes on the sliver of grey sky between buildings. The quiet wasn't unwelcome—it gave him room to think. But thinking brought questions. And questions brought doubt.

He turned to Teddy. "I need to call Francis. Head back to my flat and grab a few things."

Teddy's expression tightened. "Archie, this is beyond dangerous…"

A pause hung between them before he added, "But if we don't do this, no one will. And Mum and Dad… they deserve the justice."

Archie gave a silent nod, already moving. He dressed, buttoning his coat with methodical precision, and called Francis. One ring. "This is Frank."

"I need a ride to my flat, then back to Teddy's," Archie said. "Tomorrow, we'll need a lift to the airport—me, Nora, and Eddie." "I'll be there in an hour," Francis replied. In the living room, time passed more easily.

Teddy and Eddie sat at the chessboard, their pieces slowly vanishing from the board.

Dolores sat nearby, knitting something half-finished with a faraway smile, while Nora lounged on the sofa, amused. Teddy made a calculated move. Eddie scowled. "Ah—I'm rusty," Eddie muttered, adjusting his tie.

Nora grinned. "No, looks like he's just mopping the floor with you."

Dolores laughed softly, placing a hand on Eddie's shoulder. "Darling, challenging Teddy or Archie to chess is just asking for a slow, painful death."

Eddie chuckled despite himself. "Next time I'm bringing a checkers board."

Laughter rolled through the room. Even Archie cracked a small smile from the hallway before slipping out.

The car ride felt longer than it should've. Each turn, each bump in the road, reminded Archie that he was still bruised—but he didn't flinch. Not anymore. The ache had become part of the mission.

He reached his flat and approached the door with caution. Was the Hollowed Coin watching? Had they already been here? No signs. No disturbance.

He unlocked the door and stepped inside. Everything was untouched books on their shelves, the air faintly scented with lemon oil from last week's cleaning. It almost made him feel normal.

He crossed to the phone and dialed the university. A few rings, then, "Cambridge University, Donna speaking."

"Hi Donna, it's Archie." "Mr. Chesterfield! How are you?"

He lied with ease. "Well, thank you. I need to take urgent leave—something's come up overseas. A family matter. A few months."

"Oh dear. The Dean's left for the day, but I'll speak with him first thing tomorrow. You're one of our finest, Archie. We'll make sure your classes are covered." "Thank you, Donna. You're a lifesaver." Click... Archie hangs up the phone.

In the center of the room, Archie pushed aside the coffee table, then rolled back the rug to reveal three uneven floorboards. He pried them up and retrieved a weathered canvas bag. Beneath layers of normalcy—Archie kept a second life.

He replaced the boards, the rug, the table, and carried the bag to his bedroom. From his closet he pulled an overnight bag and began to pack: a few sets of clothes, his passport, and £150,000 in cash.

Money he'd tucked away over years of private investigation work—for situations exactly like this. He chuckled, dryly. "Well... emergency confirmed."

He added rope, a harness, a compass, and other field tools. Anything else, they'd acquire on the ground.

Then he changed into a neat traveling jacket and opened a small black box in the back of the closet. Inside: his Colt .45.

He checked the slide. Loaded. He filled spare clips, then holstered it at his side.

Back at Teddy's, laughter was still floating from the living room. Nora had taken over the chessboard, demanding a rematch on Eddie's behalf while Dolores teased them both.

But when Archie returned, silence followed his entrance. His presence said everything.

Francis leaned on the car, arms crossed, watching Archie approach with a packed bag and the quiet weight of readiness. "Heading to war?" Francis asked, one brow raised.

Archie adjusted his coat and said flatly, "This is the last time they catch us with our pants down." Francis smirked. "Fair enough." He opened the door.

They drove in silence, the engine humming low beneath the falling sun. The sky blushed orange, then dipped into indigo. Archie watched it fade. Tomorrow, they'd chase the first clue. One way or another—They'd uncover the truth.

Archie stepped out and knocked on the window. Francis rolled it down, confused. Archie held out his paw—folded tightly in it was £5,000. Francis tried to protest but Archie was already walking into Teddy's house. Archie removed his hat and walked toward Teddy and Eddie, his eyes drifting to the bottle of Silver Tabby Vintage resting on the coffee table.

"You planning to share any of that fine whiskey?" he said with a grin, glancing at Eddie.

Before Eddie could answer, Teddy was already pouring a glass and handing it off to Archie with a warm smile, doing his best to ease the weight of what lay ahead.

Eddie raised an eyebrow and took a sip. "If I'd known you Chesterfields had such good taste, I would've dropped by sooner."

Archie chuckled, taking a sip of his own. "That's just because you spend too much time being a grumpy old goat. All you had to do was ask."

Teddy and Eddie both laughed. It was good to see Archie like this again—relaxed, charming. Even if just for the evening, it felt like the old him was back.

From the kitchen, Nora stepped into view. She saw the three of them laughing and drinking and cleared her throat loudly as she approached—interrupting them on purpose.

"It's not very gentlemanly to leave a lady out," she said, crossing her arms. "I thought you lot had manners?"

The three cats straightened slightly, surprised. Nora had been quiet, nervous—almost shy— since everything started. But now, there was fire in her voice. Archie smiled. "Forgive me, my dear…"

He grabbed another glass, poured her a generous measure, and handed it to her without missing a beat. Nora took it, sipped confidently.

"There's the witty author I've been reading about," Archie said. "Now where have you been hiding all this time?" Nora blushed, just a little, and smiled behind the rim of her glass.

Archie raised his and gently clinked it against hers. "Welcome to the club," he said warmly. "Take a seat. I think we're long overdue to hear your side of all this."

Teddy stood and set his glass down. "I'll go help Dolores with dinner."

He stepped into the kitchen, where Dolores had just finished arranging the last of the spread. She smiled and greeted him with a quick kiss on the cheek.

"Can you take these out to the table?" she asked, handing him two large platters.

"Of course," Teddy said, grabbing them carefully and heading to the dining room.

Back in the living room, Archie pulled out a chair and motioned for Nora to sit. He took another slow sip, then set his glass on the coffee table beside him.

"So," he said, settling in, "what led you to write that article about the Hollowed Coin?"

Nora leaned back in her seat, her tone turning serious. "Well," she said, "it started about a month ago—before the robbery even happened..."

Nora swirled the whiskey in her glass, her tone growing quieter as the room settled.

"I was working fluff pieces at The Daily Paw—light events, local profiles. Nothing that ever-made waves. Then one morning, an envelope appeared on my desk. No return address. Just a single photograph. Aged. Faded at the corners." She looked past the rim of her glass.

"It was a coin. Black. Flat. Hollow in the center. Looked ancient. On the back, written in faded ink, was one line: 'The Hollowed Coin holds what the eyes cannot.'

"I thought it was a prank. Until I took the ink to the lab. It was old. Much older than anything that should've come through the mail." She took a measured breath before continuing.

"I started digging—quietly. The Hollowed Coin kept turning up in strange places. Shipping records. Obscure academic references. I even found a redacted police report tied to a disappearance at the London Museum. Fifteen years ago. The same museum that just got hit." She set her glass gently on the table.

"Then I found a name. It wasn't in the report, but in a document connected to an archival review of an Aztec scroll. A consultant listed as James Chesterfield." She turned her eyes toward Archie.

"I didn't include the name in the article. It wasn't confirmed, and I didn't know who he was.

But when I saw your name, and the timing of the robbery... I started connecting the dots." Her voice dropped further.

"A few weeks later, another envelope came. No note. Just a torn piece of map and a coin replica—same hollow center."

She paused. "That night, I had a strange feeling something was off. The locks looked untouched. But when I walked into my flat..." She looked up at both of them, serious now. "...the coin was sitting on top of my typewriter." Eddie leaned forward, brows furrowed.

"They didn't break in. They just got in. Quiet. Clean. Left it there like a message." She nodded. "Whoever it was... they were warning me. Telling me to stop."

"But I didn't," she added, voice firmer now. "I couldn't. I needed to know what it meant." She turned to Archie.

"I wrote the article, hoping someone out there knew more than I did. Someone who might understand the pieces I couldn't put together." She hesitated for a moment, then met his gaze fully.

"I didn't expect it to be you. But I'm here now. And I'm not walking away."

Archie sat there, paws slowly spinning the empty glass in front of him. The weight of Nora's story lingered in the air—the reach of the Hollowed Coin sinking in deeper than he'd expected. Dolores finally broke the silence. "Dinner's ready," she said gently.

The words pulled Archie from his thoughts. He blinked, looked up, and offered Nora a nod. "Thank you... for telling your part," he said.

His stomach let out a low growl. He looked at Dolores with a sheepish grin. "Guess it really is time to eat."

The table had already been set with care, and the smell of roasted vegetables and seasoned cuts filled the room. Archie couldn't help but start to salivate.

Dinner passed with a quiet comfort—warm memories shared, new bonds forming. They laughed in short bursts, ate until the plates were bare, and ended the meal with a rich apple crumb dessert served warm with brandy caramel and a scoop of vanilla ice cream.

Later, Archie and Teddy stood by the fireplace, watching the occasional spark drift upward and disappear into the chimney's shadow. The phone rang.

Archie stepped away and answered calmly, "Chesterfield residence."

Teddy watched, curious about the caller. Archie spoke quietly, his tone deliberate but not tense. It was clear he recognized the voice on the other end.

While he listened, Teddy let his thoughts wander. Archie had connections—plenty of them. Old clients, debtors, people who owed him favors from his private investigation days. Cats in high and low places.

Archie returned to the fire, poking at the embers with the iron.

"That was my flight broker," he said to Teddy. "We've got a private flight to Cempoala."

Teddy raised an eyebrow. "How'd you swing that? I doubt it was free."

Without saying a word, Archie grabbed his overnight bag, unzipped it, and flipped it open. Teddy leaned in, then froze. "Blimey..."

Inside was a stack of bundled cash—tens of thousands of pounds.

Archie didn't flinch. "Private investigations have paid off over the years. I've been saving this... just in case."

Teddy stared. "I knew you were doing well, but I didn't think you had a stash like that just lying around."

"It should cover most of our expenses," Archie said, zipping the bag closed again. "And if I can help it, I don't want Nora or Eddie paying a single coin. This isn't their mess—it's ours."

Teddy nodded slowly as Archie pulled out his pipe and began packing it with catnip. Teddy chuckled and reached for the cigar box on the mantel—the same one they'd dipped into just weeks ago.

He cut himself a cigar. "If we're doing this, we're doing it right."

Eddie came downstairs, now dressed more casually—slacks and a fitted tee. He raised an eyebrow as he spotted Archie lighting the pipe. "What've you got there?" Eddie asked.

Archie blew a lazy smoke ring into the air. "Simple pleasures," he said.

Teddy handed Eddie a cigar without a word. Eddie took it, rolled it under his nose, and gave an approving nod.

"Quality," he muttered. "Thanks." He lit the tip with a match, gave it a few puffs, and exhaled a full-bodied cloud across the room.

Then he looked at the brothers. *"Where'd you get these?"*

Teddy, cigar clenched in his teeth, mumbled, *"Fumar."*

Eddie laughed. *"You Chesterfields are something else."*

Archie smirked and blew another smoke ring. "You can't put a price on quality."

The three sat and smoked by the fire, trading stories and quiet conversation. Dolores and Nora had already turned in for the night. Outside, the wind had softened, and the house felt still.

As the final ember glowed faintly in the hearth, Archie stared into the fire. His pipe hung loose from his mouth, the last curl of smoke drifting upward. Tomorrow, they'd leave the safety of home behind. And step into the unknown.

He chewed softly on the stem of his pipe, jaw tight with resolve.

He would uncover the truth. And if he could... he'd stop the Hollowed Coin.

7

Archie was up early, his nerves taut with focus. The warmth of the previous night's laughter had faded, replaced by the weight of the journey ahead. He descended the stairs from the guest room, the muffled sounds of morning preparation rising to meet him.

Teddy sat at the table, quietly eating a bowl of cereal, his coffee steaming nearby. Dolores sipped her tea, already dressed, her usual cheerful energy subdued. There was no time for one of her famous breakfasts this morning. They were leaving soon.

Without a word, Dolores stood and poured Archie a cup of coffee. He gave her a grateful smile. The warmth in the mug felt grounding—just what he needed to steady himself.

Not long after, Nora and Eddie came down the stairs, bags in tow and ready for departure. The group gathered for one last quiet moment together. Outside, the sharp honk of Francis's horn cut through the air.

They stepped out onto the drive. Hugs were exchanged, words too heavy for full expression passed in glances and grip. Teddy hugged Archie tightly and whispered, "Come back, you hear me?" Archie held him just as fiercely. "I will, Ted. I will."

They climbed into Francis's car and began the drive to the airport. The ride was quiet. Traffic streamed by in blurs, each passing car marking the seconds slipping away. When they arrived, Francis helped unload the bags. One by one, they gathered their things and made their way inside.

A flight administrator approached them near the check-in desk. "Is one of you Mr. Archibald Chesterfield?"

Archie raised a paw, flashing a dry smile. "That'd be me."

"Please follow me," the man said, gesturing for them to come along.

They followed him through a long hallway, past restricted doors and onto the tarmac. Waiting for them was a modest private plane, its engine humming faintly in the morning light. The administrator tipped his cap. "Safe flight, Mr. Chesterfield."

Archie nodded and led the others up the steps. Inside, the plane was a bit cramped but clean and serviceable. He unzipped his bag, removed a neat bundle of £3,000 in crisp notes, and tucked the bag beneath his seat.

He made his way up to the cockpit, where the pilot turned with a nod. "We'll be taking off shortly, Mr. Chesterfield. Do you have the payment?"

Archie handed him the money. The pilot thumbed through it quickly, gave a curt nod, and slipped it into a leather pouch beside his chair. "Thank you, sir. Please buckle up and enjoy the ride."

With a polite tip of his hat, Archie returned to his seat. Moments later, the hum of the engine rose, and the wheels began to roll. The sky ahead waited—untamed, uncertain, and full of secrets.

The flight stretched on, the drone of the engines filling the cabin with a steady hum. Archie leaned back in his seat, tugged his hat low over his eyes, and let the motion of the plane lull him into rest.

Across the aisle, Nora glanced at Eddie. "So," she said, her tone light but curious, "what made you want to become a cop?"

Eddie smirked. "That an interview question, or are you working on a story?"

Nora grinned. "Maybe both. You're more interesting than you let on."

He wasn't sure if she was teasing or serious. He let out a short breath, then said, "My folks were both on the force. It was the world I grew up in. Kind of felt natural to follow the badge."

He paused, eyes narrowing slightly as memories pulled at him.

"Back when I was a beat cop, I lost my partner. We walked into an arms deal that had inside connections—real dirty stuff. Turned out some of the rot was inside the department. Nearly cost me my life." He leaned back, jaw clenched briefly, before shaking it off. "Anyway, that was a long time ago."

Nora leaned in slightly. "That's heavy. I'd love to write something like that one day—real, raw. The kind of story that sticks."

Eddie gave a half-shrug. "It's all ancient history now. Made the papers, sure, but trust doesn't come easy when the damage is done. Took years to clean up the mess."

Nora's smile turned a touch nostalgic. "Reminds me of my first real story. Not as intense, but I got my share of threats. Guess truth's never as welcome as people say."

Eddie met her eyes, something unspoken passing between them. Then he nodded. "Yeah. That's the truth."

Archie drifted in and out of sleep for most of the flight— more tired than he cared to admit. The weight of everything—his father's legacy, the Hollowed Coin, and the journey ahead— pressed heavier with each mile they crossed. A sudden voice snapped him out of his thoughts. "Hey, Chesterfield!" the pilot called from the cockpit.

Archie jolted upright, briefly disoriented before recognizing the voice. He blinked, rubbed his eyes, and stood, making his way forward. "We'll be landing soon," the pilot said. "Time to get ready."

Archie nodded, turned back, and roused Nora and Eddie from their dozing seats. They stirred with quiet groans, still stiff from the long flight.

He returned to his seat and buckled in. The engines dipped in pitch as the plane began its descent. They were finally here.

The plane bumped and shuddered to a halt, its wheels skidding slightly on the uneven dirt runway. Outside, a haze of dust rolled past the windows, thick and red as clay. Archie blinked against the light, the dense heat already seeping into the cabin before the door had even opened.

"Not exactly a tourist landing," Eddie muttered, rolling his shoulder and glancing out.

Archie stood, straightened his coat, and led the way down the steps.

The air hit like a wet towel—thick, hot, and heavy with jungle scent. They stepped onto the packed earth, their paws crunching against loose gravel. Off to the side, parked beneath the crooked shadow of a drooping tree, sat an old jeep, rust chewing at its edges. Leaning against it, like She'd been waiting all morning, was a cat unlike any Archie had ever seen.

She wasn't tall—short-legged, in fact—but carried herself with a presence that immediately drew the eye. Her fur was thick and wild, a swirl of black and burnt orange that shimmered like dying embers under the Cempoala sun. She wore a wide-brimmed hat that shaded sharp amber eyes, a loose cream shirt rolled at the sleeves, and cargo pants that had seen their share of mud and dust. She looked ready for a trek into hell, and maybe back again. "You Chesterfield?" she called out. Archie stopped, ears flicking. "Who's asking?"

She pushed off the jeep with practiced ease, her movements slow, confident. "Name's Mabel. Your father and I crossed paths once. Long time ago."

That landed harder than Archie expected. He didn't flinch, but his jaw tightened.

"I heard someone with your name was flying in," Mabel continued, her tone even. "And around here? The name Chesterfield still stirs things up."

Eddie stepped up beside Archie, arms crossed, eyes locked on her. "And who exactly did you hear that from?"

She didn't bother looking at him. "Let's just say I know where to listen. This place doesn't like strangers snooping. When someone like you shows up, it kicks the dust up."

Archie narrowed his eyes slightly. "And what makes you think we're here for anything more than a quiet holiday?"

Mabel gave a faint smile. "Because I knew your father, and James Chesterfield wasn't the type to take quiet holidays. From the look of you... neither are you." That shut him up for a beat.

Then, without another word, Mabel reached into a weathered side pouch and pulled something small and black. She gave it a casual toss toward Archie.He caught it instinctively. Cold metal met his paw.

He turned it over slowly—a coin. Flat black. Hollowed center. The Hollowed Coin.

His breath caught. Nora leaned closer, trying to glimpse it. Eddie tensed.

Mabel's tone dropped. "He gave me that once. Told me if anything ever happened to him, to wait for someone else to come asking. I figured I'd know when the time came."

Eddie stepped forward, voice sharp. "You show up out of nowhere with one of those, and expect us to just hop in your jeep?"

"I don't expect anything," Mabel said coolly. "You're free to walk into the jungle blind if you want. But if you're really following your father's trail, that coin's just the beginning. What's ahead makes it look harmless."

Eddie looked to Archie, eyes tight. "This is bad. Every part of this scream's setup."

Archie stared at the coin a moment longer, then slipped it into his coat pocket. "Yeah, I know."

Mabel moved to the back of the jeep and opened the hatch.

"You coming, or planning to melt out here in that coat?"

Archie looked at her one more time—measuring her, weighing it. She wasn't lying. But she wasn't telling him everything, either. Still, they needed her.

He climbed in without another word. Nora followed, and after a long pause, Eddie threw his bag in and climbed aboard last, still glaring at the back of Mabel's head.

The jeep engine roared to life, coughing smoke, and rolled forward into the dust and heat— toward the unknown.

As the jeep disappeared into the horizon, deep in the brush just out of sight, a lone figure adjusted a pair of field binoculars, tracking the vehicle until only dust remained. Quietly, he slipped back into the jungle.

Far from the surface, buried beneath the roots of the rainforest, flickering torchlight danced along the walls of an underground network. Tunnels twisted like veins, filled with crates, stolen relics, faded maps, and weapons from forgotten times. It was more than a lair—it was a cathedral of crime.

In its heart stood a *towering statue—a massive Hollowed Coin*, carved in stone, its center open and ringed with Aztec glyphs. *Before it, tall and silent, stood a she-cat cloaked in shadow. Her fur was a haunting mosaic of black and sandy gold, swirling together like fire and smoke.* She traced a claw across the weathered design, lost in thought. She didn't turn as footsteps echoed behind her. *"Speak," she said, voice sharp as obsidian.*

A tomcat approached and knelt. He was lean, gray-striped, with scars across one ear and a long, nervous tail. He kept his eyes low.

"The Chesterfield group has landed. I followed as instructed."

She hissed softly at the name, the sound low and venomous. He hesitated. "Perhaps… it would be wiser to strike now. Kill them before they get too close.*" Silence. Too late, he realized his mistake.*

In a blur, she was on him—faster than instinct. His back hit the stone wall with a crack, her claws wrapped tight around his throat. His breath caught. His legs thrashed.

"You presume to advise me?" she whispered, her eyes glowing like coals, breath curling like steam between her fangs. *"No. You presume I forgot."* Her claws tightened, digging in.

"I lost James Chesterfield once," she hissed. *"He escaped with a scroll fragment—he never even saw the full truth— and left this—"* she raised her free paw, revealing three deep scars down her ribs that used to be there, *"—as a reminder. But I remember."* She leaned in close, her voice now a whisper behind clenched teeth. *"I never forget."* The tom tried to speak—eyes wide, panic setting in. She whispered, tenderly now, *"What's my name?"* He wheezed. "R-Roxanne…" The sound of bone snapping echoed through the chamber. His body dropped in a heap.

Another servant, younger, already waiting in the shadows, stepped forward and bowed low.

"Follow Chesterfield," Roxanne ordered. "Keep your distance. Watch everything. Report only what matters." "Yes, mistress," the young tom said, already retreating.

Roxanne stood in the torchlight, her breath steady, her claws still stained.

She turned and strode deeper into the cavern, until she reached a ledge—overlooking a deep chasm with a narrow tunnel mouth on the other side. The distance was impossible for most. She didn't hesitate. She leapt.

Her paws landed silent on the far side, as if the laws of nature didn't apply to her. She straightened, staring-into the dark ahead. *"Chesterfield..."*

The name still tasted like blood and failure. Not this time. This time, he would lose.

The jeep rattled along the winding trail, tires crunching over gravel and roots. Jungle surrounded them on all sides— dense, wet, and loud with life. Mabel drove with one paw on the wheel and the other casually resting on the gear stick, her eyes shielded by the brim of her wide hat.

She didn't talk much. Just kept her gaze forward, the wind brushing her fur back in lazy streaks.

Archie sat up front, poring over a faded field map. His claws tapped gently over a worn spot. "This ridge here... it guards the ruins. If the temple's still standing, the key should be hidden inside."

Eddie, from the back seat, muttered, "Hidden's one word for it. So's buried."

Next to him, Nora adjusted the strap on her satchel and leaned forward. "Actually, I think you're off by a mile." She pointed to a notation on the edge of the map. "Mortimer's field notes mentioned an auxiliary site—some Spanish mission ruins that were co-opted by the Aztecs. He thought the key may have been moved during the raids."

Archie blinked, his eyes narrowing. "That report was in the museum's archive vault. Misfiled under restoration logs." "I dug a little deeper," Nora said, her ears flicking modestly. "It stood out." He smiled. "Good work." Eddie gave her a glance, still not sure what to make of her. "All that digging, and you didn't mention it until now?"

"I wasn't sure it mattered," she replied, brushing a leaf off her jacket. "I am now." Mabel suddenly slowed the jeep. "Hold."

Up ahead, the trail ended abruptly—a massive tree blocked the path. Its trunk was cleancut, not toppled or rotted. Deliberate. Eddie cursed under his breath. "That's no accident."

Archie stepped out, scanning the treeline. The jungle had gone quiet.

"They're trying to force us off course," he said. "Maybe even trap us." "The Hollowed Coin," Mabel said flatly. Eddie answered before Archie could. "No doubt."

Archie crouched near the tree, examining the axe marks. "Fresh. They were here not long ago."

Nora looked at the map again. "There's a narrow footpath just east—probably used by hunters or surveyors. It skirts the ridge and leads toward the ruins."

Mabel was already slinging a bag over her shoulder. "We'll have to hoof it. Jeep can't climb those rocks."

Eddie grunted. "Fan out when we go. If they're watching, I want them wondering who's watching back."

Archie gave Nora a nod. "Stay close but keep your eyes open. That sharp head of yours may save us yet."

Nora returned the nod, her grip tightening on her satchel.

Eddie reached into his coat and pulled out a compact sidearm. He held it out to her. "You ever fire one of these?"

Nora hesitated, then took it. "At bottles," she said quietly. "Not Cats."

Eddie gave her a hard look. "Point and breathe. You won't have time to think." She nodded again and tucked the pistol into her bag.

They left the road behind, vanishing into the overgrowth. Behind them, the ruined path lay still—until, far above, a faint shimmer of movement flicked through the leaves. Watching. Waiting.

The trail turned mean fast—narrow, overgrown, steep in places. Vines reached like arms, tugging at fur and gear, while the heat soaked through their coats like a second skin. Birds screamed above. Something hissed in the brush.

Mabel led the way, machete swinging. She didn't speak, didn't glance back. Just moved, sure and steady.

Archie followed, his map folded and tucked away now—this was instinct and memory. Eddie came next, every few steps glancing over his shoulder, paw near his sidearm.

Nora brought up the rear, eyes sharp, breath even, satchel held tight across her shoulder.

"This is too smooth," Eddie grunted. "No Hollowed, no pressure. Doesn't sit right."

"They're watching," Mabel said without turning. "I'd bet the fur off my back on it."

Eddie's eyes narrowed. "Funny. That almost sounded like you'd know firsthand."

She stopped just long enough to look over her shoulder, slow and deliberate. "Careful, cop. You think too loud."

Archie didn't stop walking. "We'll need both of you thinking in sync if we're going to survive this." They crested a ridge—and there it was.

A clearing, just as the map suggested. And in the middle, wrapped in vines and age, stood the crumbled bones of a stone church. A bell tower leaned at a bad angle, half-eaten by moss. Windows gaped like open wounds. The jungle had tried to erase it, but the frame held. Archie exhaled. "We're here."

Nora stepped past him and ran her paw along the stones near the doorway. "Spanish carving. A prayer. But beneath it— see this?" She brushed aside moss to reveal faint lines cut into the wall. "Aztec. Different hand."

"Overlayed after the conquest," Archie said, stepping closer. "Mortimer thought the site had been reused by native groups, but this—this is proof."

Eddie scanned the treeline while they talked, his tail twitching. "Let's keep the lecture short, yeah?"

They moved inside. The pews were cracked and rotting, light bleeding through holes in the ceiling in dusty shafts. Moss crept down the walls like long-forgotten fingers, and the silence wasn't peaceful—it was watchful. Like something was waiting.

Archie moved slowly down the aisle, his paw brushing a ruined bench as his eyes scanned the sanctuary. He paused at the altar, staring at the wall behind it. "This is it," he muttered. "But no stairs."

Nora stepped up beside him, already pulling the leather-bound journal from her satchel. "Your father mentioned a sun carving near the altar. Said it would cast a shadow on 'the mouth of the earth.'"

Archie blinked, then stepped around to the side. He spotted it—half buried beneath tangled vines and lichen: a faint carving of a sunburst just above the base of the altar. "There," he said, pointing. He pressed it with his paw. Nothing.

Nora studied the wall. "Wait… the journal said 'sunlight at its peak shall split the stone.' Not the carving. The shadow."

Archie looked up. A jagged hole in the roof let in a shaft of light. He stepped back, scanning the debris until he spotted a broken mirror fragment near a shattered column.

He picked it up, angling the glass until the beam caught and bounced toward the altar. He adjusted slowly, carefully, until the light struck the sunburst carving dead on. Click.

The floor shuddered beneath their paws. A section of the altar rumbled back, stone grinding against stone as a narrow stairwell creaked open beneath it, dark and stale with forgotten air.

Archie looked at Nora, something proud flickering in his expression. "Clever." She gave him a small smile. "Wasn't just me." They descended into the darkness.

The chamber below was small, round, the walls close and damp. Carvings wrapped around the stone—cats in robes, performing rites with masks and strange symbols. In the center stood a pedestal. A circular socket at the top. Hollow in the middle.

Archie stepped closer. "This is where the Hollowed Coin fits."

Mabel crouched beside him, her tone low. "Looks like a pressure plate. You trip that wrong, you'll end up skewered or worse."

Nora leaned forward, studying the base. "There's writing here. Barely readable—but I think it's a warning. Something about trespassers feeding the earth."

"Charming," Eddie muttered, keeping a firm watch near the entry.

Archie traced a claw around the socket rim. "This isn't just a trigger—it's a sequence. See these shallow grooves? Some kind of locking mechanism."

Mabel studied it beside him. "Mechanical design. Primitive but smart. You press here—then here—then counter with that notch."

Archie nodded. "Inverse calendar lock. My father wrote about something like this in his Veracruz field notes."

Together, they worked in silence. Mabel's paw hovered over the left press; Archie's over the right. He glanced at her. "On three." "One." "Two." "Three." They pressed.

A deep, low click sounded from the pedestal. Then a second panel slid open at its base.

Inside sat a coin. Smaller than expected. Silver, flawless, with a hollowed center. Symbols— Aztec glyphs— curved around the inner edge like teeth. Archie lifted it carefully. *"The key."* A sudden snap echoed from above.

"Company," Eddie growled. He raised his pistol and stepped toward the stairs.

"Time to move," Mabel said, slinging her satchel across her shoulder.

"There's a break in the back wall," Nora said, spotting a split in the stone. "Could be another way out."

They followed her, slipping into a narrow tunnel that ran behind the chamber. The air turned damp and sharp. After a few winding steps, it spilled them out into a dense patch of jungle behind the ruins.

Bright sunlight slammed into them like a wall. The sounds of voices shouting somewhere behind followed. Eddie took point. "Go. Now."

They moved fast, ducking beneath vines, weaving between trees and broken columns. Branches snapped behind them— someone was giving chase.

Archie kept the coin tight in his paw. His mind raced, but his feet were steady. Beside him, Nora ran silent and focused. She didn't falter. Mabel brought up the rear, eyes sharp, checking every angle. Somewhere in the canopy above them… something watched. And waited.

8

They sprinted into the jungle, branches lashing their faces, pursuit crashing through the undergrowth behind them.

Archie risked a glance over his shoulder. Through the tangle of vines and shadow, dark figures emerged—Hollowed Coin cultists, closing the gap. "We've got company!" he shouted, breath short.

Eddie didn't look back. "I see it." His voice was tight, focused.

Mabel pointed ahead, toward a jagged rock formation nestled between thick-trunked trees. "There—by the stones. We hold them there. We can't outrun this." No one hesitated.

Archie veered toward the outcrop. Eddie followed close, sidearm already drawn. Nora kept pace, her satchel bouncing against her back, eyes locked on the clearing ahead. Mabel broke ahead, silent and swift.

They reached the rocks just as the first of the cultists burst through the treeline.

Gunfire split the air, sharp and loud against the hush of jungle heat. The clearing lit with chaos.

Archie dropped behind a crumbling boulder, Colt .45 gripped tight. He rose just enough to fire—two quick shots. One landed. One didn't. It didn't slow them.

Eddie moved with calculated speed, firing controlled bursts, every shot a threat. Nora crouched behind a fallen log, hands trembling but focused. Her shots were cautious—but effective. One cultist yelped and fell back.

Mabel moved like a ghost, darting between cover. She took down two in the time it took Archie to reload, her blades flashing like teeth in the sunlight. "Left!" Eddie barked.

Archie spun and fired—dropping a tom mid-charge The body thudded to the ground just feet away.

His heart pounded. He hadn't shot at another cat in years— maybe ever. But this wasn't a choice. It was survival.

There was no time to think. Another wave came crashing through the brush. Then something shifted. The air turned heavy. The jungle held its breath.

Birds stopped screeching. Even the cultists paused, their wild momentum slowing like animals sensing a predator. A figure stepped from the brush—tall, poised, silent.

Her fur shimmered black and sandy gold, streaked like smoke licking across fire. Her eyes burned—a gleam of molten yellow that saw too much. She moved slowly.

Deliberately. As if the world had been waiting for her arrival. Roxanne.

A wounded cultist stumbled into her path. "Forgive—" he gasped, dropping to one knee. She didn't stop. She reached out, lifted his chin with two claws. There was a sickening pop.

He seized up—paralyzed. Not by magic, but by horrifying precision. Neck twisted, spine locked, body frozen in breathless silence. Then she let go. He dropped like a puppet with cut strings. The other cultists stepped back. So did Mabel.

She exhaled sharply. "Run," she said. Her voice had changed. No swagger. Just warning. Archie didn't question it. Neither did Eddie. "Back path—cut right!" Nora shouted.

They ran. Crashing through vines, ducking beneath low branches. Heartbeats pounding. Footsteps pounding louder. Roxanne didn't chase.

She stepped into the clearing, eyes sweeping the ruins of the ambush. Broken branches. Blood in the dirt. Footprints leading away. Her gaze rose. And locked on Archie—just visible through the trees. She smiled. Not mocking. Not amused. A promise.

They didn't stop running until their lungs burned and their paws bled. Vines snapped underfoot, tree limbs clawed at their coats, and the jungle closed around them like a fever dream.

Finally, Mabel raised a paw, signaling a stop near a moss-covered outcrop that jutted from the hillside like a broken tooth. The canopy thickened above them, darkening the clearing. No sounds followed. No pursuit. For now.

Archie bent over, catching his breath, Colt .45 still clutched in a trembling paw. Nora leaned against a tree, her shirt torn at the shoulder, a shallow scratch bleeding sluggishly down one arm.

Eddie didn't relax. He paced the edge of the clearing, eyes sweeping the trees, his paw never leaving the grip of his weapon.

"We're clear—for now," Mabel said, wiping blood from her blade. "Yeah, no thanks to you," Eddie muttered. Mabel's ears twitched. "Excuse me?"

"You led us right into that ambush. You knew the jungle too well. Too fast to dodge those cultists. And that reaction—" he jabbed a claw toward her. "You knew her. Roxanne."

Mabel's golden eyes narrowed, but her voice stayed level. "I've crossed paths with her. That's all." "Convenient."

Archie raised a paw. "Enough. She helped us fight. We're not in one piece without her." "Barely," Eddie grumbled, but let it drop—for now.

Nora sat cross-legged in the moss, already digging into the satchel. "Let me check everyone's wounds. We don't know what those blades were laced with."

Archie sat beside her, unbuttoning his coat to reveal a gash along his ribs. "Just a graze. The adrenaline's starting to wear off, though."

"Same," Eddie said, easing down beside a rock and tossing his bloodied overcoat aside. "I took a nick or two. I'll live."

As Nora cleaned and wrapped wounds, Mabel crouched by the fire pit Archie had just struck up with a flintstone.

"She's worse than I remember," Mabel said quietly. Eddie looked over. "You're talking about Roxanne."

Mabel nodded. "That was years ago. I was working in the Yucatan dealing in relics, artifacts, old trade. Back when I thought I could stay neutral." "What happened?" Archie asked.

"I stumbled onto a dig site that had gone quiet. Too quiet. Turns out, Roxanne had already been there. She didn't like unexpected guests." Eddie tilted his head. "You walked away from her?"

"Barely," Mabel said. "Three broken ribs, a fractured paw, and a message if I crossed her again, I wouldn't walk away next time." Archie frowned. "But why target you?"

"Because I knew what she was building. Before anyone else. The Hollowed Coin didn't exist back then—only an idea. Roxanne was shaping it. Not with spells or sorcery, but with symbols, control, obsession. She was pulling old world myths and turning them into something people could follow. Worship. Fear." "And you?" Eddie asked.

Mabel shrugged. "I decided some things were better left buried."

Nora pulled the wrapped key fragment from her satchel and handed it to Archie. "We should check this. Make sure it's intact."

Archie turned the silver coin fragment over in his paw. The hollow center shimmered faintly in the firelight. The glyphs, Aztec in nature, curled like serpent coils along the inner rim. He held it close to the firelight, tilting it until he could see the faint engravings better.

"There's a marking here see this?" he pointed. "It's not just a fragment. It's half of a locking disc. A dual-key system. Whatever's waiting out there, it takes two pieces to open it." "Where's the other half?" Eddie asked.

Archie tapped the journal still tucked in his coat. "There's a second ruin, deeper into the valley. My father marked it as *El Paso del Fe nix* the *Phoenix Crossing*. It was too dangerous to reach alone." Nora leaned closer. "Then that's where we go next." "After we rest," Archie said, easing back against the stone. "We're no good to anyone half dead." The fire cracked quietly between them. No one argued. The jungle had grown quiet again.

Not haunted like before just tired. Like the land itself had let out a long breath and decided to rest. The four of them sat in a small crescent-shaped clearing, walled by thick stone and heavy vines that drooped like curtains from the trees above. A fire burned low at the center, casting just enough light to hold back the dark.

Archie leaned against a boulder, his coat half-unbuttoned and a thin cut on his shoulder freshly bandaged. Nora worked in silence, tying the last strip of cloth snug around the wound. "Hold still," she murmured.

He gave her a small nod; eyes still fixed on the coin in his paw. The metal felt heavier now, like it carried more than just weight.

Eddie sat a few feet away, reassembling his sidearm with the kind of focus that kept thoughts at bay. His side was wrapped tight, the dark patch on the cloth seeping slowly. He didn't wince, didn't complain. Just kept working.

Mabel sat near the edge of the firelight, sharpening a thin blade with slow, measured strokes. Sparks flicked off the whetstone in rhythm. Her hat sat beside her on a fallen log, and her eyes were on the jungle—not the fire, not the others. Eddie broke the quiet first.

"She moves like she's been doing this her whole life," he said, mostly to Archie. "Fights like it, too. Doesn't blink. Doesn't flinch. That doesn't bother you?" Archie didn't look up. "Of course it bothers me."

"She knew Roxanne," Eddie pressed. "Had a name for her, knew her face, didn't ask questions when she showed up. You really think she's on our side?" Nora looked between them but stayed quiet.

"She got us out," Archie said simply. "That counts for something."

"Or maybe she got us in just deep enough before deciding to switch sides again." Eddie's voice was low, steady. "I've seen that kind of game before."

Across the clearing, Mabel didn't respond. Just kept sharpening.

Later, deep into the night, the fire had shrunk to glowing coals. Eddie was out cold, his pistol still close. Nora had curled under her jacket and fallen asleep not long after. The jungle sounds had returned—soft chirps, a breeze through the vines but nothing too close.

Archie sat awake, hunched over his father's notebook, flipping pages and scribbling thoughts in the margin with a dull pencil. The coin lay beside him on a flat stone. A shift in the wind made him look up. Mabel's spot was empty.

Her blanket still held the shape of her form, the fold where her shoulder had been, but her satchel, her blade gone. Archie stood quietly, listening. "Mabel?" he called, just above a whisper.

No answer. The jungle moved gently, as if nothing had changed.

He stepped to the edge of the clearing. There were no prints, no snapped branches, no sign of movement. Just night. She was gone. And this time, she'd taken the silence with her. The morning crawled in, damp and heavy.

Light filtered through the canopy in soft streaks, barely enough to shake off the night's chill. The fire had burned down to ash and glowing embers. Smoke curled lazily above it.

Archie sat close to what was left of the warmth, flipping through his father's journal. He hadn't slept. Not really.

Behind him, Eddie stirred with a grunt. "Tell me someone's got coffee."

Nora sat up next, brushing hair from her face and blinking at the clearing. "Where's Mabel?"

Archie didn't look up. "She's gone." That stopped them both. Eddie sat up straighter. "Gone how?"

"She left sometime during the night. Took her satchel, her gear… didn't make a sound."

Nora stood, turning a slow circle as if expecting Mabel to step out from behind a tree. "Why would she leave now?" Archie closed the journal. "She was never planning to stick around."

Eddie muttered something under his breath and stood. "Should've known. The way she always kept one eye on the shadows." "She did save us," Nora offered, her voice softer now.

Eddie didn't answer right away. Then, "Maybe. Or maybe she just didn't want Roxanne killing us before she got what she needed." "We don't know that," Archie said. "No," Eddie agreed. "We don't."

A pause settled in. Heavy. Thick as the jungle air around them.

Archie unfolded the map and laid it flat on a flat stone. "We don't have time to second-guess her. We still have a key. We still have a trail."

Nora stepped beside him, kneeling down. "This symbol matches the etching from the pedestal."

Archie nodded. "And the markings along the rim here? They form a path north ridge.

There's a second site mentioned in my father's notes. Something with a twin lock system. This key only gets us part of the way."

"Perfect," Eddie said flatly. "Half a key and no guide." "We'll manage," Archie said, sliding the coin back into his coat. "We've come this far."

Nora pulled a bundle from her satchel—cloth, dried herbs, a bit of salve. "Before we move on, let's deal with those cuts. I'm not letting either of you bleed out halfway to the next ruin."

Archie cracked a smile. "You're starting to sound like my brother." "You're worse than your brother."

They patched wounds. Nothing serious, but enough to slow someone down if they didn't take care of it. Nora did most of the work, gentle but quick. Eddie tightened a wrap around his arm, grimacing as it pulled tight. They checked their supplies low on food, nearly out of clean water, and down to a few clips of ammunition. Still, no one suggested turning back. And no one spoke about Mabel again. Not yet.

Not until the path took them deeper, and the next ruin whispered her name in stone. The jungle thickened, closing in around them.

Vines dangled from the canopy, and roots twisted across the ground like traps waiting to be sprung. Every sound bird calls, distant rustling felt just a little too deliberate.

Archie led, the coin key gripped tightly in his paw. He studied the map and his father's journal; both now marked with sweat and wear.

"This ridge line here…" he said, lowering his voice as the slope began to rise. "My father called it the Spine of the Watcher. Supposedly leads to the temple." "Of course it does," Eddie muttered, adjusting his holster. "Always another climb." "It's better than bullets," Nora said, brushing a branch aside.

Archie offered a small nod. His focus stayed on the terrain. Patches of old stone poked through the soil— fragments of an ancient road long claimed by nature. Fallen statues lined the overgrowth; their features weathered beyond recognition.

He slowed near a crumbled column. "Inscription here. Same pattern as the coin's markings."

Nora crouched beside him. "Looks like a warning 'Only the wise pass untouched. The beast devours the reckless.'

"Charming," Eddie said. "So we're about due for another warm welcome."

Archie stood and moved ahead. The trees parted, revealing a rocky slope where sunlight pooled over jagged stone. Something jutted from the incline a half-buried doorway, strangled in vines and packed dirt.

He moved toward it with measured steps. "This is it. The Temple of the Hollow Gate."

Nora inspected the stone. "Same type of socket as the last one."

Archie retrieved the key from his coat, its silver edge catching the light.

Eddie scanned the trees behind them. "Let's crack it open before something else shows up." The coin slid into place with a soft click.

A low tremor rolled through the earth. Somewhere beneath them, gears shifted. Dust spilled from the cracks as the doorway gave way with a grinding groan.

The stone slab receded, revealing stairs descending into darkness. Cold, stale air drifted out from below.

Archie stared down into the gloom, one paw tightening on his satchel. Then, without a word, he stepped inside.

Archie lit the torch himself strips of cloth wrapped around a splintered branch, soaked in oil from one of the flasks Nora kept in her pack. The flame flared with a sharp hiss, casting flickers of orange light against the stone around them.

The tunnel ahead sloped downward, tight and humid, the kind of place that felt like it hadn't seen light in years. Roots snaked through the cracks in the stone. Dust hung in the air.

"Watch your steps," Archie muttered, holding the torch forward.

Eddie followed close, pistol in paw, every muscle on edge. He'd taken a hit during the last skirmish—a glancing swipe across the shoulder but said nothing. Nora came behind him, her posture upright, satchel slung tight across her chest. She moved quietly, carefully still steady.

They reached a small chamber round, low-ceilinged, with carved pillars stretching up from the floor like the ribs of some buried beast. Vines curled down from the stone above. At the center, half-covered in dust and moss, sat an altar.

Archie stepped toward it slowly, lifting the torch to get a better look. "This matches the sketch," he said, pulling James Chesterfield's journal from his bag. "Second vault."

"Still feels like a trap," Eddie said. His eyes swept the corners, pistol raised. "Probably is," Archie replied.

Nora knelt beside the altar, brushing away the grime. "These carvings they're the same as the ones in your father's notes."

Archie flipped through the pages, stopping on a faded entry. Four symbols in a diamond: a jaguar with closed eyes, a snarling face, a figure with an open mouth, and one that had no mouth at all.

He read the scrawl below: "One lies. One guards. One sleeps. One bites. The key is the tongue that stays silent." Nora pointed to the altar's edge. "They're all here."

Archie pressed the one with the sleeping jaguar. Nothing. He tried the fanged mouth next. Click. And then a sudden crack stone giving way.

Nora yelped. One of her legs dropped through a hidden gap in the floor, her satchel swinging with the motion. As she tried to pull herself up, her foot twisted sharply against the edge of the stone. She cried out and sagged.

"Hold on," Eddie snapped, dropping his pistol and grabbing her under the arms. He pulled her back just as the floor crumbled further.

She hit the ground beside him with a wince, one paw clutching her leg. "I'm alright. Just twisted it," she said, her voice tight. But her face was pale, and the way she tried to stand confirmed the pain was sharp.

Archie wiped his brow. "They're not just testing memory. They're baiting us."

He stepped closer to the altar again. One symbol remained: the blank face with no mouth. He pressed it. Click.

Stone scraped against stone. A panel at the center of the altar rolled back, revealing a circular disk resting on a short metal post. Ornate. Clean. Out of place among the dust. Archie leaned in, lifted it carefully with his good paw. The moment he raised it snap.

A dart shot from the wall and sliced across his arm. He recoiled with a hiss, torch nearly falling from his grip. "Damn it" Eddie was already beside him.

"Just a cut," Archie muttered, holding the torch with one paw and pressing the wound with the other. "Shallow."

"We don't wait for a second one," Nora said, limping now as she moved toward the exit, every step slower than before.

They made their way back slowly. No one said much. The air felt tighter, like the walls were closing in behind them.

Archie stared down at the coin-shaped key in his paw, still warm from the altar. This one felt different.

The others had seen what Roxanne could do. And now... they had something she wanted. Mabel was still gone. And time was running short.

9

Dawn unfurled over London in a wash of gold, its rays spilling through the tall windows of Teddy's bedroom. He stirred, his ears twitching as he looked around and noticed Dolores wasn't there.

But not long after, the familiar scent of sausage, eggs, and bacon—his favorite—wafted through the crack under the door, curling into the room like a warm invitation. Teddy breathed it in and licked his lips.

He rolled out of bed, stretching his back and flicking his tail lazily before moving through his morning routine. When he finally made it downstairs, the rich aroma of coffee met him headon. Dolores stood at the bottom of the stairs, tail curled neatly around her ankles, a steaming cup in hand.

Teddy embraced her, took the cup, and kissed her on the cheek. "Thank you," he murmured.

Dolores padded softly back toward the kitchen. "Did you sleep well, dear?" she asked over her shoulder.

He hesitated.

He hadn't had a proper night's sleep since Archie had left for Cempoala. It had already been a week. No contact. Not a word. He didn't want to say it out loud, but worry had started to settle deep in his bones. Still, he smiled and played it off.

"Like a rock," he said, tail flicking behind him as he took a long sip from the cup.

But before he could say anything else, Dolores was already beside him. Her whiskers twitched as she studied his face, and she reached out, gently taking his paw.

"You forget, dear—I sleep next to you. I know you haven't been resting. Last week, you nearly sobbed yourself to sleep."

Teddy let out a small grunt. His ears drooped slightly at the memory. That day had been a particularly rough one. No progress at work. No sign of his brother. Just the creeping realization that he might never see Archie again. That thought alone had nearly broken him. He sniffed and straightened his posture. "I'm fine, Dolores," he said softly. "I have to be. Otherwise, I'm no good to any of them."

Dolores nodded, offering him a warm hug before returning to the kitchen. A moment later, she returned with a plate of breakfast and the morning paper, setting them gently in front of him.

Teddy gave her a faint smile, but his tail flicked once more behind the chair, betraying the unease still curling in his chest.

Teddy finished the last bite of sausage, his mind already drifting to the day ahead. The taste barely registered. He folded the paper under one arm, sipped the rest of his coffee, and gave Dolores a quiet nod of thanks. She said nothing more—just brushed a paw along his arm and let him go.

The city met him with a damp chill, the kind that settled in your fur and made your bones ache by mid-morning. He pulled his coat tighter around his chest and stepped out into the London bustle, his ears alert beneath the brim of his hat. The streets were already humming— carriages rattling, shop doors opening, voices echoing off wet stone.

Parliament loomed ahead, its spires cutting into the pale sky like watchful eyes.

He walked the path like he had hundreds of times before, but today something felt different. His whiskers twitched at every passing glance. The echo of Dolores's words lingered in his mind: You haven't been sleeping. Of course I haven't, he thought. How could I?

The great iron gates gave a groan as he passed through, flashing his credentials with a practiced flick of the paw. Inside, the building smelled of varnished wood, old paper, and dust just barely kept at bay. He nodded politely to a few passing aides, ears flicking at whispered conversation he couldn't quite catch.

He took the long way to his office—through a narrow corridor most staff didn't bother with. He liked the quiet. The walls here bore portraits no one looked at anymore, and above them, pipes and beams crisscrossed the ceiling like a forgotten web.

It was beneath these halls—deep in the records annex— where he hoped to find what Archie had left behind. Or what their father had.

Teddy had heard whispers. Buried votes. Sealed committees. And one name that came up too many times in too many forgotten documents: The Hollowed Coin. The old annex hadn't changed in years.

Down here, the noise of Parliament faded into the creak of floorboards and the faint hum of overhead gas lamps. Teddy's footsteps were soft against the worn carpet, his tail brushing the edge of dusty filing cabinets. He passed shelves stacked with forgotten ledgers, yellowing scrolls, and documents with seals so faded they looked like stains.

This was the kind of place people avoided—unless they were looking for something no one wanted found.

Teddy moved with purpose, ears swiveling at every rustle. He knew what he was after. Last week, while combing through a budget ledger, he'd spotted a strange entry tied to a now-defunct intelligence subcommittee—something called Project Azimuth. He hadn't had time to chase it down, but it had bothered him ever since.

He reached the far cabinet, a hulking thing labeled Archives: Foreign Interests (Classified Review – 1887–1902). The lock was old and rusted, but not enough to stop someone who knew how Parliament's filing systems worked. Teddy pulled a thin ring of keys from his pocket and worked quickly, muttering as he flipped through them. Click.

The cabinet groaned open. Inside were dozens of file boxes, each marked in the same faint handwriting. His eyes scanned until one caught his attention:

Special Committee Records – Section D / Internal – Restricted

He slid the box out carefully, coughing as a puff of dust lifted into the air.

Inside, a leather-bound journal lay atop a stack of typed summaries. The spine cracked as he opened it, revealing neat cursive writing—meticulous and cold. His fur bristled.

There, scrawled in the margin of a page that appeared otherwise redacted, were five letters: *COIN-R* He stared. The handwriting... it looked familiar. His pulse quickened.

Teddy flipped rapidly, pages sliding under his claws until he stopped on one with a name that turned his blood cold:

Chesterfield, James M. – Clearance Issued 1892 – Oversight Removed 1894. He stepped back, tail flicking sharply behind him.

"Bloody hell..."

Before he could take in more, the sound of a shoe scuffing against stone made his ears perk. He froze. The hallway was supposed to be empty.

Teddy closed the box slowly and pressed it under one arm. He slipped the journal into his coat just as a shadow appeared at the far end of the hall. A tall figure stood there— still, silent, watching.

Teddy didn't speak. He only turned, walked past the creaking shelves, and disappeared out the annex's back door without looking back.

Teddy hung his coat on the back of the door and moved to his desk. He took the journal from inside his coat and set it down carefully. The leather was dry and worn, the corners curled with age. He stared at it for a moment, then opened it. The pages gave off the faint smell of dust and ink.

The handwriting was clean and methodical. Each entry dated, each note carefully placed in the margins. This wasn't a diary. It was a record. Intentional. Controlled.

He flipped through the early pages—nothing more than logistics and committee names— until something stopped him cold:

Chesterfield, James M.

Assignment: Section D – Project Azimuth – Oversight Removed.

Teddy's paw hovered over the ink. He turned the page slowly.

A hand-drawn map filled the center of the sheet— sketched in black pencil. It showed a stretch of land near Veracruz. The lines were rough but purposeful. Someone had been there. Just to the side, written in firm block letters:

KEY FRAGMENT
To be retrieved. Do not log coordinates in ledger.

He kept going.

A page later, a single line scrawled in red ink stood out in the margin—shaky, but urgent:

"Local contact compromised. Trust no one inside the committee." "The order has eyes beyond London."

Teddy's ears pulled back slightly. His tail twitched. The penmanship here was different— rushed, pressured. He turned one more page. What he saw next sent a chill up his spine.

At the center of the page was a crude sketch, almost gouged into the paper:

THE HOLLOWED COIN

A hollow circle.
A triangle pointing downward through its center.
Two curved branches flanking it like laurel leaves.
Dark. Uneven. But unmistakable.

And beneath it, just visible beneath a thick line of black ink meant to hide it:

Roxanne, Teddy stared at the page, jaw tight. A knock at the door broke the stillness.

He snapped the journal shut and slid it into the bottom drawer of his desk, locking it as he called out, *"One moment."* He straightened his vest and opened the door. One of the aides stood outside, holding a folded message. "The Speaker's office asked for you this afternoon, sir."

Teddy took the note, nodded, and shut the door behind him. His eyes drifted to the locked drawer. *Roxanne. What were you doing in my father's journal?*

Dolores tucked her scarf tighter around her neck as the wind picked up on the corner of Brook and Mason. The grocer's awning flapped above the windows, and the smell of fresh bread drifted into the street. She adjusted the bag over her shoulder and stepped inside, the little brass bell chiming above her head.

She waved to the shopkeeper and made her way down the aisles—milk, onions, two tins of tuna. She paused at the tea shelf, running a paw over the Earl Grey canisters. Teddy had always preferred black tea, but lately he hadn't touched it. She added one to the basket anyway. Near the end of the aisle, a familiar voice called out. "Dolores? Is that you?"

She turned to see Marion Tilby, one of the neighborhood regulars—older tabby, always dressed like she was heading to church even on a Tuesday. "Marion! How are you, dear?" Dolores smiled.

They chatted for a few minutes—about the weather, a neighbor's sick tom, and how the baker's prices had climbed again. Dolores laughed politely, grateful for the company, even if just for a moment. Marion's voice always made her feel like things hadn't changed much.

"Well," Marion said at last, adjusting her shawl, "I'll let you get on. Don't let that tea go cold before Teddy gets his paws on it."

Dolores gave a soft laugh. "He'll be lucky if he remembers to eat, let alone make tea."

They said their goodbyes, and Dolores moved to check out. The shopkeeper packed her items into a paper bag, and she stepped back onto the street. The wind had picked up. The clouds had thickened.

She crossed the road, her ears twitching against the breeze. A carriage rolled by, then another. She didn't notice anything unusual at first—but as she passed the bakery and turned down her street, something made her glance back.

A tall figure in a grey coat. Walking her pace. About twenty paces behind.

She looked forward again. Her steps quickened, just slightly. So did the sound behind her. Her paw tightened on the handle of the bag.

She turned onto her block—six more houses to go. She passed the lamppost, then the mailbox. When she glanced back again, the figure was gone. Vanished.

Dolores stood still for a second, breath caught halfway in her throat.

She shook her head. "Don't be ridiculous," she muttered.

At home, she locked the door behind her, set the groceries down on the counter, and went straight for the phone in the hallway. She dialed Teddy's line—his Parliament extension.

The line rang once. Then twice. Then went to voicemail. She closed her eyes and sighed.

"Love," she said softly, "I don't want to worry you, but... something strange just happened. Call me back when you can."

She hung up and stood there for a moment, staring at the phone. Her ears twitched toward the living room window. Nothing. Still, she drew the curtain closed. The meeting had dragged.

Teddy stood in the corner of the Speaker's office, arms crossed as a half-dozen voices circled around figures, policies, and committee assignments that had nothing to do with what he'd found in the journal.

The Speaker—older, sharp-suited, and unreadable—barely glanced his way through most of it.

When the final papers were passed around and signatures taken, the room began to thin. Teddy waited until the last assistant left before speaking.

"I had a few follow-up questions regarding Section D oversight—specifically Project Azimuth," he said, calm but direct.

The Speaker didn't look up. *"Old records. No longer in review."* "I came across something I think deserves a second look."

The Speaker finally met his eyes. *"You're not in foreign intelligence, Mr. Chesterfield."*

"I'm not trying to be. I'm trying to understand what my father was involved in." A pause.

Then: *That assignment was decommissioned over thirty years ago. No further discussion is necessary.*

Teddy held his stare for another second before nodding and stepping back.

The Speaker straightened his cufflinks. *We appreciate your dedication to institutional memory, Mr. Chesterfield. But I suggest you focus your efforts elsewhere.* The message was clear. The meeting was over.

Teddy walked the long corridor back to his office, the heavy footfalls of staff echoing off stone and wood. Late sun filtered through the tall windows, casting sharp lines across the marble floor.

He stepped into his office, shut the door, and crossed to his desk. As he reached for the journal drawer, he noticed the blinking red light on his desk phone. One message. He pressed the button.

Dolores's voice played softly, faint static humming behind her words.

to worry you, but... something strange just happened. Call me back when you can."

He stood there for a moment, the quiet buzzing in the receiver holding longer than it should've. Then he was out the door.

The ride home passed in silence, broken only by the clatter of wheels and the occasional shout from a newsboy on the street.

By the time Teddy stepped onto his front stoop, the light was fading. He unlocked the door with a shaking paw and stepped inside. "Dolores?" No answer.

The groceries were still on the counter. A half-unpacked bag. A cracked teacup on the floor near the hallway.

His eyes swept the room—no broken furniture. No signs of a fight. No forced entry.

Just the silence. And the feeling that someone had been here. And taken her. Teddy stood still for a moment.

Then he walked to the desk, pulled out the journal, and opened it again to the page with *Roxanne's* name. He reached for the phone and began dialing. The phone clicked softly as the call connected.

Teddy stood beside his desk, the journal tucked just out of sight. His ears stayed alert, his tail low and still.

"Parliament switchboard."

"Chesterfield. Put me through to *Arthur Latch— Internal Affairs."* *"One moment, sir."*

The silence stretched. He drummed a claw once against the wood, eyes drifting to the groceries left on the counter. A cabbage had rolled out of the bag, resting against a jar of tea. The line clicked again. *"Teddy?"* Arthur's voice came through, worn and flat. *"Didn't expect to hear from you this late."* *"I need today's entry and exit logs. From the west gate. Three to five o'clock."*

There was a pause. *"You working a clearance check?"* *"No,"* Teddy said. *"I'm working a personal matter."* Another pause. *"What kind of matter?"*

"My wife didn't return home. Something's off. I think she may've been followed."

Arthur's voice shifted slightly. *"You think this ties back to work?"*

"I don't know," Teddy said. *"But I need those records—gate logs, visitor registry, and anyone who left without a return mark."*

"You know that sort of request needs to go through a form and a handler."

"You'll run it under Section 8C: domestic safety, emergency discretion. I'm invoking it officially."

Arthur let out a breath. *"Alright. I'll pull the gate ledger myself. It'll take some digging."* *"I'll wait."*

Teddy placed the receiver gently back in the cradle and turned from the desk.

He walked the hallway again, slower this time. Looking, not just seeing.

The front door's lock had been engaged. No scratches around the frame. No sign of force. But near the floor, beside the cracked teacup, something caught his eye. He knelt.

Two shallow scratches in the hardwood. Clean. Parallel. Fresh. Claw marks.

He followed them to the molding along the baseboard. *There—caught in the seam—a loose thread. Black. Coarse.* Not from Dolores's coat. He brought it to his nose. *Smoke. And a sharp trace of cologne. Not hers.*

He rose and made his way to the back room. The curtain was still drawn. The window was unlocked. That wasn't right. Dolores never left it that way.

He unlatched it fully and stepped outside into the yard. The grass was damp. The wind had quieted. *Then he saw them.*

Two paw prints in the dirt. Deep, uneven. Boots—broad, heavy, not hers. The spacing was wide, the kind of stride that didn't sneak. They hadn't crept in. They'd come through the back.

Teddy looked up and down the narrow alley behind the fence. Empty now, but it had seen something.

He returned inside, locked the door, and crossed back to his desk. He opened the drawer and looked at the journal, the page still marked where Roxanne's name had been scratched out. He closed it. The phone rang. He answered on the first ring. *"Arthur."*

"I've got part of what you asked for. A name's not confirmed, but the west gate log shows someone exited just before quarter to five. No record of return. No destination.
And the badge number?" Arthur hesitated. *"It's familiar."*
"From what?"

"It was flagged six months ago. Same corridor where those old sublevel files went missing. Thought it was a clerical error." Teddy's jaw set. *"And now?"*

"Now I don't know. But I'll bring the full ledger myself. I'll be there within the hour."

Teddy hung up the phone, then crossed the room and drew back the front curtain. Nothing on the street. No carriage. No passerby. But he could feel it. Someone had been here. And they wanted him to know it.

10

The jungle thinned at the edge of a crumbling hillside, where moss-covered stones clung to the bones of a forgotten structure. Mabel ducked beneath a low branch, her wide-brimmed hat brushing leaves slick with dew. Her paws moved quietly over the damp soil, tail low and still behind her.

She hadn't told the others. Not because she didn't care— because they wouldn't understand. Not yet. They didn't know what it was like to owe a dead man a promise and still be deciding how to keep it.

The path curved around a broken slope and flattened near a shallow ravine. Nestled into the hill, a crooked stone shack leaned into the brush, its tiled roof sagging, half lost to rot. A perfect place to be forgotten.

She paused, scanned the trees. A flash of silver—a medallion, just lifted—winked near the doorway. She gave a small nod and approached.

Inside, the air was dry and still. Dust coated the stone floor, and the sharp scent of lime oil mixed with parchment and wet cloth. An orange-furred tomcat sat at a narrow table, unwrapping a bundle of folded linen. His coat was sun-faded and scuffed at the joints, a few tufts sticking up from a long travel. His whiskers twitched faintly, but he didn't rise. "You're late," he said.

"I took the long way," Mabel replied. "Didn't want company."

The tom didn't smile. He unwrapped the cloth: brittle maps, scraps of parchment, fragments of inked diagrams. Mabel pulled a slim leather notebook from her satchel—not the one with the key. This one held transcriptions. Notes James had left buried in the margins of his journals. Names. Coordinates. Symbols the others hadn't seen. She set it on the table. "That's all you're getting."

He flipped through it slowly, claws tapping softly at the corners. "It's enough. For now."

From inside his coat, he withdrew a narrow wooden box, worn smooth from years of handling. He set it down and flicked open the latch.

Inside, nestled in faded linen, lay a disk of dark obsidian— round, palm-sized, and cool even in the heat. Gold inlays traced a jagged sunburst along the outer edge, but the center held a more curious mark: two spirals interlocked into a sideways figure-eight. Mabel leaned forward. "That's not local."

"Correct," the tom said. "Came through Lisbon under a false trade manifest. Labeled a map weight." She scoffed. "It's not."

"No," he agreed. "The gold traces to a vein in central Veracruz. And the spiral—the pattern— it matches a sketch pulled from one of James Chesterfield's field journals."

He slid a copied page across the table. The lines were rough, unfinished, but the resemblance was clear.

"James didn't know what it was," he continued. "But he kept drawing it."

Mabel studied the disk a moment longer, then closed the lid with a click. "I want more than scraps next time."

"You'll get more," he said, tone still even. "Once you find what's hidden in that cave." "I didn't say I was bringing it back to you."

"You haven't said much ," he replied, eyes narrowing. "But you've already started bringing us pieces.
The Hollowed Coin won't wait. They take."

Her ears flicked. Her jaw tightened. "I know what they do." "You're not far ahead of them."

Mabel bared her teeth. Her next words came out low and sharp—a hiss more than speech.

"Then your people better keep their side clean. Because if they're followed—"

"They won't be," the tom interrupted, his tail flicking once behind him. "As long as you hold your line."

She didn't answer. She turned and left him in the dim stone room without another word.

Outside, the sun had climbed above the tree line, casting long shadows across the ravine. The jungle buzzed with heat and insects and secrets. Mabel adjusted the strap of her satchel, feeling the weight of the obsidian disk pressing against the worn leather journal. She moved fast but quiet, fading back into the green. Not yet, she thought. But soon. I'll have to choose.

Late afternoon, near the ruined site mentioned in James Chesterfield's journal.

The jungle narrowed around them, branches clawing at their coats as they followed the overgrown trail. Nora walked just ahead of Archie, her machete swinging low, cutting through the tangle with practiced rhythm. Eddie was a few paces behind, silent but watchful, his revolver tucked close.

They had passed another marker—stone worn to its bones by time, but still bearing the faint sigil that matched their keys. And yet, the mechanism it connected to remained sealed. Unmoving. Something was missing.

Archie crouched to examine the worn base of the pedestal. He ran a claw across the inner groove.

"There's a circular slot here," he said. "Small teeth, like a gear was meant to sit here and drive it."

"Which we don't have," Nora muttered, leaning in beside him. "We've got both keys. We followed the journal. But something still isn't lining up."

She stood and rested her hands on her hips, brow furrowed. "We've come all this way just to be locked out?" "Not yet," Archie said, squinting toward the shifting canopy. "There's always something overlooked." Nora's voice lowered. "You think she took it?" Archie didn't respond right away.

It had been almost a day and a half since Mabel slipped away. No explanation. No tracks. Just an empty bedroll and a fading trail through the brush.

Nora kicked at a root. "I told myself I wouldn't care if she didn't come back." "But you do," Archie said softly. Nora didn't answer.

They stood quietly for a moment, the late light casting long shadows between the trees. A bird shrieked overhead, startled by something unseen. Eddie stepped forward. "We should set camp before dark. No point wandering blind."

Archie nodded absently, still focused on the base of the pedestal. Then a branch snapped behind them. Three heads turned at once.

A figure stepped out of the undergrowth—cloak tattered, fur streaked with dust, eyes unreadable in the shade. Mabel. Alive. Silent. Watching them. No one spoke at first.

Archie straightened slowly. "You picked a dramatic moment." She gave a dry smile. "Timing's everything."

Eddie's hand hovered near his weapon, but he didn't draw it. Nora stood like stone. Archie's eyes narrowed. "Where did you go?" Mabel's gaze swept past him toward the pedestal. "Somewhere I needed to." "And did you find what we need?" Nora asked coldly.

Mabel didn't answer. She dropped her satchel beside the fire pit and sat down as if she'd never left. "Depends," she said. "How much do you trust me?"

The silence stretched taut, only broken by the steady crackle of the fire and the occasional rustle of the jungle just beyond their makeshift camp.

Eddie stepped forward first, his paw resting near the grip of his revolver. "Where the hell have you been?"

Mabel didn't flinch. She leaned back slightly, her cloak catching the light. "Scouting," she said simply. "Making sure we weren't walking into another trap."

"Funny," Eddie muttered. "We weren't worried about traps until you left."

Nora moved to stand beside Archie, her arms crossed tightly. "You vanished in the dead of night, Mabel. No word. No direction. And now you stroll back in like you never left?" "I figured you'd manage without me," Mabel replied, brushing a leaf from her sleeve. "You did find the mechanism, didn't you?" Archie's ears flicked. "You knew we would."

Mabel met his eyes, her own unreadable. "You have James Chesterfield's journal. I trust his son could follow a map."

That drew a sharp look from Eddie, but it was Nora who spoke next.

"We're missing something," she said evenly. "The mechanism won't activate. There's a groove, a gear system. You wouldn't happen to know anything about that, would you?"

Mabel's silence lingered just a heartbeat too long.

Then, she smiled—not warm, but not cruel either. "Let's just say the ruins didn't give up all their secrets in one go."

Archie stepped forward, voice low and measured. "If you have something, Mabel... something we need... this isn't the time for games."

She stood then, slowly, brushing off her knees. "If I had something, I'd want to be sure I was still part of this team before I offered it." "You walked away from the team," Eddie snapped.

"I came back," she replied, cool and quiet. "That counts for something." A long pause.

Then, Mabel reached into her satchel—but not deeply. Just enough to pull out a cloth-wrapped bundle and place it on a flat stone near the fire. She didn't open it. She didn't say what it was. Just let it sit there between them, like an unopened truth.

Archie's gaze dropped to it, then back to her. "We break camp at dawn. That mechanism opens tomorrow." Mabel nodded once. "Then I'll be ready."

Eddie turned away with a low growl, moving to the edge of camp, paw resting again on the hilt of his weapon. Nora's eyes lingered on the bundle. Then she looked to Mabel. "I don't trust you."

"You don't have to," Mabel replied softly. "You just have to get inside."

The fire had burned low, its glow barely touching the stone pedestal at the center of camp. No one spoke after Mabel laid down the cloth-wrapped bundle. No one touched it.

By morning, the clearing was heavy with mist. The jungle around them clicked and stirred, but the group was quiet.

Archie was the first to move, stretching his limbs with a low groan as he rose to his paws.

His tail flicked once behind him as he buckled his satchel and turned toward the pedestal. He gave the bundle a glance, then looked away, ears angling slightly toward the others behind him.

Nora stirred next, shaking out her fur with a sharp twitch of her shoulders. She pulled on her coat, the tip of her tail thumping once against the ground. Her eyes were already locked on the wrapped cloth.

Eddie rolled onto his side and gave a grunt. "We really doing this?" Archie didn't answer. He padded toward the pedestal.

Mabel was already up. She hadn't slept—at least, no one had seen her do it. Her ears were alert, posture calm, but her eyes tracked Archie's every move.

He crouched beside the bundle, claws lightly unsheathing as he pulled back the cloth. Inside lay a gear—bronze, weathered, the teeth still intact. Dust clung to the grooves, but it looked solid.

Nora stepped in beside him, whiskers forward. "That's it." Archie said nothing. He turned the gear in his paw pads, lining up the teeth with the shallow slot in the pedestal. It slid into place with a low click.

He drew the two keys from his coat, gripping one in each paw. With a glance at the others, he turned them.

The mechanism resisted at first, then gave. Stone ground beneath them. Dust puffed into the air as part of the floor began to shift, grinding open with a deep, echoing scrape. A narrow stairwell dropped into darkness. All three stared down. Eddie's tail lashed once. "Well. That's not ominous at all."

Nora flicked her ears toward Mabel. "Where did you find it?" Mabel didn't answer.

Archie rose to full height, brushing dirt from his coat with the backs of his paws. "We've got what we need."

Nora didn't break her stare. "Doesn't mean we have answers." Mabel shrugged, adjusting her satchel. "Some things can wait."

The stairs waited too, steep and black beyond the first few steps.

Archie pulled a small torch from his bag, lit the end, and stepped forward. The flame flickered against his whiskers as he looked down. "We've come this far," he said. "No turning back now." Mabel lit a second torch and nodded once. "After you, Professor." Archie didn't wait. He moved down the steps in silence, claws gripping stone.

The others followed, one by one, tails low, ears high, shadows stretching behind them. The steps grew colder the deeper they went.

Archie led the way, torch in paw, ears flicking at every creak of shifting stone. The air thickened as they descended— wet, stale, and heavy with the scent of soil and time. Moss crept along the walls. The quiet felt older than anything they'd found above ground.

Eddie followed, one paw resting near the grip of his revolver. He scanned the shadows with the slow, practiced rhythm of someone who'd seen too much already.

Nora came next, steps light, her claws half-extended for balance. Her eyes flicked to every carved surface, every crack. Mabel brought up the rear, tail low, paws silent.
The stairwell finally leveled out into a stone chamber.

Archie stepped forward first, raising the torch. The walls bloomed to life in flickering light— murals of feathered jaguars and high priests, some feline, some human, stretching across the stone in layers of paint and carving. Scrolls, blood, and fire. Symbols of knowledge—and control.

Two panther statues flanked a central pedestal. Their obsidian eyes glinted with firelight, catching every motion.

"This is it," Archie said, his voice barely above a whisper.

Nora stepped beside him. "These glyphs... They're not just records. This room's a threshold." "Or a trap," Eddie muttered, tail twitching once.

Archie moved to the pedestal and cleared a layer of dust. There it was—a narrow slit, no wider than a knife blade. Not the same as the lock above.

He pulled both keys from his coat. Tried them one at a time. Neither fit.

Nora leaned in, whiskers twitching. "It's not a keyhole. It's a draw lock—meant to be pulled."

Mabel stepped forward, finally. She pulled a slender metal pin from the inner lining of her cloak—worn, bronze-colored, etched faintly with circles.

Without asking, she slid it into the slot. A click echoed through the chamber. The top of the pedestal hissed open.

Archie opened it the rest of the way and carefully peeled back the oilcloth. Inside was a single length of ancient bark parchment, pressed flat, rolled and bound with string. He unrolled it slowly. Symbols. Maps. Margins inked in two distinct hands—one Aztec, the other older Latin, almost clerical. No one spoke. Then Archie exhaled. "It's the first half."

Nora stepped forward but didn't reach for it. "We can't take it."

"No," Archie agreed. "It wouldn't survive the trip. Not in this state."

He knelt, tail curling tight behind him. "We copy it here. As much as we can. Light exposure is already doing damage."

Nora was already digging in her satchel. "I've got parchment. Graphite. Charcoal rubs if we need texture detail."

Eddie stayed back, watching Mabel with narrowed eyes. His paw lingered near the grip of his revolver.

Archie's holster creaked softly as he adjusted his coat—the polished wood grip of his Colt .45 just visible beneath the fold. He didn't reach for it. Not yet.

Mabel didn't move. She just stood there, eyes on the scroll, expression unreadable.

"We get what we can," Archie said. "Then we seal it again.

This doesn't leave here until we know what it means."

Eddie muttered, "Assuming we don't get jumped before we figure it out."

Archie didn't respond. He just reached for the graphite stick and began tracing.

They gathered around the flat stone where Nora had unrolled the tracing. The scroll's symbols, now copied in graphite and charcoal, looked almost alive in the shifting light beneath the canopy.

Nora crouched low, tail twitching as she read the lines. Her brow furrowed.

"It's dense," she muttered. "The ink-work layered. Like it was meant to hide something unless you already knew how to read it."

Archie knelt beside her. "This is older than I expected," he said. "Parts of it are in Nahuatl, but there's a separate hand— Latin script. Probably from a priest who got his hands on the original."

Nora pointed to one side of the page. "This right here—it's not a full translation. More like shorthand. Markings of a path or process."

She tapped again, claws brushing lightly against the parchment. "This word repeats four times—*lengua*. And here, a paired glyph. The fire symbol." Archie nodded slowly. "The *Tongue of Fire.*" "You've heard of it?"

"My father found a similar reference in a ruined codex. He thought it referred to a ceremonial passage—something hidden in a place of danger."

Nora glanced up at him. "You think it's literal?"

"I don't know. But if this scroll was split for safekeeping, the path to the second half won't be simple."

Eddie paced a few steps off to the side, arms crossed. "So we follow the fire tongue. Where does it lead?"

Archie scanned the bottom row. "There's a fork symbol here—river icon, then a split line. But the lines drawn beneath it... they're contour lines. Elevation."

"North fork," Nora said. "Slight rise. Matches the ridge we saw from the bluff yesterday." Archie nodded. "That's our direction." No one spoke for a moment.

Then Nora rolled the tracing up carefully and slid it into her satchel. "Let's move. I'd rather get ahead of anyone else who might be reading the same map."

Eddie checked the strap on his gear and gave a short grunt. "Lead the way, professor."

Archie stood, dusted off his coat, and looked once more at the fireless camp. His paw rested briefly on the grip of his Colt .45, but he didn't draw it. "Let's find the rest of the scroll."

They left the clearing in single file, the trees swallowing their trail.

11

Teddy didn't look up when the door opened. He recognized the knock short, sharp, followed by a pause. Arthur Latch always knocked the same way. Measured. Intentional.

Latch stepped in, coat damp from the rain, a flat bundle tucked beneath one arm. He shut the door behind him without a word. "You're late," Teddy said, not turning from the table.

Latch dropped the bundle on the wood with a dull thump. "You're lucky I brought it at all. These weren't easy to pull. Most were locked behind departmental clearances I'm not supposed to touch."

Teddy flipped the cord loose. Three books, thick and old, wrapped in waxed cloth. He peeled it back and ran his claws along the spine of the top volume. "These are clean copies?"

Latch nodded once. "Originals. Hand entries. Not the edited logs filed through the general archive. These came from a side vault in Internal Affairs. Had to pull a few strings."

Teddy opened the first book. The smell of dust and ink rose from the pages. Travel records, shipping ledgers, diplomatic manifests—standard-looking, at first glance. But Teddy had learned to read between the lines. "You find anything marked *HC?*" he asked.

Latch raised an eyebrow. "You'll find enough of it in there to keep you buried for days. *HC-V, HC-B, HC-R. Same code stamps. Multiple locations. Different decades.*"

Teddy flipped through quickly. "So it's not just modern. This goes back." "I told you. Whatever this is, it's been running through Parliament's veins for a long time."

Latch pulled a small folded slip from his inner coat pocket. "Found this, too. Misfiled. Didn't show up on the pull list."

Teddy unfolded it. *A routing note. Dated two months prior. "Secure transfer approved. Directive HC-V. Contact: Arthur Latch."* His eyes froze on the name. Latch frowned.

"They're using my name?"

"They're covering their tracks," Teddy said.

"Borrowing yours to redirect heat."

"That means someone inside Internal Affairs is ghosting paperwork through under my clearance."

Teddy closed the book. "And that means we're getting close."

Latch moved to the door. "This is the last favor I can do for a while. You need to move quietly, or not at all."
Teddy nodded. "I'll keep my head down."

Latch lingered a moment, then slipped out without another word.

Teddy sat in the quiet, claws drumming lightly on the page.

If they were using Latch's name, they weren't just hiding—they were inside.

He pulled the ledger close again and went back to reading.

Teddy sat at the kitchen table, sleeves rolled, the fire behind him reduced to a low flicker of orange. The bundle of logs Arthur Latch had delivered earlier that evening lay open across the tabletop, their parchment edges curled and brittle with age. The flat was silent, save for the occasional pop from the hearth and the soft scrape of pencil across paper.

He leaned closer to the page, squinting at an older manifest. *Diplomatic clearance. Cargo marked "private"— originating from Veracruz. No consignee. No receiving signature. But stamped in the lower corner, faint but visible: HC-V-9.*

Site Nine again.

He turned back to his notes—three pages deep now. Cross-referenced routes. Overlapping seals. Identical pen strokes appearing in documents from supposedly different hands.

The pieces didn't fit cleanly, not yet. But Teddy saw it. The pattern. A quiet infrastructure humming beneath the surface of official channels. He marked three more notations on his hand-drawn map. All pointed inward. Toward central holding sites. Nothing ever left. Everything gathered.

He flipped through a second ledger, this one older. His claws slowed as he found the Hollowed Coin symbol etched lightly in a shipping margin. Not printed. Scratched in by hand. His eyes narrowed.

Another document—one of the newest—listed Arthur Latch as the approving agent. But Arthur had sworn he hadn't signed anything in weeks.

Teddy let the paper rest in his paws, mind turning. "They're using him," he whispered. "Borrowing names. Scrubbing trails."

The fire cracked behind him, casting shadows against the cabinets. He didn't move. Just stared at the pages spread out like a crime scene.

Dolores was taken clean. No sign of a struggle. No ransom. Just silence. Not a random attack.

They wanted something. Or someone. And now they were covering the evidence.

Teddy's tail curled slowly beneath the chair. He looked at the map again—at the X marked outside London, just past the old freight lines. The depot hadn't been used in years. But the paperwork told a different story.

She might be there. And if she was, he'd find her.

___

The room was damp. Stone walls. A single gas lamp hung from a chain overhead, its flame twitching with each draft that slipped through the cracked ceiling. Dolores sat bound to a wooden chair. Her coat was gone. Fur ruffled. A dried cut near her temple. Her wrists raw where the rope had rubbed her too tight. Two cats stood across from her.

One was wiry, tall, and thin, with sharp cheekbones and a leather notebook under his arm. The other, broad-shouldered and dark-furred, paced slow circles around the room, wrapping and unwrapping a length of cord around his paw. The wiry one spoke. "You've been quiet, Mrs. Dolores. I expected more spirit." She didn't answer. Her tail flicked once behind the chair.

He stepped closer. "You work records in Parliament. A quiet post. Clean. But lately, your name's been popping up in all the wrong margins."

She met his eyes. "Then maybe your margins are wrong." The pacing one stopped. Watched her. Said nothing.

The wiry cat gave a smirk. "You're clever. But this isn't about you. It's about your husband." Dolores blinked once, slowly.

"Where is he keeping them?" the wiry one continued. "The documents. The logs Arthur Latch passed to him. You two talk, don't you? Share everything?" She tilted her head. "Not everything." He stepped in, but she didn't flinch. "You're going to make this harder than it has to be." "No," she said. "You just thought I'd be easier." The pacing cat grunted. "She's stalling."

"Maybe." The wiry one glanced at him. "Or maybe she really doesn't know."

Dolores tuned them out. Let their words fade into the hum of the gas lamp above her.

She studied the ceiling. Plaster cracked. Damp from rot. The lamp's chain was loose where it hooked into the wood.

She shifted her wrists again. The rope had slack, just barely. They hadn't tied it clean.

Her fingers probed the edge of the knot, slowly working at it. The chair creaked. One leg felt weak splintered at the joint. She gave it a small test push with her heel. Still holding. But maybe not for long.

She glanced at the floor. A dented metal bowl sat under the edge of the table—kicked aside earlier. If she could knock it just right...

The pacing one noticed the shift in her posture. "She's moving."

Dolores didn't wait. She threw her full weight to the side. The chair tipped, slammed to the floor. One leg cracked clean. They lunged.

She twisted—her wrist finally slipping free—and rolled. Grabbed the broken chair leg. Swung.

The wiry one caught it in the shin. He stumbled back, cursing.

The big one tried to pin her, but the chair splintered beneath them. She kicked hard, claws catching him across the cheek. Enough space to break loose. She ran. Still half-bound. Still bleeding. But running.

Down a narrow corridor lit by torches. She didn't know where she was. Didn't care. Just moved. One door. Steel. Locked. She slammed into it once. Twice. On the third try—it gave an inch. She screamed. "TEDDY!" Her voice rang down the stone hall. Loud. Raw. Then—a sharp crack to the back of her head. The flame from the torches blurred. And the world went black.

———

The hallway was too quiet. Teddy slowed, his paw hovering near the door latch, ears forward, breath still. Something felt wrong. Then Thud.

A sharp, sickening impact against the other side of the door. And a voice, cracked but unmistakable: *"TEDDY!"* His name, torn from Dolores's throat. Everything inside him snapped taut.

He backed up fast, planted his hind legs, and launched forward with a full-bodied slam. The wood groaned but held.

He hit it again, harder. The frame cracked down the middle.

On the third hit, the door gave with a splintering shriek, blown clean off its hinges. Teddy stormed through—eyes blazing, breath sharp.

Dolores lay sprawled near the threshold, bound at the wrists, her fur streaked with dust and blood. Her body was limp.

Two toms stood over her. One still had his paw raised, fresh from the blow. The other was already reaching for her shoulders. Teddy didn't shout. He moved.

The first tom turned just in time to see a wall of fur and fury bearing down on him. Teddy struck with a lowered shoulder, and the tom lifted clean off the floor before crashing through a stack of crates. The sound of splintering wood was swallowed by his scream as he hit the back wall and crumpled.

The second came at him with claws drawn. A slash aimed for Teddy's chest—but Teddy caught the tom mid-swing, snatched him by the collar, and drove him spine-first into the stone wall with a roar. The crack echoed like thunder. Teddy didn't stop.

He slammed the tom again, once—twice—until the fight left him. The cat dropped to the ground like a sack of wet cloth.

Chest heaving, Teddy turned and dropped to his knees beside Dolores. His paw trembled as he tore at the bindings around her wrists. She stirred. "Took you long enough..." she rasped.

He leaned close, voice low and tight. "You have no idea."

He swept her into his arms with a strength that was no longer just physical—it was the kind born of fear, rage, and love colliding at once. Behind him, the first tom let out a wheeze. Teddy slowly turned his head. "I should finish it," he growled. The tom crawled back against the wall, eyes wide.

"You're lucky she needs me more," Teddy turned away.

He stepped through the splintered doorway, tail flicking behind him, Dolores cradled tight against his chest. And not once did he look back.

The kettle whistled in the background, sharp against the otherwise quiet flat.

Teddy poured two cups, careful with the chipped mug Dolores always favored. He slid it across the table toward her. She caught it with both paws—still trembling slightly— and gave a faint nod of thanks.

She was wrapped in a blanket, hunched in the same chair she'd fallen asleep in after the medics had cleared her. Her cheek was bruised, lip split, but her eyes were steady again.

Teddy sat opposite her, a thick stack of notes and records spread across the table between them. Parliament seals. Internal affairs tags. Arthur Latch's handwriting scribbled in the margins.

Dolores took a slow sip, then looked at him. "You're not going to rest, are you?"

Teddy shook his head. "I've had enough rest for both of us. Besides..." He tapped the top file. "This doesn't wait."

She set her mug down carefully. "Tell me what you knows."

Teddy leaned back, running a paw through his thick chest floof. "Latch came through. Slipped me the restricted logs the same evening you were taken. Internal memos, disciplinary records, blacked-out transfers. I went through all of it again after..." He paused. "After I got you back."

Dolores didn't flinch. She just waited.

"It's them," he continued. "Hollowed Coin has people inside. Not many. Not at the top. But they're embedded—clerks, aides, record keepers. People who can slip a document, reroute access, or make a paper trail disappear."

She frowned. "Then how did they even know about me?"

Teddy flipped to a clipped report. "Because of me. They've been watching me. Watching who I talk to. Who I live with. You became a target because you're close to someone snooping in the wrong corners." Dolores's ears folded. "So I was leverage."

He nodded. "They wanted to scare me off. Slow me down. Maybe test what I'd risk. But it tells us something— they're nervous."

Teddy opened another folder and placed it gently on the table. The cover was stamped in thick black ink: Coin. "There's a name that keeps surfacing," he said. "Not in full records. Just fragments. Encrypted side notes. She's buried deep, but the pattern's there." He tapped the folder. "*Roxanne.*" Dolores shook her head. "Never heard of her."

157

"Didn't think you had," Teddy muttered. "No department. No record. But others answer to her.

Whatever's moving behind the scenes, she's not a foot soldier. She's pulling strings."

Dolores studied the name on the folder. "Then that's where we start."

Teddy leaned forward, tail curling around one chair leg. "We don't go through Parliament. It's not safe. I'll work with Latch and keep it off the books."

He paused, his voice quieter. "But I need you safe, Dolores." "You want me to stay out of it." "I want you alive," he replied.

Her claws tapped against her mug. "Fine. But if this is war, then we both fight."

A beat of silence passed before Teddy closed the folder with a quiet snap.

"We start with *Roxanne*," he said. "And figure out who she's working for."

12

One Week Earlier♦

The jungle never slept. Even in the dead hours before dawn, something rustled.

Archie sat cross-legged in the corner of the crumbling outpost, James Chesterfield's journal open across his lap. The candle beside him had burned low, its flame flickering with every shift of the wind. Pages curled in the damp heat, ink bleeding into paper softened by age.

He turned to one of the more chaotic pages, a clutter of notes, symbols, and a hastily drawn sketch — a serpent coiled around the sun. Ordinary enough, in isolation. But not now. Not after what they'd just found.

Earlier that evening, Nora had helped him unfurl the first half of the scroll they'd retrieved from the temple vault. The parchment was ancient — older than anything Archie had ever seen firsthand — brittle yet strangely preserved. And near the top, embedded in a web of geometric glyphs and celestial diagrams, had been with same mark.

A serpent, circling the sun like a wheel turning inward.

Archie blinked, then looked back down at the page in his father's journal. The symbol was nearly identical. Even the style of carving — the way the serpent's head pointed toward the sun's center — matched the scroll's illustration. He flipped the page, then stopped.

There, scribbled faintly in the margin, were words he hadn't registered before:

"The mark returns. The same feline — calm, composed, with eyes like glass. Cloaked in white. She moved like she belonged to no era." He stared at it. Once. Then again. Behind him, Nora's voice was soft. "You're breathing faster."

He looked up. She stood in the doorway, outlined by soft rain light and carrying two tin mugs of bitter brew roasted chicory root, the closest thing to coffee they could find this deep in the jungle. She handed him one without a word and crouched beside him. "You find something?" she asked, quietly. He didn't speak. Just turned the journal so she could read it.

Her eyes narrowed . "That's the same symbol from the scroll, isn't it?"

Archie nodded. "Father drew this in 1933. Veracruz. Forty-two years ago." "And he saw someone wearing it?" she asked.

"He never named her," Archie said. "Just described her. The way she moved. Her eyes. Like she didn't belong to any era."

Nora studied the sketch again, her voice lower now.

"You think it was her."

"I didn't—at first. I thought maybe it was coincidence. Or a misinterpretation. But now…" He turned back to the scroll, the symbols still etched in his memory. "That artifact isn't just old. It predates the Aztecs." He paused. The realization hit slow — and then all at once.

"Nora… if the scroll's as old as it looks… we're talking at least three thousand years." He looked at her. His voice dropped.

"She would have to be over three thousand years old."

The outpost felt suddenly smaller. The fire hissed in the hearth, casting shadows against the walls, as if recoiling from the thought. Nora didn't speak. Her silence said enough.

Archie stared into the flame, his voice barely above a whisper.

"We haven't stepped into a conspiracy. We've stepped into a legacy."

Archie didn't speak for several minutes. Then he reached into his satchel and pulled out a fresh sheet of parchment.

Nora remained close but silent as he began to write, the candle beside him burning lower with each word.

Dearest Teddy,

I haven't heard from you. I'm guessing you're either tied up in the investigation or didn't want to risk a letter getting lost.

I understand — trust me, I've had the same hesitation.

Still, I need you to hear this.

I don't know if you've come across her name yet Roxanne but if you've found mentions of a tall, black-coated feline tied to multiple events and locations, that's her.

If you're working under the idea that she's just another agent in the Hollowed Coin, I'm afraid you're off the mark. She's not a subordinate. She's the one giving orders.

We found a mark in the first half of the scroll a serpent circling the sun. It matches a symbol I found in one of Father's journals, drawn during his 1933 expedition to Veracruz.

He described a feline cloaked in white. Said she moved like someone unstuck from time, and her eyes were like glass.

I've seen her now. She wears black. But the eyes the presence they're the same. The mark is the same.

I don't know what she is. But I'm starting to believe she's been behind this far longer than any of us realized.

Be careful, Teddy. Whatever you're uncovering in London she's already ahead of it.

—Archie

Rain had returned by dawn. Archie sealed the letter in wax and wrapped it in oilskin. Outside, Mabel stood beneath the overhang, arms crossed, watching the jungle trail.

The courier waited at the edge of the path — a broad-shouldered ocelot with golden fur marked in black rosettes.

His satchel was already slung over one shoulder. "You're sure he can be trusted?" Archie asked.

Mabel gave a slow nod. "He works old channels. Quiet ones. Embassy runners. Mercenaries. Doesn't matter to him — so long as the coin is clean." Archie handed the letter over.

"Private residence in London. Chesterfield name will get it through."

The ocelot took the letter, sniffed the seal, then tucked it carefully inside his satchel. "I'll run silent. No stops."

Mabel pressed a coin pouch into his paw. "If you get caught, you were never here."

The ocelot dipped his head and disappeared into the mist.

Archie stood at the edge of the trail, rain tapping lightly against his coat. Behind him, Nora stepped beside him.

"You think Teddy will believe it?" she asked.

"He'll want to," Archie said. "And maybe that'll be enough."

They stood in silence as the jungle swallowed the courier's tracks. The mark had returned. And now, it had a destination.

———

Teddy – London, One Week Later

The letter arrived in a weather-stained envelope, hand-delivered by a quiet gray courier in a diplomatic coat. No return address. Just a name: Teddy Chesterfield – Private Residence Teddy didn't open it right away.

He set it on the desk in his study and stared at it for the better part of ten minutes, as though the seal itself might shift or fade if he looked long enough. It had been weeks since he'd heard a word from Archie. No calls, no notes, no sightings. Just a series of dead ends, unanswered leads, and Dolores— God, Dolores—only recently returned, shaken but alive.

He hadn't written to Archie. Couldn't. Between the kidnapping, the investigation, and the fear of every channel being watched, he hadn't dared put pen to page. Not when he couldn't guarantee it'd get through—or who might read it first. Now this.

He broke the seal and unfolded the letter. His eyes scanned the page slowly, steadily. He read it twice. By the end, his claws had lightly pierced the paper.

He stood and crossed to his desk, retrieving a folder of compiled leads. Inside were weeks' worth of findings: half-legible shipping logs, photographs of Hollowed Coin meeting places, blurred figures entering guarded buildings under nightfall. But one document stood out — a security report marked up in red ink, with a still frame of a tall, black-coated feline striding across a marble floor. No name. Until now.

Roxanne, he thought. It fit.

If Archie was right, she wasn't working for anyone. She was giving orders. Which meant—

Teddy reached for a separate folder: his father's Veracruz expedition notes. Mostly untouched. He wasn't the historian in the family. That had always been Archie's obsession.

The drawing was there — *a serpent wrapped around the sun.* The same symbol Archie had mentioned. The same one they'd found in the scroll. Teddy's eyes narrowed.

He opened a book of Mesoamerican timelines he'd dug up from the university archive two weeks ago and thumbed through until he reached a comparison chart. *Olmec. PreOlmec. Early Formative Period. He traced his paw across the estimated date ranges. The scroll predates the Aztecs...*

His brain worked through it out loud now, slow but deliberate.

"The Aztecs rose around the 1300s... this symbol is preclassical... That puts the scroll at... eleven hundred BC?" He paused. "Three thousand years..." He leaned back slowly, eyes unfocused. "No one lives that long."

Yet—his father saw her in 1933. Archie had seen her now. Her image—her presence—ran like a seam beneath all of it. He didn't want to say it aloud. Didn't need to.

He slid the letter into the folder with the photograph and closed it.

"Whatever you are," he muttered, "you've been doing this a long time."

He stood still for a moment, as if waiting for the room to settle.

Then he moved to the window, watching the overcast city shift and hum below. "I'm coming for answers." And this time, he wouldn't be asking politely.

Teddy leaned over the desk, letting the room settle around him. The rain had softened into a steady whisper outside, blurring the glow of the gaslights through the fogged windowpane. *Roxanne.*

She wasn't just a name anymore. She was a force—one that had moved through history like a shadow behind the curtain.

He stared down at the photograph. Grainy. Overexposed. But unmistakably her. Three thousand years. That was impossible. It had to be. And yet...

He opened a drawer and pulled out a fresh notebook. Flipped past the blank pages. Began sketching the serpent and sun. He didn't have Archie's eye for history, but he knew patterns when he saw them. Repetition wasn't coincidence. It was design.

If she had orchestrated this for that long, then London wouldn't just be a location — it would be a keystone. Something she meant to control. Or already did.

Teddy reached for the phone, his paw hovering. He had a few names left. People who still owed him favors. A few in Parliament. A few closer to the floorboards. He wouldn't leave. Not yet. There was still more to uncover here. More knots to untangle. And one of them would eventually lead back to her.

He slid Archie's letter into the folder beside the photo, closed it, and locked the drawer.

"Let's see what you missed, Roxanne.

13

The fire in the Chesterfield sitting room crackled low, its warmth fighting a losing battle against the damp London air. Teddy was already lacing up his boots when Dolores entered with two cups of tea.

"You're really going, then?" she asked, setting one beside him.

"I need to see it myself," Teddy said, standing. "The last set of records—expedition manifests, redirected funds—they all pointed to Parliament. If Roxanne missed something, it's going to be there."

Dolores crossed her arms. "And what exactly are you planning to do? Walk in and ask for the Hollowed Coin floor plans?"

Teddy allowed a dry smile. "More like walk in and pretend I never left. Still have a few favors owed." "You know they're not going to let me in."

"I know." He pulled on his coat. "But if I'm right, it won't end there. And when I call, I'll need you ready. Grab the maps, the old floor plans—the ones I marked with red. And bring the bag with the crowbar. Just in case." Dolores arched an eyebrow. "Subtle."

"Always," Teddy said, kissing her cheek. "Keep the fire going."

The rain hadn't let up. It came down in a fine mist, the kind that clung more than it fell. Teddy didn't bother with an umbrella. He moved through the quiet streets with his coat drawn close, tail low behind him. Westminster wasn't far—just a few blocks, but long enough for the damp to work its way into his fur.

Parliament loomed through the fog, its towers standing dark against the gray sky. Teddy approached the main gate with calm familiarity, flashing his old credentials to the guard, who gave only a cursory glance before waving him through.

Inside, the halls were beginning to fill with the early rhythm of a workday. Staff moved briskly through wide corridors, papers under arms, conversations clipped and half-whispered. Teddy passed them all without pause, cutting away from the main stairwell and toward the Document Archive Wing—currently closed for renovation, and long neglected.

He slipped through a temporary barrier and into a quieter hall. Dust lined the baseboards. A drop cloth had been forgotten over a disused bench. The lighting was dim, and the air smelled faintly of old stone and varnish.

At the end of the corridor, near a patch of exposed wall, he stopped.

There, beneath a section of cracked plaster, a ring had been carved into the stone. It wasn't whole—split cleanly at the top—and along the edge, faint notches had been etched in regular intervals. Not just decorative. Functional, maybe. Or symbolic. A fractured wheel.

Beneath it, just visible in the light, someone had scratched a line of text:

The twin rests beneath the bell.

Teddy crouched, studying it silently with no references about Roxanne. No mention in the files. But it fit. A second scroll. A counterpart. And beneath the bell—only one place came to mind.

He stood, turned without a word, and made his way to a small corner office on the second floor. Technically abandoned, but the key still worked. No one had bothered to reassign it.

He closed the door behind him, drew the curtain halfway, and picked up the old rotary phone on the desk. One ring. Then two. Click. "Hello?" Dolores's voice—even but listening.

"They still haven't changed the wallpaper in the archives," Teddy said. A pause.

"Maybe they're waiting for the bell to ring before they do." He allowed himself a quiet smile.

"Wouldn't be the first time something got buried beneath layers." Another pause. "I'll take the west entrance," she said. "I'll bring the torch," he answered. She hung up without saying goodbye.

Teddy stayed still for a moment. Then he tucked his notebook back into his coat, folded up the loose map, and slid it into his satchel. He checked the time.

Three meetings before lunch. A finance review after that. Half a dozen eyes watching every exit. He wasn't going anywhere. But Dolores would know what to look for.

Dolores didn't bolt out the door or throw things into a bag. She moved with a quiet, practiced calm—each step measured, her tail gliding behind her in a slow curve. Teddy's call had given her all she needed. Not in words, but in tone. In timing. He had found something. It was her turn to move.

She packed light: maps folded twice and marked in red ink, a pocket torch, gloves, and a field notebook. She slipped in a small pry tool—just in case—and tucked a folded cloth around it to stop the metal from rattling. Her claws clicked softly on the kitchen tile as she passed through the flat. Before she left, she paused at the front window, eyes narrowing, ears flicking at the soft hiss of rain against the sill. No one was watching. Not yet.

She slipped into the street with her coat drawn tight and the satchel tucked close. The rain flattened her whiskers and clung to her fur in droplets. She didn't shake them off. Instead, she adjusted her pace and let her body fall into rhythm—lean, low, and silent, her paws light on the pavement.

No cab. No Underground. She preferred the street, where she could hear her own thoughts.

The walk to St. Paul's gave her time to focus. Water pooled in the grooves of the cobblestones, catching bits of light as she passed under flickering gas-lamps. Her ears rotated at the creak of a window above, then pinned back as a cab splashed past. Her senses were alert—always had been. She didn't walk with hesitation. She walked like someone who could vanish if needed.

As she turned off Ludgate Hill, the fog began to thin just enough for the shape of the cathedral to rise in full view. St. Paul's. Its dome loomed like a great, silent bell—one that no longer rang but still knew how to listen.

Dolores slowed, her claws briefly unsheathing to grip the edge of a slick curb as she stepped up onto the square. Tourists lingered beneath umbrellas across the plaza, but no one looked twice at the black-furred figure crossing the stone. Her coat blended with the shadows.

She stopped at the base of the steps and tilted her head upward. The bell. The twin.

Teddy hadn't told her where to look, but she knew. It wasn't just a phrase. It was a challenge. Something had been hidden beneath all this weight and reverence, and Roxanne had either missed it… or walked away from it. Dolores didn't plan on doing either.

She flexed her claws once inside her gloves, took a breath, and began to climb.

The cathedral doors gave a reluctant creak as she slipped inside, just wide enough to avoid drawing attention. Dolores moved through the threshold with care, her tail flicking once as the air shifted around her. The interior swallowed sound.

Stone columns reached toward the domed ceiling above, disappearing into dim light. Her ears twitched against the sudden quiet, catching only the occasional footstep, the rustle of a page turned by a visitor seated at one of the pews. She stayed close to the side aisle, her steps soft on the smooth stone floor, her claws sheathed but ready beneath her gloves.

No one looked twice at her. She moved like she'd been there before.

She scanned the side chapels as she walked, taking in the names carved into the plaques, the weathering of old dedications, the symmetry of the marble lines in the floor. Her eyes weren't on the grandeur—they were watching the details. The places where the old structure and the newer restorations didn't quite match.

At the far end of the south transept, she paused in front of a visitor's placard listing historical renovations. She ran her paw slowly along the bottom edge of the board, then stopped when she saw it:

"South Crypt Access: sealed in 1971 during structural stabilization efforts."

She glanced to the left. Just past a velvet rope and a discreet *STAFF ONLY* sign, a low stone staircase descended into shadow. That was it. Dolores waited a moment; ears angled for movement. Nothing.

She crouched low and slipped beneath the rope in one fluid motion. No fuss. No sound. By the time a tourist turned to glance in her direction, she was already gone—vanished down the stairwell into the dark.

The descent was steep and close. The stone steps were slick from condensation, the walls tight enough that her coat brushed them. Each step echoed softly, but never more than a whisper.

She didn't need a light yet. Her eyes adjusted quickly. At the bottom, the crypt opened into a long, arched chamber with a vaulted ceiling and rows of low-set tomb markers carved into the floor. Dim wall sconces lit alcoves on either side—enough to cast shadows, but not enough to see clearly into the corners. It was silent. Completely. Her claws slipped out just slightly as she walked.

She wasn't expecting company—but Roxanne had a habit of being two steps ahead.

Still, the space felt untouched. Preserved, even. But not empty.

Dolores's gaze swept along the floor until it landed on a single stone slab—near the back wall, larger than the others. It wasn't misaligned. Not obviously. But something about the finish was off. Too smooth. Too clean.

She crouched beside it, ran a paw along the seam, felt the faintest shift beneath her claws. It had been moved—maybe even opened—though not recently. But there was no latch, no mechanism. No keyhole. She sat back on her heels and stared at it. This had to be it.

The second half of the scroll—if it was still here—was under that slab. But how to get to it without drawing attention, or worse, triggering something meant to keep it hidden?
She glanced once over her shoulder. Still alone. Her ears lowered slightly. "Almost," she murmured. "But not quite."
Then she moved into the shadows.

She chose an alcove far enough from the stairs to remain unseen but close enough to watch the slab. She crouched low, knees tucked beneath her coat, one paw resting lightly on her satchel, the other tracing the ridge of the stone beside her. She'd wait. Quiet. Still. Teddy was coming.

And she'd be ready when he got here.

———

While Teddy and Dolores searched beneath the stones of London, Archie crouched under a different kind of weight one of heat, dust, and ancient warning.

Archie crouched beneath the narrow overhang of a weathered column, brushing loose soil from a carved edge with the side of his paw. He narrowed his eyes against the sun. The glyphs here weren't as deep as the ones near the temple—they had been worn by centuries of wind, of rain, of moss. Still, a pattern was forming.

Nora stood a few paces away, flipping through the pages of his father's journal. Her brow was furrowed, her ears turned slightly outward—she was in full focus mode, and Archie knew better than to interrupt.

"Does anything match the diagrams?" he asked without looking up.

"No," she said, flipping another page. "At least, not in the way I expected. It's all out of balance. James mapped everything as a mirrored system. Dual paths. Dual seals. But this site—it's not complete. Half of it's been untouched."

Eddie paced nearby, eyes on the trees more than the ruins. "Feels like we're being watched," he muttered, paw resting just above his sidearm. "And not by the usual jungle things."

Archie rose slowly. He could feel it too. The air wasn't still. It pressed in from all sides— quiet, but not peaceful.

Mabel appeared at the edge of the clearing, brushing dirt from her gloves. "Path ahead's clear, but there are paw prints. Deep ones." Nora stopped flipping pages. Her ears lifted slightly. "Archie." He turned.

She held out the journal, tapped her claw on a single line in the margin—James Chesterfield's handwriting, nearly faded with time.

"The second gate rests where the bells no longer ring. Too loud for them to find it."

Archie blinked. "That's… London."

Nora nodded. "St. Paul's. It fits the geometry. The old city was built in concentric layers, just like the outer ring here.

But this site doesn't have the anchor."

Archie didn't answer. He just stared past her shoulder, into the tree line. Eddie's ears perked. *"Movement."* Mabel tensed. *"We need to go. Now."*

They packed quickly—journals, notes, the rest of the mapping equipment. Archie didn't speak again until they were back on the trail, deeper into the brush.

"They were never meant to find both pieces here," he said quietly. "Just one. The rest... was hidden closer to home."

Nora walked beside him, her steps careful, her eyes scanning the undergrowth. "Then we get it back before they do." Eddie fell behind, guarding their rear. Mabel led from ahead. But even in motion, Archie could feel it. The Hollowed Coin was closing in. That night he knew now it wouldn't just be shadows in the trees. *The Arrow Struck first.*

No sound. No warning. Just the sharp crack of bark splitting inches above Archie's head.

He dropped fast, yanking Nora down with him behind a shattered arch. His paw found the Colt .45 beneath his coat. Hammer back. Ready.

"Ambush!" Eddie called out. A single shot answered— one masked figure collapsed in the brush.

Shadows moved fast—black coats, curved blades, no words. Hollowed Coin.

Archie stood, fired. Missed. Fired again. The second shot hit a shoulder—dropped one clean. He ducked back, breathing steady, ears twitching. "Two on the ridge!" Nora shouted, sharp and clear.

"I've got them," Eddie replied. He shifted left and fired twice more. Another dropped. The rest scattered.

Mabel flashed past them—silent, quick. A sharp cry followed. She returned with a shallow cut along her cheek and blood on her claws. "They're cracking," she said. "We push now, we finish it." And for a moment—they were winning. Then the jungle went quiet. Not still. Hollow. *Roxanne stepped out.*

She moved like fog—measured, precise, untouched. Her coat flowed open, and the Hollowed Coin insignia sat on her collar like a brand. She didn't draw a weapon. She didn't need one.

Archie raised the Colt.45. Eddie mirrored him. Mabel went low, wide, knives in both paws. Roxanne didn't speak. She acted.

Eddie fired. Before the sound finished, Roxanne moved— inside his guard, struck his wrist hard. The gun flew.

Archie fired. She knocked his aim wide, drove a sharp elbow into his side, and kicked the Colt from his paw. It clattered across the dirt. Mabel lunged. She came fast, low— classic strike pattern.

Roxanne stepped around the first blade, caught Mabel's arm mid-swing, and twisted. Mabel dropped one knife.

The second never got near.

A blow to her ribs. A slap to the muzzle. Mabel stumbled back, raised her paws to block

Roxanne struck with a brutal hook to the jaw, then swept her legs clean out.

Mabel hit the ground flat. Breath knocked out. She reached for her last blade—

Roxanne kicked it away and drove a heel into her ribs.

"You were dangerous once," she said, cold. *"Now you're just tired."* Roxanne turned—no hurry. Nora had just stood, trying to disappear into the trees.

Roxanne was on her before the others could react. She grabbed her by the collar and hauled her off her feet.

Nora fought—furious, wild—but Roxanne didn't flinch. She simply dragged her through the clearing like a sack of cloth. Archie took a step. She didn't even look back.
He stopped.

Mabel groaned, still on the ground. Eddie stood empty-pawed, tense, frozen. Roxanne walked into the jungle, Nora still kicking.

She didn't speak. She didn't threaten. Her taking Nora was enough. Then she was gone. Trees swallowed them whole. And in the silence that followed, no one moved.

Archie stared into the green. His Colt lay bent in the dirt. Mabel's paw trembled against her ribs. Eddie's ears were flat.

And Nora was gone.

14

The cathedral was quiet. Not silent, but still in the way old buildings sometimes were — the kind of stillness that settled into the walls after centuries of holding secrets. Dolores stood near the stairwell leading to the crypt, half in shadow, one hand resting on the cold stone. She hadn't moved in hours.

She'd slipped inside earlier that afternoon, waiting until the corridors emptied out. Now she kept low and out of sight, tucked behind a narrow column just off the lower level. From here, she could still see it — the section of wall that looked just a little too smooth, a little too intentional. She didn't know for sure what it was.

There was no handle, no lock, no engraving. Just a subtle mismatch in the stonework and the faint outline of a faded circle — almost invisible in the dim light. But something about it felt wrong. Or maybe right.

The paper in her pocket was soft from wear. A torn fragment of journal — her father's handwriting, tight and exact: "Second vault. Sealed chamber beneath the dome. The altar does not face it — the wheel does." She didn't know what the wheel was. Not yet. Footsteps echoed above. Steady, familiar.

Teddy Chesterfield appeared at the top of the stairs, coat damp from the late rain, face drawn with exhaustion. When he spotted her, he descended quickly, his steps careful but urgent. "You picked a fine place to disappear to," he said as he reached the bottom.

"I had reason," she answered, nodding toward the patch of wall behind her. He followed her gaze. "That it?"

"Maybe. No seams. No markings. Just... wrong. I don't know how else to put it."

He handed her a folded page. "This might help. Dug it up in the old Parliament files. Took forever to cross-reference."

She opened it. Thin paper, fading ink. Latin text bracketed by two rough circles, marked in pencil: *"Through the turning of the wheel, stone opens to memory.*

He who bears the mark may descend; the rest must remain."

Dolores exhaled through her nose. *"Matches the journal."* *"So?"* he asked. *"It's not a door,"* she said. *"Not exactly. But it wants to be."*

She turned toward the wall, eyes narrowing. "We're not getting through it yet. But we're close."

Teddy stepped in close, eyes narrowed as he examined the wall. The stone looked ordinary at a glance, but something about the mortar lines bothered him. Too clean. Too deliberate. He pressed a paw flat against the surface.

"There's weight behind this," he said. "It's not just wall. Something's braced behind it." Dolores moved beside him, crouching low again. She drew a small blade from her coat and ran it gently along the seam she'd uncovered earlier. The dust

gave way to a fine groove etched into the base—an arc, maybe a half-circle. "It curves," she said. "It's part of a larger pattern."

Teddy reached into his bag and pulled out a short, worn crowbar. "I figured we'd run into something like this."

He wedged the end into the groove, adjusted his grip, and nodded toward her. *"On my count," she said. "One."*
Teddy braced the bar. "Two. Three."

She pushed while he leveraged the bar forward. The metal groaned against the stone, and for a moment nothing gave— then a soft click echoed through the wall. Dust spilled from the seam. The wall moved. Only an inch, but it moved.

"Again," Teddy said.

They pressed together this time, shoulder to stone. The slab rotated slowly on a hidden axis, grinding over old hinges buried deep inside the wall. As it turned, it revealed a narrow space behind it—a dark passage slanting downward into deeper stone.

Dolores clicked on her flashlight. The beam cut through the dust, catching glimpses of carved walls and uneven flooring. They stepped in slowly, careful not to disturb anything.

The passage widened into a circular chamber. Cracked columns ringed the space, most half-swallowed by earth. The air was cold, dry, unmoving. At the center of the floor was a large stone ring—flat, smooth, and marked with unfamiliar symbols. Teddy knelt beside it. "It's a second mechanism."

Dolores was already examining the edges. "There's no lock, no lid. This is a cover. Whatever's down there... this is keeping it shut."

She brushed more dust from the edge, revealing a faint emblem—three interlocked circles, and the wheel again, carved dead center.

Teddy looked up at her. "This is the chamber. The box must be beneath it."

She nodded. "But without the key... we're not getting any further." Teddy sat back. "So we're close. But we're stuck."

Dolores stood slowly "Then We break it down, piece by piece."

She circled the ring again, eyes scanning every carved detail — the overlapping circles, the broken sun, the shallow notches etched into the outer rim. There were five of them, evenly spaced.

Teddy crouched near one of the notches and ran a claw along the groove.

"None of these symbols match the ones above," he said. "This isn't ceremonial. It's mechanical."

Dolores didn't respond. She was studying the floor near the second column — where a faint line cut into the stone like something had dragged across it a long time ago.

Teddy muttered, "I hate not knowing what we're looking at." The words barely left his mouth before a voice echoed in his memory — something Archie had said more than once, usually while neck-deep in things they didn't understand.

"The absence of context doesn't mean chaos. It just means someone else understood it before you." He didn't say it out loud, but it stuck.

"Dolores," he said instead. "What if this isn't meant to be solved in one go? What if it's supposed to slow us down?" She glanced over. "Then it's doing a good job."

She tapped one of the outer notches. "These turn. But they're not going to move freely. Not until we align them with something else."

Teddy looked up toward the rear wall. Part of an old mural had crumbled to ruin, but half a symbol remained — a fractured wheel, embedded in stone. Dolores followed his gaze. *"We're missing the rest of it."*

Teddy let out a slow breath. "I should've copied the scroll fragments before we left."

"No," she said quietly. "We don't need the scroll."

Teddy blinked. "We don't?"

She reached into her coat and pulled out a folded slip of parchment — a torn journal scrap. She held it beside the carved wheel on the floor.

"It's not identical," she said, *"but it's close. James Chesterfield left this behind.* I don't think it was meant just for Archie. I think he knew someone else might have to come looking."

She crouched again and held the paper steady beside one of the notches. "The altar does not face it — the wheel does."

She whispered it under her breath, her eyes tracing the chamber's edges.

"There," she said, pointing. "That ridge near the second column. It lines up with this mark on the outer ring."

Teddy crouched beside it. "You're right. It's a fixed point."

Dolores stepped back to the center, placed her paws on two of the notches, and gave him a glance. "One turn at a time," she said.

He almost smiled. The tension that had clung to him all afternoon eased, just slightly.

"Sometimes the only way out of a puzzle," Archie had once told him, *"is through it. Just not all at once."*

Together, they began to rotate the notches slow, deliberate adjustments. Dust stirred from the grooves as the rings shifted. When the final notch clicked softly into place, the floor beneath the wheel gave a low, grinding sound.

The stone ring sank with a slow, grinding shudder, revealing a spiral staircase carved into the rock beneath. The steps were narrow, uneven, slick with the damp chill of undisturbed air.

Dolores took the lead, flashlight in one paw, the journal scrap tucked into her coat. Teddy followed a step behind, one hand steadying himself against the wall.

They descended in silence, the weight of the chamber pressing tighter with every turn. About halfway down, the air shifted — colder, stiller. Dolores paused, one paw raised. Teddy stopped just above her. "What is it?"

She tilted the flashlight downward. The beam caught something thin and metallic stretched across the step below — almost invisible unless you were looking for it. A wire.

She crouched, examined it, then looked back at Teddy. "Tripwire," she said. "Tension's fresh. This wasn't built with the rest of the stairwell."

Teddy's voice dropped. "Which means someone's been down here more recently than we thought."

Before she could respond, her paw slipped slightly on the edge of the step, and her shoulder nudged the wire.

It snapped. A sharp, mechanical click echoed through the stone. Teddy didn't hesitate.

He moved fast, grabbing Dolores by the coat and shoving her against the inside wall just as the trap triggered. A section of the ceiling gave way — stone shards and rusted iron teeth slammed down toward the stairwell.

The edge of a broken plate caught Teddy across the side as he turned his body to shield her. He let out a sharp breath, staggered, but didn't fall. The debris clattered and settled. Silence returned.

Dolores shoved him back just enough to get a look. "You're hit." "It's nothing," he muttered, gripping his side.

She pulled his coat open. Blood, but not deep. A long gash along his ribs, shallow but painful. "It could've taken your arm off," she said.

"Would've made paperwork easier," he said, through clenched teeth.

She tore a strip from the inside lining of her coat and wrapped it tight. "You should've let me take the hit."
He looked at her, wincing. "Not how I work." She tied the knot. "Then start adjusting."

Teddy steadied himself, bracing on the stone wall. "Still with me?" She nodded. "Still with you."

They moved forward slower now, careful with every step, watching the walls and ceiling like predators. When they reached the bottom of the stairwell, the space opened into a long, vaulted corridor. The air was cold and dry. No movement. No sound.

At the end of the corridor stood a raised platform — a single pedestal, square and solid, wrapped in faded carvings and half-swallowed by shadow. Teddy exhaled. "Tell me that's it." Dolores stepped forward, gaze steady. "Let's find out."

The corridor opened into a wide stone chamber, circular and echoing, its walls carved with faint, winding script. Most of the room had been reclaimed by time — stones cracked, floor uneven — but the pedestal at the center remained untouched. Solid. Waiting.

Teddy limped slightly, one hand pressed to his side. Dolores took point, flashlight in a steady grip. As they approached the pedestal, it became clear this wasn't the resting place of the scroll itself — not yet. The top was flat stone, bordered by four inset plates. Each one held a different symbol: the wheel, the broken sun, a snake eating its own tail, and a pattern of nine dots in a circle. Dolores leaned closer.

"Another lock."

Teddy crouched with effort, wincing as he steadied himself. "Pressure plates?" "Maybe. Or a sequence."

He glanced at the far wall. More of the winding script — almost decorative, but not random. He narrowed his eyes. "Looks like there's an order here. A progression."

Dolores moved beside him, eyes following the carvings.

"They're stories," she said. "Phases of something. The wheel comes first. Then the sun breaks. Then the snake. Then the stars."

"Cycle of collapse," Teddy muttered. "History repeating itself."

She nodded toward the plates. "Then we press them in that order." Teddy hesitated. "If we're wrong—" "We're not." She placed her paw over the wheel and pressed. The stone clicked. Nothing moved. Then the sun. Another click. She reached for the snake. Teddy reached up with his uninjured arm and stopped her.

"Wait," he said. "The snake's eye—it's closed in the carving on the wall, but open here." She frowned. Looked again. "You're right. The order's reversed for this version."

"Deliberate," he said. "Someone expected a wrong answer first." She stepped back, thinking. Then: *"Try the stars."* Teddy pressed the nine-dot circle. *Click. A low grinding sound echoed under the pedestal.*

They stepped back as a small stone panel slid aside near the base. Dust spilled out. Beneath it, tucked in a carved recess, sat a thick stone box — flat, sealed, and etched with the complete wheel symbol, fully formed, raised at the center. Dolores crouched. "We found it." Teddy let out a slow breath. "Finally." She studied the surface. "No hinges. No keyhole." "No way in," Teddy said. Dolores stood slowly, her voice low. "Not yet." They stood over the box in silence.

Dolores didn't touch it right away. Neither did Teddy. But leaving it here wasn't an option — not now. She crouched beside it, checked the sides. "It'll move." Teddy knelt, winced. "Heavy?" "Solid. But manageable."

They wrapped it in a piece of canvas from Teddy's bag and lifted it together — one paw each, tight grip, no wasted motion. The box gave no resistance. No sound. It just came up like it had been waiting.

They started back. The air in the corridor felt tighter than before. Dolores kept her flashlight low, beam steady. Teddy didn't speak. His side burned, but he kept moving.

At the crypt level, the silence hit different. Not peaceful — expectant. "Should we cover the wall?" Teddy asked. Dolores shook her head. "Let them waste time." When they reached the stairwell, she stopped. A figure stood at the top.

Tall. Smoke-colored fur. Neat dark coat. No visible weapon, but the way he held himself — still and balanced — said he didn't need one. His eyes were pale, unreadable. He didn't flinch at the light. Just watched.

Teddy stepped up beside her. Quiet. Ready.

The tomcat stepped forward slowly, one paw resting just below his coat-line. *"You've been busy,"* he said. Dolores didn't answer. "This level's closed," she said evenly. *"Not for me."*

Teddy kept his voice low. "You're not with the Hollowed Coin." The tom's mouth curved slightly. *"No. I'm not."* He glanced down the passage behind them. *"You found it, didn't you?"* Dolores didn't blink. "You're in the way." *"I could be,"* the tom said. *"But I'm not."*

He looked at them both, taking his time. Then, quietly, he stepped aside.

"Safe travels," he said. *"Mrs. Chesterfield. Mr. Chesterfield."*

Neither spoke. They passed him without pause, the box held steady between them.

Outside, the air had cooled. Rain in the distance, just starting to spit. Dolores stared ahead. "He wasn't there for the box." Teddy nodded once. "No. He was there to see who got it."

They kept walking, the street pulling them back into London's noise and shadow. They didn't speak much on the ride back.

Teddy kept one paw pressed to his side. The bleeding had slowed, but not enough for comfort. Dolores sat across from him, arms folded, eyes out the window. The box sat between them on the floor of the cab, wrapped tight, unmoving.

When they reached the flat, she locked the door behind them and went straight for the small first aid kit beneath the kitchen sink. No lights on — just the low lamp in the corner and the distant hum of traffic. "Sit," she said. Teddy lowered himself onto the couch without a word.

She peeled his coat away carefully, then his shirt. The gash along his ribs was angry and red, torn clean but deep enough to sting for days. She didn't speak. Just cleaned the wound with a steady hand, wrapped it in tight layers of gauze, and taped it down. When she finished, she sat back on her heels. "You'll live," she said. He nodded. "You've done worse." "Not lately." They were quiet a moment.

Then he looked toward the box, still wrapped and set against the far wall. "Let's have a look."

Dolores stood and brought it over, setting it gently on the table. She unwrapped the canvas, folded it back clean, and stepped aside.

The stone surface was darker now in the low light — no longer buried in dust, but just as sealed. The wheel emblem in the center was smooth and cold, raised half an inch off the surface. No hinge. No lock. Just weight. Dolores ran a paw along the edge. *"It's older than the vault,"* she said.

Teddy leaned in. "But it's not just sealed. It's designed to stay that way." She nodded. *"Until the right key comes along."*

He sat back, wincing slightly as he adjusted against the bandage. "We've done all we can." "Not quite," she said.

She took a small notebook from the shelf, opened to a clean page, and began sketching the emblem — every curve, every marking around the edge, each slight variation in the stone's face. Teddy watched her work in silence.

After a while, he said, "He knew what he was leaving behind."

She didn't look up. "And he knew someone would come for it."

15

Nora sat on the cold stone floor, tail looped tightly around her ankles, paws bound in front of her with coarse rope. Her shoulders ached from the earlier struggle. The flickering bulb overhead did little to warm the concrete room, but her fur had dried from the damp. She hadn't spoken since she was taken. No one had. The bolt scraped. The door creaked open.

A pair of guards entered—large toms, both clad in dark coats. One of them stepped forward and yanked her to her feet with more force than necessary. Nora winced. Her claws flexed instinctively.

As they turned to leave, the taller one shoved her forward with a muttered growl under his breath.

They walked in silence down a long, winding corridor. Older stone now. Dry, heavy with the scent of dust and iron. Her pawsteps echoed. She counted them again. Left. Right. One paw in front of the other. At the end of the hall, a door opened without a knock.

Inside was a clean, sparse chamber. A table. Two chairs. A wall of old shelving behind it. Roxanne sat waiting. She didn't rise. She didn't need to.

Her coat was immaculately buttoned to the throat, fur sleek, ears still. She watched Nora enter with the calm of someone who'd already seen this play out a thousand times. "Unbind her," she said, without looking at the guards.

The shorter one hesitated. The other didn't move. "She bit one of ours on the way in," the tall one said. Roxanne's eyes didn't shift. "And I am not one of yours." He moved, reluctant.

As he approached, Nora flinched slightly — and he seized her arm with unnecessary force, claws biting into the fur at her elbow. Then he staggered back with a sudden cry.

Roxanne stood — her paw outstretched, claws red. She'd moved without warning, faster than the eye could follow, and raked her claws across the side of his face with a precision that didn't spill blood but cut deep enough to humiliate.
The other guard froze. Roxanne's voice was flat. "You'll heal."

She stared the tall one down, who now gritted his teeth, tail rigid with pain and fear.

"If you ever put your paws on her like that again, I'll make sure the next scar can't be hidden under fur." Silence. Tense, absolute. The tall tom stepped back, trembling now, ears low.

The shorter one cut the rope from Nora's wrists quickly and without a word. Roxanne didn't look at either of them. "Out." They obeyed immediately. The door clicked shut behind them.

Roxanne gestured to the seat across from her. "Please." Nora sat slowly. Silence hung between them for a few seconds.

Then Roxanne stepped toward the shelf, removed a tin cup, and poured water from a tall clay pitcher. Her movements were precise — almost ceremonial.

"I imagine you have questions," she said, still turned slightly away. "I have plenty," Nora replied. Roxanne offered the cup. Nora took it cautiously.

"What is this really about?" Nora asked. "The scroll? The wheel? Why go this far?" Roxanne didn't answer immediately. She moved to the windowless wall behind the table and traced one paw slowly across the stone surface.

"I've lived long enough to know that knowledge doesn't change the world. Control does. Cycles repeat. Empires rise, fall, and rot in their own arrogance. But if you can shape the rhythm— tilt the wheel slightly—you don't need to rule. You just need to adjust the balance." Her tail flicked once. "The Scroll?" Nora pressed. "What's on it that matters so much?" "Not What. Where." Nora tilted her head slightly.

"You want the artifact." "I want what it guards."

Roxanne sat again, folding her paws neatly. "The wheel is real, Nora. Not metaphor. Not myth. The scroll reveals part of its pattern. There are still pieces buried across the world… locked. Lost. But when joined—" She didn't finish.
Nora leaned forward. "You beat Mabel like she was a kit."

Roxanne's whiskers twitched faintly. "Mabel used to be dangerous. When I first encountered her, she was clever. Fast. Confident."

She looked to the chair across from her, then slowly stood and moved behind it.

195

"She relied on chaos. Kept her enemies guessing. Kept herself guessing. It worked—until she stopped learning."

She placed a paw lightly on the top rail of the chair. "The mistake most fighters make is assuming unpredictability is the same as control."

In a single fluid motion, she tipped the chair forward, pivoted on the back leg, and brought it down with a soft knock — perfectly balanced on one leg, unmoving.

"That's what Mabel lacked. Balance. Precision. The moment she hesitated—she lost."

Roxanne stepped away, leaving the chair balanced as if it defied gravity.

"She still believes she can improvise her way out of discipline. But instinct dulls. Old tricks become habits. And habits are easy to break."

Nora swallowed, unsure whether the chill she felt came from the cold room or the truth in Roxanne's tone.

"And how do you fight like that?" Nora asked quietly. "You made it look effortless."

Roxanne's eyes didn't blink. "Because I don't fight for effect. I fight to end things."

Nora hesitated. "Archie said you were ancient... Is it true?"

Roxanne tilted her head slightly. "What matters is that I remember. Every mistake. Every outcome. Every door that was once closed." It wasn't a yes. But it wasn't a no either.

Her gaze drifted momentarily to the side wall, eyes narrowing as if caught in a memory.

Nora followed her line of sight—just a shelf. Books, a dusty globe, a rusted key ring with half the rings empty. A small polished mirror lay among them, angled just wrong enough to catch the light from the ceiling. Roxanne's ears flicked.

She stood and walked over to adjust the mirror. The light bounced away—an old habit, maybe. Or a memory that had nothing to do with this moment. And Nora saw it.

The key. A small bronze shape tucked into the inner pocket of Roxanne's coat. The same one that had shifted earlier.

Nora's pulse quickened.

As Roxanne turned away from the shelf, the mirror slipped slightly and clattered down. Roxanne knelt to pick it up.

In that second—quiet, quick, focused—Nora moved. Her paw brushed the coat near the chair. One claw, precise, looped the chain and slipped the key down into her sleeve, tight against her forearm.

By the time Roxanne turned back, the coat had shifted. The key was gone. She said nothing. "Thank you for the water," Nora said.

Roxanne looked at her a moment longer, then nodded to the door. "You'll be taken back. Rest. You'll need it." Nora stood. The guards re-entered.

The larger one kept his distance this time. No claws. No growls. Only silence.

"She walks," Roxanne said, not bothering to glance at him. They obeyed.

Nora didn't look back. Her ears stayed high. Tail even. But her heart hammered in her chest. Because this time… she wasn't empty-pawed.

The torchlight faded behind her as the guard dragged her down the corridor. Nora kept her head low, her breathing steady. She had the key. And that meant there was still a chance.

―――

Elsewhere, deep in the jungle

The night had fallen hard, wrapping the trees in silence. Archie crouched at the edge of the firelight, one paw wrapped around his knee, the other resting on the satchel by his side. The fire cracked softly, spitting embers into the thick air. Every so often, a branch creaked above them, or something small rustled through the underbrush, but none of them reacted. She was gone. They all knew it. No one said it aloud.

"She didn't even draw a blade," Eddie muttered, tail twitching behind him. "Took us apart like we were nothing." Archie didn't look up. "Nora tried to stop her." "She never had a chance," Eddie said. "None of us did."

Mabel was perched on a rock across from the fire, arms folded, jaw set tight. Her eyes hadn't left the flames since they'd stopped moving.

Archie finally turned to her. "You've fought her before." Mabel didn't respond.

He pressed. "You said she let you live. Back at the ridge." A long pause.

"She did," Mabel said. "And she could've ended me. Same as tonight." Archie stood slowly. "Why didn't she?" Mabel's ear twitched.

"She wanted me to remember. Wanted me to know I couldn't stop her then, and I won't stop her now."

Eddie stepped closer, arms folded. *"You said it happened years ago. Where?"*

"Barcelona," Mabel said. *"I was working a case.* Thought I was chasing down some smuggler skimming from a local fence. Turns out, he was working for her. I didn't know it until it was too late." *"You fought her?"* Eddie asked.

Mabel gave a slow nod. "I thought I had the upper paw. Speed, traps, everything. I even got her to react—once. But the moment I did... the fight was over. She adjusted. I didn't.

She knew every step I'd take after that."

Eddie scoffed. "No one fights like that without training."

Mabel didn't look up. "It wasn't just training. It was instinct. Control. She moved like she'd already fought me in her head and was just playing it out for the second time."

Archie's voice was quiet now. *"That's why you froze tonight."*

Mabel's eyes finally lifted. "Because I remembered what it felt like to lose. And I knew we weren't going to win." The fire cracked again, louder this time.

"She disarmed all of us," Eddie said. "Clean. Fast. We couldn't even track her movements." Archie didn't move. "We're getting Nora back." "Not if we're fighting blind," Mabel said.

Archie looked at her. *"Then talk. Tell us everything. Every detail. Every mistake."* She didn't speak for a moment. Then she nodded. "All right." Mabel didn't speak at first.

The firelight played gently across her fur as she sat still, eyes fixed on the jungle beyond their makeshift camp. One claw tapped quietly against her arm—a rhythm she didn't seem aware of.

"She doesn't fight to win," she said finally. *"She fights to end it. No hesitation. No excess. Just enough to make sure you don't get up."*

Eddie crouched beside the fire, his ears flat. "Like she's done it all before."

"She has," Mabel said. "Not in body. In mind. That's how she moves. Like the fight already happened and she's just... walking through it."

Archie watched her closely. "You're not predictable. Not in the slightest."

"She didn't need me to be," Mabel said. "Every trick I tried, she adjusted. Mid-strike. Like instinct. Like she'd already mapped out how to beat me—and then chose when to do it." She shifted, sat a little straighter.

"I wasn't always like this," she said. *"Didn't grow up with a sword. I was a food critic. High-end. The New York Ledger.*

Private tastings, velvet ropes, menus that changed lives and ended careers." Eddie raised a brow. "So how'd you end up here?"

"There was a supper club in Midtown," she said. "Invite-only. No phones. No names. You got a card in the post, and if you showed up, you didn't talk about it afterward." She let her voice drift for a moment before continuing.

"One night, I was seated across from a tom I didn't recognize. Quiet. Wore a brown coat. Just listened. Never interrupted, never joined in. When the final course came out, he looked across the table and said:

This place—it's not about food. It's about watching who comes hungry. And what they're really starving for.'"
Mabel's voice dropped.

"Then he said: 'You think power's found in what people say about your words? Try holding a truth no one believes. Try standing alone when the silence gets too loud. That's where power starts.'" *She glanced at the fire again.*

"'You're sharp,' he told me. 'But sharp gets dull without purpose. If you're going to cut something, make sure it's not yourself.'"

Archie's eyes narrowed. "That was him."

Mabel nodded. *"James Chesterfield.* He didn't say the name 'Hollowed Coin,' but he didn't need to. He warned me without warning me." "What did you do after that?" Eddie asked.

"I chased it," Mabel said. "That idea. That maybe I was too comfortable in someone else's room.

I started paying attention. Who showed up to the clubs. Who paid for what. Who disappeared." Her claws stopped tapping.

"I started seeing patterns. The same faces. The same symbols. People who should've been on opposite ends of the world suddenly dining in the same hall." She looked at Archie.

"I remembered what your father said. About purpose. About knowing how to hold a truth even when no one listens. And I realized... I needed to be more than sharp. I needed to be ready." Eddie leaned forward. "So you trained?"

"Harder than I ever thought I could," she said. "Kyoto. Lisbon. Istanbul. I found instructors who didn't ask questions, just handed me bruises until I figured out how not to get hit. But none of them trained me for *Roxanne.*" Archie's voice was quiet. *"And Barcelona?"*

Mabel gave a slow nod. "I thought I was ready. Tracked one of their middlemen to the coast. Got too close. And she showed up. Ended it in less than a minute."

"She didn't even look surprised," she added after a beat. "Just disappointed. Like I'd wasted her time." The fire popped softly. Archie sat forward. "We're going to get Nora back."

Mabel looked him in the eye. "Then we need to know what we're up against." "Then start talking," Eddie said. "We're listening." Mabel nodded. "All right. From the top."

16

It was Tuesday evening, and the rain hadn't let up all day.

Thin ribbons of water slid down the tall windows of the Chesterfield townhouse, blurring the city into a gray wash of lights and outlines. The house itself was quiet, save for the ticking of the brass mantel clock and the soft pop of logs in the hearth.

Dolores heard the door shut and knew it was Teddy by the rhythm of his steps—measured, heavy, the kind he only used when his thoughts were louder than the street.

She didn't call out. Just met him in the sitting room as he shrugged off his coat and dropped his bag by the chair.

He looked worn. Not exhausted, not injured—just stretched thin. His ears twitched at some thought he didn't share. His expression was that familiar mix of worry and calculation that Dolores had learned to read better than any journal. She didn't ask.

Instead, she crossed to the liquor cabinet and pulled down the Highfang Select he kept hidden behind the polite bottles. She never liked the stuff—said it tasted like peat and regret— but tonight she poured two fingers into each glass without comment. Teddy raised a brow. "You're drinking this?" "Not by choice," she said, handing him a glass. "By necessity." He managed the faintest smile.

She set the other glass down and walked to the drawer beneath the sideboard, pulling out a slim wooden box marked Fumar. She opened it and held out the last cigar— dark, well-kept, untouched since the night he'd planned to celebrate a vote that never came. "You kept that," he said.

"You were saving it," she replied. "Figured this counts as an occasion."

Teddy lit it without another word. The ember glowed, and the smoke curled up into the soft light of the study. He exhaled and leaned back, letting the moment settle.

Dolores sat across from him, both watching the rain carve slow lines down the glass. The moment held. Then the phone rang.

Not the hallway phone. Not the desk line. The gray phone in the drawer—his direct line from Parliament.

Teddy froze, then reached for it, the cigar still between his fingers. *"Chesterfield."* *"It's Halstrom."* Teddy sat upright. *"Sir?"*

"This isn't an official call," Halstrom said. *"You're being placed on leave. Effective immediately."* *"What? For what?"*

"I wasn't told," Halstrom said. "Just that the order came down this morning. Higher than me. You're not to report in again until contacted."

Teddy's voice went flat. "And I'm supposed to accept that?" "I'm telling you as a favor, Teddy," Halstrom said. "Keep your head down. Don't ask. Don't fight it. Not yet." The line went dead.

Teddy sat for a long moment, the phone still in his paw.

Dolores didn't ask. She just nudged his glass closer again.

He took it, staring at the fire, the cigar smoldering low between his claws. "They're trying to box me out," he said.

Dolores leaned forward, voice steady. "Then we change the shape of the board."

The silence lingered, broken only by the soft hiss of rain and the quiet crackle of the fire.

Teddy took another long draw from the cigar, eyes still fixed on the flames. The smoke curled upward, slow and deliberate—thick with the sharp scent of aged tobacco and a distinct undercurrent of catnip. It was a Fumar blend, the kind reserved for dignitaries and gamblers with reputations to maintain. *Rich, earthy, tinged with spice.* The scent drifted across the room, warm and strange, like memory wrapped in heat. Dolores sipped her scotch. No wince this time. *"They know,"* she said quietly. *"Or they suspect."*

Teddy didn't answer right away. He rolled the glass in his paw, letting the amber liquid catch the light.

"They're making sure I can't move freely," he said. "Parliament was the last place I had reach. Pulling me now… means they're ready to act."

Dolores set her glass down gently. "So what do we do?"

Teddy looked at her, the flicker of the hearth dancing in his eyes. "We pack a bag," he said. "Tonight. Just in case."

Her ears twitched, but she nodded once and stood without a word.

Teddy reached for the phone again, the older one tucked into the desk drawer—not Parliament's, but his own line. No notes, no names—just one number scratched on a card he kept behind the drawer liner. He stared at it a moment before dialing.

"Francis," came the voice after two rings. Calm. Low. The sound of someone already expecting trouble. "They've pulled me," Teddy said. A pause. "Understood," Francis replied. "You need cover?" "Not yet," Teddy said. "But something's coming." Another pause. Then, with quiet weight: "I'll be ready." Teddy hung up.

Dolores returned with a satchel and side case, setting them gently by the coat stand. She glanced at him but didn't speak.

He let the silence hold a little longer before saying, "Archie gave me that number before we left for Cempoala. Said if things went sideways, Francis would know what to do." Dolores raised an eyebrow. "He always that cautious?"

Teddy smiled faintly. "He called it 'being prepared.' Said he wasn't planning for betrayal— just didn't want to be surprised by it."

Dolores shook her head once and handed him his glass again. "Smart cat," she muttered. Teddy nodded. "Yeah."

Outside, the rain thickened, tapping harder against the windowpanes. The fire dimmed, and the house settled into stillness again, but it didn't feel like peace. It felt like waiting.

Two hours had passed since the call. The fire had burned down to low embers, pulsing red in the grate. The rain had stopped, but the slick quiet outside hadn't lifted. Shadows moved only when the light did.

Teddy sat forward on the couch, elbows on his knees, jaw tight. Dolores watched him from the other end, legs curled beneath her, the empty glasses still resting between them. The last of the Fumar cigar had turned to ash in the tray, leaving behind its bitter, catnip-sweet haze.

No one said a word. Then—two knocks. Sharp. Close.

Teddy stood in one motion. Dolores was right behind him. "No one should be here," she murmured. "I know."

He motioned for her to stay back and crossed to the coat closet. From the bottom, beneath an old duffel, he pulled out the sealed box they'd taken from St. Paul's. It looked heavier than it was. Still sealed. Still quiet. He tucked it under his arm.

Dolores was already in the kitchen, eyes scanning for anything she could use.

Teddy stopped at the front door. No voice followed. No footsteps walked away. Just that knock. He unlatched the lock and eased it open.

The attacker came through fast—a tall gray tabby in a long coat, blade in paw, eyes blank. Teddy had braced for it.

He stepped into the strike, slammed his shoulder into the cat's chest, and drove him sideways into the wall. The knife came in again, low and quick—Teddy caught the wrist and twisted hard. The blade hit the floor, and a follow-up strike from Teddy's paw sent the attacker crumpling beside it.
A crash rang from the kitchen. Dolores shouted—then snarled.

Teddy turned as another figure lunged from the side hall—a smaller, wiry black cat trying to pin her arms. She twisted, grabbed the pan from the stove, and brought it up under his chin. The cat reeled. She didn't wait. One more swing and he went down.

Teddy grabbed the sealed box with one paw and motioned toward the back door.

They left fast. Out the alley. Through puddles and lamplight. A cold wind chased them for six blocks, but no footsteps followed. When they reached the payphone, Teddy dropped a coin and turned his back to the street. Francis answered on the second ring. "They found us." "You followed?" "No."

"Corner of Holt and Marbury. Five minutes."

Teddy hung up.

The black sedan pulled up quiet, headlights off. Francis reached across and pushed the door open from inside.

They climbed in, soaked and silent. Teddy placed the sealed box on the floor between his feet.

Francis didn't say anything for the first two blocks. Then he reached behind the seat and pulled out a plain canvas satchel. He handed it back without looking. Dolores unzipped it.

Inside: a thick envelope of cash £20,000 in neatly stacked bills. Two temporary passports. Two small revolvers in worn holsters. No names, no questions. "If you need to disappear," Francis said, "don't wait." Teddy met his eyes in the mirror. "Understood." No one spoke again. The box stayed between Teddy's boots. The weight of it seemed to grow with each mile.

———

Far from the rain-soaked streets of London...

The cell stank of damp stone and fur.

Nora shifted in the dark, her back pressed to the cold wall. The torch in the hall cast a flickering glow across the floor, but none of it reached her. Her paws were still sore from the restraints, now gone, but the pressure remained in her joints like a phantom grip. She hadn't moved in ten minutes. Maybe longer.

They'd brought her back an hour ago—maybe two—after that strange, clipped conversation with Roxanne.

The memory still crawled beneath her fur: the way the older cat had studied her, sharp-eyed and quiet, as if measuring something she hadn't spoken aloud. But it had worked. Roxanne hadn't noticed the missing weight. The key was no longer in Nora's possession.

She'd slipped it onto the belt of the guard with the crooked tail as they passed through the second archway. Just a brush of her paw as he'd shoved her forward, a motion she prayed looked clumsy enough to ignore. He hadn't stopped. Hadn't checked. Not yet. Now it was a waiting game.

The floor was rough beneath her legs. The air stale. Every so often, something shifted down the corridor—a guard pacing, the scrape of claws, the grunt of conversation. But here, in this part of the holding cell, it was quiet. Too quiet.
Nora's ears twitched at a sudden creak. Footsteps. Two sets. No armor. Heavier than before.

She stood slowly, brushing dust from her trousers with the side of her paw.

The lock turned. A hinge groaned. The light grew brighter. They were coming for her again. And she already knew who was waiting.

They didn't speak as they moved through the corridor. The taller guard kept a paw heavy on her shoulder, not rough, but firm in a way that made it clear who was in control. The other walked a few paces ahead, tail flicking side to side, ears sharp for movement. Their steps echoed dully, swallowed by the stone walls and the mildew-soaked air.

Nora kept her head level and her ears slightly turned. Every sound mattered now. Every turn in the hallway burned itself into memory.

They stopped in front of a tall wooden door bound in blackened iron. The lead guard rapped once with his knuckles.

A voice answered from inside—measured, calm. "Bring her."

The door opened without ceremony. Nora was guided in, then left alone. It shut behind her with a heavy, final sound.

The chamber inside was spare, lit by a single hanging lantern that swayed just slightly from a recent draft. A long table stretched across the back half of the room, crowded with worn documents and stone fragments. The light touched the corners of several unfamiliar symbols. Roxanne stood behind it.

She didn't look up at first. Her paw moved across a page, marking something with the tip of a steel-tipped stylus. She looked composed fur smoothed, collar folded crisp at her neck. Her coat was buttoned. Tail still. Then her eyes lifted, and they found Nora's without effort. "You've been quiet," Roxanne said. Nora didn't answer.

"That's good. Most cats start rattling off apologies or questions. I don't have much patience for either today."

She walked around the table, unhurried, her steps soundless on the old stone. She stopped a few feet from Nora, tilting her head slightly.

"There's something missing," she said. "A detail. A weight. I feel it."

Her tone didn't rise, but the temperature in the room dropped. Nora blinked once but said nothing. "You've got guts," Roxanne added, as if offering a compliment. "I like that. But I don't like being lied to." She stepped past her, slow, her back briefly turned.

"You're not the first to try and pull something clever under my roof. You're just the only one still breathing afterward." She stopped at the far side of the table again, then gestured toward a single chair placed across from her. "Sit." Nora didn't move at first.

Roxanne tapped a claw against the tabletop. Just once. A sound more patient than threatening.

Nora crossed the space slowly and sat. She kept her back straight, ears neutral. Her tail stayed low behind the chair.

Roxanne studied her a moment longer before sitting as well, folding her paws neatly in front of her. The table between them looked suddenly vast.

"You think you're the first to sneak something past me," Roxanne said. "You're not." Nora said nothing. "But you might be the first to believe it matters." A pause.

"Why am I here?" Nora asked. Her voice didn't shake, but it carried weight.

Roxanne didn't answer right away. She tilted her head, eyes narrowing—not with suspicion, but thought.

"Because I'm curious," she said. "You're not Hollowed Coin. Not a relic hunter. Not some mercenary with a blood-debt. You're a field agent, maybe. Smart. Loyal. But not a threat on your own." "Then why not just kill me?" Nora asked.

Roxanne smiled—not wide, not kind. Just enough to show the faintest glint of fang.

"Because killing someone with no value is a waste. But killing someone who had potential?" Her claws tapped the table again. "That makes a statement."

Nora looked at her. "And you think that's what I am? A statement?"

"I think you're useful," Roxanne replied. "But you've made that difficult." She leaned forward. "Where is it?"

"I don't know what you mean." "Yes, you do."

The room went still. A long breath passed between them. Roxanne didn't raise her voice. She didn't need to.

"I can tear apart every room, every wall, every breath between here and the next mile. But we both know I don't need to. It's close." Nora's ears flicked once, involuntarily.

Roxanne noticed. Of course she noticed. But she didn't act. Instead, she reclined slightly, as if bored.

"You've bought yourself a little time, Nora. That's all. But time's a funny thing. It doesn't slow down when you need it to."

She reached across the table and gently slid a stone fragment toward her.

"I found this in a city older than any map you've ever read. Do you know what it means?" Nora glanced down at the strange carving. She said nothing.

"It's part of a whole," Roxanne said. "Like the scroll. Like the wheel. Like me." A beat.

"And whether you understand your place in it or not... you're already inside it."

214

Roxanne stood, pushing back her chair with slow precision.

"I'll see you again tomorrow. Think carefully about what that meeting will look like." She tapped the table once more. "Don't let someone else pay for your choices." Then she turned and left the room without another word.

The guards returned seconds later and hauled Nora to her feet. She didn't resist. Her eyes never left the stone fragment. And as they led her away, she kept her breathing steady. The key wasn't on her. But it was close. And the clock had just started ticking.

17

Roxanne, Hidden Compound, Yucatan Peninsula

The monastery compound had been awake since dawn, crawling with motion and noise beneath its ancient stone walls. Guards turned over crates in the supply room. Search dogs sniffed through the barracks. Every corner, every chamber, every forgotten crawlspace had been combed, and still nothing.

The key was gone.

Roxanne already knew that. She'd known the moment Nora refused to speak.

Not out of defiance Roxanne could've broken that. No, it was something else. A silence born of calculation. Fear, perhaps. Not fear of her, but fear of what the key meant.

She stood on the upper balcony, overlooking the narrow courtyard. The sun had begun its slow descent, spilling golden light across the cracked flagstones. The jungle beyond rustled with distant movement, but here, at the heart of her domain, all that remained was the hunt. A futile one.

Her eyes followed the movement below, but her thoughts had already drifted. She wasn't thinking of the girl anymore.

Not directly. Her mind was further down the path— past the doors they hadn't yet found, past the puzzle pieces they thought they had stolen. In the end, it would all come back to her. It always did. They were still playing her game, whether they knew it or not.

Below, another patrol assembled. Their shoulders were tense. None dared look up.

The key had been slipped into the compound. She was sure of it. Not handed off to some ally that was laughable. No one in the Hollowed Coin would be foolish enough to turn traitor. No, the girl had hidden it. Somehow. And now it was here, somewhere under her own roof.

Roxanne let her claws tap the railing in a steady rhythm.

Behind her, an aide appeared in the doorway. "Still no sign, ma'am. We've expanded the search to the west storehouse and the water tunnels. Permission to rotate the handlers?" "No," she said without turning. "Keep them running." The aide hesitated. "We may be wasting time."

She finally turned to face him. Her expression was unreadable. Calm. Cold. "Exactly." The aide gave a slight nod and disappeared.

She stepped back inside, where a long table waited scrolls, charts, and fragments laid out in symmetrical precision. In the center, the map of the Wheel. One spoke still missing.

They thought they were gaining ground. That they'd stolen something important. That she was off-balance. Let them think that.

She adjusted a mark beside one of the ruins sketched into the southern quadrant. The trap was already laid. When they opened that door whenever they reached it she would be on the other side.

The council chamber was buried beneath the oldest part of the monastery—stone walls cold to the touch, silence so deep it seemed carved into the room itself. A ring of torchlight circled the chamber, casting uneven shadows across the table and the seven tall-backed chairs that surrounded it.

Above the door, carved into the stone lintel, was the symbol Roxanne had chosen when she formed the council: a wheel with seven spokes. No names. No titles. Just the shape. A reminder that the strength of the Hollowed Coin came from reach—not equality. She was the last to enter. No guards. No announcement.

Just the soft rhythm of her steps, paw pads soundless across the stone. They were already waiting.

Marius Greaves glanced up first. Heavy in the shoulders, muzzle streaked with gray, his thick tail curled neatly around one leg. He wore a coat too fine for jungle heat and rings that caught every flicker of firelight. Marius controlled the accounts—the flow of money, clean and dirty, that passed through a hundred banks across three continents. If it could be financed, insured, or buried under numbers, it ran through him. He didn't smile. "You've kept us waiting,".

To his left, Madame Havel traced the rim of her glass with a single claw. Black lace veiled part of her face, ears held high and rigid beneath the fabric. She was old, though she refused to admit how old, and still carried herself like a feline used to being listened to in private rooms. Havel controlled leverage—secrets, blackmail, and everything too delicate for a gun. She didn't speak yet, but her pupils had narrowed, and her gaze followed Roxanne's every move.

Roth Thorne reclined two seats down, golden fur sleek and trimmed close, cufflinks gleaming at the joint of his slender wrists. His tail flicked lazily against the back leg of the chair. Young, fast-talking, and sharp when it came to acquisition— land, goods, silence— Roth had grown the Coin's reach faster than anyone else at the table. He grinned like this was sport, baring the edge of one fang.

Across from him sat Sabine DuMorne, upright and unmoving, her fur so black it absorbed the light. Her tail lay still against the floor. She ran intelligence—movement, surveillance, asset control. She didn't blink. She never did.

Nico Virelli slouched beside her, boots planted wide, chewing on something brittle between sharp molars. His coat was rougher, patched in places, and his left ear bore a notch from an old fight. Virelli ran enforcement. Hired guns. Field teams. Disposals. He looked bored, but his claws were half-unsheathed, tapping rhythmically on the arm of the chair.

Dame Celeste Halbrook sat immaculate in ivory, her Snow White coat brushed to perfection, posture regal. A silver pin gleamed at her throat, shaped like a dagger tucked behind a lily. She ran the Coin's political operations—senates, courts, diplomats. Her tail was wrapped tight around both ankles, unmoving, but her ears were tilted slightly back. Listening.

Elias Crane sat last. Quiet. Gray-furred. His expression didn't shift, but his claws flicked once across the pages of his ledger. Scribe of the Council. Secrets. Mistakes. Punishments. He did not speak, but his eyes tracked every motion in the room with flat, methodical calm.

Roxanne took her seat. Her tail curled neatly along the back leg of the chair. They didn't wait long.

"We're no longer aligned," Marius began. "The girl. The scroll. The professor. Each of these missteps leads back to you."

"You've lost objectivity," Celeste said. "You're chasing shadows while we're trying to maintain control." "You've lost control," Havel added.

"And now you've lost the key," Roth said, lounging deeper into his chair. "It's time we address what happens next." "There is no vote," Roxanne said.

"You don't get to decide that anymore," Roth replied. "Not when your failures are costing us real ground."

"She built this," Sabine said, voice even, her gaze steady. "And she's still the only one among us who has never been compromised."

Roth turned toward her. "You're siding with her?"

"I'm stating a fact," Sabine replied. "None of you would've survived what she has."

"We're not talking about survival," Marius said. "We're talking about leadership."

"She isn't leading," Celeste added. "She's improvising."

"She's unraveling," Havel said. "We've all seen it." Sabine's tail curled tighter, but she said nothing more.

"I say we remove her now," Roth said. "Formally. Publicly. The organization needs stability. Not a ghost story."

Virelli nodded. "I agree. Whatever this was supposed to be— it's gone off the rails." Celeste looked toward Elias. "You'll record the vote?"

Elias's eyes met hers, then shifted to Roxanne. He didn't speak. But he nodded.

Roth leaned forward and gave the smallest signal with one claw. The doors opened.

Six guards entered—black-clad, visors down, rifles and blades ready. Their tails swayed low in unison, disciplined. They lined the wall in practiced formation. "You came unarmed," Marius said. "And alone." "Wasn't that foolish?" Roth asked. Roxanne stood. Calm. "I understand," she said.

One of the guards stepped forward. "You'll come with us." She looked at them. Then at the council. Then back again. And nodded once.

She turned, coat trailing softly behind her, ears forward, posture effortless. The doors closed behind her.
The council remained in their seats. For a moment, all was still.

Then the sounds came—muffled voices, claws scrambling, the bark of a rifle shot. Another. Then something heavier— a dull, sickening thud. A scream, raw and feline. Then a final, crunching snap. Then silence.

Roth exhaled through his nose and leaned back in his chair, tail flicking idly.

"Well," he said, adjusting his cufflink, "that settles that."

Celeste was already reaching for her notes, claws gliding across the page. "We'll need to reassign her operatives. Fold her remaining cells back into the larger structure."

Marius nodded. "Her name will remain in the history. But the direction of the organization—The doors opened. And Roxanne walked back in.

Dust clung to her coat. A dark smear crossed her cheek. Her ears were forward. Her breath steady. No weapon. No guards. She crossed the chamber in silence. Then she stopped behind Roth Thorne.

He had just started to rise when her paw gripped the back of his skull and twisted. The crack echoed.

He slumped forward across the table, neck snapped cleanly, mouth still open.

Virelli surged up with a snarl, claws bared, blade in hand.

Roxanne caught his wrist mid-strike, slammed it into the edge of the stone so hard the joint shattered. The blade dropped. She didn't stop.

Her other paw drove up beneath his chin, lifted him off his paws, and threw him against the wall. The impact left a dent. He dropped like a felled tree and didn't move again. She returned to her seat. Two chairs sat full—but lifeless. No one else moved. Havel set her glass down with both paws. Celeste's ears tipped backward. Slight. Silent. Sabine blinked, just once. Elias turned the page in his ledger, tail twitching faintly. Roxanne looked at them.

"You believed the stories were exaggerated," she said. "Now you've seen the beginning of them." Her gaze swept across the survivors.

"The next time you try that, there won't be a council left to recover."

She folded her paws over one another and rested them on the stone. "Now. Let's continue." The silence lingered.

Dust settled on the floor where Virelli's body lay crumpled near the wall. Blood pooled slowly beneath the broken curve of Roth's neck, soaking into the grain of the stone table.

Roxanne's paws remained folded, one thumb idly brushing over the edge of the other. Her gaze had returned to the center of the table as if nothing had happened.

"Now," she said, her tone dry and smooth. "As I was saying."

"We have narrowed the location of the sealed chamber. Chesterfield is likely headed there. He believes he's outmaneuvered us."

Her eyes flicked toward Marius, then Celeste. "Let him."

Celeste gave the smallest nod, her posture stiff. Marius said nothing. Havel reached for her glass again, but her paw shook when it lifted. "Elias," Roxanne said, without looking.

The gray-furred scribe tilted his head. "Recording resumed." "Good."

Roxanne stood. "We'll reconvene tomorrow. Sabine, remain."

Chairs scraped softly as the others rose. None dared look her in the eye as they filed out— each with tails lowered, ears still. Marius was the first to leave. Celeste followed, silent and straight-backed. Havel hesitated, then left quickly. Only Sabine remained.

She hadn't spoken since the violence. Her black coat was immaculate. Her silver eyes calm.

"You were outvoted," Roxanne said. "You stayed seated anyway."

"I understood the vote," Sabine replied. "I didn't respect it." That earned a rare glance of approval.

Roxanne stepped past Roth's body without pausing. She stood beside Sabine now, not above her. The light from the torches reflected faintly in her blood-slicked coat. "I need two names," Roxanne said. "One to control Virelli's networks. One to manage Roth's holdings." Sabine didn't flinch.

"Choose wisely," Roxanne said. "They don't need to be obedient. But they need to be terrified." Sabine nodded. "When?"

"Soon. I want them seated before the next gathering. And Sabine" she paused, voice quieter, "they don't have to be council material. Not yet." Sabine's tail shifted once. "You want placeholders."

"No," Roxanne said. "I want leverage. No one rises without blood in their teeth." She turned to leave. Then paused. "You served me today without being asked." Sabine didn't respond.

"Keep doing that," Roxanne said. "And there may not be a council above you much longer." Then she was gone. The door closed behind her, quiet as a breath.

Sabine stood alone. Her ears turned toward the silence, listening.

Then she reached into her coat and removed a small, silver notebook. Not as thick as Elias's, but precise. Private. She opened it to a blank page. And began writing names.

Roxanne didn't move for a long time.

The council chamber, emptied of its cowards and corpses, felt heavier. The torches burned lower.
The stone seemed to breathe.

She stood slowly, paws deliberate, her tail curling once behind her. "Bring them out," she called.

Two guards entered different from the six that had been sent in earlier. These ones kept their eyes down, shoulders low, weapons holstered. They said nothing as they approached Roth's slumped body and began the process of lifting him with care neither earned nor deserved.

Roxanne watched as they slid Virelli's limp form into a canvas wrap.

"Burn them," she said quietly. "Not here. Far from this place."

The guards nodded and exited, leaving the air thick with smoke, blood, and memory.

She stood alone again, ears twitching at the faint hiss of the torches.

Her claws flexed just once—against the table's edge.

James Chesterfield.

She could see him, clear as day, seated across from her at a different table, in a different life. His coat was dusted with desert sand, his amber eyes sharp behind those battered spectacles, paw scribbling notes even as she explained what he'd never be allowed to keep.

"You can't control it, Roxanne," he had said, voice low but steady. "You can manipulate symbols, rewrite history, shape the truth—but you can't control the cost."

He'd been wrong. She had controlled it. For a time. Long enough to outlast men like him.

But now—now that cursed bloodline sat across from her again. With sharper eyes. With his father's mind. With his name.

She paced the perimeter of the chamber, tail low, steps soft. A line of blood still darkened the corner where Virelli's skull had cracked. Roxanne paused beside it, staring.

Archibald Chesterfield.

Every time she turned a page, he was there. Peeling back truths that should have stayed buried. Chasing relics he shouldn't understand. Unraveling work that had no business surfacing again. It wasn't the scroll that frustrated her. It was the mirror.

James had defied her out of arrogance. But his son… he was fueled by something else. Curiosity. Integrity. Maybe even vengeance. Traits far harder to extinguish. She exhaled softly.

The council thought she was chasing shadows. But it wasn't the scroll she feared losing it was control. Over what this boy represented. Over how far his reach might grow.

The stories of her were fear. But he was story-proof. He wasn't afraid. Not enough. Not yet.

She turned back toward the Wheel etched above the door. A design she had carved into stone herself long before any of these other names existed. It was meant to center her. To remind the others. But it reminded her too. That every wheel turns. Even when you built it.

Sabine walked the hallway in silence, the echo of her own footsteps following close behind. The notebook felt heavier in her paw than it should have. She hadn't realized until now just how tightly she was gripping it.

She had left the council chamber without a word. Roxanne had remained behind—calm, unshaken, alone among the bloodstains. That image would stay with her.

Sabine reached the outer corridor where the air cooled slightly, a whisper of night slipping in through the narrow windows carved into the stone. Only then did she stop. Only then did she breathe.

She opened the silver notebook again beneath a hanging lantern. The page she'd started moments earlier was still marked with her first attempt at names. She stared at them now, and for a moment, simply let the pen hover above the page.

She had always known Roxanne was dangerous. Everyone in the Hollowed Coin did—how could they not? But this… this was something beyond danger.

Sabine had watched six trained guards descend upon her. Heard the shots. Seen the flicker of motion. And when the doors opened not a scratch.

Roth's neck had broken like driftwood. Virelli's body had barely twitched after the final impact. Roxanne hadn't roared. She hadn't raised her voice. She had just moved.

Sabine closed her eyes. The fear was there but it was clean now. Focused.

She wasn't afraid of dying. She was afraid of miscalculating.

Roxanne had always said the Wheel turns. That you can be replaced. That nothing is permanent. But Roxanne had never turned with the Wheel. She had made it turn for her.

Sabine glanced back down the hall, just once, toward the chamber where the wheel symbol sat above the door where Roxanne remained, surrounded by the ghosts of her council.

Then she pressed pen to paper again. This time, the names stuck.

18

No words, no explanation just rough paws on her arms and a shove toward a stairwell she hadn't seen before. The descent was long, each step colder than the last. Wherever they were taking her, it wasn't meant for recovery. It was meant for forgetting.

At the bottom, a heavy metal door waited. One of the guards unlocked it, the other gave her a hard nudge between the shoulders. She didn't resist. Not yet.

Inside: stone walls, low ceiling, no cot. No chains, either. Just a room that could close in around her without making a sound.

The door shut behind her. No bolt. Just a clean, final thud.

She didn't move at first. Just listened. Counted her breaths. Let the quiet settle. They weren't watching. Or they thought they didn't need to. That would be their mistake.

She dropped to one knee and reached into the seam of her coat. Her claws caught on the thin length of wire she'd tucked away before the jungle. She hadn't used it until now.

She crouched at the door, not bothering with the lock just the hinge at the bottom. It took longer than she liked. But eventually, the pin slid free. No alarm. No creak. Just silence. She eased the door open and slipped into the corridor. Now came the harder part. She needed the key back.

The same one she'd passed off during the last transfer tucked into the guard's belt pouch when he wasn't looking. It was a gamble then, but she hadn't expected to be buried this deep so soon.

She didn't even know his name just the slight limp in his left leg, the scent of rust on his armor, and the black gloves he wore even indoors.

She'd have to find him. Quietly. Quickly. Before the others knew she was loose.

The hallway split in two ahead. She picked the darker path.

The corridor was narrower than she expected walls pressed close, ceiling low enough to brush her ears if she straightened up too tall. Pipes ran overhead, rusted and dripping. The air was damp and stale, full of copper and mildew. No windows. No light except the occasional flicker of old bulbs hanging from wires that swayed without wind. Each step echoed.

She padded forward anyway, ears pivoting at every sound. Her tail stayed low, twitching only when the shadows shifted ahead of her. She didn't know how many turns she'd taken, or how far she'd gone from the cell. The compound felt like a maze, deliberately built to confuse. Like something ancient had been carved over and over until it no longer resembled a place, just a trap.

She stopped near an intersection and pressed herself into the shadows. A soft hum buzzed through the wall. Machinery? Or surveillance?

She waited. Listened. Nothing but the quiet hiss of air ducts and the distant, irregular drip of water.

Her thoughts darted ahead of her body. If she was lucky, he still had the key had not passed it along or noticed it missing. If she was wrong... well, she'd worry about that later.

She crouched lower and moved again, pawsteps light, careful. The next turn opened into a wider corridor with break rooms or staff alcoves branching off to either side. She paused at the edge, eyes adjusting to the faint green glow from a bulb above. Then movement. A silhouette at the far end, slouched and walking slow. She narrowed her gaze.

Left leg dragging slightly. Gloves on. Same thick belt with pouches too full. Still favoring his right side. It was him. Her claws curled lightly.

He hadn't noticed her yet. She had one shot to follow and act before he rejoined anyone else.

Her fear stirred again, clawing at the base of her spine but it didn't stop her.

She slipped into the open hallway, moving like she had back when she used to sneak through windows at university after curfew. Only this time, she wasn't hiding for mischief.

She was hunting.

She followed him low, her body close to the ground, tail flicking gently behind her for balance. Each step was silent, practiced. Her ears tilted forward, tracking the rhythm of his uneven gait—left leg dragging just enough to confirm it was him. She kept her pupils narrowed, adjusting to the dim hallway glow, and her whiskers twitched as she slipped closer, taking in the faint scent of metal and sweat trailing in his wake.

He turned into a break room, and she pressed herself to the wall just outside the doorway. Her fur bristled along her spine not from fear, but focus. The kind that came from knowing the odds weren't in her favor. Her claws flexed slightly, catching the stone floor as she steadied her breath.

Inside, the guard grunted. A mug scraped. She saw the edge of his silhouette. She pounced.

Her paw was halfway to his belt when his ear twitched—too sharp, too fast. "Hey!" He spun, snarling.

She ducked under his reach and swiped at the pouch, her claws slicing the strap clean. But he grabbed her arm and yanked her forward with a snarl. She twisted her hips and drove her head into his jaw—skull meeting muzzle with a wet crack.

He hissed and staggered. She landed on all fours, crouched low. His claws came out. So did hers.

He lunged, but his bad leg faltered again. She darted sideways and lashed out with her back paw, catching the injured limb and driving him to the floor with a yowl. Before he could rise, she sprang onto his back, all four claws digging into his shoulders.

He roared—more from rage than pain and reached back wildly. She ducked and hooked her arm under his neck, dragging him down into a chokehold, her legs wrapped around his chest, claws raking against his vest.

"Where is it?" she growled into his ear, fur brushing his cheek. He bucked beneath her, but her grip didn't slip. The pouch spilled open. A small clink hit the floor. There.

She reached, claws snapping around the cold shape of the key just as he broke free and twisted toward her. Too slow.

She slashed across his snout—not deep, but enough to bleed and pivoted. He bared his fangs, furious and panting, but she saw the tremble in his leg. Saw the weight shift. He was going to strike

She leapt, over his shoulder, landing behind him.

Before he could turn, she kicked his leg out from under him and cracked her elbow into the side of his neck. He hit the wall hard and slumped, his breath wheezing out. Not dead. But done.

She stood over him, claws still out, fur ruffled along her shoulders, tail lashing once in the dark. The key glinted in her paw, her heart racing with the aftershock. She hadn't meant to fight. But she had won.

She turned, ears still swiveling, and melted back into the shadows of the corridor. There was still a long way to go.

The guard lay sprawled behind her, out cold, his weapon kicked aside and his injured leg twisted awkwardly beneath him. Nora didn't wait to see if he would wake.

The key was in her paw now warm from the rush of blood and the fight. She didn't know what it unlocked. But it had been on Roxanne. That alone made it important.

She wiped the metal clean on the inside of her shirt, then tucked it deep into the fraying seam she'd worn through weeks ago—a small slit along the inner waistband. She pressed the key flat against her side, tight beneath the fabric.

If they caught her, they'd search her. But if they didn't search well... She moved.

The corridor ahead narrowed, its flickering lights humming above in staggered bursts. The pipes along the ceiling hissed and dripped. The air reeked of mildew and grease, layered with something faintly metallic—like old blood in stone.

Her ears perked at a voice in the distance. Two voices. Arguing. One said something about "the breach." Another mentioned Roxanne's name.

She flattened herself behind a row of cracked utility bins, fur brushing metal, and waited. The voices faded.

She crept forward, paws light and deliberate. Her tail flicked once behind her as she passed deeper into the underbelly of the Hollowed Coin's compound. These walls were older, grimier. Some doors had long since rusted shut. Others were sealed with thick bolts and unfamiliar runes.

None of them mattered. The key she carried wasn't meant for anything down here.

She didn't know what it was for yet. But she had stolen it from Roxanne. That was reason enough to guard it with her life.

A soft alarm echoed two corridors back—faint, but growing louder. Her stomach twisted. The guard must've come to. She bolted.

Ahead, the corridor split. One direction sank downward into complete blackness. The other curved up—slightly, but enough to feel the grade shift beneath her paws. She followed the incline.

The shadows thinned. A faint draft whispered through the vents. For a heartbeat, she thought she smelled the outside world—wet stone, soil, a trace of night air.

Every pawstep now felt like it might be her last. But she didn't stop. She couldn't.

The tunnel narrowed until it was barely wider than her shoulders. A rusted hatch stood ahead—unlocked, cracked just slightly open. A chill breeze slid through it, stirring her fur. She pushed it open.

Damp grass. Night air. Wind in the trees. It was a service exit, hidden in the side of the compound's foundation. A miracle. She was free.

Her paws hit the earth running, sprinting across uneven stone toward the treeline. Mud clung to her pads. Her lungs burned. She could still feel the shape of the key pressed against her hip. One more hill. Just one—

Two tomcats burst from the shadows, knocking her to the ground.

They were bigger than the others broad-shouldered bruisers with scarred muzzles and thick, dirty coats streaked with dust and dried blood. One had a chunk missing from his right ear.

The other wore a cracked leather harness stained dark across the chest. Their claws were already out, smeared with something that glinted red in the moonlight. These weren't guards. They were enforcers.

"Well, look what we got here," one snarled, pinning her arm beneath his weight. His breath reeked of rotgut and raw meat.

"The witch herself," the other spat. "Should've run faster." "I thought the orders were to keep her alive," the first grunted, raising a jagged blade.

"Sure. But who's watching?" he sneered. "She slips, she falls... nobody's fault."

Nora bucked under them, her claws scratching dirt. Her mouth opened to scream— But she didn't have to.

The first tom froze, eyes wide.

A line of crimson bloomed across his throat, and he dropped soundlessly. The other turned—And was lifted clean off the ground by the neck.

Roxanne stood behind him, one paw curled around his jaw, the other braced against his chest. With a sudden jerk, she snapped his spine with a sickening crack and let him fall. She didn't speak. She didn't look at Nora.

She cleaned her claws on the fabric of her cloak and stepped back into the shadows.

Nora scrambled upright. Her heartbeat like thunder in her throat. She ran faster than before clawed her way over the grass, up the slope, gasping for air. She crested the hill. And froze.

Roxanne stood there, waiting.

No weapon. No guards. No breath drawn heavy from the chase.

Just her—silent and still, tail flicking once behind her.

"You got farther than I expected," Roxanne said, voice calm, almost amused. *"But you should've known better."*

Nora screamed and turned bolting sideways through the trees. She made it three steps.

Then Roxanne caught her by the back of her collar, yanking her from the air like prey caught mid-pounce. Nora thrashed and kicked, claws slashing but Roxanne didn't flinch.

She dragged her back down the hill one brutal, wordless pull at a time. The wet ground tore beneath Nora's paws. Mud streaked her face and arms. Her breath came ragged, hoarse. When they reached the hatch, Roxanne stopped. "Next time," she said, pressing the door open with one paw,

"I won't be so generous."

Then she hauled Nora through the opening and slammed it shut behind them cutting off the night, the air, and any thought of escape. Darkness swallowed them both.

19

SHE SCREAMED.

It came from somewhere deep inside the compound one sharp, broken sound that split the jungle and cut straight through Archie's chest. He didn't move.

Neither did Eddie or Mabel. The three of them stood at the edge of the clearing, breath caught, hearts pounding. It had been days since the ambush, but that scream was fresh real.

No mistaking it.

"She's alive," Archie said. His voice was low, like he didn't want to disturb the stillness around him. Mabel didn't answer. Eddie's jaw tightened.

"She's alive," Archie said again, this time firmer. "And that means we're not too late."

Eddie shifted. "You think Roxanne let her scream on purpose?"

"Maybe," Mabel said. "Or maybe she slipped. Either way, we don't get another warning."

Archie stepped away from the trees and knelt beside their gear. He unrolled the weathered map they'd been studying for the past two days. It was incomplete stitched together from old civil planning records and hand-drawn sketches they'd pieced together from locals who remembered the compound before the Hollowed Coin took it over. He flattened it out on a patch of dry ground.

"South wall's our best shot," he said, pointing to a faded section marked in pencil. "There was an old aqueduct here. It was sealed up decades ago, but the foundations unstable. If the layout's still close to what it was..." "We can get under it," Mabel finished.

Archie nodded. "Not walkable, but enough space to crawl through."

Eddie crossed his arms. " You're sure Roxanne doesn't know we know?"

"She's guessing where we'll come in," Mabel said. "We've been too quiet for her to be certain."

Archie stood and slung the satchel over his shoulder. "She's waiting somewhere. But it won't matter if we're faster."

He didn't look toward the compound. They couldn't even see it from this part of the jungle. But he heard the scream again in his mind sharp, pained, and very much alive. It hadn't faded. "Ten minutes," he said quietly. "Be ready." No one argued. Ten minutes later, the jungle closed behind them.

They moved in a low line, tails brushing the dirt, ears twitching at every crack of underbrush. Archie led with his nose low and eyes sharp, stepping lightly over roots and wet leaves. Mabel followed like a shadow, her coat streaked with dew, one paw always near the knife strapped across her chest. Eddie brought up the rear, shoulders hunched, whiskers flicking as he scanned behind. No one spoke. The compound was close now. The scent of rust and oil clung faintly to the breeze.

They followed the slope down, moving where the earth dipped just enough to shelter their approach. What had once been a path was now overgrown and half-swallowed by the forest. But Archie's memory held. So did the map.

After a slow descent, Archie stopped short and raised one paw. Ahead, buried in vines and rot, was what they'd come for. The wall.

Old stone, broken and slick with moss. Its foundation had cracked decades ago, maybe longer. Roots had pulled it apart over time but not completely. One section had slumped inward, revealing a narrow gap beneath the rubble. Just wide enough for a cat to crawl through if they flattened themselves. Mabel eyed it and twitched an ear. "That's a squeeze."

Archie crouched, sniffed the entrance, then clicked on a compact lantern and held it low. The air that pushed out was stale dry, musty, and laced with something metallic.

"About forty feet," he said. "Straight shot, no branches. You'll feel it widen near the end."

Eddie stepped beside him and narrowed his eyes at the hole. "You really think this leads inside?"

Archie nodded once. "It's part of the old aqueduct. Hollowed Coin built the compound right on top of it."

Mabel gave a low hum. "They always did like digging up history to hide behind it."

Archie glanced back. "No talking once we're in. Keep low. Claws in. Watch for roots."

He slung his satchel across his back, dropped to his belly, and slid forward. The stone scraped at his sides. Dirt crumbled around his whiskers. Behind him, the others followed.

The tunnel pressed close fast. Roots tangled overhead, brushing their ears. The ground was uneven and cold beneath their paws. Once, Archie had to stretch flat to slide under a fallen beam. His fur caught on a jagged edge, but he kept going. At last, a faint flicker of light. Not daylight. Firelight warm, orange, dancing. Archie stopped just before the exit and peered out.

Stone corridor. Damp. Mold climbing the walls. Ten yards ahead, two Hollowed Coin guards in patchy uniforms leaned near an iron gate, talking low. Their rifles were slung but close. One of them had a scar down his snout. The other was chewing something and spitting it out between words.

Archie pulled back and whispered, "Two. Armed. Slow patrol." Mabel and Eddie nodded. They were in. And the hunt had begun.

Archie held still, one paw pressed to the floor just inside the crawlspace's mouth. The torchlight ahead wavered, casting long shadows across the corridor. Two guards. Felines, both. Rough coats, patchy armor. One was nodding off against the wall while the other paced in a slow arc, muttering to himself as he picked at his claws.

Eddie crept up behind Archie and leaned in, voice barely audible. "We can't risk a fight here. If they call for backup, it's over."

Archie nodded once. "We wait for the right moment. Then we move." The pacing guard turned, giving them a narrow window.

Archie slithered forward, paws silent against the mossy stone. Mabel followed, hugging the wall with practiced ease. Eddie waited half a beat longer, then slipped out after them, tail low and still.

The corridor bent left just past the guards sharp enough to block their line of sight. The moment they cleared it, Archie ducked behind a rotted column base and exhaled. His pulse pounded in his ears. They'd made it through the first checkpoint. But the compound was far from quiet.

Voices echoed in the distance muffled commands, footsteps moving in rhythm. The Hollowed Coin was active tonight. Guard rotations. Watch shifts. The kind of movement that meant someone important was inside. Roxanne hadn't left.

Mabel sniffed the air. "This place stinks of blood and ash. There's a furnace running somewhere."

"She's expecting something," Eddie said. "She knows we're coming. Just doesn't know when." "Or how," Archie added. "That's the only edge we've got."

They pressed on, moving deeper into the compound. The walls changed old stone gave way to patched reinforcements. Welded steel, repurposed fencing, rusted doorways sealed with sliding locks. This place was once ruins. Not anymore. It had been reshaped into a fortress.

At one corner, they passed a doorway left ajar. Inside, the floor was lined with crates.

Symbols branded into the wood same coin sigil etched onto the necks of the guards. Weapons. Supplies. Tools for something larger than this one site.

Mabel paused. "They're gearing up for something. This isn't just about the scroll."

Archie didn't answer. His attention was on a mark scratched into the wall ahead. barely visible in the low light. Three short lines. One longer one curved underneath. Cat writing. Prison slang. A sign. "She was here," he whispered. "This is fresh."

He stepped closer, ran a paw across the grooves. "It's a signal. She left it." Eddie leaned in. "Means they moved her.

She's still alive."

Mabel scanned the hallway ahead. "Then we're close." Archie closed his eyes for a second. Nora's scent lingered in the stone. Faint. Recent. "We keep moving." They turned the corner and froze.

A third guard was blocking the corridor ahead lean, wiry, and far more alert than the others. His ears twitched once, and his paw went to the blade at his belt. He hadn't seen them yet. But he'd heard something.

Archie backed up slowly, pressing against the wall. The hallway behind them was too narrow to retreat without making noise. The guard stepped forward, head tilted, sniffing the air.

Mabel moved first.

She darted forward in a blur low, controlled, utterly silent. Her paw struck the guard's wrist before he could draw his weapon, twisting it hard enough to pop the joint. He let out a breath, but nothing loud enough to echo. Before he could react, her back leg swept his footing, and she slammed him hard into the wall. The crack of his skull hitting stone was quiet, but final.

She caught him before he dropped, easing him to the ground in a heap. Eddie was already there, checking his pulse. "Out cold. Might have a fracture."

Archie looked down at the mercenary, eyes narrowed. "Tie him."

Mabel stripped a cord from her belt and secured the guard's paws behind his back, then gagged him with a strip of cloth torn from his own uniform. It wasn't elegant, but it would hold long enough.

"Coin's getting sloppy," she said, brushing dust off her shoulders. "He shouldn't have been posted here alone."

"Maybe they didn't expect us to come through the wall," Archie said. "Or maybe Roxanne wanted us to." They kept moving.

The corridors grew colder, more narrow. The flickers of firelight were gone now just darkness and the sound of their own breathing. Then came something worse. A smell.

Blood. Faint, but unmistakable. It caught in Archie's throat before he even realized what it was. His fur bristled. "She's close," he whispered.

The corridor ended in a heavy steel door, cold to the touch. Reinforced hinges. Fresh scrape marks along the frame. Someone had tried to claw their way out. Eddie stepped forward and tested the handle. "Locked."

Mabel moved past him without a word. She knelt, paw steady as she pulled a slender tool from her belt. One ear cocked forward, the other twitching as she listened. Her claws worked quick, precise. Click. The door creaked open an inch. She peeked through, then said one name. "Archie."

He was beside her in a heartbeat.

The room beyond was small bare walls, a single flickering torch, and the copper sting of blood thick in the air. In the far corner, chained to a cot, Nora lay curled on her side. Her fur was matted, bruised, streaked with dried blood. A gag pulled tight across her muzzle. One eye swollen shut. Her wrists raw and bound with cord. Archie pushed the door wide and ran to her. "Nora"

He dropped to his knees beside the cot. His voice cracked. "We're here. You're safe now. I've got you."

Her head moved, barely. Her ears twitched at the sound of his voice.

Eddie crossed the room and pulled a knife from his belt, slicing through the restraints. "Hang in there," he said, low. "We've got you." Mabel stayed at the door, blade drawn, eyes on the hall. Archie loosened the gag.

Nora gasped. Then her eyes snapped wide.

She clutched Archie's shirt, claws catching fabric. Her mouth moved, but no sound came at first. Then she forced out a single cry.

"Trap"

The door behind them slammed shut. Locks clicked into place. Boots pounded the stone.

"Move!" Eddie shouted, gun raised. Mabel backed into the room, blade up, breathing sharp.

From a dark panel in the corner, a voice filled the air. "You always were predictable." Roxanne stepped out.

She wore black, same as always coat brushed clean, eyes cold. Three guards followed, rifles ready.

Archie stood slowly. One paw still rested on Nora's shoulder. Mabel didn't move. "You knew we'd come."

Roxanne's gaze drifted to Nora. "I was counting on it." She turned to Archie.

"Tell me. Was it worth it?"

Archie didn't answer. He stayed crouched beside Nora, one paw steady on her arm. Her breathing was shallow, her chest rising in short, painful bursts.

Roxanne gave a slow shake of her head, ears flicking in distaste. "You never were very good at picking your battles."

She looked past him briefly to Mabel and Eddie.

"The stray and the burnout," she said, unimpressed. "Still following your tail, I see."

Mabel shifted, claws barely unsheathed, golden eyes locked on Roxanne. Eddie stayed near the door, muzzle tense, tail down, finger on the trigger. But Roxanne wasn't watching them.

"You still think you're the hero in this story?" she asked, her voice low. "You think saving one girl changes anything?" Archie didn't move.

Nora did.

Her paw reached up barely a flick of fur and claw and slipped inside Archie's coat. She pressed the key into his paw. He caught it, heart pounding.

Her eyes met his. One was swollen, nearly shut. The other glistened.

She pulled him close, just enough for her whiskers to brush his. "Don't stop," she whispered. Then louder-so everyone could hear, voice cracking with pain but clear as glass

"Don't. Stop."

She shoved him back.

With the last of her strength, she twisted, snatched the torch from the wall, and threw it to the floor.

Flame burst across the rags. Smoke surged up the far wall. Roxanne moved. A blur. A shadow.

Then a brutal, sudden crack.

Her paw slammed into Nora's throat. One strike. No hesitation. Nora's body dropped from the cot like a puppet with the strings cut. Silence.

Roxanne stood over her, unmoving. Blood dripped from her claws.

"She made her choice," she said.

Archie didn't breathe. Couldn't. The key felt like fire in his grip. Mabel yanked him up. "Archie. Now."

Eddie fired into the corridor one shot. Enough to make the guards hesitate. The flames rose higher. They ran.

Roxanne didn't follow. She stood there in the firelight, tail low, staring down at the girl who had outmaneuvered her if only for a moment. Smoke curled around her. She said nothing.

20

The city blurred past in streaks of muted gold and wet gray, rain curling against the cab windows in slow rivulets.

Teddy sat in the back seat, his frame rigid, ears drawn slightly back beneath the brim of his cap. One paw rested on the duffel Francis had handed him. Canvas, old. Full of cash, pistols, and the last thread of a plan his brother had tucked away years ago just in case.

Dolores sat beside him, her shoulders square, expression unreadable. Her tail was curled tightly around her leg, claws brushing the grip of her sidearm. She hadn't spoken since they left. Neither had he.

Francis drove in silence, his paws steady, his eyes flicking between the road and the rearview mirror. He hadn't said much. Just one line after they'd climbed in:

"Fifteen minutes. Safe house. Archie's orders."

That was ten minutes ago.

Outside, London didn't feel right. The streets were too quiet, the shops too dark. Lamps sputtered overhead, casting dim halos across the wet stone. Everything looked... held. Like the city was waiting for something. Teddy flexed his claws against the side of the duffel.

He remembered the conversation clearly now. Archie had poured two cups of tea, then looked him in the eye and said:

"If it all falls apart really falls apart go to Francis. He'll know what to do. But don't use it unless you have no other choice."

At the time, Teddy had brushed it off as overcautious. Now it felt like prophecy. "You trust this place?" Teddy asked, voice low.

Francis didn't look back. "I trust Archie,". "If he told me to drive into the Thames, I'd ask which pier."

The car dipped into a narrower lane brick pressed in on both sides, soaked and soot-streaked. A flickering streetlamp buzzed overhead. Somewhere in the distance, a train cried out across the city like it was in pain. Francis slowed the cab. "Next right."

Teddy glanced down at the bag again. Still there. Still sealed. Still heavy.

Not with steel but with the knowledge that this was never supposed to be used. And yet here they were.

The cab slowed to a stop outside a worn, narrow building wedged between a shuttered bakery and a locksmith's shop long since abandoned. No name. No number. Just soot-dark brick and a door with peeling paint. Francis cut the engine but didn't move.

Teddy stared at the place. His ears twitched once. "This is it?"

"This is it," Francis said, eyes on the rearview. "No one here knows your name. The ones who did? They don't speak anymore."

Dolores opened her door without a word, her coat catching the wind, tail trailing low. She scanned the empty street with the kind of stillness that came from training. Teddy followed, stepping out with the duffel still clutched in his paw.

It felt heavier now—not from the steel inside, but the history. Every ounce of it was Archie's preparation. Quiet insurance from a brother who never assumed they'd be safe forever.

Francis leaned out the window slightly, voice low. "I'll circle back in two days. If I don't come back, assume they got to me."

Teddy nodded, paw tightening on the bag. "We'll hold." Francis gave him one last look. "Take care of her."

Then he pulled away, tires hissing in the rain, taillights vanishing into the night.

Teddy turned toward the door. Dolores was already at it, paw on the rusted handle. Her ears were pinned back, her stance ready. She looked at him a silent check. He gave the nod. She pushed it open.

Inside, the air was cool and still, like a place that had waited patiently to be needed. The stone walls were rough, the light low a single lantern glowed near the base of a staircase. Dust clung to the corners, but the room was clean. Maintained. Safe.

Teddy closed the door, letting the sound settle into the silence. He unslung the duffel and knelt by the table. Dolores stood watch near the far wall, her ears turning with each creak of the building. Teddy unzipped the bag.

Pistols. Ammunition. Folded currency. Rations. A first aid kit. Clean shirts, a small flask, two maps of London with routes circled in red ink one to the train yards, the other toward St. Paul's.

At the bottom, wrapped in a handkerchief, was a pocket watch. Old. Dented. Teddy flipped it open with a claw. Archie's handwriting was scratched inside the lid:

"Time's not on our side. Use it well."

Teddy exhaled through his nose, ears softening. For the first time since they'd fled, a flicker of calm broke through the pressure. He didn't know if Archie was alive but this... this was like hearing his voice again. He looked to Dolores. "We'll be safe here." She didn't answer. But she nodded. For now, that was enough.

Teddy sat back on his heels, still holding the watch in one paw. He let it swing gently by its chain, the faint tick sounding louder than it should. "You think he's still alive?"

Dolores didn't look away from the window. "You'd know if he wasn't."

Teddy didn't answer. Just let the watch settle in his palm before tucking it into his coat. The duffel still sat open on the table, half-unpacked. He reached inside again, checking the side pockets for anything he might've missed. He paused.

Two slim leather booklets. No names on the front. Just a faint national seal stamped in gold foil—one for him, one for Dolores. The kind of document you didn't ask questions about. Blank identification pages, forged entries, fabricated travel stamps. Different names. Clean aliases. Teddy stared at them for a long moment. "He really thought this through," he said. Dolores didn't respond. Not right away.

He turned to look at her. Her shoulders were still squared, but her paws were clenched at her sides. Her ears had dropped just slightly.

"He was always so damn calm," she whispered. "Even when it was falling apart... he made it feel like it wasn't."

She finally turned to face him, and there was something in her eyes—wet, but refusing to fall.

Teddy stepped forward and placed the passports down gently, then crossed the room. He didn't say anything. Just pulled her into a hug. Dolores stiffened, just for a second. Then she melted against him, silent but trembling.

They stayed like that breathing the only sound in the room.

When she stepped back, she wiped her eyes with the back of her paw and gave a small nod. "Right. Maps."

Teddy didn't push it. Just nodded once and sat back down, unfolding one of Archie's routes.

The routes were marked in clean, crimson strokes. Hidden turns. Narrow alleys. Safe zones. All mapped out in Archie's exacting hand.

"We'll still have to move eventually," Teddy murmured, claw tracing a path east. "Even with Parliament off my back, the Hollowed Coin has long arms."

Dolores tapped a narrow alley near the Thames. "We slip through here. Quiet. If someone's watching, we'll know."

Teddy looked at her. "You think this is regroup or retreat?" "Depends," she said. "If Archie's alive, it's regroup. If not"

"He's alive."

She met his eyes, then gave a small nod. "Then we keep moving."

A gust of wind caught a loose shutter, slapping it once against the outside wall. Neither of them flinched.

Teddy folded the map and tucked it into his coat. "Get some rest. I'll take first watch."

Dolores turned without a word, her silhouette vanishing into the stairwell's gloom. The hours passed slowly.

Teddy sat alone now, the lantern dimmed, casting long shadows across the table. The pocket watch lay open beside him, ticking quietly in the dark.

He stared at it. Then at the passports. Then at nothing at all.

His breath hitched.

One paw came up and pressed against his eyes, ears folding back. A single sob slipped out before he could stop it low, broken, and sharp around the edges. The floor above creaked.

He straightened quickly, swiping at his face, but he didn't look up when soft paws stepped into view. Dolores stood in the doorway. She said nothing. Just crossed the room and sat down beside him.

After a moment, she leaned her shoulder against his. They didn't speak. They didn't need to. Together, they kept watch as the night wore on.

The light that filtered in through the crooked shutters was the pale blue of a London dawn— soft, muted, and cold. Dust drifted through the beams like ash. Teddy stirred, his coat wrapped tight around him, one paw resting on the duffel like a soldier guarding a post even in sleep.

He blinked the haze from his eyes. His back ached, and his tail was stiff from curling too tight against the chill. The room was quiet too quiet. Only the occasional creak of old wood and the low tick of a clock in the next room kept it from feeling dead. Dolores was up.

He sat up slowly, ears twitching toward the stairwell. A moment later, she descended, one paw on the banister, the other gripping the pistol Francis had given them. Her expression was unreadable locked in routine, as if letting her guard down now might let everything else break too.

She crossed to the corner table without a word, crouched beside the bag, and started checking its contents. Rations, clothes, spare ammunition. Her movements were slow but sure, keeping her paws busy like she was keeping something buried.

Teddy stood with a soft grunt and stretched, bones popping one by one. He moved to the window and pulled the curtain back just enough to peek out.

The alley outside was slick with last night's rain. Empty. Still. "How's the pistol?" he asked, voice low and even. "Cleaned and ready," she replied, not looking up. He nodded faintly. "Did you sleep?" she asked after a moment. "Some."

"Liar."

He gave a tired half-smile, the kind that didn't reach his eyes. "You?" She didn't answer.

Teddy let the curtain fall back into place and turned toward the room. "We're going to need more than what's in that bag. Can't sit on our tails for two weeks."

Dolores zipped the bag halfway closed, then paused. "There's a shopfront a couple blocks down. Saw it when we came in with Francis. Looked like it might've been a grocer." "You think it's still stocked?"

"I doubt it," she said plainly. "But it might be worth a look. Could be something we can use." Teddy stepped away from the window and crossed to the table, claws tapping against the wood as he leaned forward. "We check it tonight. No noise, no risk unless it looks safe. Then we make the run tomorrow." Dolores gave a small nod. "We don't wait on Francis?"

"He said two weeks. We'll be dry in five days if we're careful. Three if anything goes wrong." He lowered his voice. "We're on our own." She finished zipping the bag. "Always were." Silence hung again.

Teddy leaned on the edge of the table, letting his paws fall to his sides. His tail swayed once, then settled still. Dolores stood, arms crossed. "You think Archie made it out?" she asked quietly. He didn't respond at first.

His eyes flicked to the bag, then to the folded map resting near it still marked, still hopeful. His ears twitched, but his voice didn't waver.

"I have to," he said. "Because if he didn't… none of this matters."

Dolores sat cross-legged on the dusty floor, her back against the safe house's cracked wall. A flicker of dawn crept through the torn curtain, stretching pale across the room. She hugged her knees to her chest, ears twitching every so often at the faint sounds outside birds, wind, the creak of the old floorboards.

Teddy was across from her, seated at the corner of the dining table, poring over a sheet of notes by lantern light. The map Francis had given them lay folded nearby, but his attention had drifted. Dolores broke the silence. "We shouldn't have split up." Teddy looked up. "It was the right call," he said after a moment.

"Still feels wrong." Her voice was soft, but steady. "Archie always said that kind of instinct meant something. That even if logic said one thing… you trust that quiet pull in your gut." Teddy gave a faint nod. "That sounds like him."

She stared down at her paws for a long beat. "I remember once, years ago well before any of this mess. We were walking through Hyde Park, I think. He stopped mid-sentence, squinting at this old memorial plaque everyone else passed without a glance. He tilted his head, ears twitching, and said, 'There's a date missing.' I thought he was joking, but he wasn't. He said the inscription listed every battle but one a major one and he couldn't understand why they'd leave it off."

A faint smile touched her face. "Next thing I knew, he was scribbling notes on a napkin from a hot dog cart, saying it was probably deliberate. 'History isn't what happened,' he said. 'It's what gets remembered. And who gets to decide what's worth remembering." Teddy didn't speak for a moment.

"That's where we're alike," he finally said. "Different strengths, maybe. But we both see threads. Patterns."

He pushed the page aside. "I've been thinking a lot about those lately. Not just the scrolls or the symbols but the people. The ones I saw in Parliament. Names that didn't fit. Meetings that felt… staged. The further back I look, the more it starts to feel like… they've always been there." Dolores sat up straighter. "The Hollowed Coin?"

He nodded. "Maybe not under that name. But something. The shape is always the same quiet influence, erased details, people who vanish without a sound."

He tapped the table once. "I think they were in Parliament long before I got hired. Maybe even before my father." Dolores frowned. "That's… terrifying." Teddy didn't argue. She looked at him, her tail curling slightly. "You think Roxanne's part of that thread?" He didn't answer right away.

"I don't know what she is," he said at last. "But I know she didn't just appear out of nowhere."

They sat in silence for a while, the quiet stretching between them like a blanket neither of them could pull close enough.

Then Dolores leaned her head back against the wall and closed her eyes.

"I hate not knowing," she muttered. "I hate sitting still."

"You're not," Teddy said quietly. "You're still here. You're still fighting."

She didn't respond, but her ears flicked slightly toward him. It wasn't a plan. Not yet. But it was something.

Teddy didn't sleep.

Once Dolores drifted off curled in her corner, one paw still half-clenched he remained at the table, eyes scanning the dark room as if it might whisper answers. The lantern had long since burned low, and the chill of morning settled into the floorboards.

He stood quietly, slipping on his coat. The map was folded in his inner pocket, along with a list of possible contacts Francis had scrawled in shorthand. Most were scratched out.

Before heading for the door, Teddy crouched beside the worn satchel Francis had left them and unzipped the side pocket. The pistol was still there, heavy and cold in his paw. He checked the chamber loaded and tucked it into the inside of his coat, hidden but ready. Just in case.

He crept to the front door, ears alert for any sign of stirring from Dolores. Nothing. Just her steady breathing and the occasional twitch of her tail.

Outside, the alley was still. Grey sky pressed in overhead, and the air smelled faintly of rain and brick dust. Teddy pulled his collar up and moved.

The store was only three blocks off at least, what passed for a store in this part of the city. Francis hadn't said much about it, just that "it's good in a pinch" and "don't ask for anything flashy." Teddy hoped that meant food. Maybe something for protection.

He kept his steps light, sticking close to the shadows, ears twitching at every distant shout or clatter. London had always held danger in its bones. But lately, the city felt like it was breathing heavier, watching.

The building didn't look like much. Cracked green paint, a sagging awning, and a half-lit sign that flickered with a few dying letters. It was barely open. Teddy stepped inside. A bell gave a half-hearted jingle.

Dust hung in the air, catching the low lamplight. Shelves leaned precariously under the weight of supplies canned goods, dry paper packages, odd tools, and things that didn't have labels at all. A figure emerged from behind a sliding curtain. Older cat, dark fur gone patchy around the muzzle, one eye milky white. Teddy nodded once. "Looking to stock up."

The figure didn't respond at first, just gave a grunt and stepped behind the counter. The shopkeeper didn't ask questions. That was promising.

Teddy moved through the aisles slowly, checking expiration dates, weighing cans in his paw. A few tins of fish. Some bandages. A small, collapsible kettle. Nothing elegant, but it would stretch their supplies another week.

He paid in cash, said nothing more than necessary, and left with a burlap sack over one shoulder.

The walk back was slower. Not because he was tired but because he didn't like how many windows were open. How many doors were cracked, just slightly. They weren't followed. Not yet. But the city wasn't asleep.

Teddy locked the door behind him with a soft click, doublechecking the deadbolt before slipping out of his coat. The burlap sack hit the table with a dull thud, but he didn't unpack it right away.

Dolores stirred from the other room but didn't rise. A soft grunt. The rustle of a blanket. Then stillness again.

He stepped softly past her and into the corner of the main room, near the cracked window that overlooked the alley. The curtain was drawn, but he peeked between the folds. Nothing moved outside, but that didn't mean no one was watching. He'd felt eyes on him more than once during the walk. Real or not, it stayed with him.

The pistol came out of his coat and sat beside the window frame, close to paw. He flexed his claws once, just to feel them.

It wasn't the first time he'd felt like this like he was being hunted without ever hearing a sound. But this was different. This wasn't the instinct of a cat with something to lose. It was the instinct of someone who had already lost too much.

Teddy pulled the map from his coat, spreading it across the small table. His claws traced the edge of the river, then the circle around St. Paul's. The scribbled notes Francis had added in haste still clung to the page in fading ink. He saw patterns where others saw only ink. Movement. Disruption. Names that didn't belong. The Hollowed Coin wasn't new. And it wasn't just around the edges anymore. It was inside. Rooted deep.

He sat down heavily, the chair creaking beneath him. A gust of wind rattled the glass, and his ears twitched before settling. Then silence.

His eyes drifted to the bag Francis had left. He'd already pulled supplies and passports, but there were little things too. A familiar tin of tea Archie used to keep in his flat. An old lighter. A compass shaped like a pocket watch with a cracked dial. Things that didn't need to be there—but were.

Teddy ran his paw along the edge of the compass, his ears folding back. He hadn't heard from Archie since that last letter.

The thought struck hard, faster than he was ready for. He felt the tightness rise again low in the throat, heavy in the chest but he swallowed it down.

He had to keep moving. For Dolores. For Archie. For all of them. But in the quiet, that didn't feel like enough.

21

The jungle whispered around them, but none of the four cats spoke.

Archie walked at the front, his boots pressing into the damp earth without urgency. His tail dragged behind him, limp and dust caked. Nora's satchel hung from his shoulder still fastened tight but every jostle felt like it might tear his heart clean open.

Behind him, Mabel said nothing. Her hat low, the jungle's dying light casting shadows across her face. She moved like a ghost—no complaints, no comments, not even a glance at the others.

Eddie brought up the rear, one paw hovering near his coat pocket where his revolver waited. His ears flicked at every sound, but his pace matched the others. He kept watching Archie, waiting. Not ready, but waiting. No one mentioned Nora. They couldn't. Not yet.

They reached a clearing just before dusk, the last of the sun straining through the canopy. Eddie gave a quiet nod and slipped off into the trees to check the perimeter. Mabel sat against a log and reached for her canteen. After a moment, she offered it toward Archie without a word. He didn't take it. Didn't even look at her.

"She was brave," Mabel said, her voice low. "Braver than any of us."

Archie froze. His ears flattened.

He turned, slow and sharp, like something snapping loose inside.

"She shouldn't have had to be," he rasped. "None of this should've happened." Mabel didn't respond. Her expression didn't change.

Archie's voice rose. "You damn it you were supposed to help us! You knew Roxanne. You should've warned us!"

Mabel blinked. Once. "I did." It wasn't a defense. It wasn't an argument.

Archie stared at her a second longer, then shook his head and stumbled back a step, like the weight of it all had finally landed.

"I saw her throat" he choked. "I keep seeing it. Her eyes she was trying to scream but she couldn't and I"

His legs gave out.

He dropped to his knees in the clearing, breath shallow, claws digging into the dirt. "I should've protected her. I should've gotten her out." Mabel stayed still, her eyes cast down.

Eddie reappeared from the tree line just as Archie's shoulders started to shake. He didn't say a word—just moved to his side and crouched down, placing one paw on Archie's back.

"She knew the risk," Eddie murmured. "She chose to be there. Just like we all did."

"I dragged her into this..." Archie gasped, his voice breaking. "She trusted me. And now she's gone. Because of me."

Eddie didn't argue. He just sat there beside him in silence, steady and unmoving while Archie sobbed into the jungle floor. Tail curled tight around his side, breath coming in ragged gulps, the professor was gone left in his place was a friend shattered by loss. Night crept in around them.

Mabel turned her face toward the trees. Not away from Archie, but away from the grief like she couldn't bear to look at it. Or didn't feel she had the right to. No one slept that night. But for the first time since it happened, Archie wept. The jungle was quiet, but Archie didn't sleep.

He dozed for minutes at a time, slipping in and out of a restless haze as the fire crackled low and the insects hummed beyond the clearing. Each time his eyes shut, something pulled him under—not sleep, but something colder. Blacker.

Nora's scream came first. Always the scream.

Then the jungle bled away.

He stood in the compound again not as it was, but as it lived in his mind. The walls twisted higher. The stone bled. A thousand hollowed coins glittered in the darkness like watching eyes. And there she was. *Roxanne.*

She stepped from the shadows without sound, her coat whispering behind her like silk across a grave. Her eyes glowed a molten, sickly gold. Not catlike. Something older. Something wrong.

"You led her to me," she said, circling him. Her voice echoed even though her mouth never moved. *"You handed her over."*

Archie backed away, but the floor dissolved beneath him. He fell through staircases, ruins, old lecture halls, down into the pit where Nora's body waited, her crushed throat frozen in time.

"I didn't know," he choked. *"I I tried"*

"She screamed for you," Roxanne said, appearing behind him. Her claws touched his shoulders. *"And you didn't answer."*

He spun around but she was gone.

Now he stood in Parliament. But it was wrong too. Twisted. Fire clung to the stained glass. Figures in suits with coin-branded faces watched him from above. And at the center... a throne made of bones.

Roxanne sat upon it, smiling.

"We're just getting started, Professor Chesterfield." He jolted awake, gasping. The fire was low. The jungle was quiet again.

Archie sat up slowly, wiping the sweat from his brow. His fur was damp. His paws shook.

But the worst part—the part that chilled him deeper than the dream itself wasn't the fear. It was that somewhere in the nightmare... he believed her. She wasn't done. Not with him. Not with London. Not with history.

And he didn't know how to stop her.

The jungle stirred with early light, soft gold spilling through the canopy and brushing the edges of the clearing.

Archie sat near the ashes of the fire, unmoving. His eyes were hollow, tail curled tight, shoulders hunched beneath the weight of memory. Every time he blinked, she was there.

Nora...

Not as she had been, but as she had ended. Eyes wide. Throat crushed. Paw reaching for him through the dark.

"Don't stop."

The words clung to his ribs, soaked into the soil beneath his paws.

A crack of branches. Mabel froze mid-step. Eddie crouched, paw hovering near his pistol. "We've got to move," he said.

"Now."

Archie didn't flinch.

"You think this is what she wanted?" Eddie's voice was low, sharp. "You think she gave up her life so you could sit here waiting to die too?" Archie's ears flattened. "You didn't know her."

"I didn't," Eddie said, voice steady. "But I know what she meant to you. And I know you've got a brother back in London who still might be alive because she gave you the chance to save him."

That broke through.

Archie blinked, dazed. "Teddy..."

Eddie stepped closer, eyes locked on his. "And Dolores. Don't forget what we're up against, Professor. If we don't get home, they're next."

Archie slowly stood, claws curling into the earth. His breath shuddered, but his legs held.

"I'm not losing anyone else."

Mabel scanned the treeline. "South ridge. Movement. We've got minutes."

Archie nodded, voice hardening. "We get to the landing strip. We get home."

They moved fast packs half-secured, paws pounding through brush, the hush of leaves broken by distant voices hunting behind them.

Mabel glanced at him as they ran. "And then?" Archie didn't slow. He didn't look back.

"Then we make sure she didn't die for nothing."

The jungle thinned, trees parting like curtains to reveal the small dirt landing strip— sunlight baking the cracked earth, the edges lined with rusted barrels and half-covered tarps. A twinprop plane sat idle at the far end, its nose pointed toward the horizon as if already prepared to leave them behind.

Archie stumbled out of the brush, breath ragged. Mabel was beside him, fur matted with sweat and dust. Eddie brought up the rear, checking behind them every few steps.

They reached the tarmac. The heat off the ground shimmered like a mirage. A single tabby in a worn flight vest stepped from the shade of the supply shed, ears flicking back at the sight of the group. "You weren't scheduled," he said flatly.

Archie didn't waste a second. He marched up to the pilot, pulled a bundle from his satchel, and slammed it into the cat's paw.

"Ten thousand pounds," he said. "We're getting on that plane."

The pilot looked down, then up eyes narrowing at Archie's blood-streaked coat, the shadows in his face, the way Eddie's paw still hovered near his pistol. "You bring heat with you?"

"They'll be here soon," Archie said. "And if we're still on the ground when they arrive, you won't get the chance to spend a single note of that money."

A long silence passed between them, broken only by the whine of cicadas and the thrum of distant birds.

Finally, the pilot tucked the money into his vest. "Engine's been fussy. You'll have to help push." Eddie exhaled. "We'll push."

Mabel turned toward the trees. "No time to waste. Let's move."

Behind them, the jungle still stirred with memories, with ghosts, with things left undone. But ahead? Home waited. And maybe answers with it. Gunfire cracked from the trees—closer this time.

Eddie swore and dropped behind the landing gear, returning fire. "They've got us pinned!" Mabel spun, loosing two shots from her revolver.

"Push the damn plane!"

Archie was already at the wing, shoulder low, paws digging into the metal. "Pilot get it moving!" The pilot leaned out of the cockpit, furious. "She's not ready! I need"

He was cut off by a hiss of steam and the sudden whine of the engine sputtering to life.

Then the guards broke cover five, maybe six of them, closing fast.

One lunged toward Mabel. She ducked, slammed an elbow into his ribs, and kicked him square in the jaw. Another tried to climb onto the wing—Eddie knocked him back with the butt of his pistol.

The wheels finally lurched forward.

They had movement—but not enough. Then the jungle parted.

Roxanne stepped through.

Her black coat moved like liquid shadow, ears upright, whiskers twitching in the humid air. She didn't shout. She didn't run. She simply walked forward calm, unstoppable. The guards saw her and backed off instinctively. "Get in!" Archie shouted. The ramp began to lower again too slow.

Roxanne's eyes locked on Archie. Her voice, when it came, was like ice sliding under the skin.

"You're not going to make it."

Archie stood tall, chest heaving, fur damp with sweat and blood.

"You already lost."

She blinked once almost amused. Then she moved. Faster than anyone should be able to move.

Eddie fired but she was already past him. Mabel drew her blade, but Roxanne sidestepped with a blur, snatching her wrist and slamming her into the fuselage. Only Archie was left staring her down.

"I'll take it back myself," she snarled.

Archie didn't flinch. Instead, he hurled the small smoke grenade from his coat pocket to the ground one of Eddie's, unused until now. It burst in a thick, stinging white fog that blinded everything.

"NOW!"

The pilot didn't wait. The plane lurched forward as the last of them dove in.

The ramp rose slow, agonizing and through the swirling smoke Archie caught one last glimpse of her silhouette. Still. Watching.

Then she lunged.

A single clawed paw slammed into the closing ramp, catching it mid-shut.

But Eddie was already there, driving a metal crate into the edge. The ramp slammed closed with a final hiss.

The plane lifted, wheels peeling off the ground, engines screaming into the sky.

Inside the cabin, Archie collapsed against the wall, chest shaking. He had outmaneuvered her. Just barely.

The plane thundered into the sky, jungle shrinking beneath them as the canopy broke into clouds. No more gunfire. No more footsteps. Just the wind. Inside the cabin, no one spoke at first.

Mabel leaned back, eyes shut, one paw clutching her ribs.

Eddie lowered his weapon, jaw tight, watching the hatch as if expecting it to blow open again. It didn't.

Archie sat on the floor, head against the vibrating wall, paws trembling. The smell of smoke still clung to his fur. They had made it. They were alive.

He closed his eyes, but all he could see was her face Nora's. The flash of her final scream. The weight of the key in his coat pocket.

A quiet sniff came from Mabel. Eddie muttered something and slumped beside him. They didn't speak but they didn't have to.

Archie opened his eyes again, staring forward, past the rows of crates and rusted bolts and scuffed metal walls.

"Teddy," he whispered.
His claws curled against the cold steel floor.
"I'm coming."

22

The clouds over London looked heavier than Archie remembered.

He hadn't said much since they'd left Cempoala. The hum of the aircraft filled the silence between the three of them, but none seemed eager to speak. He sat by the window, watching the gray sky ripple past like waves on a stone sea. His paw curled instinctively around the key in his coat pocket.

Nora's key.

Beside him, Mabel sat with arms crossed, eyes closed not asleep, just conserving energy. Her normally sharp posture had sagged ever so slightly, but her mind was clearly elsewhere. Eddie sat one row back, scribbling in a beat-up notebook. Another new habit.

Archie's reflection in the window looked wrong. The soft edges of the professor were still there somewhere, but something sharper had taken root. His shoulders no longer sagged under uncertainty. His frame, still lean, had grown wiry. He hadn't been trained for what came in that jungle but he'd survived it anyway.

He blinked, and saw her again just for a moment. Nora, standing in the temple chamber, holding out the key like it was nothing. Like she hadn't just risked her life to get it.

"Don't stop," she'd whispered.

He hadn't. Not then. Not now.

Eddie leaned forward slightly. "What's the plan when we land?"

Archie didn't turn. "We check the first safe house. It's the most likely fallback if they're still in London, they'll go there first. If not, we head to Teddy's home. He'd have left something behind." Mabel opened one eye. "And if it's compromised?" "Then we improvise," Archie said. "We stay moving." Eddie nodded. "Right." Another minute passed in silence. Eddie shifted again. "You think we'll even recognize it? London, I mean." Archie finally glanced at him, his voice low but firm. "London's not different." "No?" Eddie asked.

"No," Archie said. "We are."

The plane touched down in silence. No applause, no welcome. Just the hiss of brakes and a sky that had forgotten how to be anything but gray.

By the time Archie's boots hit the London pavement, his plan was already in motion. The streets near Holloway Market were steeped in fog.

Teddy walked fast, his coat collar up, one paw on Dolores's shoulder to keep her close. The courier's message had burned to ash hours ago, but the words still echoed in his mind.

"You're exposed. Move now."

They hadn't spoken much since they left the Camden flat just kept to side alleys, back stairwells, and dark corners. London didn't feel like home anymore. It felt like something was watching.

"We're almost there," Teddy muttered, eyes flicking toward the storefront ahead.

A faded chalk mark green, barely visible was scrawled along the base of the brick. The door it marked was metal, slightly ajar. Then came the noise. A shoe scraped behind them. A soft cough, too close. Dolores turned hand already on her pistol. Muzzles flashed through the fog. *"Down!"* she shouted.

They dove behind a dumpster as silenced gunfire split the alley. Stone cracked. Sparks burst off metal. Dolores yelped grazed along the shoulder. Teddy shielded her, pressing low behind cover. "We're boxed in," he said between breaths. "One exit. They're pushing us into the kill zone."

Dolores checked her wound, then gritted her teeth. "I'll run left draw them" "No." Teddy scanned the shadows.

"We stay together"

Another shot rang out, closer this time. The sound of boots on wet pavement.

Then suddenly a body flew through the fog, crashing into the brick wall behind them. Another blur slammed into the second agent, knocking him flat before he could raise his weapon.

A streak of black cut past them. Mabel. Knives flashing. One takedown. Two. A voice barked from deeper in the alley:

"Get down!"

Teddy recognized it Eddie.

Then Archie emerged. Not stumbling or breathless. Precise. Efficient. Cold.

He moved like a soldier, not a scholar coat flaring, pistol raised, body low to the ground. He fired two shots, two clean hits then pivoted, elbowed an attacker in the throat, ducked low, disarmed another in a blur of motion, and slammed him to the pavement.

Mabel swept behind a stack of crates and cleared the left flank. "Three more!" she called out.

Eddie moved like clockwork on the opposite side, his revolver cracking through the fog.

Archie didn't flinch. He stalked forward and grabbed the next attacker by the coat—ripped the gun from his grip, struck him across the head, and didn't look back. The last agent raised his weapon shaking now.

Dolores tried to aim, but Archie had already fired. One clean shot. Center Mass. Silence.

For a moment, the only sound was the wind moving between alley walls. "Clear," Mabel said quietly, checking her sleeves. Eddie nodded once. "Let's move."

Teddy stepped out from behind the dumpster, stunned. The fog still hung low, curling around his boots.

Archie stood over one of the fallen agents. Still. Unshaken. Alive but transformed.

Teddy whispered, "Archie?"

Archie didn't answer. He turned instead, stepped past them, and said, "We're not safe. We move now."

Dolores was bleeding but upright. Mabel helped her steady.

They fell in behind him, no one questioning the sudden shift in command. Teddy lingered, eyes still locked on his brother. Dolores, quiet now, asked, "Did you see what he just did?"

Teddy's voice was low. "Yeah... I saw."

The safehouse above the tailor's shop smelled of dust and old thread. The stairwell creaked beneath them as they entered—one at a time, silent, eyes scanning every corner out of habit.

Archie moved first. He cleared the front room without a word, a Colt .45 gripped tightly in his paw. Mabel swept through behind him, silent and methodical. Eddie shut the door and wedged a chair under the handle, then posted up near the window.

Only then did Archie lower the weapon.

Dolores dropped into a worn armchair, her breathing shallow, coat damp from the mist and blood. Mabel crouched beside her, unrolling gauze. "You'll live," she said gently. "It'll scar, but it's clean." Teddy paced slowly, his eyes fixed on his brother.

Archie remained standing in the center of the room still alert, still wired, like his body didn't realize the fight was over. He hadn't said a word since the alley. Not to Teddy. Not to anyone. Teddy stepped closer. "Archie..." No response. He moved in, slower this time. "We're okay now. You got us out." Still nothing.

He laid a paw on Archie's shoulder.

The Colt .45 slipped from Archie's grip and hit the hardwood with a dull, solid thud. Then he crumpled. Teddy caught him.

Archie collapsed into his brother's chest, chest heaving, his frame trembling beneath his coat. His paws hung uselessly, gripping at air.

Dolores stood halfway from her chair, alarmed. "Archie?

What's wrong?"

He didn't lift his head. His voice cracked on the edge of breath.

"I tried..."
A pause painful, raw.
"I tried to save her."

Dolores froze. Teddy did too, arms still locked around him. "No," she whispered, eyes going wide. *"No. Where is she? Archie where's Nora?"*

Archie shook his head once against Teddy's chest. Just once.

Dolores staggered backward like she'd been hit, then sank to the floor beside him. Her paw clutched the edge of his coat like she could pull him out of it—out of what he was saying. What she didn't want to believe. Teddy's voice was barely audible.

"She's gone."

Archie didn't respond. He didn't have to.

Mabel stepped out of view, disappearing into the next room without a word.

Eddie stayed by the window, one paw resting on the sill, his jaw locked tight. And in the silence that followed, Archie wept.

Not for the key.

Not for the scroll.

For her.

For Nora.

For the cost of coming home.

They didn't leave the safehouse that day.

No one asked. No one suggested it. The moment the door was bolted and the last curtain drawn, it was as if the whole flat exhaled with them.

Dolores dozed on the couch, one paw resting lightly over the bandaged graze on her shoulder. Teddy had found a small kettle in the back room and boiled water on a rusted burner. Mabel sat on the windowsill, one leg dangling, sharpening a blade in slow, deliberate strokes. She hadn't introduced herself yet. No one had asked.

Archie had collapsed in the corner armchair and hadn't moved for an hour. Then two.

Finally, he stood and gave a nod toward the back room. "I need a few hours." Teddy only said, "Take them."

Upstairs, Archie lay down in a small, creaking bed that smelled like dust and iron. He didn't expect to sleep. But he did. And when sleep came, so did the dreams.

It was just past two in the morning when Archie crept down the stairs.

The safe house was quiet, wrapped in that deep stillness only found in the hours before dawn. A single lamp glowed over the kitchen table, casting soft light across worn wood and tired faces. Teddy sat with a half-empty mug, his shoulders sagged with exhaustion. Across from him, Dolores cradled her own tea, wrapped in a blanket, eyes rimmed with grief and sleeplessness. Neither spoke when Archie entered.

He moved like someone still coming down from survival mode slow, sharp-eyed, shoulders taut. Without a word, he pulled out the chair between them and sat. Dolores slid the teapot toward him.

He poured carefully. Let the warmth settle into his paws. After a long pause, Dolores broke the silence. "What happened to her?" Archie kept his eyes on the steam rising from the mug.

"The camp was hit in the late afternoon," he said. "We were gathering gear, prepping to move deeper into the jungle. We'd stayed too long. Got too comfortable." Teddy looked up, frowning.

"They struck fast. No warning. Hollowed Coin units armed, trained. They had been watching us for days. Maybe longer."

His voice stayed level, but there was something brittle just beneath it.

"We tried to scatter. Mabel and Eddie held the line. Nora stayed with me we were cutting north through a ridge path, trying to regroup at the fallback site." Then, his tone shifted. "And that's when she appeared."

Dolores sat up slightly. "Who?"

Archie looked up at them. "A cat. But not like any I've seen." He took a breath. *"Her name is Roxanne."*

Teddy went still.

Archie noticed immediately. "You know that name."

Teddy stood, stepped into the next room, and returned holding the wooden box. He didn't set it down just yet.

"I saw it in old files at Parliament," he said. "Her name kept appearing. Different countries. Different decades. No records, no birth. Same name, always in the background. I thought it was a ghost story. Or a title passed between leaders."

"She's not a story," Archie said. "And she doesn't pass anything down." Dolores leaned in. "What did she do?"

"She didn't come in guns blazing. She walked in like she already knew where we were. Like she didn't need to rush."

He flexed his paw slightly still remembering the feel of that moment.

"Mabel engaged first Roxanne dropped her instantly. No wasted motion. Like she'd already seen the fight before it started. Eddie tried next she disarmed him mid-step. I moved in to shield Nora..." His voice thinned. "And then she was gone. Nora was gone. Just like that." Dolores whispered, "She took her?"

Archie nodded. "Took her. And made it clear we weren't going to get her back." Teddy finally set the box down. His voice was quieter now. "You think she's... something else?"

"I don't know," Archie admitted. "What I saw wasn't normal. Her reflexes. Her strength. Her presence. It's not magic. Not like that. But she fights like she's had a thousand years to practice." He looked down at the box.

"She didn't kill us because she didn't need to. But she knew what she was doing." Teddy sat back slowly. "And she's still out there." Archie gave a single nod. "Yes."

They let the silence stretch, the three of them circling the truth. Then Archie reached out and touched the box lightly. "You found it," he said. Teddy nodded. "Dolores led us in. I almost missed it."

"There was no guarantee it was still here," Archie said. "Even knowing the second half was in London... it was a shot in the dark." "But we got it," Dolores said. Archie didn't open the box not yet.

He just leaned back, the weight of the tea still warm in his paws and let the moment hold. They were together now.

And Roxanne didn't know what they had.

23

By eight o'clock, the safe-house had begun to stir. The kettle on the stove whistled softly, steam curling into the cold morning air. The scent of tea mixed with the must of old floorboards and worn upholstery. Sunlight broke through the kitchen window, casting warm streaks across the floor. London outside was its usual gray blur, but inside, there was a fragile stillness. A pause between storms.

Archie stood at the kitchen table, already dressed clean shirt, pressed coat, fur combed back into order. The collapse of the night before was gone from his face, replaced by something quieter, sharper. The box sat in front of him, still unopened.

He glanced up as the others began to trickle in. Dolores entered first, pulling her coat tighter around her shoulders. Teddy followed, rubbing the sleep from his eyes and still shaking off the weight of the last twenty-four hours.

Archie gave a short nod toward the corner, where Mabel leaned against the wall, sharpening a short blade against a flat stone.

"For those of you who haven't been properly introduced," he said, "this is Mabel. She's been with us since Cempoala. And before that, she knew our father."

Teddy blinked. "You knew Dad?"

Mabel didn't look up from the blade. "Briefly. We met in New York about seventeen years ago." Teddy frowned. "At a conference?"

"No," Mabel said. "At a restaurant. He showed up while I was reviewing it. Sat down at my table without asking, ordered the most expensive bottle of wine they had, and started talking about Aztec astronomy like we were old friends." Archie raised an eyebrow. "That sounds like him."

Mabel chuckled. "He left after one meal, but not before convincing me to look into a symbol I'd never seen before. I never forgot that conversation."

Teddy narrowed his eyes. "Wait. Was that the trip where he came back raving about lamb and wearing that ridiculous silver scarf?" Mabel smirked. "That would be the one."

Teddy crossed his arms, still studying her. "So how'd you end up in Cempoala?"

"I was chasing my own trail. Symbol fragments. Vanished ruins. Stories that didn't match the official timelines." She shrugged. "The Chesterfield name came up more than once. I figured if James was gone, one of his sons might still be chasing ghosts." "And you recognized Archie?" Teddy asked.

"The second I saw him step off the plane," Mabel said. "Same look in his eyes. Like he was already ten steps into a puzzle no one else could see." Teddy looked over at Archie. "That tracks."

Archie stepped forward, turning his attention back to the box.

"Let's get to work."

He ran his paw along the carved edges of the lid, inspecting the surface. "There's no keyhole.

Which means the key we found in Cempoala isn't for unlocking it the usual way." Dolores tilted her head. "Then what's it for?"

Archie tapped the wood. "There's too much space beneath the lid. Hollow. That means there's a hidden compartment some kind of trigger." Teddy stepped up beside him. "Weight plate?"

"Close," Archie murmured. He pressed a paw against the left edge and twisted just slightly. A faint click echoed through the wood. One of the side panels shifted.

He retrieved the carved key from his coat pocket. "This was never meant to open a lock. It was meant to complete a mechanism."

The key slid into the narrow opening with a soft snap flush, seamless. Another click followed. The lid rose by a hair. Archie lifted it slowly.

Inside, nestled in worn black cloth, was the second half of the scroll. No one spoke as he lifted it out.

He unrolled it beside the first, smoothing the edges with deliberate care. The parchment was faded, but the ink layered, detailed still held its shape. Symbols wound across it like veins. Archie and Teddy leaned in together.

The others gathered around silently. Dolores hovered at Archie's side. Eddie stood off to the left, arms folded. Mabel shifted closer to the table, but kept quiet, observant.

"The outer edge orientation lines," Archie murmured. "Used in early guild mapping. Meant to sync with celestial coordinates."

Teddy was already taking notes. "Here river route markers.

This curve matches maritime trade routes from the 1500s." Archie nodded. "But it's been altered. See how this layer overlays the original glyphs? This was redrawn. Someone adapted it." Mabel tilted her head, intrigued.

Archie traced a symbol with his claw. "This isn't just a translation it's a puzzle. The original author encoded location data. Whoever added the second layer corrected the orientation."

Teddy pointed to a twisted knot-like pattern. "That's an old calendar anchor. If we align that with the previous segment"

"Then the two halves lock," Archie finished. He shifted the scroll slightly. Click.

Even the parchment seemed to breathe.

Together, the brothers aligned the symbols. A shape emerged. A path. Then

"Guildhall," Archie said.

Teddy nodded slowly. "Right beneath London. Hidden in the vaults under the old Masonic structure."

Dolores stepped forward. "That's where the artifact is?" Archie nodded. "That's the site. The scroll confirms it." But then his eyes narrowed. Teddy followed his gaze. "What's wrong?"

Archie's paw hovered over the lower section of the scroll.

"This… I can't read this."

Curved symbols unlike the rest of the scroll. Older. Fainter. They formed a language that looked like it belonged to something even more ancient than the maps themselves.

"It's not Nahuatl," Teddy said. "Not anything we've cataloged."

"No," Archie replied. "I've only seen pieces of it once. Madrid archive. They didn't have a name for it. Just a notation: pre-contact anomaly." Dolores asked quietly, "Can anyone read it?" Archie didn't hesitate. "Maybe. I know someone. A friend Vince. He's studied lost linguistic roots for decades." Teddy raised an eyebrow. "You trust him?" "I do."

Mabel said nothing, but her eyes remained on Archie. The scroll lay open between them now half decoded, half unknowable. But they had a path.

And for the first time in days, the next step forward didn't feel like a leap into the dark.

Archie stepped away from the table as the others lingered over the scroll. He retrieved a sheet of stationery from his satchel, unfolded it on the counter, and uncapped his pen. He didn't say much just started writing. A few lines. Concise. Direct.

It was a letter only one cat in the world would understand, addressed to someone who had once studied languages too old for academia, and too strange for acceptance.

When he finished, he folded it, sealed it, and wrote one name on the front in careful script: Vince.

He tucked it into his coat pocket and turned back to the group. "We'll get it to him on the way to the Guildhall." Dolores glanced at the scroll. "And in the meantime?"

"We plan our move," Archie said. "Guildhall isn't just a location. It's bait."

Teddy sat on the edge of the table. "The Hollowed Coin's probably already narrowing in."

"They will be soon," Archie said. "Once they realize we've gone quiet."

Mabel stepped closer, arms crossed. "Assume they're already looking. If they've got people embedded in Parliament or the archives, the Guildhall would've been flagged." Eddie nodded. "So we hit first. Quiet. Fast." Dolores frowned. "And if Roxanne's there?" A silence settled.

Mabel didn't flinch. "Then we make a plan." Teddy raised an eyebrow. "To... what? Fight her?" "To stop her," Mabel said. "Whatever that takes."

Dolores leaned forward. "You saw what she did to Nora. What she did to all of you."

"I did," Mabel said calmly. "And I know she's strong. Fast. Brilliant, probably. But she's still just one cat. She's not invincible." Archie nodded. "She's not a ghost. She bleeds."

Mabel continued. "With the right plan timing, terrain, coordination we can distract her long enough to land a killing shot."

Teddy glanced between them. "We're seriously planning to... kill her?" No one answered.

Dolores looked to Archie. "Even after what she did are we sure that's the only option?"

Archie didn't look away. "You don't know her. I barely do. But what I saw in Cempoala wasn't someone playing power games. Roxanne doesn't just want the artifact. She's part of something older. Bigger." He paused. "If we don't stop her really stop her no one will." The weight of his voice landed hard.

Eddie broke the silence. "Then the artifact becomes our only leverage."

"Right," Archie said. "If we get it first, we can deny her access. Use it to draw her out or force her hand." Teddy sighed. "Or she takes it from us by force." "She'll try," Mabel said. "But that's what the plan's for."

Dolores looked between them, her voice low. "And if we get it... what then?" Archie shook his head. "One step at a time."

Teddy spread a folded map of London across the table, laying a finger on the heart of the city.

"Guildhall. Beneath it are a series of sealed vaults. Some were never reopened after the Blitz. We're talking stone walls, reinforced ironwork. Deep."

Dolores frowned. "So it's not just about finding the chamber it's about getting in without being seen." "Exactly," Archie said. "We don't want to trigger alarms. And we can't risk tipping the Hollowed Coin."

Mabel leaned forward. "We split the approach. One group moves inside, one stays above to monitor movement."

Eddie pointed to the surrounding streets. "There's a service tunnel entrance two blocks away.

Old utility access. If the vault connects to it, we can slip in beneath their surveillance grid."

Teddy nodded. "And there's scaffolding on the east wing restoration project. Could give us cover if we need to exfiltrate above ground."

Dolores tapped the scroll. "If Roxanne's watching the site already, we're walking into a trap." "We don't walk," Mabel said. "We ghost it."

Archie looked between them all. "So here's the breakdown." Archie stood over the table, both paws pressed against the old city map. His eyes scanned every line, every alley, every variable that could go wrong. When he spoke, his voice was composed—measured.

"All right. Here's how we run it."

He looked around the room, pausing to meet each of their eyes.

"We split into two teams. Eddie, Mabel, and I will infiltrate through the service tunnel. Teddy, Dolores you will stay above as our overwatch."

Teddy frowned slightly. "You sure splitting up is smart?" "No," Archie said. "But it's necessary."

He tapped a narrow alley leading toward Guildhall's eastern wing. "There's scaffolding here. Still active from the last restoration. Teddy found it while working through Parliament site access logs. It'll give us cover going in and an escape route if needed."

Teddy gave a small nod. "It connects to a maintenance stair that drops beneath the foundation. Old utility shaft. Not on modern blueprints." "We'll use that to hit the vault access," Archie said. "Quiet. Low profile." Eddie nodded, already mapping it out in his head.

"We're assuming the Hollowed Coin has narrowed in on the site," Archie continued. "They might not know the exact location yet but if they're nearby, we'll draw attention fast." Dolores leaned in. "What about comms?"

Archie shook his head. "We'll use short-range radios but down there, with stone and metal, we can't count on them. Expect dead zones." Teddy sighed. "So no backup if something goes wrong."

"That's why you two stay mobile," Archie said. "One block out. You'll have the signal beacon, fallback maps, and the scroll copy. If things go sideways, you guide us out or you disappear and mail the letter to Vince. That's priority one. No one else knows what's on that scroll yet. It stays that way."

Teddy didn't like it. But he nodded. "Understood." Archie turned toward Mabel. "You'll be on point with Eddie and me. Fast entry, silent movement. If Roxanne's there" "We don't engage," Mabel finished. "We delay. Disrupt."

"Exactly," Archie said. "Long enough to grab the artifact and vanish." Dolores crossed her arms. "And if we can't delay her?" A silence settled over the room. Archie's voice lowered. "Then we make a choice." Mabel said it flatly. "We put her down."

Teddy looked between them, unsettled. "You're really saying we kill her?"

"We don't want to," Archie said. "But if we don't stop her, no one else will."

"She killed Nora," Mabel added quietly. "And she didn't hesitate."

Dolores's eyes were on the map. "But we're not assassins."

"No," Archie agreed. "We're not. But this isn't war. It's worse. Roxanne doesn't just want control. She wants the artifact and if she gets it, it's over." He tapped the map again.

"We don't fight to win. We fight to outsmart her. Disrupt her rhythm. Keep her guessing."

Eddie broke his silence. "Because that's the only time she's vulnerable."

"Right," Archie said. "If she sees you coming, you're already dead."

Mabel gave a quiet nod. "So we hit her from three angles. Fracture her focus. Then go for the heart."

Teddy looked down, then back at Archie. "And if she's already waiting?" "Then we find another way in. Or we walk away." "And the artifact?"

Archie's eyes hardened. "We get it before she does. No matter what." He looked at them all.

"We move at dawn."

24

The rain had just let up, leaving the London pavement slick with reflections—lamplight rippling across cobblestones like ghosts in evening-wear. Outside a discreet corner of La Violetta, a French-Italian fusion restaurant tucked in the heart of Mayfair, a black car slowed to a graceful stop. The rear door opened, and Roxanne stepped out.

She wore a sleek black dress, tailored to perfection and matched to the midnight sheen of her fur. Her long tail swept once behind her, and the tips of her claws clicked softly on the wet stone as she moved. There was no umbrella, no handbag, no rush. Just presence. Intentional and unmistakable.

The valet stiffened slightly but said nothing as she passed. Her eyes didn't meet his. They didn't need to.

Inside, La Violetta glowed in soft golden tones—crystal chandeliers shimmered above white linen tables, violins whispered from a tucked-away mezzanine, and polished wood floors stretched beneath fine Italian loafers and silk slippers. The scent of white truffle and veal ragu curled through the room like a lover's hand. Roxanne slowed slightly as she entered.

She took it in—the elegance, the texture of it all. The way candlelight danced across polished surfaces. The hush of wealth and reputation in every flick of a napkin or soft-spoken order. These were the things she remembered. The maî tre d' didn't even glance up.

"I'm afraid we're fully booked this evening," he said without pause.

Roxanne didn't speak. She only smiled—not wide, not warm. Just enough to be remembered.

From across the room, the restaurant manager looked up. His expression froze mid-turn. Within seconds, he was at the host stand.

"Madame," he said with a breathy, apologetic tone. "Your usual table?" Roxanne nodded once. "Merci."

She was guided toward the back, past diplomats and magnates and old nobility. No one stopped her. Some watched. Most looked away too slowly.

Her private velvet-lined booth sat in the corner, with rich drapes ready to be drawn— though she left them open. She slid in without a sound, her tail curving beside her, one paw resting on the polished tabletop. Her claws were sheathed but unmistakably present. A sommelier approached, wine list in hand. *Do you still carry the 1982 Margaux?" she asked without looking up.*

"Yes, madame," the sommelier said at once, bowing slightly. "Then don't waste time." He disappeared with practiced speed.

Roxanne leaned back slightly and let her eyes roam again. Not searching—remembering. The velvet of the booth beneath her. The soft clink of glasses and distant laughter. The hush of power, dressed in manners. Moments later, Sabine arrived.

Silver-furred and trim, she walked with the posture of a career tactician—measured but alert. Her coat draped neatly over one arm, her whiskers still faintly wet from the drizzle outside. "Don't be so stiff," Roxanne said gently before Sabine even reached the booth. "It's just dinner."

Sabine raised an eyebrow, easing into the seat across from her. "And I wasn't sure if it was a warning."

Roxanne gave a low, amused chuckle. "If it were, I'd have chosen the wine myself and poured only one glass."

The sommelier returned with the bottle, uncorking it with care. Roxanne didn't bother with a tasting pour. She watched him. Sabine did, too.

Once poured, Roxanne lifted her glass with slow appreciation. "Margaux '82. Earthy on the nose. Violet and dried plum. Slight tobacco finish. It tastes like history." She took a sip—just enough to savor.

Sabine followed with a more tentative taste. Her eyes widened slightly. "I've never had anything like this."

"Most haven't." Roxanne's voice was soft now. "It was a good year. Not for governments. Not for armies. But the vines? They remembered something the rest of the world forgot." Sabine raised her glass. "To rare things, then."

"To rarer company," Roxanne replied, and the clink between them was quiet, not ceremonial— just sincere.

A moment passed in silence. Then the edge returned— not sharp, but unmistakable.

"So," Roxanne said, swirling her glass. "The business before dessert."

Sabine nodded, straightening slightly. "The replacement names are coming. Slowly. No one's eager to volunteer after the... demonstration."

"They'll come around," Roxanne said without concern. "Terror fades. Survival doesn't." "And the artifact?"

Roxanne's eyes drifted toward the candlelight.

"Exactly where I left it. Still untouched. Still singing to those who can hear." "You think anyone else is listening?" "I know they are. But not well enough." Sabine took another sip of wine. "There's interference."

Roxanne's voice was even. "Chesterfield?"

Sabine nodded. "Closer than ever."

Roxanne's expression didn't change. She took another small sip of Margaux and exhaled slowly. "He's not the business at hand." "You sound tired of him."

"I'm tired of pretending he's the real threat." Sabine didn't press.

"Barrow," she said after a pause. "He's been siphoning from the docks. Files. Crates. Funding. Thinks you're just a ghost story." Roxanne's whiskers gave a slow twitch.

"He's getting bold," Sabine continued. "Not subtle. Not scared." "I know." "You're letting it happen?" "Until dinner is over." Sabine blinked once. "You're handling it?" Roxanne set her glass down gently. "Personally." Sabine leaned back, letting that settle.

"I forget sometimes how calm you are when you say things like that."

Roxanne tilted her head, the faintest smile returning.

"You shouldn't," she said. "It's when I'm calmest that you should be afraid."

A quiet laugh escaped Sabine not nervous, just tired. She reached again for her wine.

"I suppose I should be honored you asked me to dinner instead of Barrow."

"You're not dinner," Roxanne said, almost gently. "You're company." Sabine looked at her. "You're lonelier than you let on." Roxanne didn't answer. She simply raised her glass again. "To silence, then," she said. "Before the storm."

The main course arrived without a sound. Poached sea bass in saffron broth for Roxanne, lamb loin over white truffle mash for Sabine each plated with such delicate precision, it could have been framed. The candle between them flickered slightly as steam rose from their dishes.

Roxanne smiled at the presentation, tail lightly brushing the leather of her seat. "La Violetta hasn't lost its touch."

She cut a slow piece of fish, savoring the aroma first, then took a bite without ceremony. Sabine followed, chewing with the caution of someone aware of the company she kept. "The expansion plans in Paris," Sabine said, dabbing at her mouth with a napkin. "They're moving along. We've already secured property discreet, off the main avenues. We'll need new staff, of course. Ones we can trust."

Roxanne nodded without looking up. "Handpick them. No locals unless they come with loyalty proofed in ink and fire." "Understood." Sabine paused. "You'll be there next month?"

"If only to see if the wine holds up." Her voice was light, almost amused. "And to be present when the foundations are laid."

Another sip of Margaux. Another quiet breath. Then Sabine shifted slightly in her chair.

"About Chesterfield…"

Roxanne's eyes flicked toward her not hard, but enough to still the air between them.

Sabine kept going. "I know he's just a professor, but he's… tenacious. And clever. He's not far off."

Roxanne leaned back, folding one leg over the other. "That's always been his charm," she said, as if amused by the memory of it. "He learns. He studies. He bleeds. And then he keeps going."

Sabine narrowed her eyes slightly. "And the artifact when we secure it what exactly will it fetch? Something like that, with the right buyer…"

Roxanne didn't answer immediately. She took another bite, chewed, and let the moment stretch. When she spoke, her tone remained soft. "It's not for sale." Sabine hesitated. "But it could be. If we had to."

"No." Roxanne didn't raise her voice. But the quiet finality of it cut like ice through wine. Sabine recovered quickly. "Of course."

Roxanne refilled both their glasses with a fluid, elegant motion, then softened her gaze again. "Enjoy the moment, Sabine. I don't get many of them."

"You could," Sabine said, watching her carefully. "If you let Chesterfield go. If you'd just... end him. Like you did his father."

Roxanne's paw paused over her fork. For a heartbeat, the room felt colder. *"I didn't kill James,"* she said. Sabine blinked. "I thought"

"He died chasing ghosts." Her voice was flat. "I merely set the table."

Sabine stayed quiet, unsure if that was metaphor or confession.

Roxanne sipped again, as though the wine might smooth the sharp edges. "James was a fool, but not a weak one. And Archie..." she let the name hang for a second too long, "...isn't a child anymore." Sabine's eyes narrowed. "Then why is he a problem?"

Roxanne looked across the table at her not angry, not cold, but something in between. Something older. Sadder.

"Because the world keeps giving me Chesterfields," she said softly. "And each one refuses to stay buried." That ended the conversation.

The plates were cleared. Dessert menus offered, declined. And Roxanne sat back, glass halffull, gaze distant as the city lights twinkled beyond the restaurant windows.

London Docklands – 11:52 P.M.

The air was damp with salt and diesel. Wooden planks creaked beneath their steps as Roxanne and Sabine crossed the length of the old Camden Pier. A rusted sign swung on broken hinges above a long-shuttered customs house now repurposed—barely—into Barrow's makeshift command center.

Roxanne said nothing as they approached. Her hands stayed at her sides, the soft sway of her black dress whispering against her legs. She let Sabine move ahead, let her knock on the iron door, let her voice call the meeting to order.

Barrow would never listen if she opened the conversation. But Sabine? Sabine still had a sliver of diplomatic capital.

The doors opened. Warm, sour air poured out cheap liquor, sweat, and wet fur.

Inside, Barrow's crew lounged around stacked crates and battered tables. They snapped to attention only halfway, most still gripping drinks or half-drawn weapons. At the center, Barrow sat like a king on his crate-throne, his gray tabby coat stretched tight across a wide chest. A thick gold chain hung around his neck, too flashy to be tasteful.

He raised a brow at Sabine. "Look what the wind dragged in." Sabine stood tall, ignoring the jeers. "We need to talk."

Barrow laughed. "Talk? Thought you council types were all bark these days." He gave Roxanne a quick once-over without interest. "Who's your date?"

Roxanne didn't answer.

Sabine kept her composure. "You've been skimming the last three shipments. Taking more than your allocation. That ends tonight."

Barrow rolled his eyes. "Allocation. Like I work in a bakery. I'm the one running this end, Sabine. I am the Coin out here."

"The Hollowed Coin does not belong to you," Sabine snapped. "You serve the organization you don't own it."

Barrow leaned back. "You bring her," he nodded toward Roxanne "to try and scare me? Let me guess. She gives one icy stare and I hand over my operation?"

Roxanne remained still, unreadable. The only movement was the slow, deliberate turn of her head as she surveyed the room. Barrow smirked. "I've got twenty-five good claws here. Real bruisers. Not perfume-wearing aristocrats." Sabine took a breath. "Barrow, I'm warning you"

He raised a paw. "No more warnings. I've been running this dock while the rest of you sip wine and write memos. So here's my warning." He stood. "Get out. You and your mute shadow. Or we stack your bodies in the bay."

He waved his claws. The room shifted. Crates were pushed aside. Steel flashed in the light. Roxanne's voice was soft. "Sabine." Sabine turned her head slightly.

"Step aside," Roxanne said.

Sabine obeyed. Barrow grinned. "Oh, she speaks."

He snapped his claws. They charged.

The first tabby came at her with a blade raised high, his tail flicking with overconfidence. Roxanne ducked beneath the strike, driving her elbow into his ribs. He folded instantly. She spun, grabbed the scruff of his coat, and hurled him into the next wave. She moved like she'd already seen it all unfold.

Two more lunged together one swinging a length of pipe, the other cracking a chain between his paws. Roxanne stepped between them, fluid as smoke. She struck the first in the throat with a paw, turned, and kicked the other into a splintering crate.

A burly tom with brass claws swung wide. She caught his wrist mid-air, twisted, and the snap was loud and final. He yowled. Another tried to flank her she pivoted and smashed his muzzle with the back of her heel. He dropped cold.

Barrow, eyes narrowing, reached for the pistol tucked behind his belt. He drew, aimed and fired. The crack of the shot echoed across the dock.

Roxanne moved before the sound had finished. Her body leaned into the motion with uncanny instinct—twisting as the bullet split the air beside her ear. He fired again.

She stepped forward, unblinking, and the second shot went wide too slow. By the third, she was already within reach.

Her paw struck his wrist like iron. The gun clattered to the floor. She kicked it aside and slammed her elbow into his chest, sending him staggering into the crates behind him.

Barrow's smug grin collapsed. The crew wasn't full of fighters anymore—it was full of broken bodies. And one demon in black fur. He turned to flee. She caught him before his third paw hit the floor.

Roxanne yanked him back by the collar of his coat, then slammed him face-first into a crate hard enough to splinter it. He gasped, dazed, and tried to crawl. *She rolled him onto his back. "Wait please I didn't mean"*

Her claws slid out, sharp and measured. She placed one paw gently on his throat not pressing, just resting. "You believed power came from numbers,"

she whispered.

"That was your mistake."

Her claws punched into his chest one clean, surgical strike between his ribs, angled up. He choked. Eyes wide, legs trembling.

Roxanne leaned close. "Don't worry," she said softly. "You won't feel the rest." Then she twisted. Barrow went still.

Silence returned. The surviving crew stood frozen, too afraid to breathe. Roxanne adjusted the cuff of her dress.

Sabine, a few paces behind, watched without speaking. She looked shaken. But not surprised.

Roxanne didn't look back. "Add another replacement to the list."

The ride back was quiet, save for the low rumble of the engine and the occasional hush of passing traffic. Sabine sat beside her, arms folded, the tension still fresh behind her eyes. "Twenty-five of them," she finally said. "I've seen you take out squads before, but that—? That wasn't a fight. That was... something else."

Roxanne kept her gaze on the window, the city lights brushing silver across her fur. "Speed. Timing. Experience," she said softly. "Most of them didn't know how to fight. They knew how to shoot. There's a difference."

Sabine gave a dry exhale through her nose. "I suppose there is."

"You're not going to ask again," Roxanne added, almost smiling. No. I'm not."

They pulled up to the hotel—a polished glass-and-stone retreat where names weren't asked and privacy was king. The doorman opened the rear passenger door and stepped aside without a word.

Roxanne slid out first, the pads of her paws silent against the stonework as she adjusted the sleek black dress that shimmered faintly under the awning lights. Sabine followed, brushing out her coat as she joined her at the entrance.

"Keep me informed on Chesterfield," Roxanne said. "Movements, conversations, everything. I want to know where he eats and where he sleeps." Sabine nodded. "You'll know."

With that, Roxanne turned and stepped through the doors, leaving her lieutenant on the sidewalk.

Behind velvet-paneled doors near the rear of the lobby was the hotel's after-hours bar—no signs, no schedule, and no entry without a name whispered to the right paw. The bartender stiffened as Roxanne entered.

"I'll have a martini," she said, voice calm but certain. "Stirred. Three olives. And use the good stuff—nothing bottom shelf tonight."

He nodded and turned to his private stock, disappearing briefly behind a wall of polished crystal.

She padded softly to the end of the bar, her posture fluid and at ease, tail curling once around the leg of the stool before she sat. The bar was quiet, the kind of quiet that cost more than most cats would see in a year. A warm jazz number drifted from the hidden speakers, soft enough to disappear into memory but rich enough to carry weight.

The martini arrived in its chilled glass. She took it without ceremony but didn't drink right away.

Her eyes moved toward the booth tucked in the back corner. Empty now. Candlelight played across the velvet, casting low amber shadows.

He had been there. James Chesterfield. So many years ago.

He had sat in that very booth, flanked by academic confidence and an appetite for danger. He wasn't scared of her, not really. Cautious, yes. But not frightened. And unlike so many others, he never looked away.

That night should've been uneventful. An exchange. A test of wills. Instead, it ended in fire and broken glass.

She had blamed herself, at first. Then came the truth: it wasn't her order. An overeager associate within the Hollowed Coin had deemed James too nosy to live. No clearance. No permission. Just a rogue execution from a fool who thought he understood the game. She had corrected the mistake. But the damage had already been done.

She brought the martini to her lips and paused—just for a moment—as a faint shimmer collected at the corner of her eye. She didn't wipe it away. Instead, she let it trail, silent and slow, down her cheek.

The olives shifted gently in the glass. Outside, the city pulsed on.

And in that booth across the room, the ghost of a memory refused to leave.

25

The fog hung low over the second safe house, curling like smoke through the alleyways and bleeding into the corners of the glass panes. Dampness crept into the walls, the kind that settled in your joints and made silence feel heavier than it should.

Archie stood at the front window, chewing the end of his pipe not lit, just pressed thoughtfully between his teeth. The warm light of the sitting room lamp cast soft shapes in the glass. For a breath, he saw her Nora's face, clear in the reflection. Then it was gone. Just fog and shadow again.

Behind him, Eddie sat in the corner, quietly cleaning his revolver. The metallic click of parts shifting into place broke the silence at intervals, a rhythm of readiness. He hadn't said much all day. These hours before a mission always brought out something quiet and sharp in him.

Mabel lay sprawled on the old couch, her wide-brimmed hat tipped low, one paw resting across her stomach. She hadn't moved in over an hour, but Archie could tell she was still awake. Sleep didn't come easy in houses like this.

In the kitchen, Dolores worked with what little they had. The smell of toasted bread and sliced chicken drifted into the room nothing fancy, just sandwiches. But they carried a weight, a reminder of something close to normal. Dolores could make even a rationed meal feel like home.

Teddy stepped up beside Archie, lighting a cigar with a flick of his thumb. It smelled cheap but familiar—something picked up at the corner shop down the road.

"Figured I'd even the odds," he said, tilting his head toward Archie's pipe. "You've had the good stuff since you got back." Archie raised a brow, just slightly.

"That Fumar blend," Teddy continued. "Took me ten minutes to figure out what it was. That's a small piece of home a true London cut.

"Smuggled it," Archie muttered. "Saw a tin in an old shop near the edge of town. Only thing in the whole place not covered in dust. Thought I'd get to enjoy it after all this."
"Did you?"

Archie finally looked over. "Didn't have time. We were too busy getting shot at."

Teddy gave him a sidelong smile. "Well, think of it this way you made it back. You can finally light that pipe now."

Archie gave a dry huff through his nose, a shadow of a laugh. The corners of his mouth pulled up just slightly.

"Doubt I'll taste anything for days," he said. "Still smells like gunpowder."

"Then I guess you'll have to settle for this sorry excuse," Teddy said, holding up his cheap cigar like a toast.

"For now," Archie replied. "But I'm lighting the good stuff the day this ends." "That's the spirit."

For the first time in a long while, Archie let the moment hang. It wasn't joy not really but it was something. And only Teddy could pull it from him.

They stood in silence for a moment, the fog pressing against the window like a memory trying to find its way back in. Teddy's voice came low. "You think she's beatable?"

"Roxanne?" Archie's jaw flexed.

Teddy nodded. "I mean, you read what the scroll said..."

"I read it," Archie cut in. "But it doesn't name her. It speaks in metaphor 'a shadow that endures when empires fall'... vague enough to fit a dozen figures across history. It's not proof. It's folklore stitched into record."

Teddy puffed his cigar again, considering. Archie continued. "She's not some ancient force. She's practiced. Trained. Someone who's mastered every advantage she could skill, misdirection, maybe even fear. That's how you get stories like this. You win enough battles, people start calling you invincible." "You're saying she's just good?"

"I'm saying she's one cat. Flesh and blood. We weren't ready, that's all." Teddy didn't argue. He didn't agree either.

In the kitchen, Dolores laid the sandwiches onto a tray and carried them into the room.

Mabel stirred just enough to lift her hat and sit up, one ear flicking toward the hallway. Eddie set down his gun parts and began reassembling them slowly. Archie didn't move from the window. "I miss her," he said quietly. "I know," Teddy replied.

313

They stood there together a while longer, surrounded by the sounds of a house full of quiet warriors, their hearts heavy, their mission hours away.

Outside, the fog thickened folding in like the weight of everything that had come before. Two hours passed.

The fog outside had only thickened, curling against the windows like breath on glass. Inside, the lights stayed low. Sandwich wrappers were folded, weapons cleaned and checked, and silence settled in like smoke. No one spoke much. There wasn't much left to say. Archie glanced at the clock, then at the others.

"It's time," he said.

Mabel stood and adjusted her coat. Eddie checked the cylinder of his revolver, then snapped it shut with a flick. Dolores rose from the arm of the chair, wrapping her scarf. Teddy was already reaching for his coat when Archie stopped him. "Here," Archie said, handing over a sealed envelope. "For

Vince."

Teddy took it without a word and tucked it into his inside pocket.

"Per the plan," Archie continued, "you two stay back. Post the letter. Keep watch. If we don't come back" "You will," Teddy said simply.

Dolores gave Archie a steady look as she pulled on her gloves. "We'll be ready if things go wrong." Archie gave a nod. "Let's move."

314

Outside, the city lights were little more than a dull glow behind the fog. Somewhere out there, Guildhall loomed old, silent, and waiting.

They moved like shadows through the alleyways, boots quiet on slick cobblestones. Mabel led the way, confident and unspoken. Eddie followed, revolver hidden beneath his coat. Archie brought up the rear, clutching the strap of his satchel, the journal pressing against his ribs with every step.

They reached the edge of the square and crouched behind a crumbling brick wall. Through the mist, Guildhall rose a silhouette of ancient stone and shuttered windows. And in front of it "Mercs," Mabel whispered.

Three guards near the western arch. Two more at the rear. Tactical gear. Radios. Hollowed Coin insignias. Eddie narrowed his eyes. "They were waiting for us."

Archie's ears flicked back. "They shouldn't even know we're here. Roxanne doesn't know we have the scroll..."

Mabel glanced sideways. "Unless someone told her." "She'd need more than just a name or location," Eddie muttered. "She'd have to know what it means."

Archie stared at the building, frowning. "Maybe she does. Or maybe she's guessing. Either way... she got here first."

"What do you think she wants with it?" Mabel asked. "The artifact?" Archie didn't answer right away.

"If it's what we think it is," he said, "it's powerful. Maybe it completes the map. Or maybe it's worse." "Only one way to find out," Eddie said.

Archie gave a quiet nod and pointed toward the far side of the building.

"We go in through the east side. There's a service entrance old, maybe overlooked." "And if it's not?" Eddie asked.

Archie's expression didn't change. "Then we make it work." The east side was quiet.

Mabel led them down a narrow path between two worn buildings, the walls damp with moss and soot. A rusted gate leaned open, its hinges long since broken. She slipped through first, the others close behind. No guards. No sound. Just fog.

They crossed the rear courtyard and approached a narrow service door tucked under a stone arch. Vines had overgrown the frame. Mabel tried the handle. "It's unlocked," she said. Archie frowned. "That's not right." "Too easy," Eddie muttered.

"Maybe they missed it," Mabel said, though her voice was dry. Archie didn't reply.

The corridor beyond was narrow and cold. Shelves lined the walls. Dust coated the floor. Light from overhead fixtures flickered without rhythm. The air smelled like mildew and rust. They moved quietly, checking corners, listening. Nothing.

Archie's grip tightened around the strap of his satchel. "This place should be guarded," he said.

"They're all out front," Mabel replied. "And none back here." "Which makes no sense," Eddie said.

They entered a wide room file cabinets on one side, old crates on the other. At the far end stood a heavy door, carved with faded markings. Brass around the handle had dulled with age. Archie stepped closer. "This is it." Mabel reached for the handle. "It's open." Archie hesitated. "Why leave it unguarded?" "Could be a trap," Eddie said.

Archie glanced back once, then turned to the door again. "We've come this far." He reached out and pushed it open. The door opened without a sound.

Beyond it, a narrow flight of stone steps led into shadow. Cold air met them as they descended, lantern light flickering against old stone. The stairway opened into a circular chamber domed, with walls carved in a language none of them could read. The ceiling arched high, vanishing into shadow.

Four thick pillars framed the room; each etched with jagged symbols and metal inlays dulled with age. At the center sat a raised stone pedestal black as coal, smooth as glass. Resting atop it, half-embedded in its cradle, was something none of them had seen before. A sphere. Roughly the size of a grapefruit.

Deep green emerald, but not like anything found in jewelry or museums. This was darker, layered, almost alive. Veins of gold shimmered beneath the surface like lightning trapped in glass. The outer shell was impossibly smooth, but not flawless faint scratches ran along one side, like it had been handled, or fought over. It glowed faintly, but there was no source for the light.

It wasn't just old. It felt ancient. Older than the room. Older than anything they had ever found. "Is that it?" Mabel asked. Archie nodded slowly. "It must be." But the sphere wasn't free.

It was held in place by a series of shifting metal rings, mounted around it like gyroscopic restraints. The outer ring had no visible seam. The inner ones were etched with unfamiliar symbols and shallow notches—some worn nearly smooth, others still sharp.

Below the pedestal, carved into the base, was a flat stone dial with nine rune-like characters arranged in a circle.

Archie knelt. "It's a locking mechanism. Three rings. Three positions. It's... it's like a sequence. Input the right combination, the bands disengage." "And if we get it wrong?" Eddie asked.

Archie looked at the dial again. "There are pressure marks around the wrong runes. Someone's failed before."

Mabel stepped closer, eyes scanning the chamber. "Anything in the journal?"

Archie pulled it from his coat, flipped quickly. His father had sketched something not the full mechanism, but fragments. Symbols. A pattern. He studied the shapes, cross-referenced the notches, then looked back to the dial. "The order matters," he said. "And the timing."

He rotated the outer ring slowly, aligning it with a rune. It clicked softly. Then the middle ring. Another soft click.

The inner ring resisted. Archie paused, then reversed course and chose a different rune. A low rumble vibrated through the floor.

The rings slid open. The sphere lifted an inch from its cradle, now floating freely above the pedestal.

Archie reached out. His paw hesitated above it the glow reflected in his eyes then he lifted it carefully, holding it between his paws.

It was warm. Almost pulsing. "We have it," he said.

Then A voice behind them.

"I believe you have something that doesn't belong to you, Chesterfield."

They turned as one.

Roxanne stood in the far corner of the chamber. No one had seen her enter. No sound. No movement. She stepped forward slowly, the green glow of the sphere catching in her eyes. She didn't look rushed. She looked... satisfied.

"Hand it over," she said.

Her voice echoed softly against the chamber walls calm, deliberate. Not a command. A statement of inevitability.

Archie didn't move. The sphere sat warm in his paws, its green glow casting fractured light across the stone. Eddie raised his revolver, steady but uncertain.

Roxanne barely glanced at him. "I wouldn't't," she said. "Not unless you want to find out what happens when I stop being polite."

Mabel shifted, half a step forward. "Polite? You've been hunting us since Cempoala."

"I've been cleaning up a mess," Roxanne said.

Her coat shimmered faintly in the emerald light, the fabric catching flecks of green like dew in moonlight. She didn't raise her voice. She didn't move fast. She didn't need to.

Archie's paws tightened on the sphere. "How did you know we'd come here?" he asked.

She tilted her head. "You think I haven't been here before? You think I haven't walked this place long before your father first cracked open his first history book?"

Archie blinked. "Right."

Mabel folded her arms. "Sure. You've been here before. Centuries ago, right?" Roxanne smiled, unfazed. "You can believe what you like. You're here now. Holding what I need."

Behind them, something shifted in the stone a dull grinding sound, slow and heavy. The pedestal they'd taken the sphere from began to retract into the floor. Archie turned toward it, confused. "What the?"

A second rumble followed, deep in the walls. Somewhere above them, a gear clicked. Another wall shifted slightly, then stopped.

"What's happening?" Mabel asked.

Archie stepped forward, eyes scanning the room. "I don't know. I didn't trigger anything. The puzzle's already solved." "Then it's not about the puzzle," Eddie said.

Roxanne watched the commotion with mild amusement. "It's reacting to the artifact," she said. "As it should." Archie turned back toward her, still holding the sphere. "What is this thing?"

"It's older than the scroll," Roxanne said. "Older than Guildhall. Older than anything your father ever found."

"And you expect us to believe you were there to see it made?" Archie asked, voice sharper now. "Come on."

"I don't expect anything from you," Roxanne said. "Not anymore."

The wall behind her groaned faintly. Dust trickled from a carved seam near the ceiling, but she didn't flinch.

"You've done your part," she added. "Now give it to me." Roxanne stepped forward, slow and measured.

The stone behind her groaned again, another unseen mechanism shifting somewhere in the walls. Dust trickled from the carved ceiling. Still, her focus never left Archie.

"You've done enough," she said. "Give me the sphere, and you can walk out of here breathing." Archie didn't move. Mabel stepped between them. *"No," she said. "Not today."*

Roxanne's smile faded. She looked at each of them Mabel, Eddie, Archie and her voice dropped to something flat and final.

"I'm not asking."

A beat passed. Then she moved.

Eddie raised his revolver, but Roxanne was already in motion fast, controlled, and efficient. She struck his wrist, knocking the weapon from his grip. Before he could recover, she twisted and drove a sharp blow into his ribs, sending him back against the nearest pillar with a thud. Mabel lunged.

She came in low, fast, claws ready. Roxanne blocked the first strike, dodged the second, then countered elbow to Mabel's ribs, a sweep at her legs. Mabel stumbled back but didn't fall. Her breathing was tight, but her stance held.

Archie backed toward the far wall, the emerald sphere clutched tight to his chest. "Go!" Mabel shouted.

Roxanne turned toward him calm, steady. She didn't chase. She stalked. "You don't understand what you're holding," she said.

Above them, the ceiling groaned again. A carved panel shifted, gears clicking just out of view. A low rumble vibrated through the floor. Archie's eyes flicked upward just for a second. Roxanne moved.

She crossed the chamber in three quick steps, raising one hand toward him but the wall behind the pedestal gave out first.

With a sharp crack, a section of stone collapsed inward. Dust and rubble slammed into the floor with a crash. The whole room shook. Roxanne flinched just slightly. Mabel seized the opening.

She charged, shoulder-first, and slammed into Roxanne with her full weight. The two of them hit the ground hard. Roxanne rolled, came to her feet, but this time there was no smirk. No calm detachment.

Just silence.

Her stance shifted.

Then she came forward again faster, sharper, this time without hesitation. The fight wasn't over. It had barely started. Roxanne advanced again, swift and focused. Mabel met her without flinching.

She didn't charge not this time. She moved sideways, forcing Roxanne to pivot, keeping her off center. The strikes that followed came quick one high, one low testing. Mabel wasn't just attacking anymore. She was studying.

Roxanne blocked both, wrist to wrist, footwork tight, but there was a flicker — a half-second longer than before as she recalculated. Mabel saw it. She pressed harder.

Elbow, hook, spin. Roxanne caught one, deflected the other, but Mabel's last strike grazed her coat. A hit. Not a wound but a warning.

Eddie came in fast from the other side, revolver now back in hand but held like a blunt weapon. Roxanne turned, caught his wrist mid-swing, and twisted hard.

He dropped the gun again it clattered across the floor but he didn't stop. He threw his weight into a shoulder check. It clipped her and staggered her two steps back. Mabel was already moving.

She swept low, forcing Roxanne to leap back again. For a second, just a second, the three of them froze.

Archie watched from the edge of the chamber, still clutching the sphere. He couldn't move couldn't look away. It was the first time he'd seen Roxanne off balance. The first time she looked like she might not win.

Roxanne's chest rose and fell, calm but slower now. Her eyes moved between them not panicked, not afraid calculating. Adjusting.

Mabel narrowed her stance. Sweat lined her brow. "You're good," she said. "But not perfect." Roxanne raised an eyebrow. "I'm not here to be perfect." She moved again. This time, faster.

Eddie blocked high. Mabel dodged low. Roxanne flowed between them like water twisting, striking, ducking. Her precision was relentless, but the rhythm had changed. They weren't chasing her anymore. They were cornering her.

Mabel grunted as a knee clipped her side, but she pivoted through it and struck Roxanne's arm hard enough to stagger her. Eddie followed with a straight punch that caught her across the jaw not clean, but enough to turn her head. Roxanne stumbled. Regained her footing. Then smiled. That smile again tight, cold, controlled.

"You've both learned a few tricks," she said.

She stepped back just enough to reposition, breathing steady, but this time her coat was scuffed. Her lip, just slightly, was bleeding. She licked it once and looked at Mabel. "You learned fast," she said.

Mabel steadied herself. "You're not as unreadable as you think."

Roxanne's eyes flicked to Archie again, just for a second. And then in one fluid motion she dropped her coat.

Underneath was the same black combat gear she'd worn in Cempoala, but here, under Guildhall's flickering light, it looked sharper. Sleeker. Like it didn't belong to any era at all.

"Good," Roxanne said. "Then no one has to wonder why this ends the way it does." Roxanne moved.

She struck low at Eddie, aiming for his ribs. He twisted with it, grunted from the blow, but stayed upright bruised, not broken. Mabel slid in from the side, reading the rhythm.
She wasn't testing anymore. She was finishing it.

The knife was already in her paw small, sharp, perfectly balanced. She'd waited for this opening. Eddie threw a high punch. Roxanne turned to counter. That was her mistake.

Mabel stepped in and drove the blade forward with everything she had. Straight into Roxanne's chest.

The steel slid between bone and muscle deep, centered, unflinching.

Through the sternum. Through the heart.

The sound was horrible a thick, final crunch. No echo. Just impact. *Roxanne froze.*

Her breath caught. Her mouth parted. But no sound came out.

Her eyes lowered to the hilt now embedded in her chest. Blood spread fast, darkening her fur, spilling over her forearm. Eddie didn't lower his revolver. Mabel didn't move.

Archie gripped the emerald sphere so tightly his claws ached. Roxanne swayed. Then dropped to one knee.

One forepaw braced against the stone floor. The other hovered near the knife... but didn't pull.

She collapsed forward, weight sinking into her front limbs then slumped.

Her chin dipped toward her chest. Her tail lay still. Blood pooled beneath her. Slow. Steady.Nothing else moved.

No twitch. No breath. No sign of life.

The chamber was silent now.

The gears in the walls had stopped. Even the emerald sphere had dimmed slightly in Archie's grasp. Mabel stayed frozen. Eddie lowered his revolver, just a little.

Archie exhaled the first full breath he'd taken in minutes. Roxanne didn't stir. She didn't shift. She didn't breathe. *She was dead.* No one moved at first.

Then Mabel stepped forward, slow but steady. She crouched beside Roxanne, keeping one paw on the hilt of her knife just in case. The blood was still flowing, thick and slow, but fading. She pressed two claws to the side of Roxanne's neck. Nothing.

She shifted position and tried again, lower, more deliberate. Still nothing.

"She's gone," Mabel said.

Archie let out a long breath and lowered the emerald sphere slightly, his shoulders finally relaxing. The soft warmth in the stone was fading now still present, but less urgent. Like whatever it had been waiting for had passed.

Eddie stepped closer, revolver still in his paw but no longer raised. He didn't say anything at first, just stared down at the body. The blood had pooled across the stone floor, soaking into the seams. "She's dead," Mabel said again, firmer this time.

Archie nodded, more to himself than anyone else. "We did it."

They backed away slowly, giving space between them and the body like it might still lurch but it didn't. Roxanne didn't move. Her fur was matted, soaked through at the chest. The knife stood at an angle, buried deep, untouched.

Eddie finally holstered his revolver and sat down heavily on a nearby crate. "That's done."

Archie looked at the emerald sphere in his paws flawless, heavy, laced with fine veins of gold that no longer pulsed. "She wanted this," he murmured. "Whatever she wanted," Mabel said, walking over to him, "she's not getting it now."

Archie turned the sphere over carefully, studying it in the flickering light. It no longer burned in his paws. It simply rested there, as still as everything else.

Mabel stood beside him, her voice low. "You think this is what she was after?"

"I think it's part of something bigger," Archie said. "But we keep it out of her reach."

Eddie gave a tired grunt of agreement from the corner. "Let's just get out of here before the rest of the Coin shows up." They stayed quiet for a few moments. The chamber had gone still not just silent, but heavy. No more turning gears. No more vibrations in the floor. Just dust drifting from the ceiling, and the sound of distant water somewhere deep beneath the foundation.

Mabel finally allowed her stance to ease. She holstered her second blade. "She was fast," she said. "I've fought killers.

I've never fought anything like that." Archie nodded.

"We were lucky." "No," Mabel said. "We were good."

He didn't argue.

He looked over at Roxanne's body. Still slumped forward. Still bleeding. Still unmoving.

The knife remained buried in her chest. The fur around it soaked dark, matted and slick. Her limbs were limp. Her tail was still. She wasn't breathing. He exhaled again. A real breath this time. It was over. Then—A sound. Soft. Subtle. Barely audible. Stone scraping. Archie turned his head. Roxanne's paw twitched.

Once. Then again.

Mabel spun back, eyes narrowing. Eddie didn't move. Didn't speak. He couldn't. He stood there still as the stone beneath him watching.

The knife in her chest shifted slightly, not outward, but deeper like the body beneath it had started to breathe again.

And very slowly… Roxanne began to rise.

26

She wasn't standing yet. Her body moved with quiet precision, like the ticking of some ancient mechanism realigning itself after centuries of stillness. One paw braced against the floor. Her head tilted.

And then Her eyes opened. They weren't the same.

The irises glowed not with light, but with something deeper. Something buried. Like molten gold beneath obsidian. Something that didn't belong in this world.

Mabel stepped back. "Her eyes..."

Roxanne's expression didn't shift. She reached up slowly claws steady, unshaken and wrapped her paw around the hilt of the knife buried in her chest.

Archie couldn't look away.

The blade had sunk deep right through the heart. There was no question. And yet, as she pulled it free, the wound didn't spurt or spill. It yawned, then closed. They watched it.

The torn flesh pulled together. Muscle reformed. Fur regrew.

No scar. No blood. As if the blade had never touched her. She dropped the knife.

It struck the stone with a clatter that echoed too loudly in the chamber's stillness.

Then, she rolled her neck slow, deliberate until it cracked. A deep, feline stretch. Almost casual. Her voice came softly, but it carried.

"Now, my pets..." she said, eyes gleaming like something eternal. "Where were we?"

Roxanne tilted her head, eyes still glowing faintly in the dark.

"My dears..." she said, lips curling into a smile. "You look like you've seen a ghost." Then she stepped forward.

Each step cracked the stone beneath her paws not from weight, but pressure. Raw, controlled power. The ancient floor groaned in protest as fractures spidered out with every move.

Archie staggered back. He had seen her fight. He had seen her kill. But this? This was something else. Something that should not be.

"Stay back," Mabel warned, raising her blade again, though her voice trembled. Roxanne vanished.

Not completely invisibly but with such speed it felt like the world stuttered.

The knife that had been buried in her heart slammed into Mabel's shoulder, piercing flesh to the bone.

She screamed as Roxanne twisted it, her other paw striking down in a sharp arc.

Mabel's leg gave way. Bone cracked. Her knee shattered with a sound that made Archie flinch. Then Roxanne threw her hard.

Mabel's body hit the far wall and slid to the ground in a broken heap. Eddie roared and charged.

She turned without even facing him, stepped hard on his foot The crunch was unmistakable. His howl echoed through the chamber.

Before he could fall, she spun and kicked him full force in the chest.

He flew backwards, slamming into a stone pillar so hard it shook dust from the ceiling. He collapsed in a gasping heap, ribs broken, breath stolen. Then silence.

Only Archie remained standing, trembling, clutching the emerald sphere to his chest. Roxanne looked at him. Not angry. Not wild. Just cold.

"I won't let you have it," Archie said, voice raw. "You'll have to kill me."

She stepped forward, reached out, and lifted him like he weighed nothing.

Her claws wrapped around his throat.

Archie clawed at her arm, kicking, gasping. The artifact rolled from his paw and struck the floor with a soft thud. His vision blurred. Her grip tightened.

And still her expression was unreadable. Focused. Watching. Archie's voice cracked, half a sob, half a scream.

"You murdered her!"

He coughed, choking on his own breath.

"You killed Nora hunted us"

His claws scraped against her arm.

"You killed... my father..."

That stopped her.

Her ears flicked. Her grip loosened just slightly. Not enough to let him go. But enough to hear him. The glow in her eyes dimmed for just a second. Her silence said everything. She hadn't expected that. Roxanne didn't speak. Didn't blink.

She just stared at him, her glowing eyes unreadable, the pressure of her claws still locked around his throat. But her ears twitched. Her body went still. A moment passed. Then another. And just as suddenly as she'd lifted him she let go.

Archie dropped to the floor, hitting the stone hard, coughing and gasping, paw at his throat. The artifact rolled beside him, untouched. She didn't look down at him.

She turned away. Took a single step into the dark. Then paused.

Her head turned slightly just enough for him to see her face in profile.

There was something else there now. Not rage. Not triumph. A tear. One. It rolled down her cheek in silence.

"I didn't kill James," she said softly. *But I am responsible."* And then She was gone. No flash. No gust of wind. Just absence.

Archie lay there on the cold stone floor, surrounded by the aftermath. Mabel broken against the wall. Eddie unconscious in the dust.

And the emerald sphere gleaming quietly under the flicker of gaslight. The room was still.

Archie didn't move for a long moment. He lay there, throat raw, the imprint of her grip still burning into his fur. He didn't understand what had just happened. Not really.

A knife through the heart. A body that shouldn't have moved again. And yet she had risen eyes glowing, bones healing, speaking with grief in her voice. Mabel groaned from across the chamber.

Archie turned forcing himself upright, crawling toward her. *"Mabel"*

She was conscious, but only barely. Her shoulder was soaked in blood where the blade had struck, and her leg twisted in a way it should never twist. She looked up at him with dazed eyes.

"Did we... did we win?" she rasped.

Archie didn't know how to answer. He looked past her to where Eddie was slumped near the pillar, ribs crushed, breathing shallow but steady. The revolver still hung at his side, untouched. He hadn't even reached for it. They'd all frozen. They'd all seen something that defied reason.

Archie pushed himself to his feet. His paw trembled as he reached for the emerald sphere still sitting untouched on the stone pedestal at the room's center.

Its surface gleamed with unnatural polish. Dozens of facets, none the same size. He could almost see something moving within it a shimmer, like mist caught in glass. He wrapped it in cloth, cradled it like a relic. Then he looked back. No trace of Roxanne.

Not a sound. Not a whisper. Just silence, broken only by the drip of Mabel's blood on stone and the faint wheeze of Eddie's breath.

"We need to go," Archie said at last. His voice was hoarse, quiet. No one argued.

———

They found them by instinct more than plan.

Teddy had waited, pacing the far end of the street, hands shoved into his coat. Dolores sat on the front step, one eye on the fog, the other on the time. When Archie and the others didn't return by the hour mark, she stood up.

"Let's go," she said.

They made their way to Guildhall quietly, tension growing with every step. The front entrance was unlocked. The guards, gone. No sign of a struggle. Just silence.

It was Dolores who heard it first a low, ragged sound, almost a gasp, coming from inside. They followed the noise into the heart of the chamber. The sight stopped them cold.

Eddie lay near a broken pillar, blood crusted beneath his fur, breathing shallow. Mabel was slumped against the wall, her shoulder still bleeding, one leg twisted unnaturally beneath her. Archie was seated on the stone floor, back to the far wall, one paw clenched over his ribs, the other curled around the emerald sphere. His eyes were unfocused. He looked up, but didn't speak. *Dolores moved quickly.*

She darted outside and crossed the street to the old red payphone on the corner thankfully still working. She fed it two coins with shaking paws and dialed a number she hadn't used in years. The line clicked. "St. Aelred's," a tired voice answered. "Jess. It's Dolores." Silence, then: "Didn't expect to hear from you." "I'm calling in the favor." "Off-books?"
"Off-books. No records. No questions." The voice on the line paused, then said, "Where?" "Guildhall. Back entrance. Now."

Fifteen minutes later, an ambulance pulled up in the alley behind the building. No sirens. No lights. Two medics climbed out and moved fast no clipboards, no paperwork. Just stretchers and muscle memory.

The nurse in the passenger seat never even stepped inside. She met Dolores at the edge of the street, cigarette in one paw.

"You owe me dinner." Dolores managed a nod. "Make it two."

The team was loaded quickly. Archie tried to argue. Couldn't find the words. The artifact never left his grip.

The lights at St. Aelred's were soft, muted through the hallway glass. It was an older hospital— no digital buzz, no sterile shine. The kind of place built before everything was meant to look clean.

Archie sat beside Eddie's bed. His own ribs were wrapped tight beneath his coat, but he hadn't left the room since they brought them in.

Mabel was down the hall in recovery. Her leg had been reset. Her shoulder sewn. She hadn't woken up fully yet just muttered something about knives and monsters before slipping back under.

Teddy stood at the window, arms crossed, a crease between his brows.

Dolores sat near the foot of the bed, reading over the nurse's notes with a distant, troubled look. It had been nearly twelve hours since the fight.

A month would pass before any of them walked properly again. Archie rubbed his face, voice low and distant. "She died." Teddy turned, uncertain. "Who did?"

"Roxanne," Archie said. "Mabel stabbed her. Through the heart. I checked there was no pulse. No breath." He looked up at them. "And then she got back up." The room fell silent.

Dolores blinked, the words catching up with her. "She what?"

Archie nodded slowly. "I saw the knife. Still in her chest. I saw her fall. We all did." Teddy stared. "Archie, are you sure?"

"I'm sure," he said, cutting him off. "We watched her die."

He looked down at his hands. "And then we watched her stand back up like nothing happened."

Neither Teddy nor Dolores responded. They hadn't seen Roxanne. They hadn't witnessed the fight. What they saw now was their brother exhausted, wounded, and utterly convinced of something that should have been impossible.

"She's not normal," Archie whispered. "Whatever she is... she isn't like us."

He shifted his gaze toward the window, where the artifact rested on the sill, still wrapped in cloth. "And the worst part?" he said. "She didn't try to take it." Dolores tilted her head. "What do you mean?"

"She let us leave," Archie said. "She could've killed me. She didn't. She looked right at me and left."

Teddy stepped closer now, unsure. "So... this was her plan?"

Archie nodded once, slowly. "I think she wanted us to find it."

He turned back to the window. Sunset lit the edge of the cloth, revealing a glimmer of green where the emerald sphere lay hidden.

"She's been ahead of us the whole time."

27

The scent of smoke, long soaked into the curtains and floorboards, had been scrubbed out, replaced by lavender and pine. The walls had been patched, the glass replaced, and the hallway lights flickered on without a sputter. Teddy unlocked the front door and stepped aside.

Archie entered first, pausing in the doorway. His ribs still ached when he breathed too deep, but the bruises had mostly faded. The limp in his step was barely visible.

Behind him, Eddie moved with a careful gait, a thick brace strapped around his torso and a fresh scar peeking through the edge of his shirt. He didn't complain. He hadn't since they got out.

Dolores followed, setting her bag down near the stairs. She glanced toward the living room— the rug had been replaced. No blood. No shattered glass. Just a couch, a table, and a room that looked almost like it had before.

And Mabel her shoulder now bandaged in tight surgical wraps, a cane tucked under one arm—wandered toward the kitchen and peeked into the fridge like she owned the place. "You're cleared to walk?" Teddy asked.

"I'm cleared to sneak whiskey," she said. "So mind your business." Eddie chuckled, then winced as pain caught up to the laugh.

Archie opened the envelope in his coat pocket and held it up. "He wrote back," he said. Everyone turned.

He moved to the table and laid the folded letter flat, smoothing out the creases. It was Vince's handwriting slanted, sharp, and neat. The message was short.

Received your last correspondence. I've reread the symbols. Your instincts were right. It's not just a scroll. It's a map to something older.

I'll be waiting at the cabin when you arrive. Bring the artifact.

—V.

Archie folded it again. "He's in," he said. Dolores poured tea. "When do we leave?"

Archie looked at the others wounded, recovering, and still standing. "Soon." Dolores gave a small nod, then turned toward the kitchen. "Then let's eat properly tonight."

The pantry door creaked open as she stepped inside. This time, the shelves were full— restocked and organized with care. She pulled down a sack of arborio rice, imported mushrooms, a bottle of white wine, and fresh herbs in oil-sealed jars. Within minutes, she had the makings of something far more refined than the usual pantry fare.

"Mabel," she called, already chopping shallots with fluid precision, "put the whiskey down and help—if you're able."

Mabel, lounging with her cane resting beside her, groaned theatrically before rising. "Fine, but if I fall over, you're the one explaining it to the doctor."

She moved slowly, gripping the cane as she crossed the room. Her ears twitched as she took in the scent. "That garlic?"

Dolores nodded without looking up. "Risotto. With truffle oil and lemon zest. I'm not serving canned soup to a table full of survivors."

Mabel blinked. "You're doing risotto from scratch? That's bold." "I've made it before."

"I believe it," Mabel said, grabbing the bottle of wine and pouring a splash into the pan like she'd done it a hundred times.

The simmering mix filled the kitchen with warmth earthy, bright, and indulgent. Mabel leaned against the counter as Dolores stirred the rice, one paw confidently flicking a tasting spoon.

"You could cook in New York," Mabel said, watching her work. "Like the real New York. White tablecloths. Critics that wear gloves to dinner."

"I have no interest in critics," Dolores replied coolly. "Only flavor."

Mabel grinned. "Respect. Still… if I make a comeback, you're my first call." "You'd be lucky," Dolores muttered, hiding a smile.

Meanwhile, in the den, Eddie unfastened a small silver cigar case and held it open for Teddy and Archie. "Fumar," Teddy said, his brow raising. "That's the real stuff."

Archie leaned in. "From the lounge near the embankment?" "Same roll," Teddy confirmed. "Same label."

"You actually bought these?" Archie asked, eyeing Eddie with a mix of surprise and admiration. Eddie shrugged. "We almost died," Archie said.

"Exactly," Eddie added with a nod.

Teddy walked to the liquor cabinet and reached high for a tall bottle sealed with deep green wax. He brought it down and set it on the table with care. Archie's eyes widened. "Is that...?" Teddy gave a smug little nod. "IronFang Reserve." Archie blinked. "You own a bottle of IronFang Reserve?"

"Had it for years. Was saving it for something... monumental."

Eddie looked between them, confused. "Is that supposed to mean something?"

"It means," Archie said, almost reverently, "you're about to taste something older than you." Teddy chuckled. "And twice as smooth."

He popped the cork with a satisfying crack, and the aroma drifted out oak, spice, and a warmth that promised a rare kind of comfort.

He tipped the bottle carefully, letting the amber liquid flow in a smooth ribbon. It caught the light as it poured rich and golden, with the weight of age behind it. The scent deepened as it swirled into the first glass, then the next, until three perfect measures sat glowing on the table.

He handed one to Archie, then to Eddie, before claiming his own.

Archie held his glass up to the light for a moment, then took a slow sip. The warmth hit his tongue and spread across his chest like velvet and smoke.

"Still think we should've saved it for a birthday?" Teddy asked with a small grin. Archie shook his head. "No. Tonight's right."

They settled into the den fire crackling low, shadows climbing the walls. Dolores and Mabel soon joined them, each with a plate in hand, the risotto plated elegantly with shaved lemon peel and a drizzle of oil. Eddie passed around the cigars, cutting the ends with a quiet snap, and lit each one with the tiny torch he always kept tucked in his coat.

It wasn't loud, or festive. There was no laughter echoing through the rooms. But it was warm, and for the first time in weeks, safe.

They smoked and drank in silence for a long while, each lost in their own thoughts.

Finally, as the last of the wine was poured and the coals in the fireplace glowed like dying embers, Teddy leaned forward. "So," he said softly. "Tell us everything."

Archie looked to Mabel. She nodded once. Eddie set his glass down. It was one thing for one of them to say it.

But all of them?

Dolores leaned forward, her eyes serious. "What did you see?"

Archie exhaled slowly. "We stabbed her. Through the heart." Mabel continued, her voice flat. "And she got up."

"She didn't just get up," Eddie added. "She healed. Right in front of us." Teddy blinked. "You mean she survived the fight?"

"No," Archie said, shaking his head. "I mean she died. I saw the light leave her eyes. She wasn't breathing. There was no pulse."

"And then," Mabel said, "she stood. Like it never happened. Like she was just... waking up." The room fell quiet. Dolores looked from one face to another. "You're sure?" "We're sure," Archie replied.

Teddy leaned back, rubbing a paw down his face. "That doesn't make sense." "It's not supposed to," Archie said. "But it happened." They sat with that for a while. Then Dolores spoke again. "You said... she reacted to your father's name?"

Archie nodded. "I blamed her for his death. For Nora. She let me go. And then she vanished."

Mabel glanced sideways. "Vanished is a polite way of saying she moved faster than anything I've ever seen. And I've seen a lot." Eddie stared at the fire. "So what is she?" No one answered. Not yet.

Archie leaned forward, resting his elbows on his knees. "She didn't just flinch when I mentioned our father. It was deeper than that. Like I struck a nerve she didn't know was still there."

"She said she didn't kill him," Eddie added quietly. "But she said it like someone who's... carrying something. Guilt, maybe. Or regret." Teddy's brow furrowed. "Wait, what exactly did she say?"

Archie met his brother's eyes. "She looked me in the face, and said, *'I didn't kill James... but I am responsible.'* Then she vanished." A long silence. Dolores blinked slowly. "James. She used his name."

"She did," Archie confirmed. "She knew it. Not 'your father.' Not 'the professor.' She said James."

Mabel was staring at the bottom of her glass now. "She's not just some relic-chasing lunatic. She knew your father— personally." "How long ago?" Teddy asked.

Archie shook his head. "I don't know. But if what we saw is real—if she's truly... not like us— then maybe it wasn't just years ago. Maybe decades. Centuries." "No," Dolores whispered. "That's impossible."

Eddie looked at her. "We watched her come back from the dead."

"She's not a ghost," Mabel said. "She bled. She fought. She was real. But what's inside her— whatever that is—that's not normal."

"She's older than we understand," Archie said. "And stronger than we could've imagined. But she hesitated. She could've killed us, and she didn't. She was angry. But something held her back."

Teddy's jaw tightened. "You think she knew Dad... before he died? That maybe he was involved in something we never knew about?"

Mabel gave a slow, grim nod. "If James Chesterfield was chasing the same truth we were, then she was part of it—whether he knew what she really was or not."

Archie leaned back, staring up at the ceiling, the weight of that thought settling in his chest like a stone.

"She wasn't hunting the scroll. Not really. She was watching us. Letting us find it." Dolores said it aloud: "We helped her." The fire cracked. No one disagreed. The silence stretched long after the drinks were poured.

Teddy sat with his glass cradled in both paws, staring into the fire like he could force it to give him answers. Across from him, Archie shifted in his chair, the weight of the evening finally settling on his shoulders.

"I didn't think we'd survive," Teddy said eventually. "When you didn't come out of Guildhall... I thought we'd lost you."

Dolores rested a paw gently on his shoulder. "It was almost the worst."

No one spoke for a while. The kind of silence that followed near-death wasn't the kind you could fill with small talk.

Archie set his glass down, eyes dark. "I think she knew him." Teddy looked over. "Dad?"

Archie nodded. "Not just met him—knew him. Worked with him. Maybe even... trusted him once."

Mabel stirred. "I knew James," she said. "But I never really knew what he meant to her. Whatever it was... it ran deep."

They turned to her.

"She flinched," Mabel added. "When you said his name. Her expression changed. It wasn't rage. It was... guilt."

"She said she didn't kill him," Archie muttered. "But she was responsible."

Eddie leaned forward, rubbing his jaw. "What does that mean? She gave the order? Looked the other way?"

"She wasn't there," Archie said. "That's what she meant. By the time she found out, it was already done."
Dolores crossed her arms. "Would she have stopped it?"

Archie answered without looking up. "I think she wanted to." Nobody replied. The fire crackled.

"She looked at you like she'd seen a ghost," Mabel said at last. "Not when you fought her— before that. Back in the jungle. You said she watched you from the trees. I believe it. She wasn't just following us. She was... studying you." Eddie let out a low breath. "Maybe you remind her of him."
Archie didn't speak.

Teddy took a slow sip from his glass. "You think that's why she didn't finish it? You think she saw Dad in you?"

Archie stared at the flames. "I don't know. But I don't think she wanted me dead." That settled over them like a storm cloud. It was Mabel who finally broke the silence, her tone shifting. "She wanted the artifact removed." *Eddie blinked. "Say again?"*

"She's been to Guildhall before," Mabel said. "Think about it. That vault wasn't a mystery to her. She waited for us to do the hard part. She could've taken the scroll pieces long ago. She didn't need them."

"She needed us," Archie realized. "To trigger something. To unlock it."

Dolores stood quietly at the edge of the room, her paw still resting on the back of Teddy's chair. "But why? What does that sphere do?"

"That's what Vince is going to help us figure out," Archie said. Teddy looked up. "And if it's worse than we thought?"

Archie didn't flinch. "Then we stop her."

28

Paris wore its history like perfume —
clinging to every shuttered window, every cobbled alleyway,
every whisper beneath a streetlamp. Roxanne stepped from the
car with the kind of silence that suggested she hadn't opened
the door so much as willed herself outside.

The wind stirred her coat, a tailored piece of charcoal
wool that shifted like water when she moved. Her padded paws
made no sound against the old stone street. Her tail flicked
once, then stilled.

The manor loomed ahead, draped in scaffolding and
shadows. The Hollowed Coin's Parisian outpost was weeks
from public opening, though the true work had already begun
behind its false front — an art restoration institute, complete
with forged grants and a generous endowment from a museum
that didn't exist.

She paused at the threshold, amber eyes scanning the structure. Her pupils narrowed in the dark — a vertical slit adapting to every line and lie it found.

"It will hold," Sabine said from behind her, voice soft but firm. "They built it exactly to your instructions."

Roxanne gave a small nod. She didn't speak, just turned her muzzle angled slightly toward the light, catching the gold in her fur. Sabine, taller and broader in frame, still moved with the deference of someone who knew her place in the food chain.

They passed through the heavy doors and into a smaller salon lined with tapestries older than France itself. The room smelled of lemon oil, iron, and varnish things scrubbed over secrets.

The two new council members stood as Roxanne entered. A formality. One did it with a calm elegance. The other did it with barely disguised defiance.

Dr. Lysandre Mercier was trim, composed, dressed in a sleek storm-gray coat that offset the silver streaks in his ears and whiskers. He blinked once, slowly — a gesture of thought, not fatigue.

Adelina "Della" Kovacevic was carved from different stone. Compact and muscled beneath a dark military jacket, her fur was pale at the edges and marked by a thin scar that sliced through her right brow. Her tail flicked once behind her chair. Her claws did not retract. Neither spoke first.

Roxanne walked to the head of the table, each step smooth and silent. She did not sit. "You've both been briefed." It wasn't a question.

Mercier gave a shallow nod. Della folded her forelegs, claws just slightly visible where they curled over her sleeves.

Sabine, standing just to the side, let out a slow breath the only one who seemed aware that the room's temperature had dropped by several degrees.

"Your operations here," Roxanne continued, "are not independent. You do not lead in isolation. You act under banner and seal."

"We were told we'd have autonomy," Della cut in, tone edged with cold defiance. Her ears didn't twitch. "We don't answer to intermediaries."

Sabine stepped forward, expression unreadable.

"You'll answer to me until you prove yourself," she said calmly. Della didn't blink. Her voice sharpened.

"I don't report to someone who hasn't earned my respect." In the space between words, Roxanne moved.

One moment, she stood beside the chair. The next, she was behind Della her paw already on the backrest, pressing down. Not with force. With certainty.

The chair creaked under Della's weight as her body lowered involuntarily. Not from a strike. Just from the truth of who stood behind her. Roxanne's paw never trembled. Her expression never changed.

Della froze. Her tail flicked. The chair groaned and then settled.

"Respect," Roxanne said quietly, her breath close to Della's ear, "is not a condition of survival. Obedience is." She stepped back as if nothing had happened, her paws utterly silent as she returned to her place at the table's head. Della remained seated. Quiet now.

Mercier cleared his throat delicately, realigning the conversation.

"You must understand," he said, "our hesitation is not resistance. Only caution. The Hollowed Coin is expanding rapidly. Control must follow clarity."

"Then let me be clear."

Roxanne's forepaws rested lightly on the polished table. The claw tips did not unsheath, but they hovered just beneath the surface.

"I did not build this for debate. I built it to last. And that requires obedience."

Sabine stepped forward at last, the pressure in the room loosening just enough to allow breath.

"Roxanne," she said softly, "invited you not just to meet. But to be seen. She does not grant audiences lightly." Roxanne watched them both.

"Sabine speaks for me in Paris," she added. "And where her words fail, mine will be heard." For a long moment, no one moved.

Then, imperceptibly, Mercier inclined his head. Della gave the smallest nod. It would do for now.

The manor's central wing was still unfinished. Light fixtures lay half-installed. Wood crates stacked against raw plaster walls. But the wide inner courtyard was cleared and humming with activity.

Uniformed security personnel paced the inner perimeter. A shipment of encrypted ledgers had arrived from Vienna that morning, guarded by low-level operatives still green to the Paris terrain.

Roxanne and Sabine stood on the second-floor balcony that overlooked the entire courtyard — an arched stone terrace framed by ivy-stripped columns. The vantage point gave them an unobstructed view of the operation below.

Most of the operatives didn't even realize she was there. They knew only the silhouette. The tail. The gold-ringed eyes watching from above. Whispers called her "the Architect", though no one used the name to her face.

At first, she didn't react to the raised voices beneath them.

Two guards — both Hollowed Coin, both recently transferred — stood nose to nose near the loading dock. A disagreement over patrol routes. Territory. Posturing. Sabine, beside her, turned at the noise. "Should I" "No."

The argument escalated. One guard shoved the other. The second retaliated a jab to the shoulder. Then a snarl, a tackle. The sound of claws on concrete. Dozens of heads turned. And then Roxanne moved. One moment, she was beside Sabine.

The next she was there. On the ground. Between them. It wasn't teleportation. It wasn't magic. It was speed that defied physics.

Sabine blinked, muscles tensing too late. She looked down at the now-empty space beside her, her eyes wide. She had seen Roxanne fight. She had seen her kill. But this   This was not that. This was impossible.

Below, Roxanne's paw shot forward, catching the closest guard mid-swing. She stopped his blow midair — without bracing, without shifting her weight.

His entire body locked in place. Her grip didn't tighten. It didn't have to. Her voice was quiet.

"You've mistaken this place for something common."

The courtyard fell dead silent.

The second guard the one still crouched began to rise, tail twitching in instinctive fear. She turned to him. *"Stand."* He obeyed. She released the first, letting his paw drop like dead weight.

Roxanne stepped back and looked at them both but her voice carried to everyone now.

"If you want to challenge chain of command, do it in an arena. If you want to question orders, file them through the liaison. If you want to fight in my house"

She met both their eyes in turn. A stillness settled in the air. Primal. Electric.

"You can do it bleeding in the street."

Neither spoke.

She gestured to one of the senior operatives on a third-floor balcony overhead.

"Reassign them. Separately. Patrol shifts at opposite hours. If they cross paths again without authorization, remove them." No one argued.

The crowd began to dissolve, heads down, ears flattened in quiet acknowledgment. But the whispers were already spreading like smoke. "How did she?" "Wasn't she just" "I didn't think she actually existed."

Up on the balcony, Sabine hadn't moved. She stared at the courtyard where Roxanne had landed. That wasn't reflex. That wasn't technique. That was something else.

She exhaled and when she turned, Roxanne was standing beside her again. No sound. No warning. Just there. As if she'd never left. Sabine didn't speak. Didn't ask.

"It's going to be a productive month," she murmured, half to herself.

Roxanne didn't answer. Her eyes glinted with something colder than approval.

She wasn't here to oversee Paris. She was here to remind it who built the walls.

Later That Evening — Paris

The gala was held in a repurposed museum space near the Seine — one of the Hollowed Coin's quieter investments. The event, on its surface, celebrated the patronage of art conservation in the city. Below that, it was a signal flare to allies, operatives, and silent partners: Paris is ours now.

Roxanne stood near the edge of the grand hall, her fur brushed smooth, her coat tailored but subdued. She wore no jewels, no rank insignia, no visible mark of power. She didn't need to.

Sabine was in her element making introductions, accepting praise, guiding conversations. When anyone asked about Roxanne, she gave a knowing smile and said only: "She's visiting. A patron of sorts."

Most didn't question it. A few tried to introduce themselves.

A minor state minister from Marseille, a sleek-coated silver tabby with too-bright eyes, approached with a half-bow. "I've seen your photo before, I think in an article about transnational firms and... logistics. Geneva, maybe?"

Roxanne turned her head just slightly. Not enough to dismiss him. Just enough to remind him she hadn't invited the conversation. "Unlikely," she said. "I'm rarely photographed."

The minister blinked, mumbled something about mistaken identity, and excused himself with a polite smile that didn't reach his ears.

Later, a gallery director with diplomatic credentials offered her champagne.

"You're not part of the restoration council, are you? I could've sworn I saw you in a piece about legacy funders.

The older families. You have that... presence."

"It's a trick of the lighting," Roxanne replied, her voice calm, her gaze unmoving.

The director laughed nervously and vanished into the next conversation. She didn't smile. She didn't need to.

Her presence worked like gravity. She didn't push people away they simply veered off.

A string quartet played something slow and romantic in the far corner. Crystal clinked. Politicians and collectors moved through the candlelit haze, making deals they would not remember the details of come morning.

Eventually, Roxanne crossed to the bar a temporary installation set into the corner of the great hall, framed by cut glass and ironwork. The bartender was young, but quiet-eyed. He didn't flinch when she approached. That alone was rare. "A particular vintage, madam?" he asked.

She tapped a single claw on the wine list not at the offerings, but the margins. "In the cabinet behind you. Second shelf. *The '77 Le oville.*" The bartender paused.

"The Saint-Julien?" he asked carefully. "That's... not on tonight's menu." "It's still yours to open."

He hesitated only a breath longer, then obeyed pulling the bottle out with reverent care. A cork older than he was. A label faded at the edges. He poured a single glass. "It's a rare choice." "It's not a celebration." "Then may I ask... what it is?" She looked at the wine but didn't touch it. "A tradition."

Then she turned and walked away, the glass following her on a silver tray. No one stopped her. Not even Sabine.

She slipped from the main hall through an unmarked service door and followed a narrow staircase up to a private terrace one that hadn't been part of the evening's itinerary.

Paris sprawled before her. Lights along the river. Boats cutting black lines through gold.

The barkeep had left the tray neatly on a nearby table. She picked up the glass and carried it to the edge. She didn't toast. She didn't smile.

She just stared out over the city, the glass untouched in her paw. And then

The memory came.

Not like a dream. Not like a ghost. Like a door she opened herself.

———

Many Years Ago, London

It had rained earlier that evening, and the city wore it still clinging to the pavement and rolling in off the Thames. The hotel was discreet, old enough to have forgotten who owned it, and its bar was hidden behind a velvet curtain and a wall of unlabeled books. You didn't stumble into it. You had to be invited.

Roxanne sat in the far corner, one paw curled around a glass of whiskey, her posture relaxed but alert. Her coat was dark, her fur sleek, her presence like a shadow that had simply decided to sit.

James Chesterfield arrived late.

He always did never out of disrespect, just with the persistent arrogance of a man who believed time would wait for him. He stepped in from the London night, coat damp at the hem, and shook off the rain like an old friend.

"And here I thought you'd finally stood me up," he said, pulling off his gloves with that familiar grin tired, sharp, a little crooked.

"Tempting," Roxanne said. "But I've always had a fondness for lost causes."

He smiled at that. Sat across from her without asking. Their conversations had never needed permission.

"This place hasn't changed," he said, glancing around at the firelit walls and silent staff. "Still smells like a crypt with better liquor." "That's what you liked about it." "I liked the company," he said. Then, more quietly: "Still do."

They drank. Talked. Laughed more than she expected to. For a moment, it almost felt like something close to peace two predators at rest. But James had never been able to leave well enough alone.

"I've been thinking," he said after a while, rolling his glass between his paws. "About life. About the boys."
"Still small, aren't they?" Roxanne asked.

"Archie's clever. Teddy's softer. Olivia says I'm gone too much." "She's right." "She usually is." He gave a short laugh. Drank. His gaze turned sharp again. "You've never told me what it is you really do." "And you've never truly asked."

"I'm asking now."

Roxanne didn't answer right away. She studied him. The lines in his face. The silver starting to creep into the edges of his whiskers. He had aged. She had not. That, too, had once frightened him. But not anymore.

"You know what I do," she said. "You just don't want to name it."

"I know the Hollowed Coin. I know it stretches farther than anyone understands. I know it doesn't die, and neither do its stories." He leaned in.

"I've found records. Before the war. Before the last one. Mentions of you or someone who could be you in cities that no longer exist." Roxanne tilted her head. Didn't blink. "Do you think I'm that old?"

"I think," he said slowly, "that you're older than you want anyone to realize." "And what would you do with that truth, James?"

"I don't know," he admitted. "I just know you've survived things I can't explain."

His voice was quiet now. Almost reverent. But what came next was not praise.

"I don't like what you've become. But I've never wished you were someone else."

That landed heavier than she expected.

Because years ago, long before this bar, long before whiskey and quiet questions they had fought. *He had tried to kill her once.*

Bucharest. A monastery half-swallowed by ash and fog. He had tracked her across borders and ruins, acting on orders he would later come to question. She had warned him, back then. But he hadn't listened.

And in the middle of that broken stone sanctuary, he had struck her. Cracked a rib. Nearly dislocated her shoulder.

She hadn't killed him.

But she had made sure he never forgot what it meant to draw his blade on her.

The injury had healed. His memory of it had not. Nor hers.

You were the only one who ever marked me, she thought. The only one I ever let close enough to do it.

Now his son had stood before her bloody, accusing, screaming her name like it was a curse. Like she hadn't tried to keep the sins of the father buried and untouched. She didn't respond to James's words. Not directly.

Instead, she stood. Left the glass half-full. Gave him a look that said too much and nothing at all. She was across the Channel by sunrise. *And later that night, James Chesterfield was dead.*

Back on the Paris balcony, Roxanne's paw tightened around her glass. The wine sat untouched.

The city beneath her burned gold and silent, a sprawl of light that had forgotten him entirely. *But she hadn't.*

She still felt the old pain when she shifted her weight not from the wound, but from where it once lived. That bone-deep memory. The blow he landed. The one moment he had her vulnerable, exposed, real. You always did see more than I wanted you to, she thought.

And now his son carried that same fire reckless, untamed, wounded.

She hated it. Hated that Archie had his voice. His anger. His grief. Hated that when he called her monster, it almost sounded like James. I didn't hate you, she thought. I just didn't know how to keep you. The tears came without warning. Not loud. Not broken. Just... steady.

She leaned forward against the stone railing, the wine glass held loose in her paw. Her tail curled tightly around her ankles. Her shoulders shook once, then again. She cried without sound. Without shame. No one saw her. No one but Paris.

And Paris as always said nothing.

29

The plane touched down just before sunrise. A hard landing the kind that rattled teeth and made even seasoned travelers pause. Snow clung to the edges of the runway, and the mountains beyond looked less like a backdrop and more like a warning.

They had left London behind without fanfare. No authorities. No statements. No headlines. Just bruises, questions, and the weight of a choice none of them quite understood yet.

By the time Archie and the others made it through customs and into the narrow terminal, the sun was barely a suggestion behind the ridgeline.

Teddy's contact a soft-spoken marmalade tom in a wool-lined vest met them with a rented jeep and a thermos of thick coffee. He drove them up the narrow roads without asking questions, speaking only once to confirm: "Cabin's still there. Weather's holding. For now."

They made the rest of the climb on paw. The village that waited near the edge of the valley had no name printed on any map. Only locals and cartographers knew it existed.

Teddy's house or what passed for one stood near the center. Stone and timber, tucked between wind-worn cliffs. Simple. Cold. Safe. They unpacked in silence. No one had slept much.

A few hours later...

Teddy's house smelled like wool and lemon oil the kind of clean that came from too much energy and not enough stillness. Dolores sat cross-legged on the living room floor, her backpack open and overflowing. Mabel lay nearby on the rug, her tail flicking as she squinted at a hand-drawn copy of the mountain route. Eddie had fallen asleep on the windowsill; tail curled under his chin. Only Archie moved with purpose.

He packed without speaking efficient, quiet, methodical. Books. Maps. The scroll. The nowunified pieces stored in a reinforced case and wrapped in layers of cloth. His coat was already on, collar turned up, ears slightly back.

"Food's sorted," Teddy said, stepping into the room with a large, insulated pack. "I triple-checked the elevation charts too. We're not going above the tree line until the third leg."

Archie gave a low hum. Approval, maybe. Or preoccupation.

Dolores stood, brushing fur off her trousers. "We really going to do this? Hike halfway across the Himalayas to a cabin no one's ever seen, following clues none of us fully understand?" "Pretty much," Teddy said. "Great." Mabel didn't look up. "I think it's exciting." Archie finally paused long enough to meet her eyes. "It will be cold. It will be long. It will be dangerous." "You forgot haunted," she said dryly. He didn't smile. But he didn't disagree either.

Outside, wind rattled the shutters. The storm hadn't hit yet, but it was coming. Vince had called in hours earlier grounded, waiting it out in a village two valleys over. He'd join them once it cleared. Archie stood, pulling his pack over one shoulder. "I'm leaving tonight."

Teddy frowned. "What? No, you should wait. The storm"

"I know the terrain. I want a night alone. Before everything changes." That silenced the room. No one argued.

They helped him finish packing in silence. A few more provisions. A compass. A second scarf. Dolores handed him a small tin of matches. "Don't get yourself killed." "I won't," Archie said.

Mabel padded forward and nudged his shoulder. "We'll be right behind you." He nodded. Then turned.

The front door opened with a gust of wind that pulled at his coat and pushed cold into the house. He stepped into it without hesitation.

They watched him walk down the hill, his figure shrinking against the rising white. And then he was gone. The climb had been harder than he remembered.

The air thinner, the trail steeper, the cold biting deeper into his coat. The trees had thinned as he rose, giving way to sharp ridge-line and white. Clouds clung to the cliffs like old ghosts.

By the time Archie reached the cabin, his legs ached, and his breath came in short, sharp pulls. It was still there. Unchanged.

A simple stone structure tucked between two jagged rises, half buried in snow, just as he'd left it years ago. No one came this far unless they were running from something or toward it. He pushed the door open. The hinges groaned in protest. Inside: silence. The good kind.

He lit the fire first, then the lamps. He unpacked slowly, one item at a time. The scroll case. The journal. The emerald sphere, wrapped in dark cloth, cool to the touch. And then he sat.

The wind howled through the peaks as Archibald Chesterfield struck a match with shaking fingers. The end of his pipe flared to life, casting a faint orange glow across his tired face. The fire crackled low in the hearth behind him, barely pushing back the chill that crept through the old cabin's stones.

On the table sat James's journal, worn and frayed at the edges. Beside it lay the scroll whole now. Two halves, reunited. The secrets no longer hidden. And tucked behind them, glinting faintly in the firelight, the emerald sphere.

It didn't hum. It didn't glow. It just sat there ancient, perfect, and impossibly still. Archie stared at it for a long time.

He thought of Nora.

Of her laugh. Her steady hands. The moment she slipped the key into his coat pocket without saying a word.

He tightened his grip on the pipe. And then there was *Roxanne*.

There had been a moment just one when he'd thought it was finished.

But she was still out there. Somewhere. Watching. Waiting.

He shifted in the wooden chair, the bones in his back aching from the climb. Outside, snow battered the windows. The others would arrive soon, once the roads cleared. Mabel, Eddie, Teddy, Dolores. Even Vince. All of them coming because he'd asked. Because there was still one truth left to face. Not long ago, he'd been a professor chasing footnotes. Now he was something else.

He exhaled, smoke curling like a ghost in the firelight, and rested a paw on the closed scroll.

Tomorrow, if the storm broke, he'd hike down the mountain and meet Vince before the others arrived. Just a few more hours of quiet of solitude before the final chapter began. The fire had gone out hours ago.

Archie stirred from a shallow sleep, still seated in the wooden chair, his neck stiff, one paw curled loosely over the table's edge. Outside, the wind had stilled. The storm had passed.

He rose slowly, joints protesting, and gathered only what he needed water, a flare, and a small tin of jerky. His coat was heavy with frost. He pulled the collar up, brushed a layer of ash from his whiskers, and stepped out into the cold.

The air outside was sharper than before. Clearer.

The sky above was an ocean of blue, the snow below unbroken. Trees stood like sentries in the hush. The world felt... paused.

The path down from the cabin wound along the southern ridge narrow and unforgiving, a shelf of stone threaded through the trees. Archie moved with precision, paws finding purchase through instinct more than vision. The snow was knee-deep in places, the ice whispering beneath each step.

He reached the rendezvous point just before noon a small flat of packed earth near a frozen stream. The stillness there reminded him of a cathedral. Even the birds hadn't returned yet. Then: movement.

A figure coming up through the break in the trees. Slower than usual. One ear dipped low against the cold. But unmistakable. *Vince.*

His fur was dusted white, clinging to his coat in clumps. His tail twitched with each step, flicking snow behind him. His whiskers were frosted. A scarf was pulled high over his muzzle, and his breath came in short clouds but the glint in his green eyes hadn't dulled at all. Archie felt something loosen in his chest. "There you are," he said, voice rough from the cold.

Vince slowed as he reached him, panting lightly. His paw pads left soft, staggered prints behind him.

"Didn't think I'd find the place," Vince said, tugging down the scarf. "Snow swallowed every landmark I had.

Thought I overshot the ridge."

Archie took a step forward. Not to help just to see him closer. Just to be sure. "You made it," he said. "That's enough."

Vince gave a low, rumbling laugh and shook the snow from his ears. "You look like hell." "You look worse."

They didn't embrace. Didn't need to. But their tails flicked in a way that mirrored each other — small, involuntary gestures. Old instincts. Friendship expressed in feline shorthand. "The others?" Vince asked. "They'll follow tomorrow. Weather's holding." "And the scroll?" Archie turned toward the trail. "You'll see it soon enough." They climbed back in silence.

Side by side, their breath rising in twin columns. Vince kept pace, despite the altitude. His coat caught the wind like a banner, a dark streak in the white world.

By the time they reached the cabin again, the sun had dipped low behind the ridge.

Archie opened the door and stepped inside. The room still smelled of old smoke and stone.

The emerald sphere sat on the table, still as ever. The scroll lay beside it, sealed tight. James's journal rested on top, open to a page Vince couldn't yet see. Archie walked to the hearth and struck a match. "Rest up," he said, softer now.

"Tomorrow we begin."

Vince dropped his pack near the door, stretching out with a groan, claws flexing against the floorboards. "I'm just glad to see you in one piece," he muttered.

Archie didn't answer. But his ears twitched slightly a signal. Heard. Understood. He sat down, pipe in paw, and watched the fire catch again.

The fire had caught now, low but steady. Archie sat on one end of the old bench, legs stretched out, pipe curling faint wisps of smoke toward the rafters. Vince had slouched into the armchair across from him, paws thawing near the hearth, coat unbuttoned just enough to show the edge of his scarf still damp from snow.

The cabin creaked as it settled into warmth slow, hollow echoes in old timber. Vince glanced at the table, then back at Archie. "You're quiet tonight," he said. "Even for you."

Archie tapped the pipe once against the edge of the tray, then took a slow draw. "It's been a long road." "We've had longer."

Archie didn't answer. His eyes flicked toward the scroll case, then to James's journal.

"Tell me something," he said, voice low and steady. "Have you ever heard of a group called the Hollowed Coin?" Vince sat up slightly. One ear twitched.

"The Hollowed Coin? Maybe. Old rumors. Cairo, Tangier, Paris once. No one ever seemed to have a clear picture. Just shadows. Whispers." Archie nodded faintly.

"They're real. Organized. Old. And they've been behind more than we realized."

Vince followed his eyes to the emerald sphere resting on the table. "This all ties back to them?"

"Most of it."

Vince let out a low whistle. "Hell of a revelation to drop after tea."

Archie didn't answer. He poured two mugs in silence, handed one over, then sat again. The steam drifted between them, warm and faintly floral. After a pause, Vince asked carefully: "You said we lost someone."

Archie's ears shifted. He held the mug in both paws, gaze distant. *"Her name was Nora."*

Vince tilted his head, thoughtful. He didn't recognize the name and wisely didn't pretend to. "Friend of yours?" Archie nodded slowly.

"She didn't belong in any of this," he said. "But she came anyway." "Because of you?"

"Because she believed in what we were doing. Even when I wasn't sure I did." The silence that followed was full. Not strained just honest. "I'm sorry," Vince said. "So am I."

They sat with it not the grief, exactly, but the shape grief had left behind.

Eventually, Vince leaned back with a low exhale, stretching until his spine cracked and his claws flexed against the floorboards. "We'll figure it out," he said. "Whatever this is." Archie gave a quiet nod. "We always do." Vince flicked his tail once, settling deeper into the chair.

"I mean it. You've come this far. Hell, I'm here now. That counts for something." The fire burned on.

And for a little while longer, Archie watched it not for warmth, but for memory.

30

The door creaked open just before noon. Snow spilled in behind them, cold and blinding, before Dolores kicked it shut with a grunt. Teddy shrugged off his coat, fur matted from the climb, while Mabel helped Eddie ease out of his harness. They were soaked, wind-chapped, and exhausted — but alive.

Vince straightened from the hearth, brushing soot from his paws. Archie stood at the long table, waiting for them, firelight catching the edge of his coat. The scroll case sat in front of him, beside the emerald sphere. His eyes softened as he took them in. "You made it."

Teddy grunted. "Barely. Trail was frozen over past the ridge. We walked the last mile." "You're lucky I prepped the steps," Vince muttered. "I nearly slid off the damn cliff this morning."

Mabel gave Archie a look as she unwound her scarf. "You didn't doubt we'd come, did you?" "Not for a second," Archie said, and meant it.

Dolores stepped past the fire, her sharp eyes locking onto the scroll. "So. That's it?" "That's it," Archie replied. "The scroll. And James's notes." "Is it translated yet?" Eddie asked.

"Not yet," Archie said. "I couldn't read part of it. But Vince can."

Vince raised a brow, already stepping toward the table. "You really waited on me to crack the thing open?" "Didn't trust anyone else," Archie said simply.

Vince smirked, rolled his shoulders, and opened the scroll. The ancient paper unfurled like a breath, soft and dry, the ink faded but still visible. Symbols wound through the center, some in recognizable Aztec glyphs, others far older rougher, etched with meaning layered over centuries. *The group gathered close.*

"Alright," Vince muttered. "Let's see what your mystery map says." He read aloud, translating as he went.

"The artifact you seek was once known as the Wheel of Echoes. Forged not in worship, but in warning. It remembers what was... and makes whole what was broken." His brow furrowed as he scanned further.

"Those who hold its keys may turn the Wheel. With each turn, memory bends. What once was truth may fall to silence."

Archie leaned in. "That line. There that name." Vince squinted. *"The bearer of the second key... Es'Tara."* He looked up. "That name's old. Pre-empire. Root dialect. You're saying that's Roxanne?" Archie nodded once. "That was her name long ago. Before she was Roxanne. Before any of us knew what she was." Vince blinked. "Hold on. Are you telling me she's still alive?" "Not just alive," Dolores said quietly. "She's still running the Hollowed Coin."

Vince gave a short, incredulous laugh. "Come on. No one lives that long. That's" "I stabbed her," Mabel said, voice sharp and clear. "In London. At the Guildhall." Everyone turned to her. She didn't flinch.

"I watched the blade go in. Watched her fall. And then..." She swallowed.

"She got up. Healed in seconds. And then tore through us like we were nothing."

Vince fell silent, the disbelief on his face slowly giving way to something closer to dread. "So... she's immortal?" Archie didn't answer.

Vince looked back at the scroll, reading slower now. The weight had shifted.

"Es'tara Roxanne she didn't guard the Wheel. She turned it. Each artifact... it calls to her. Not to protect it. To use it."

Teddy spoke for the first time since entering. "To do what?" "To change things," Archie said. "The past. The future. Whatever she wants."

"She's rewriting history," Dolores added. "Shaping it in her image." Mabel stepped forward. "And we've already helped her." Vince looked at the emerald sphere on the table. "We've only got one artifact. Just the sphere."

"That's all we've removed," Archie confirmed. "The scroll isn't one of them. It's just the instruction manual." "So if she gets the others..." Vince trailed off. Archie answered for him. "The Wheel turns. And history forgets what it once knew." Vince read the next line aloud, quieter now.

"When the final key is turned, the world will not remember the one before it." They stood there in silence.

The fire cracked in the hearth. Snow slid from the roof above. Outside, the mountains held their breath.

Inside the cabin, time seemed to still and then begin to move again, in a direction no one yet understood. They didn't speak much after that.

Vince rolled the scroll back into its case with deliberate care. No one stopped him. No one needed to. The cabin was quiet again, save for the wind pressing against the windows and the fading crackle of fire.

"We need more," Vince finally said. "More context. More information. If this Wheel is real — if it's really what you think it is then we need to know who built it, how it works, and what happens when all the keys are turned." "Agreed," Archie said quietly. Vince looked at him, ears angled slightly back. "And this Roxanne or Es'tara you're convinced they're the same?" Mabel didn't move. "We are."

Vince didn't argue. He didn't believe it, not completely. But he could tell they weren't guessing.

They'd seen something. Something that left a mark on all of them. So instead, he just nodded.

"Alright," he said. "Then we keep going."
They left the next morning.

By midday, the storm had fully broken, and the team split off to rest, recover, and regroup. The mountain air thinned behind them as they descended. It was the last time they would all be together until the next call came until history called them back into its grip.

For now, Archie returned to London.

It was early evening when he stepped into his flat, his coat damp with drizzle and paws aching from the train. Everything looked the same. The kettle still hung on its hook. The scent of firewood and old tobacco lingered in the rug.

He loosened his scarf, set down his satchel, and turned toward the study and froze. There, hanging on the far wall, was the painting. The one that had been stolen from the museum. The one that had set everything in motion.

It hadn't been there when he left. He was sure of it. He took a slow step forward, eyes locked on the canvas. It was clean, pristine — carefully mounted, perfectly lit. But the longer he stared, the more the warmth drained from his limbs.

There, staring back at him, half-blurred by shadow and candlelight, was a feline figure. Her eyes looked directly at him.

Even in paint, she seemed aware of him. A smirk played at the corner of her lips — knowing, amused. As if she'd been waiting to be found. "No..." Archie whispered, his breath catching.

His paw trembled as he turned to his desk. A piece of parchment lay folded on the surface, cream-colored and impossibly crisp. He opened it.

I expected you to have discovered this sooner.
In any case, Archibald Chesterfield...
The Wheel now turns and it's all thanks to you.

Enjoy this gift. You might find something familiar about it.

— R

He staggered a step back. The painting seemed to loom.

The candlelight flickered, and for a moment, her eyes Roxanne's eyes seemed to follow him. His heartbeat once. Twice. "It was her," he breathed.

The air in the flat suddenly felt too thin. Too quiet. A chill rolled through him not from cold, but from realization. From fear. She hadn't just returned the painting. She'd left him a message. She had been there from the start.

And the next move... was already hers.

Epilogue

The elevator chimed softly. Roxanne stepped out into the muted hush of the hotel corridor, her pawprints silent against polished marble. Sabine followed at a measured pace, her dark coat still speckled with rain. The air smelled faintly of lilac and stone polish sterile, expensive, forgettable. This was not a hotel chosen for comfort.

The staff hadn't questioned the reservation. No one ever did when Sabine handled the arrangements.

They moved together, silent, until Sabine broke it. "You could've stayed somewhere closer." Roxanne didn't glance back. "I don't need to be close."

They reached the suite. Sabine swiped the card and held the door open. "Did he receive it?" Roxanne asked, stepping through. Sabine nodded. "Yes. I left it exactly where he would see it." "Good. He'll be home any minute."
Sabine lingered in the doorway. Roxanne turned to face her now, one brow raised. "Something on your mind?"

Sabine hesitated. "I... just didn't expect you to return. Not like this."

"Few ever do." She unfastened her coat and handed it off. "But the Wheel has turned. And the last time it did, we were caught unaware. I won't allow that again."

Sabine accepted the coat. "Of course." "You may go."

Another pause. Sabine opened her mouth, as if to ask something—then thought better of it. She gave a slight bow and slipped away, the door whispering shut behind her. The room fell into a perfect silence.

Roxanne stood alone in the penthouse suite, its high glass walls revealing the full sprawl of London below. Lights blinked in the mist. Trains shimmered across steel bridges. The Thames cut its familiar black line through the maze of streets. Most would find the view romantic. But Roxanne was looking for something else.

She crossed the room slowly, trailing a paw along the edge of a velvet chair, and stepped to the sideboard. A crystal tray sat waiting. She selected a tall glass and poured the champagne. No rush. No nerves. The fizz crackled softly as it rose. She brought the glass to her lips but did not drink.

Instead, she turned to the window.

Far across the city miles away, lost in fog and rooftops was Archibald Chesterfield's flat. To anyone else, it would be a speck. A silhouette. Indistinguishable. To her, it was crystal clear. She blinked, and the city sharpened.

Every pane of glass. Every brick. Every flicker of movement behind curtains. Her eyes adjusted not like a lens, but like an instinct. As if her very bones remembered how to see the world as it truly was.

The gift had awakened slowly, but now it was effortless. A sight not bound by distance or obstruction. A gaze unblinking, inescapable. Archibald stepped through his front door. Roxanne raised the glass in silence.

He paused just inside the entrance, dripping with rain, coat sagging on his shoulders. He looked older than she remembered thinner around the eyes. Tired.

She watched as he moved further inside. He hadn't seen the painting yet. "Curious," she murmured. A single flick of her claw, and the view tightened.

She could see the frayed edge of the parchment on his desk. The dried wax seal, unbroken. The slow turn of his head as he spotted the frame on the wall. He froze.

Her smile grew.

He took two steps toward the painting. Stared. Stared harder. *And then... recognition.* He reached for the note.

Roxanne tilted her glass slightly in salute. *"You always were a bit slow on the reveal, Archibald. But I do admire your persistence."* He opened the parchment. His lips moved as he read.

I expected you to have discovered this sooner. In any case, Archibald Chesterfield... The Wheel now turns and it's all thanks to you. Enjoy this gift. You might find something familiar about it.

— R

He staggered back, tail bristling. From her vantage, she could see the exact moment his breath caught. The moment he knew. Roxanne finally took a sip of the champagne.

It was French. Perfectly chilled. A bottle from a private vineyard she'd once commissioned a century ago. Still exquisite.

She turned from the window, only slightly. Enough to let the firelight from a faraway flat reflect off the glass.

Her eyes glowed softly, subtly. Not with magic. Not with rage. With sight.

A quiet, dreadful knowing. She had seen him. She had always seen him. And now, he had seen her.

The game had never ended. The first move was merely... delayed.

Roxanne raised her glass once more, not in toast, but in declaration. "Let's see what you do next."

She turned away from the window entirely. Behind her, Archibald Chesterfield collapsed into a chair, note trembling in his paws, eyes still locked on the painting. She didn't have to watch anymore. The Wheel had begun to turn.

She was already ahead.